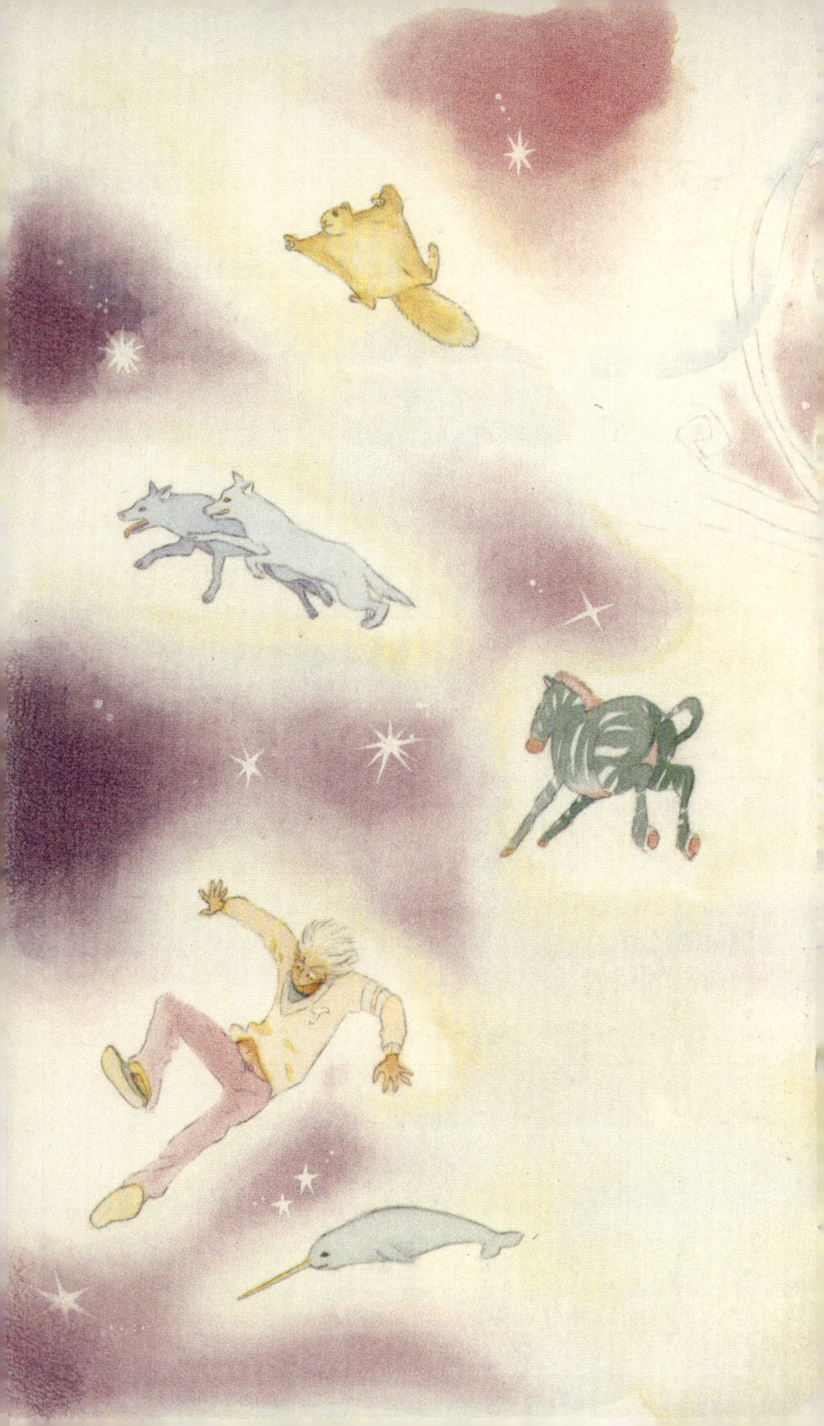

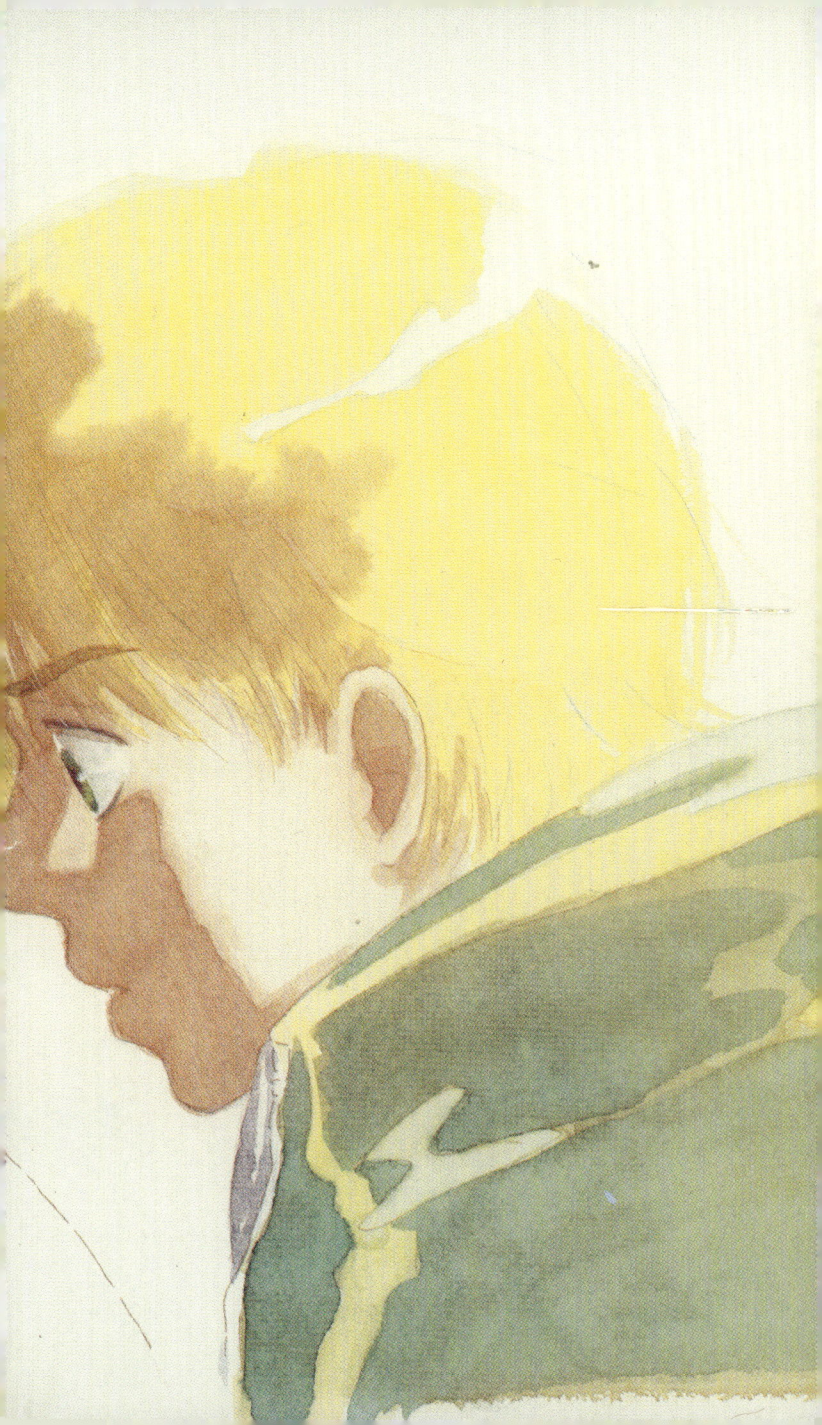

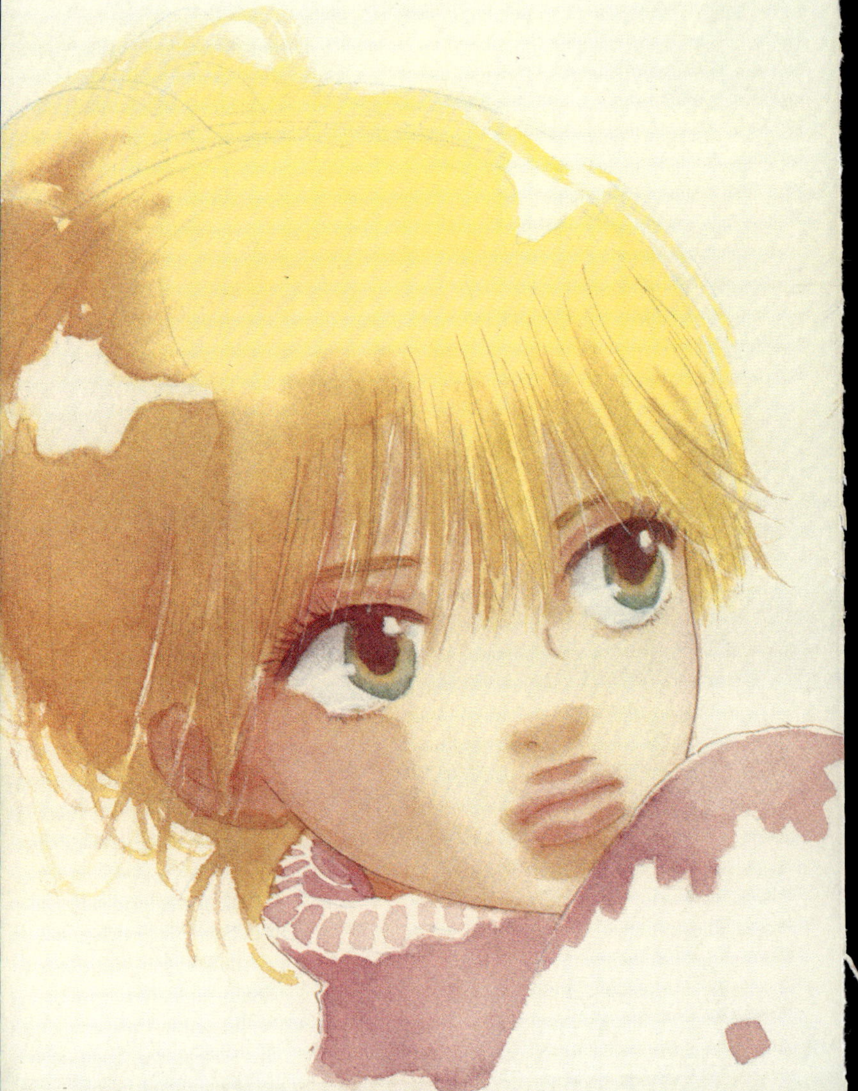

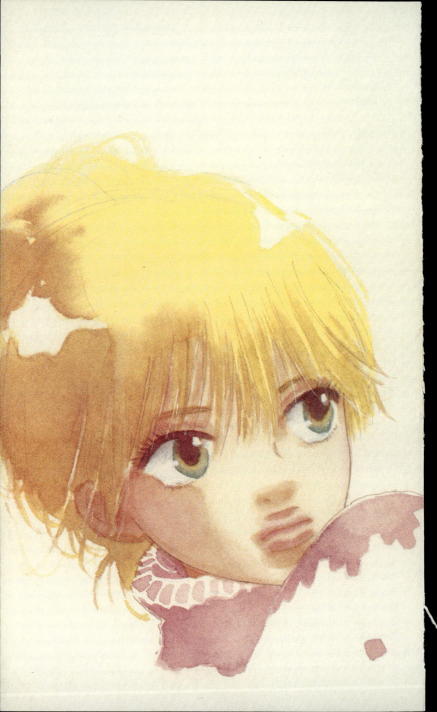

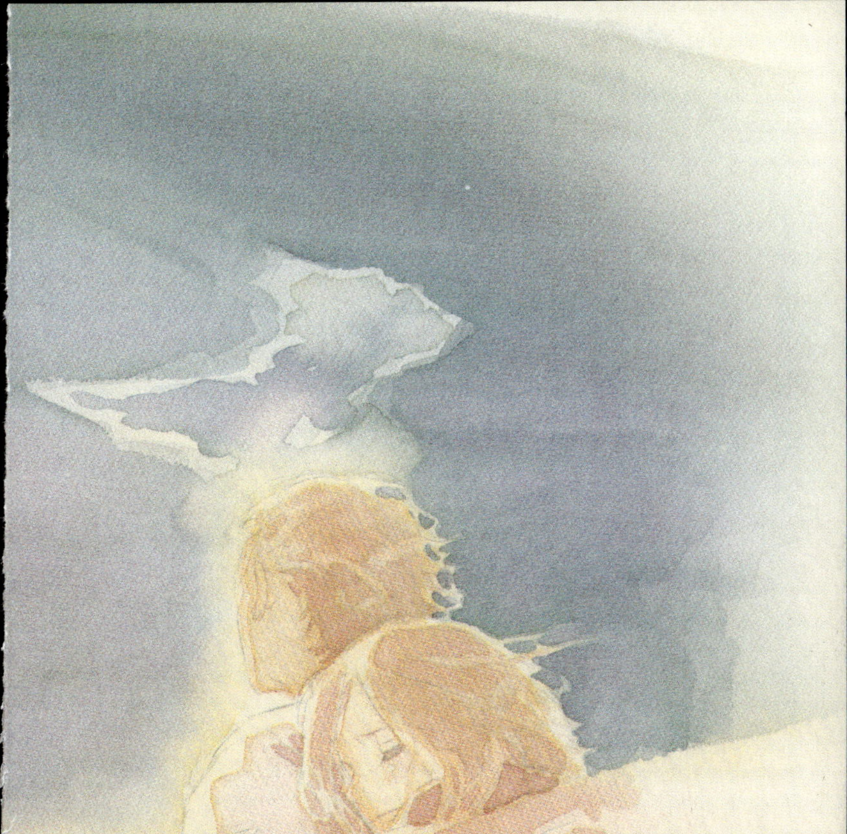

TABLE OF CONTENTS

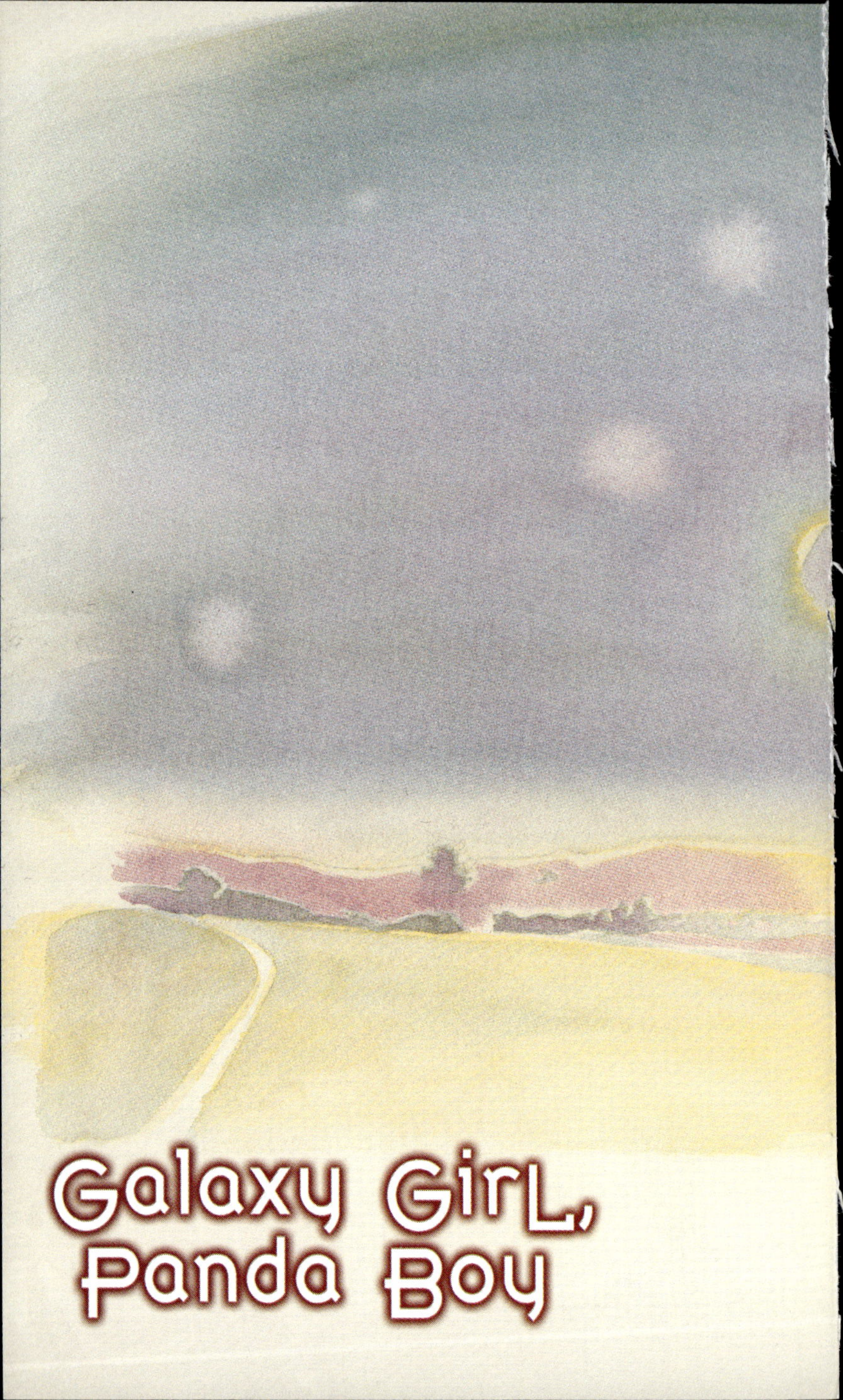
Galaxy GirL,
Panda Boy

Galaxy Girl, Panda Boy

Galaxy Girl, Panda Boy
Created by Junko Kawakami

Translation - Amy Forsyth
English Adaptation - Lori Millican
Retouch and Lettering - Irene Woori Choi
Production Artist - Gloria Wu
Cover Design - Anne Marie Horne

Editor - Julie Taylor
Digital Imaging Manager - Chris Buford
Production Managers - Jennifer Miller and Mutsumi Miyazaki
Managing Editor - Jill Freshney
VP of Production - Ron Klamert
Publisher and E.I.C. - Mike Kiley
President and C.O.O. - John Parker
C.E.O. - Stuart Levy

A  **TOKYOPOP**® Manga

TOKYOPOP Inc.
5900 Wilshire Blvd. Suite 2000
Los Angeles, CA 90036

E-mail: info@TOKYOPOP.com
Come visit us online at www.TOKYOPOP.com

ISBN: 1-59182-798-1

First TOKYOPOP printing: August 2005
10 9 8 7 6 5 4 3 2 1
Printed in Canada

Galaxy Girl, Panda Boy

by
Junko Kawakami

Passion Fruit

TOKYOPOP®

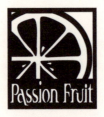

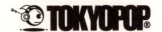

HAMBURG // LONDON // LOS ANGELES // TOKYO

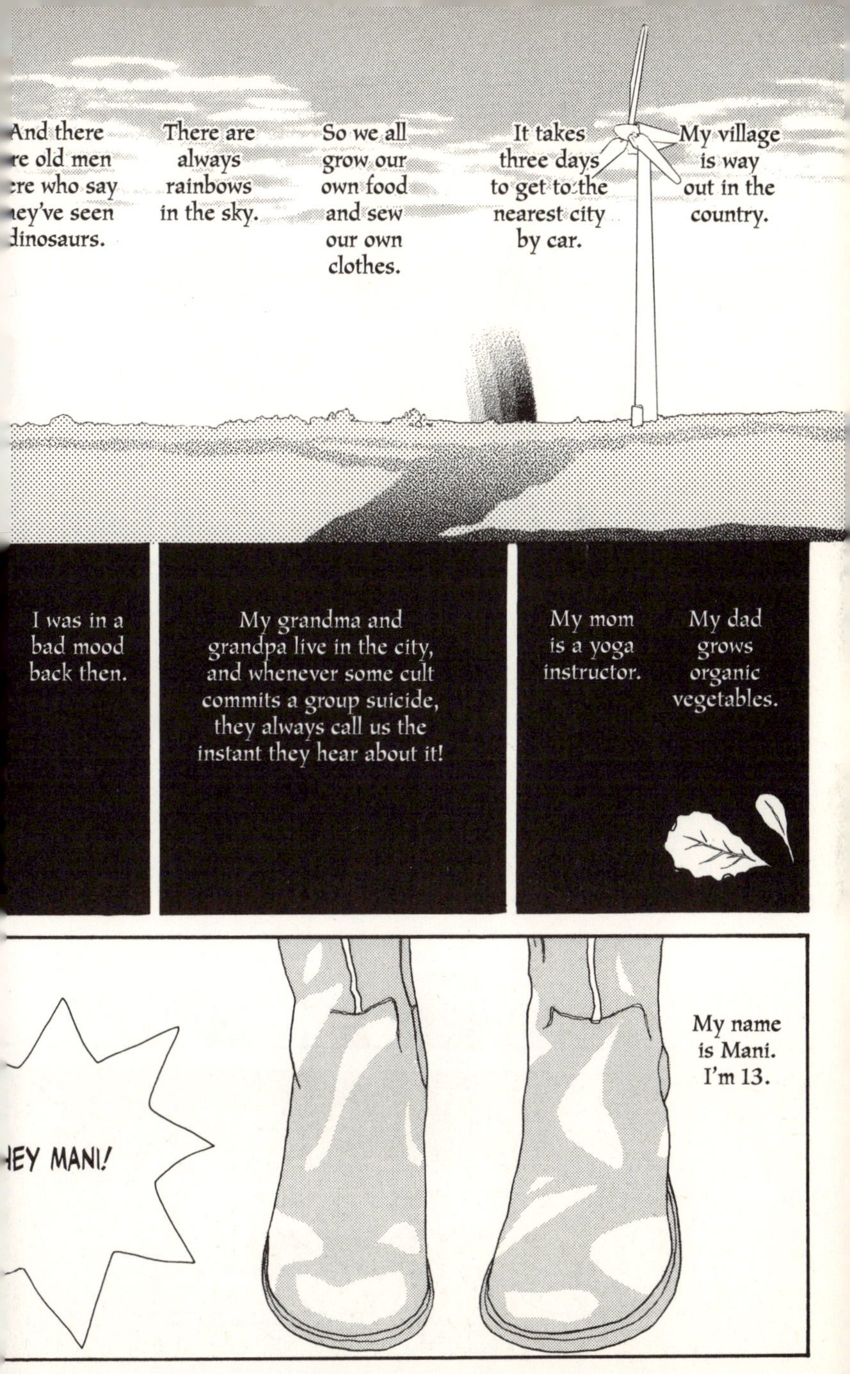
My village is way out in the country.
It takes three days to get to the nearest city by car.
So we all grow our own food and sew our own clothes.
There are always rainbows in the sky.
And there re old men re who say ey've seen inosaurs.
My dad grows organic vegetables.
My mom is a yoga instructor.
My grandma and grandpa live in the city, and whenever some cult commits a group suicide, they always call us the instant they hear about it!
I was in a bad mood back then.
My name is Mani. I'm 13.
EY MANI!

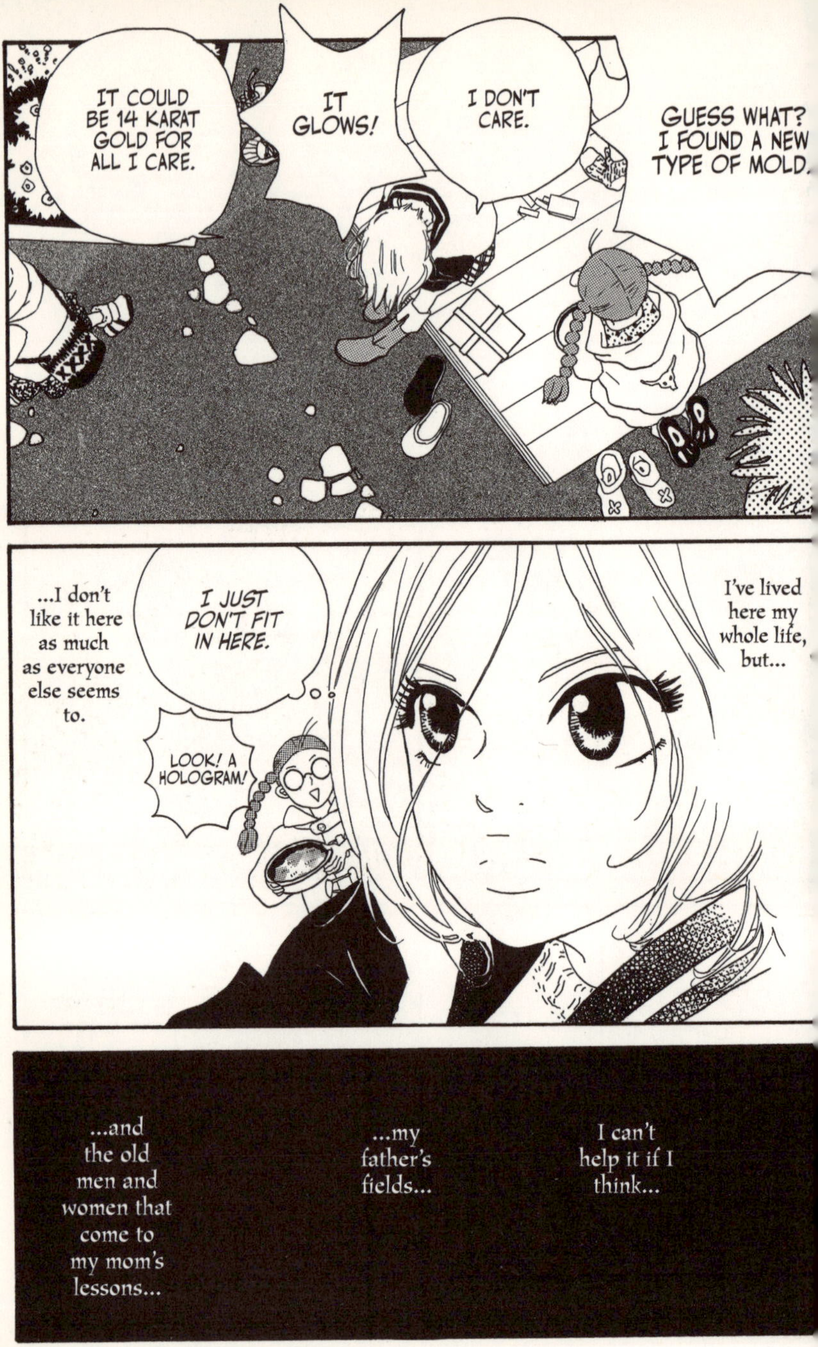

GUESS WHAT? I FOUND A NEW TYPE OF MOLD.
I DON'T CARE.
IT GLOWS!
IT COULD BE 14 KARAT GOLD FOR ALL I CARE.
I've lived here my whole life, but...
...I don't like it here as much as everyone else seems to.
I JUST DON'T FIT IN HERE.
LOOK! A HOLOGRAM!
I can't help it if I think...
...my father's fields...
...and the old men and women that come to my mom's lessons...

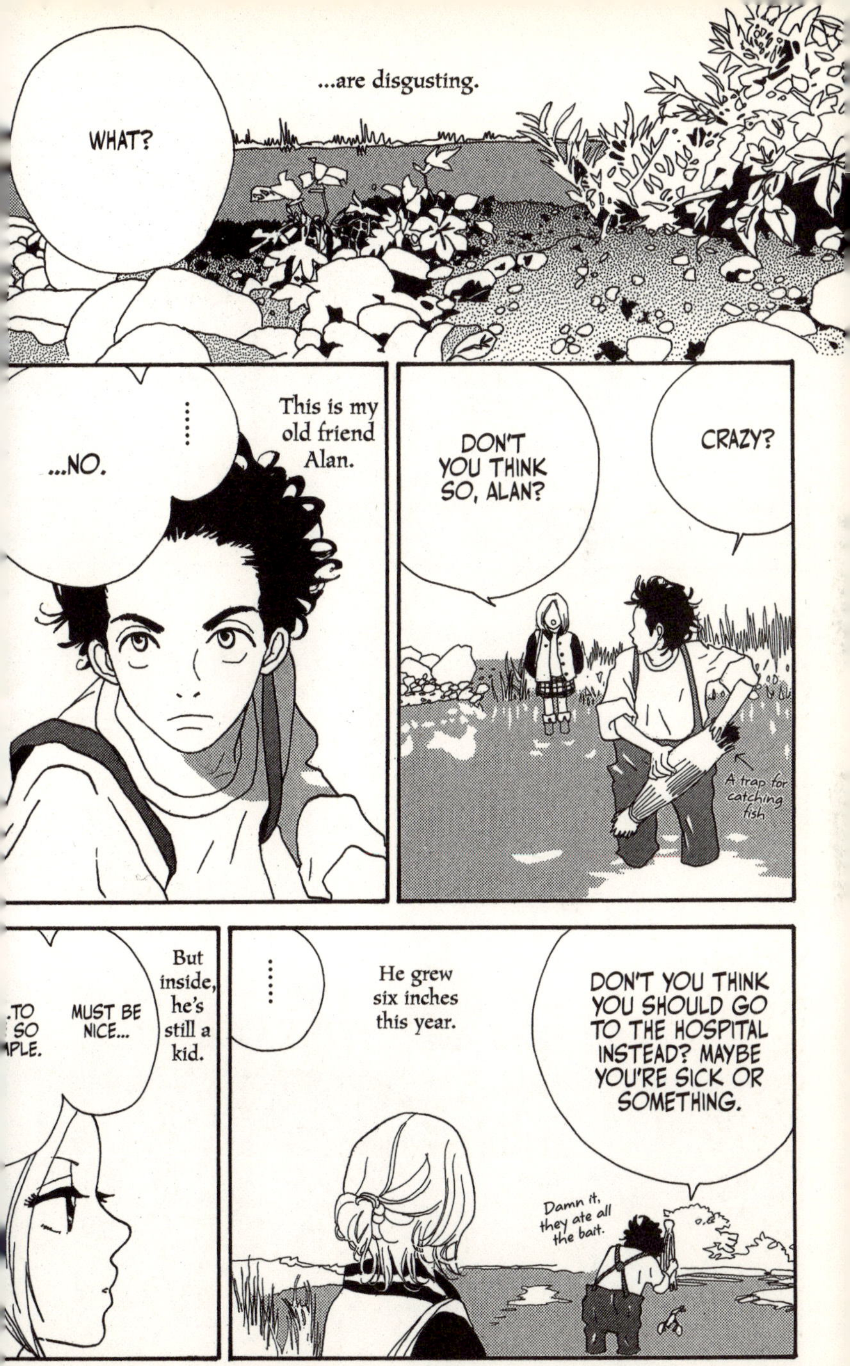
...are disgusting.
WHAT?
CRAZY?
DON'T YOU THINK SO, ALAN?
A trap for catching fish
This is my old friend Alan.
......
...NO.
DON'T YOU THINK YOU SHOULD GO TO THE HOSPITAL INSTEAD? MAYBE YOU'RE SICK OR SOMETHING.
He grew six inches this year.
......
Damn it, they ate all the bait.
But inside, he's still a kid.
MUST BE NICE...
.TO SO PLE.

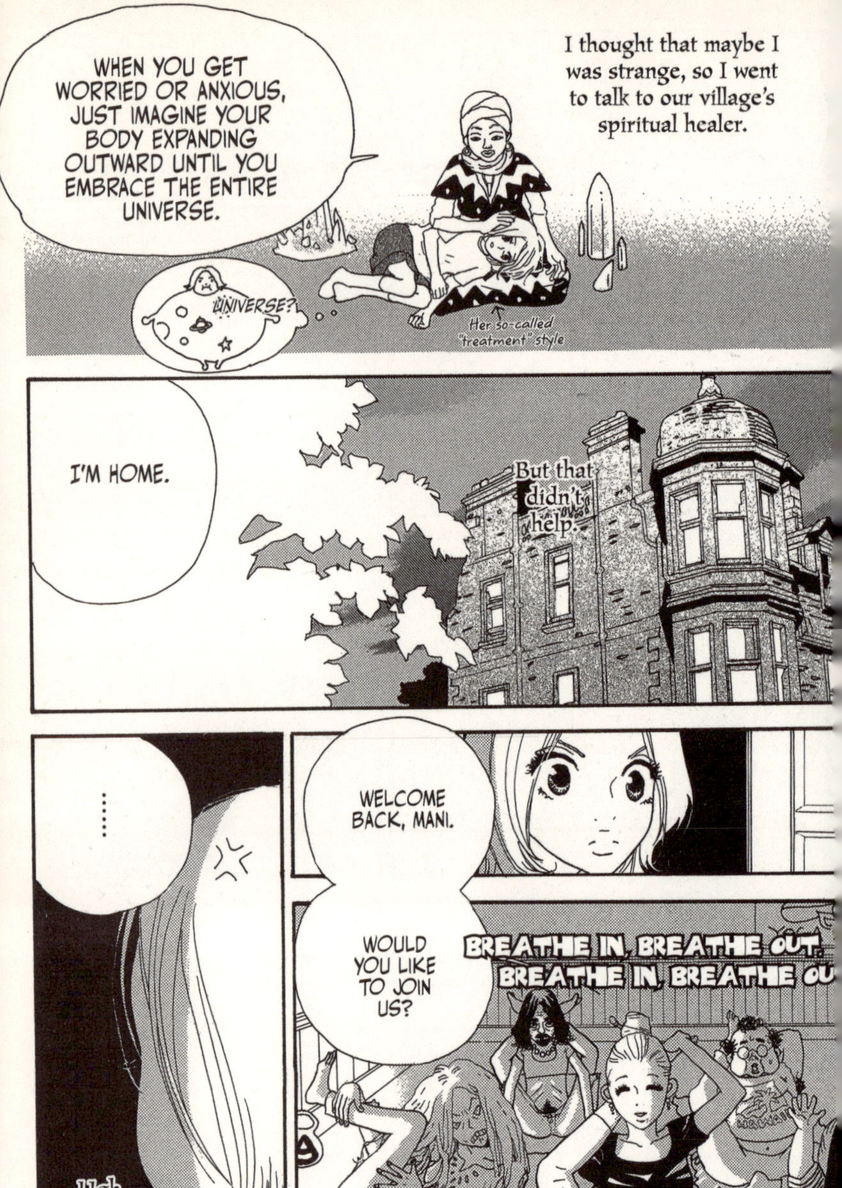
I thought that maybe I was strange, so I went to talk to our village's spiritual healer.
WHEN YOU GET WORRIED OR ANXIOUS, JUST IMAGINE YOUR BODY EXPANDING OUTWARD UNTIL YOU EMBRACE THE ENTIRE UNIVERSE.
Her so-called "treatment" style
UNIVERSE?
But that didn't help.
I'M HOME.
WELCOME BACK, MANI.
BREATHE IN, BREATHE OUT.
BREATHE IN, BREATHE OU
WOULD YOU LIKE TO JOIN US?
......
Ugh. No way.

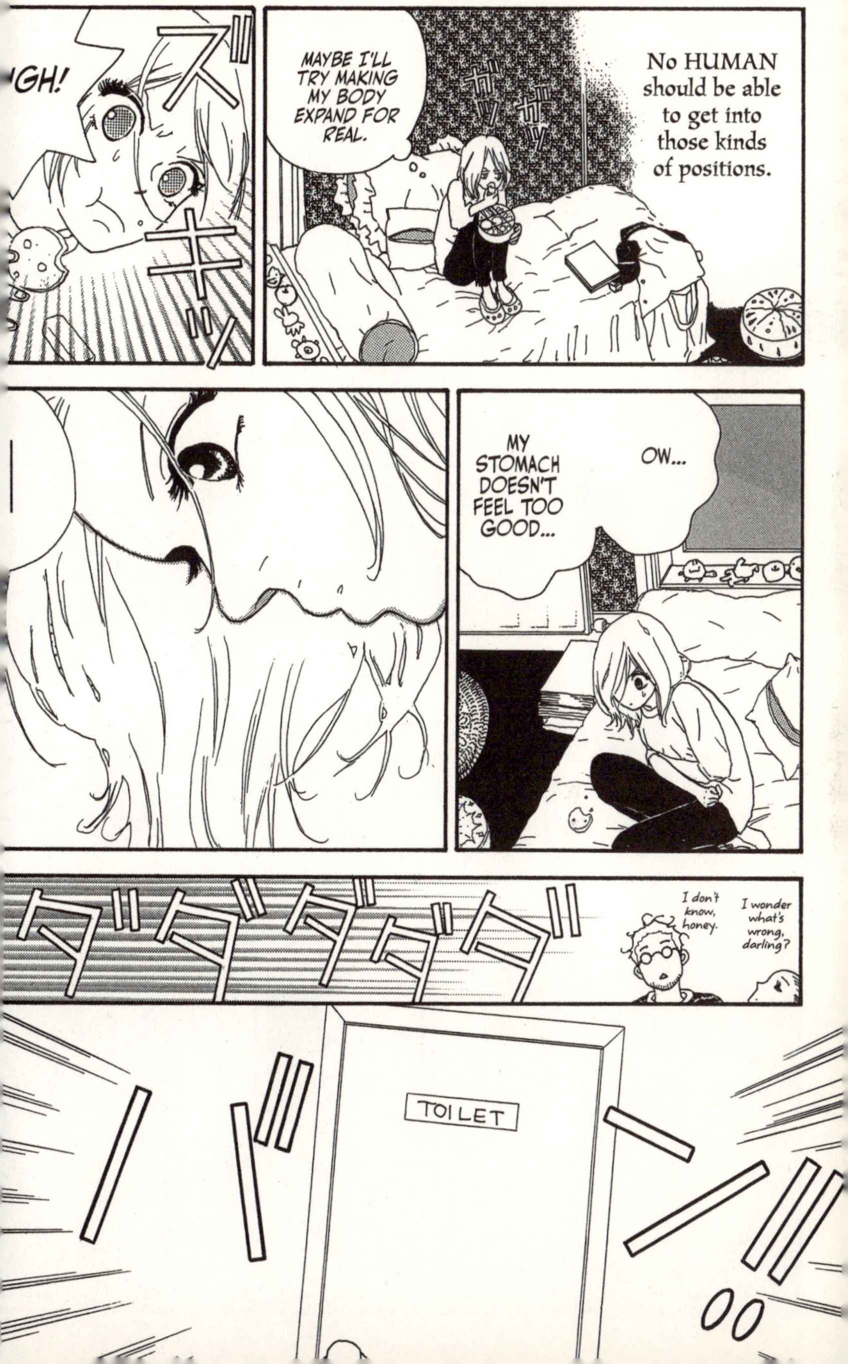

No HUMAN should be able to get into those kinds of positions.
MAYBE I'LL TRY MAKING MY BODY EXPAND FOR REAL.
GH!
OW...
MY STOMACH DOESN'T FEEL TOO GOOD...
I wonder what's wrong, darling?
I don't know, honey.
TOILET

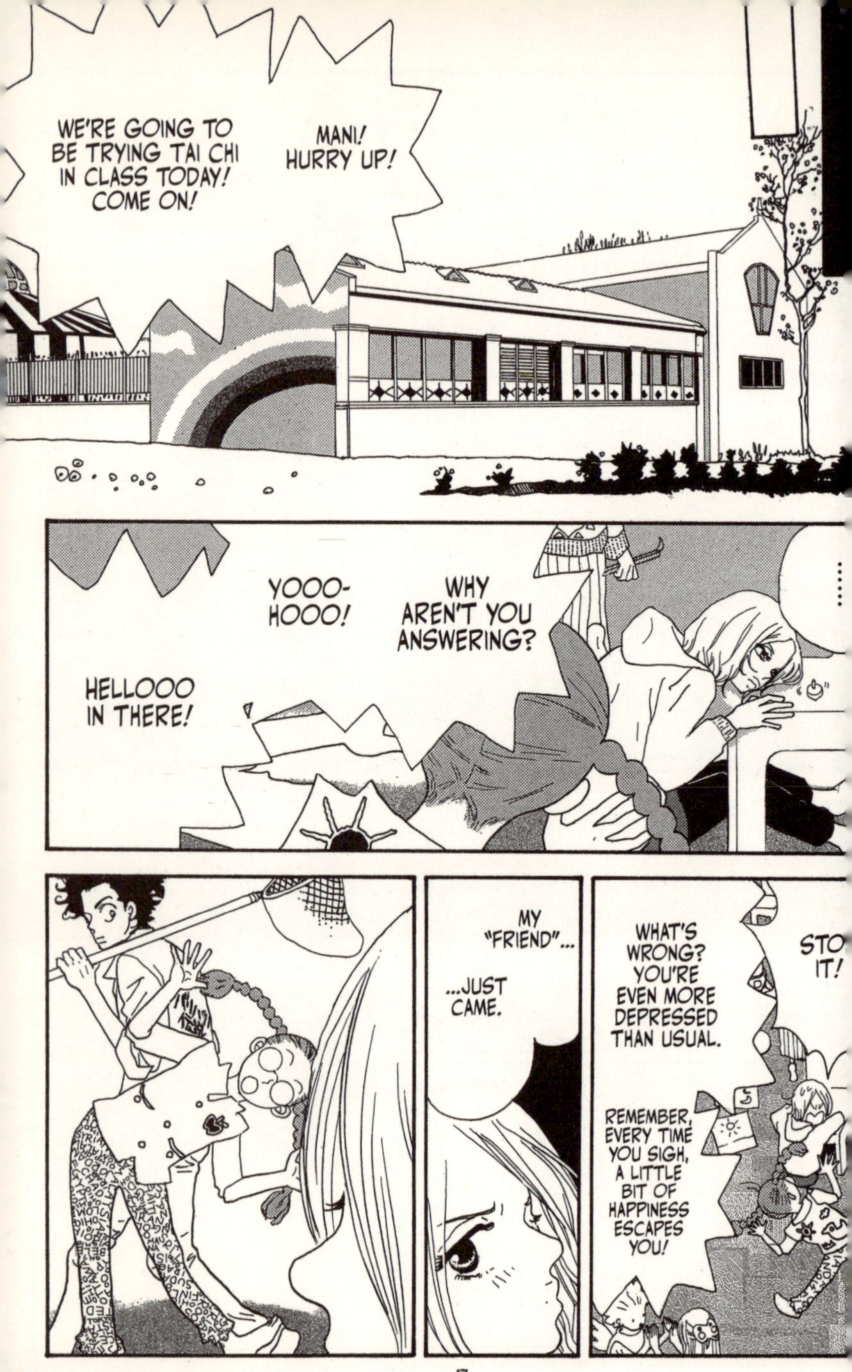
MANI! HURRY UP!
WE'RE GOING TO BE TRYING TAI CHI IN CLASS TODAY! COME ON!
WHY AREN'T YOU ANSWERING?
YOOO-HOOO!
HELLOOO IN THERE!
STO IT!
WHAT'S WRONG? YOU'RE EVEN MORE DEPRESSED THAN USUAL.
REMEMBER, EVERY TIME YOU SIGH, A LITTLE BIT OF HAPPINESS ESCAPES YOU!
MY "FRIEND"...
...JUST CAME.

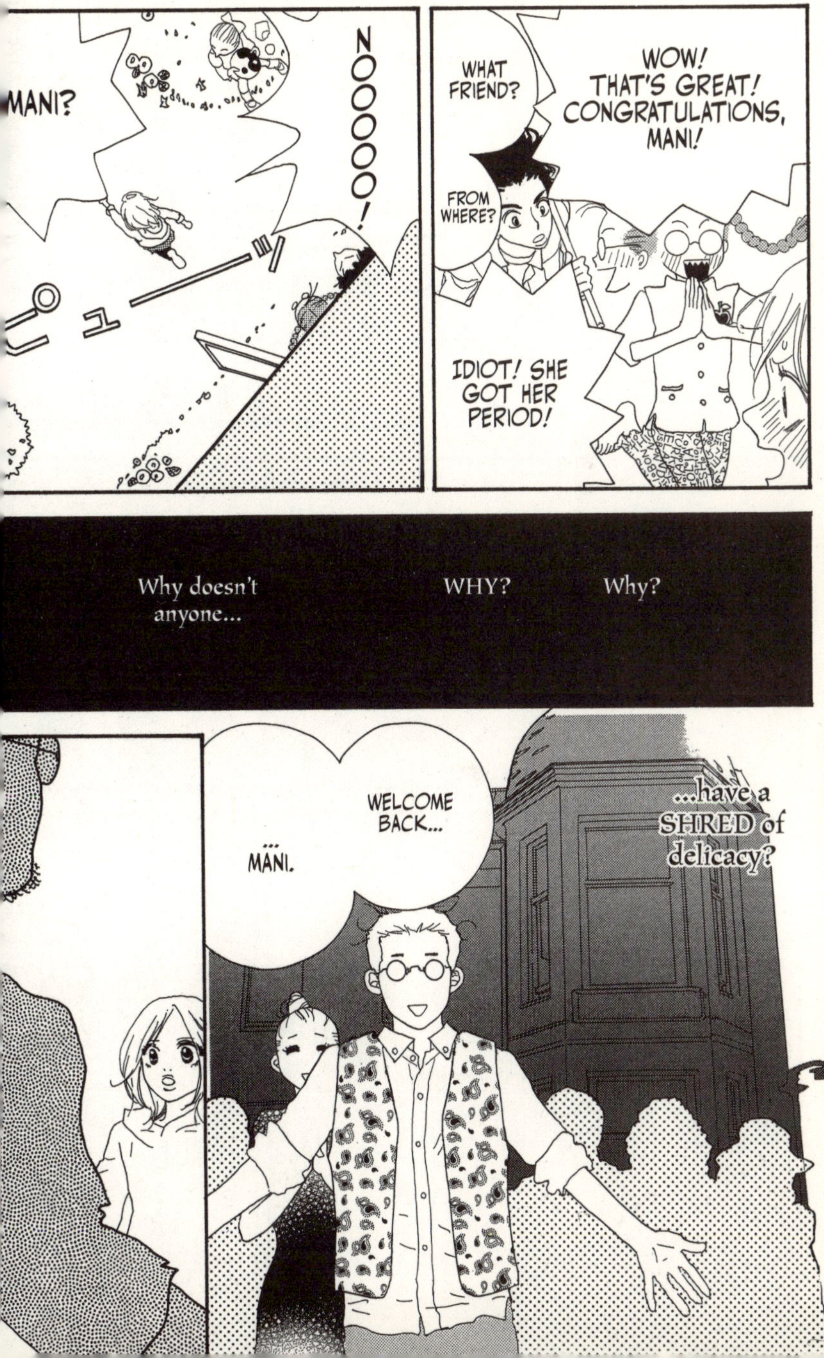
WOW! THAT'S GREAT! CONGRATULATIONS, MANI!
WHAT FRIEND?
FROM WHERE?
IDIOT! SHE GOT HER PERIOD!
NOOOOOO!
MANI?
Why?
WHY?
Why doesn't anyone...
...have a SHRED of delicacy?
WELCOME BACK...
...MANI.

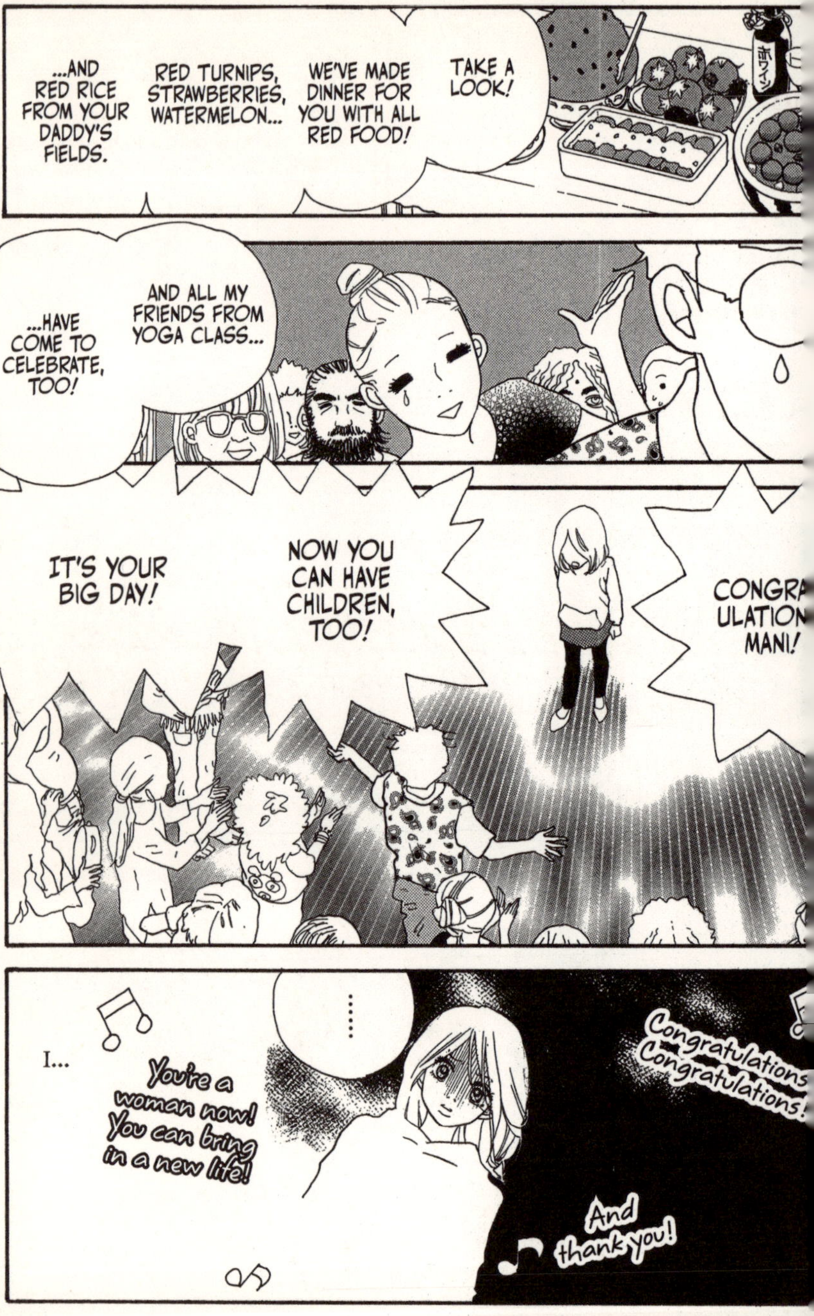
TAKE A LOOK!
WE'VE MADE DINNER FOR YOU WITH ALL RED FOOD!
RED TURNIPS, STRAWBERRIES, WATERMELON...
...AND RED RICE FROM YOUR DADDY'S FIELDS.
AND ALL MY FRIENDS FROM YOGA CLASS...
...HAVE COME TO CELEBRATE, TOO!
CONGRA ULATION MANI!
NOW YOU CAN HAVE CHILDREN, TOO!
IT'S YOUR BIG DAY!
Congratulations Congratulations!
......
You're a woman now! You can bring in a new life!
I...
And thank you!

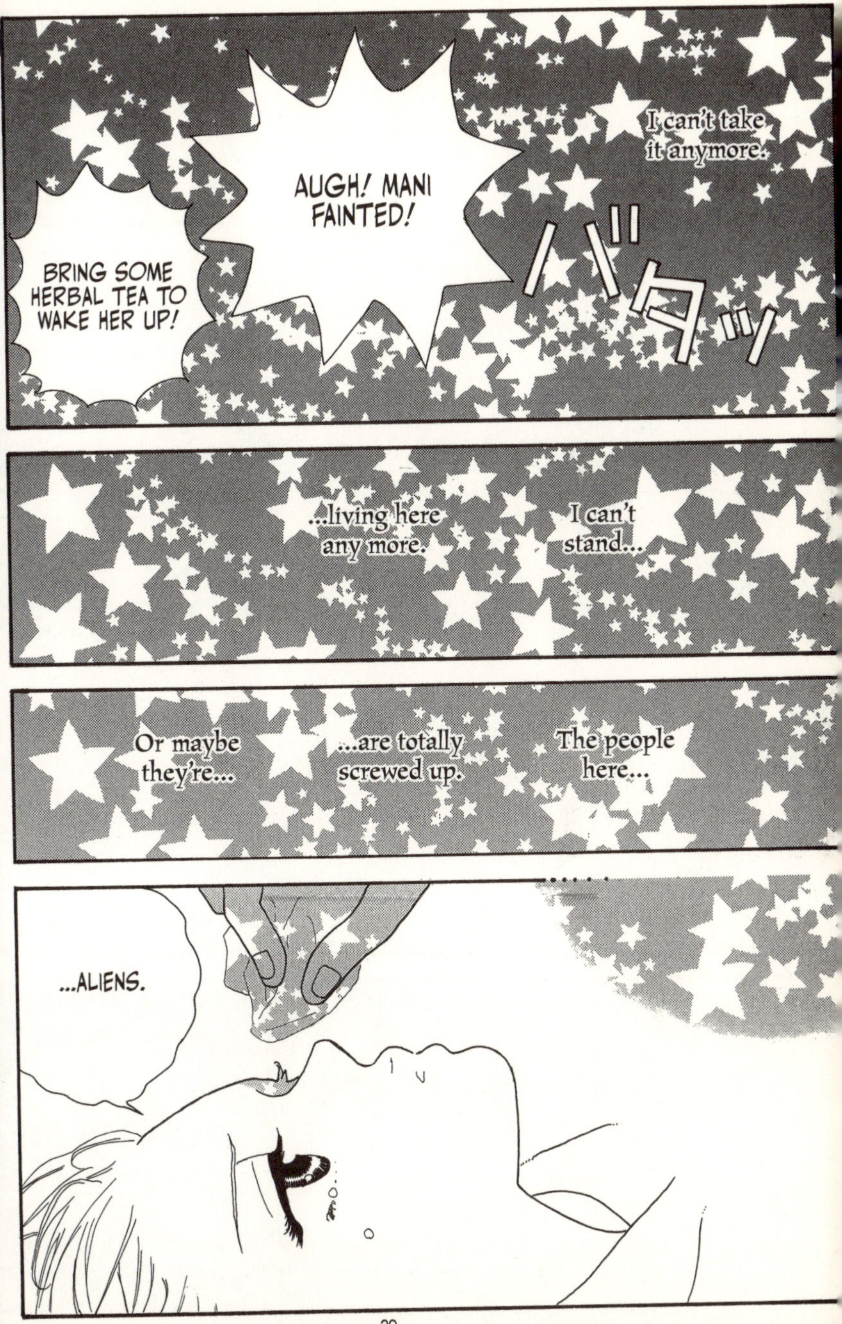

I can't take it anymore.
バタッ
AUGH! MANI FAINTED!
BRING SOME HERBAL TEA TO WAKE HER UP!
I can't stand...
...living here any more.
The people here...
...are totally screwed up.
Or maybe they're...
.....
...ALIENS.

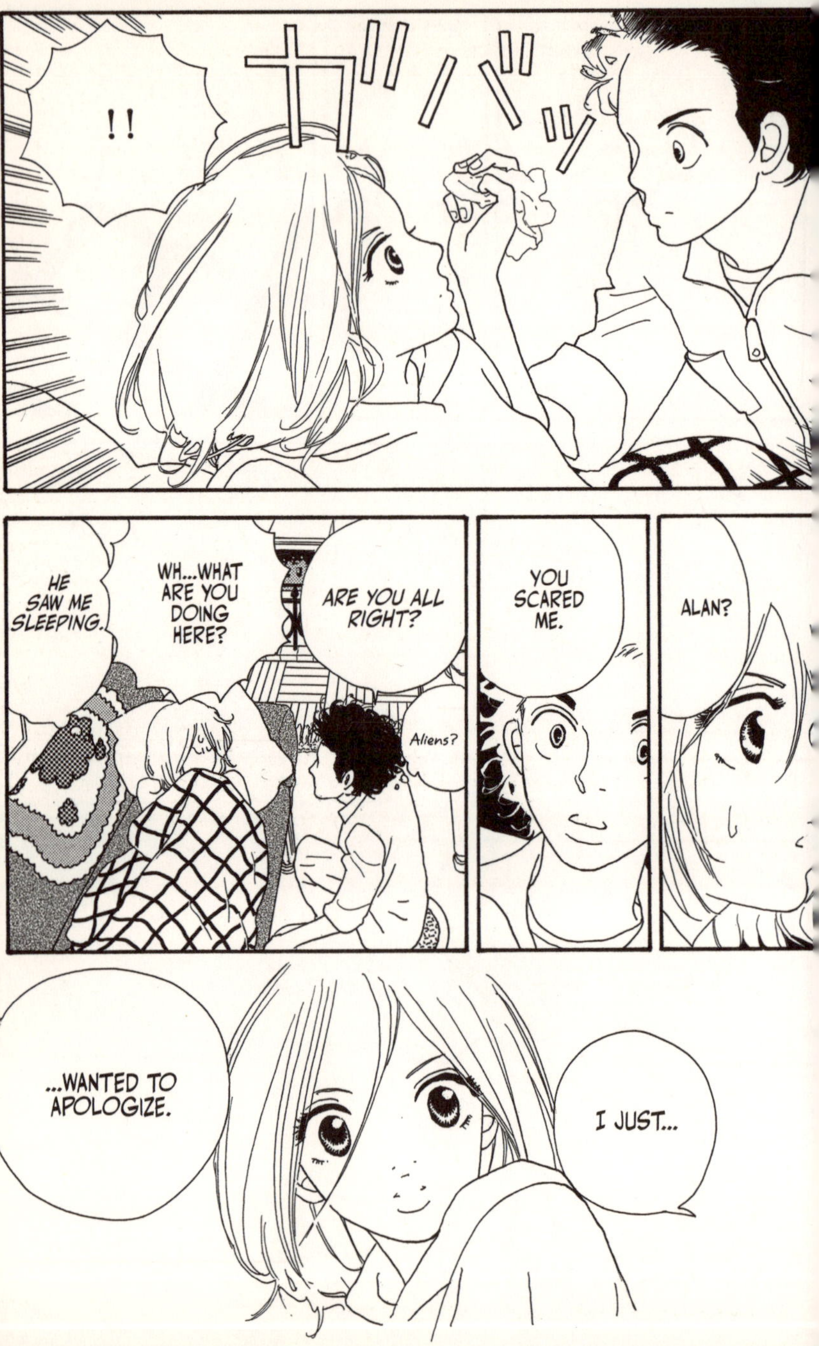
!!
ALAN?
YOU SCARED ME.
ARE YOU ALL RIGHT?
Aliens?
WH...WHAT ARE YOU DOING HERE?
HE SAW ME SLEEPING.
I JUST...
...WANTED TO APOLOGIZE.

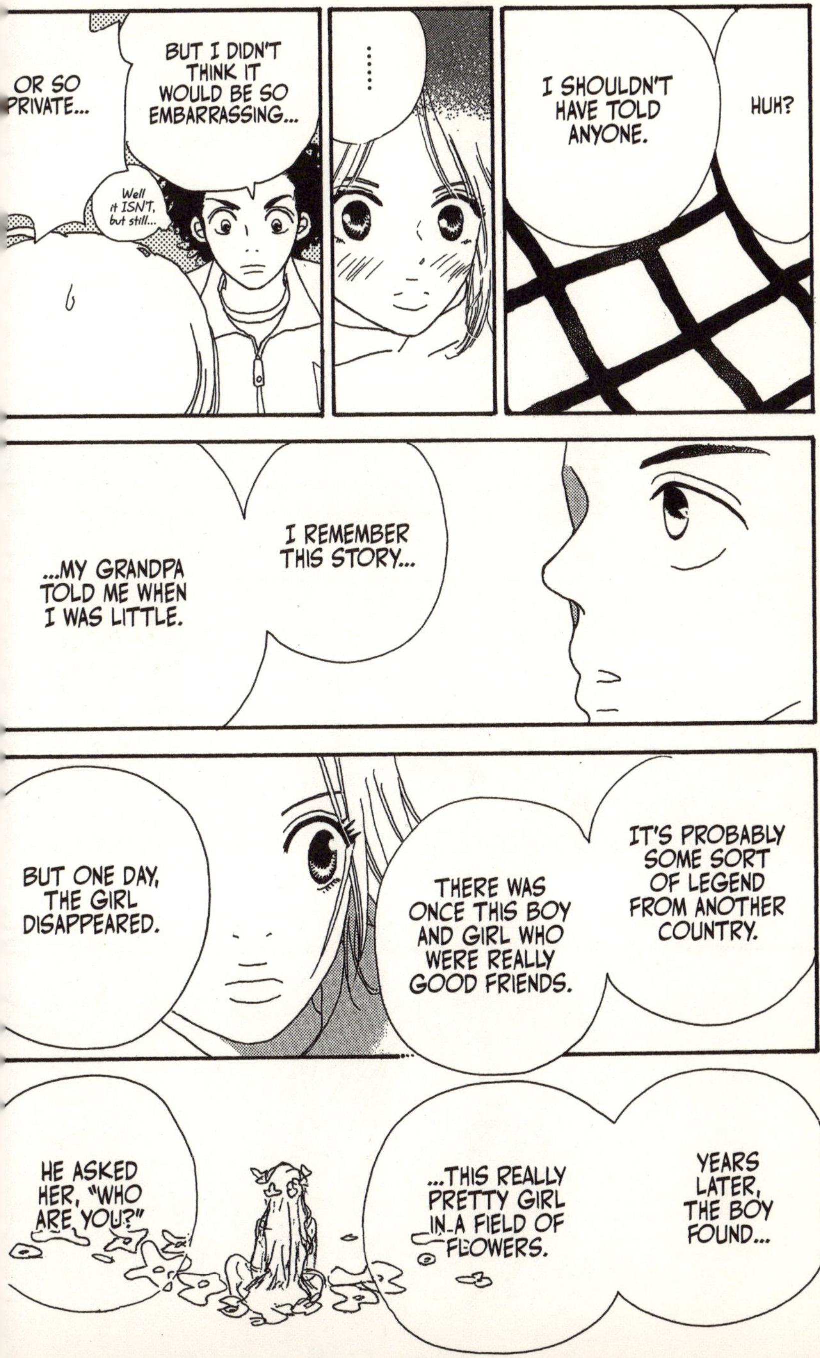
HUH?
I SHOULDN'T HAVE TOLD ANYONE.
......
BUT I DIDN'T THINK IT WOULD BE SO EMBARRASSING...
Well it ISN'T, but still...
OR SO PRIVATE...
I REMEMBER THIS STORY...
...MY GRANDPA TOLD ME WHEN I WAS LITTLE.
IT'S PROBABLY SOME SORT OF LEGEND FROM ANOTHER COUNTRY.
THERE WAS ONCE THIS BOY AND GIRL WHO WERE REALLY GOOD FRIENDS.
BUT ONE DAY, THE GIRL DISAPPEARED.
YEARS LATER, THE BOY FOUND...
...THIS REALLY PRETTY GIRL IN A FIELD OF FLOWERS.
HE ASKED HER, "WHO ARE YOU?"

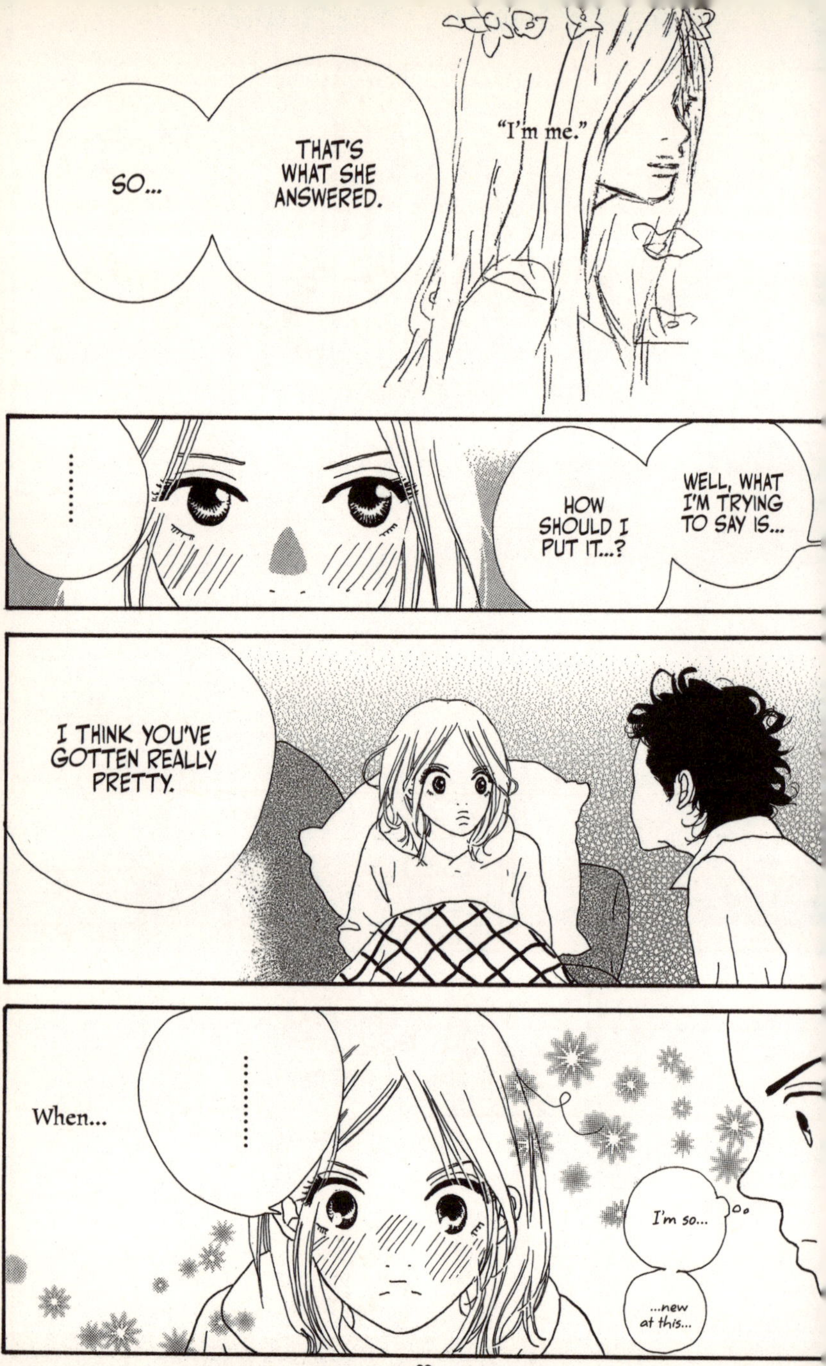
"I'm me."
THAT'S WHAT SHE ANSWERED.
SO...
WELL, WHAT I'M TRYING TO SAY IS...
HOW SHOULD I PUT IT...?
....
I THINK YOU'VE GOTTEN REALLY PRETTY.
I'm so...
...new at this...
....
When...

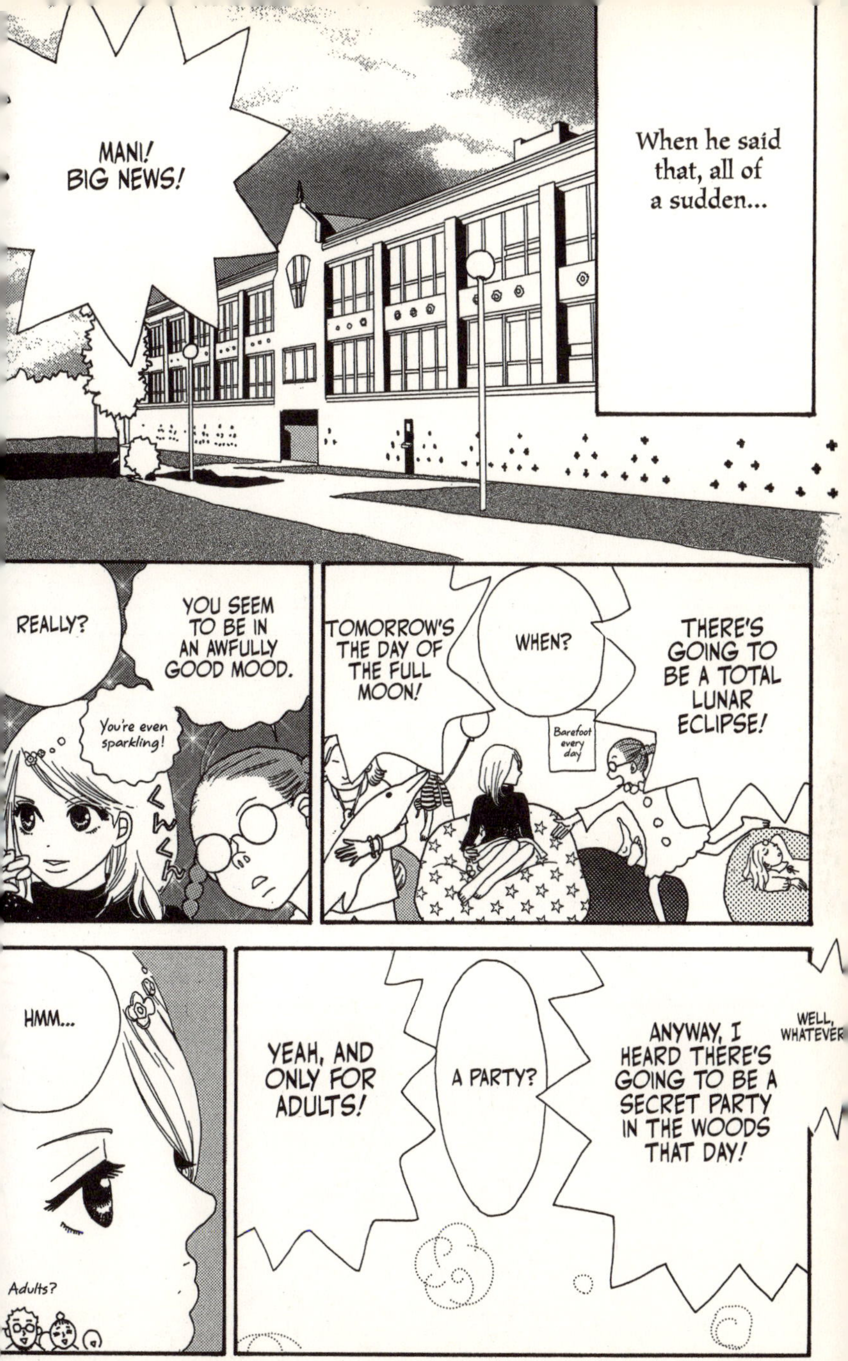
When he said that, all of a sudden...
MANI! BIG NEWS!
THERE'S GOING TO BE A TOTAL LUNAR ECLIPSE!
WHEN?
Barefoot every day
TOMORROW'S THE DAY OF THE FULL MOON!
YOU SEEM TO BE IN AN AWFULLY GOOD MOOD.
REALLY?
You're even sparkling!
WELL, WHATEVER
ANYWAY, I HEARD THERE'S GOING TO BE A SECRET PARTY IN THE WOODS THAT DAY!
A PARTY?
YEAH, AND ONLY FOR ADULTS!
HMM...
Adults?

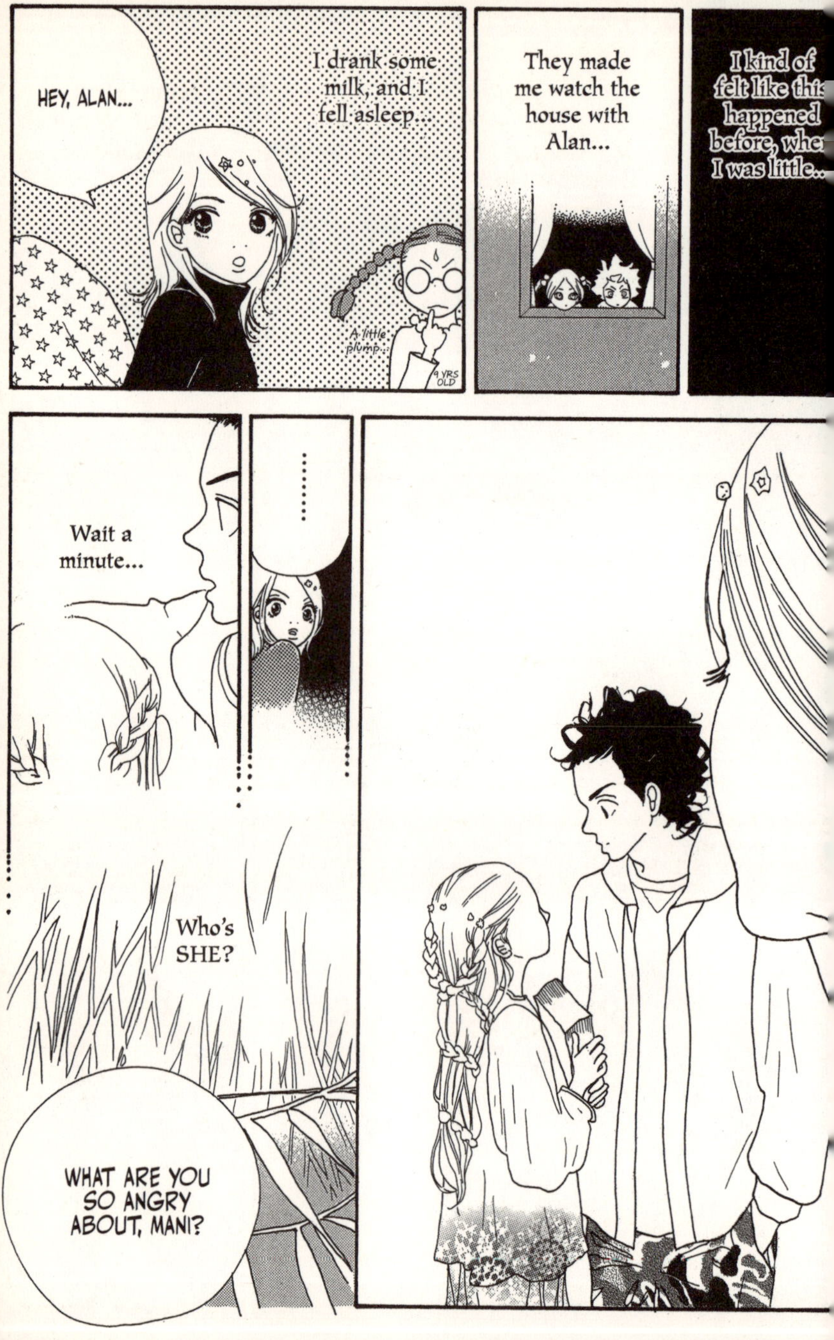
I kind of felt like this happened before, whe I was little...
They made me watch the house with Alan...
I drank some milk, and I fell asleep...
HEY, ALAN...
A little plump...
9 YRS OLD
....
Wait a minute...
Who's SHE?
WHAT ARE YOU SO ANGRY ABOUT, MANI?

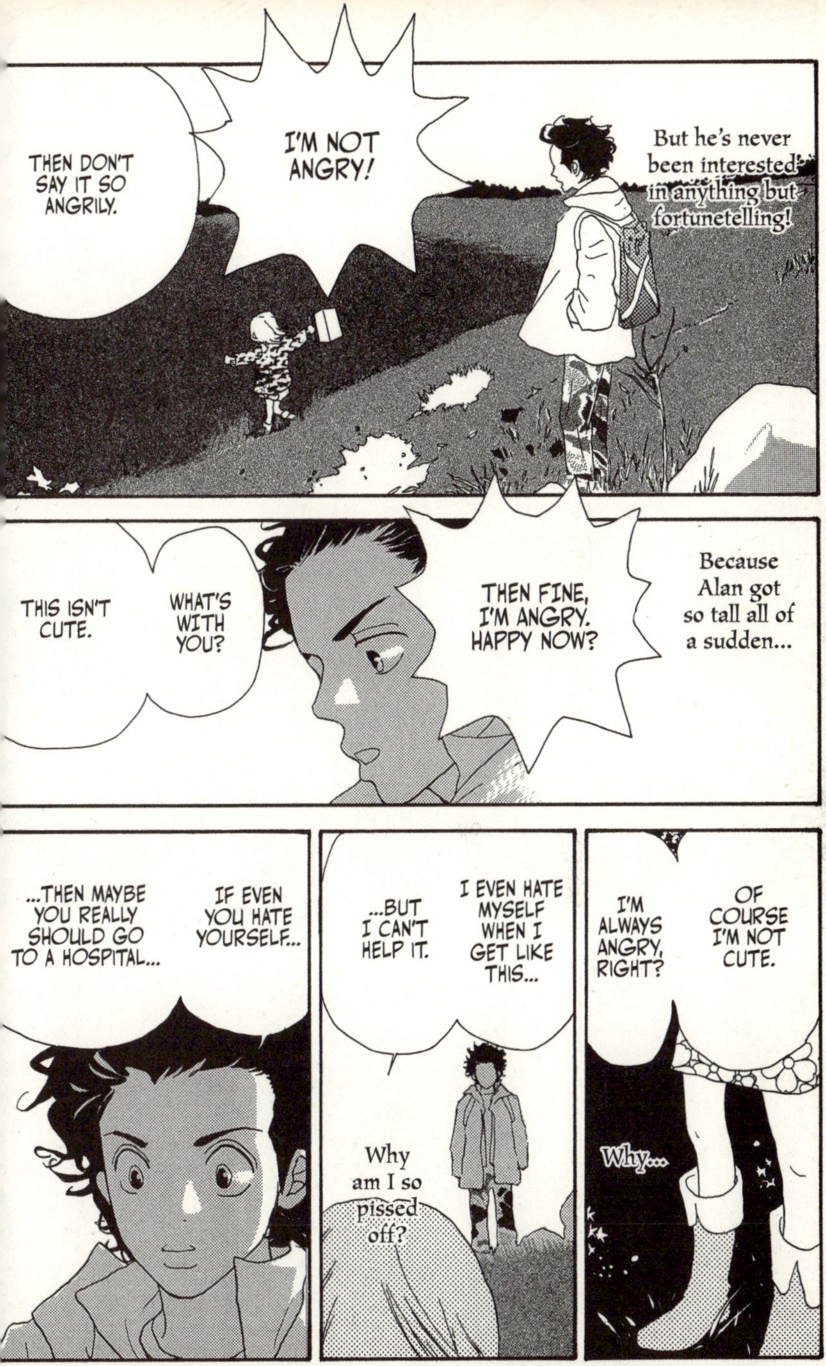

But he's never been interested in anything but fortunetelling!
I'M NOT ANGRY!
THEN DON'T SAY IT SO ANGRILY.
Because Alan got so tall all of a sudden...
THEN FINE, I'M ANGRY. HAPPY NOW?
WHAT'S WITH YOU?
THIS ISN'T CUTE.
OF COURSE I'M NOT CUTE.
I'M ALWAYS ANGRY, RIGHT?
Why...
I EVEN HATE MYSELF WHEN I GET LIKE THIS...
...BUT I CAN'T HELP IT.
Why am I so pissed off?
IF EVEN YOU HATE YOURSELF...
...THEN MAYBE YOU REALLY SHOULD GO TO A HOSPITAL...

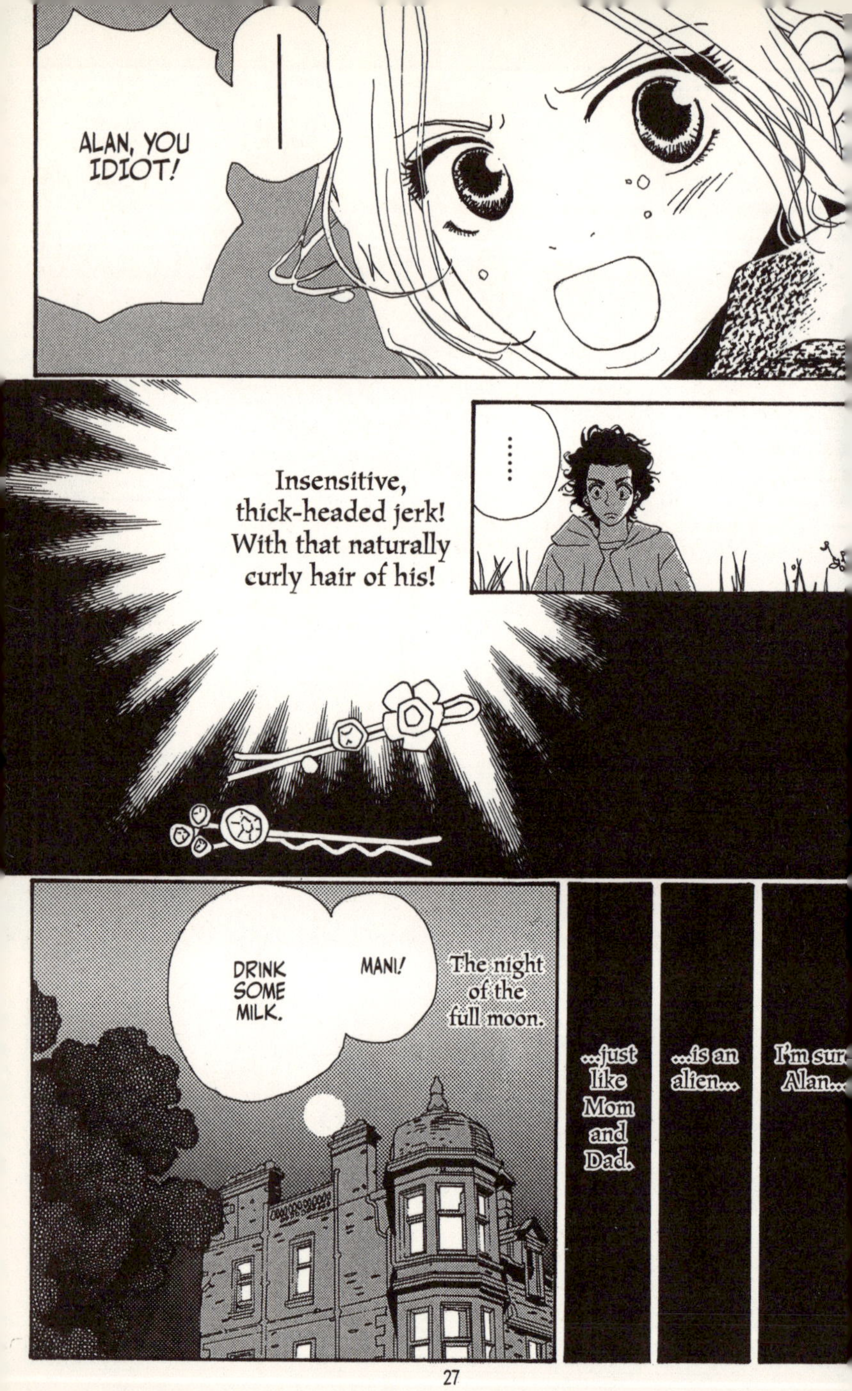
ALAN, YOU IDIOT!
......
Insensitive, thick-headed jerk! With that naturally curly hair of his!
I'm sur Alan...
...is an alien...
...just like Mom and Dad.
The night of the full moon.
MANI!
DRINK SOME MILK.

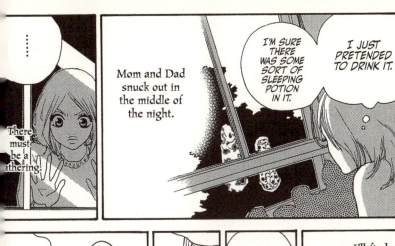

I JUST PRETENDED TO DRINK IT.
I'M SURE THERE WAS SOME SORT OF SLEEPING POTION IN IT.
Mom and Dad snuck out in the middle of the night.
......
There must be a athering.
I'll find them and see what-they REALLY are.
バサッ
(sheets)
NOT TALL ENOUGH.
カーン
......
ポックリ
ポックリ
ALAN...

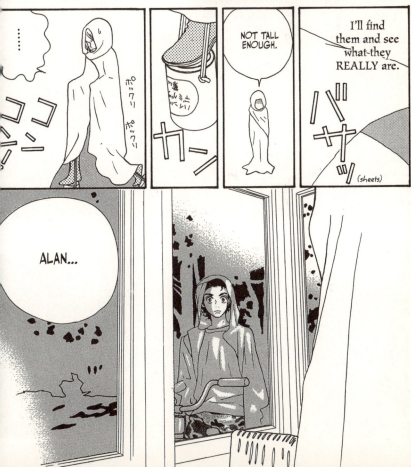

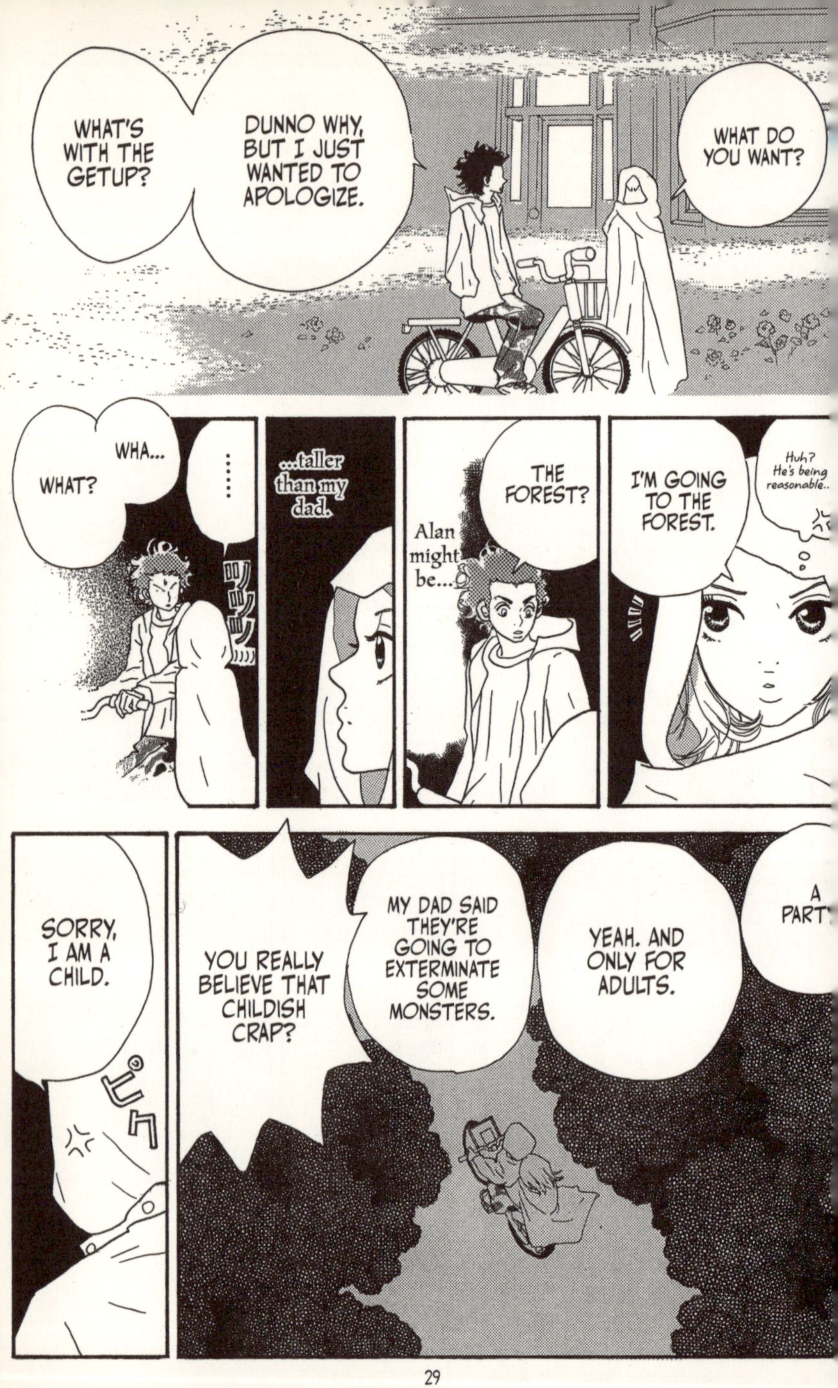
WHAT DO YOU WANT?
DUNNO WHY, BUT I JUST WANTED TO APOLOGIZE.
WHAT'S WITH THE GETUP?
Huh? He's being reasonable..
I'M GOING TO THE FOREST.
THE FOREST?
Alan might be...
...taller than my dad.
......
WHA...
WHAT?
A PART
YEAH. AND ONLY FOR ADULTS.
MY DAD SAID THEY'RE GOING TO EXTERMINATE SOME MONSTERS.
YOU REALLY BELIEVE THAT CHILDISH CRAP?
SORRY, I AM A CHILD.
ピク

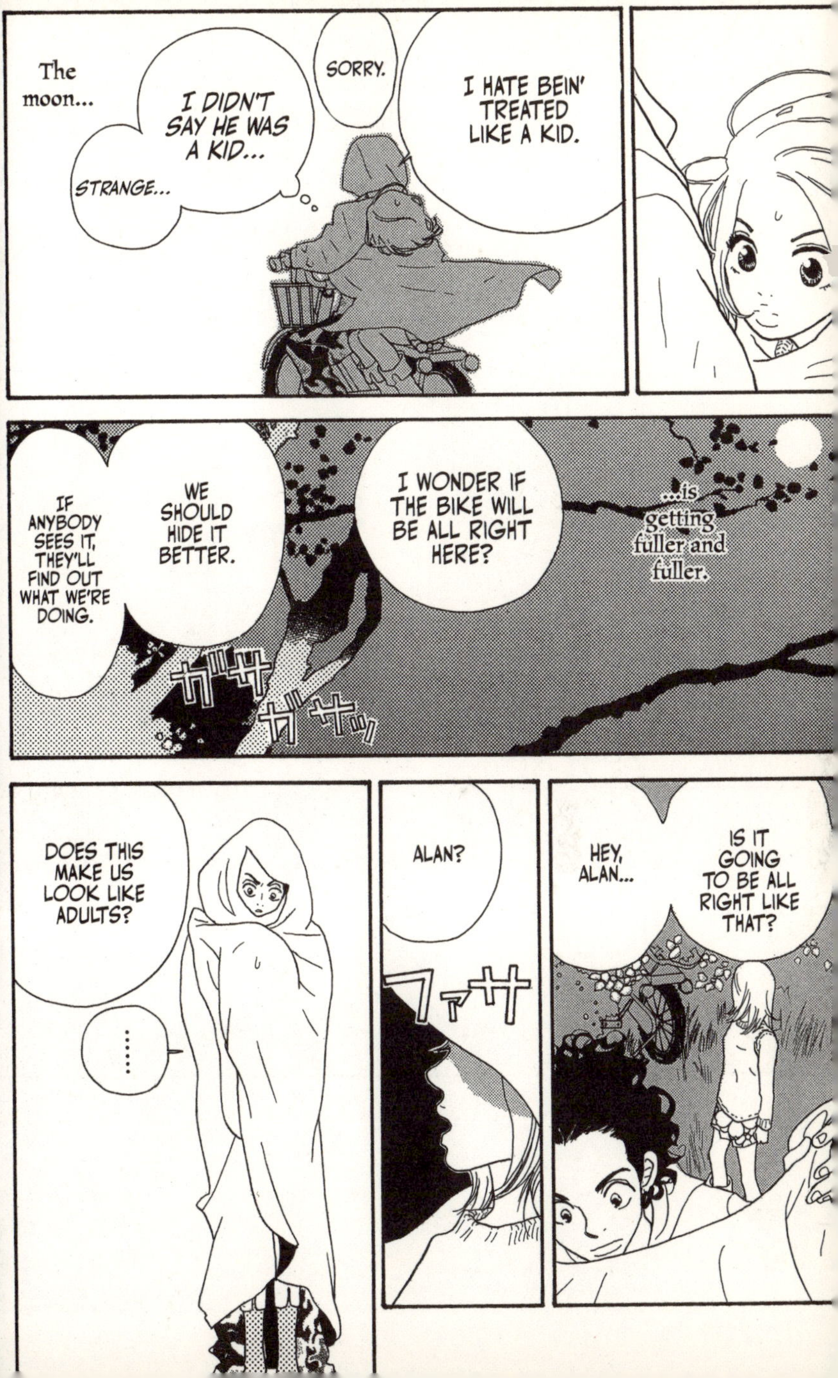
I HATE BEIN' TREATED LIKE A KID.
SORRY.
I DIDN'T SAY HE WAS A KID...
The moon...
STRANGE...
...is getting fuller and fuller.
I WONDER IF THE BIKE WILL BE ALL RIGHT HERE?
WE SHOULD HIDE IT BETTER.
IF ANYBODY SEES IT, THEY'LL FIND OUT WHAT WE'RE DOING.
ガサ
ガサッ
IS IT GOING TO BE ALL RIGHT LIKE THAT?
HEY, ALAN...
ALAN?
ファサ
DOES THIS MAKE US LOOK LIKE ADULTS?
......

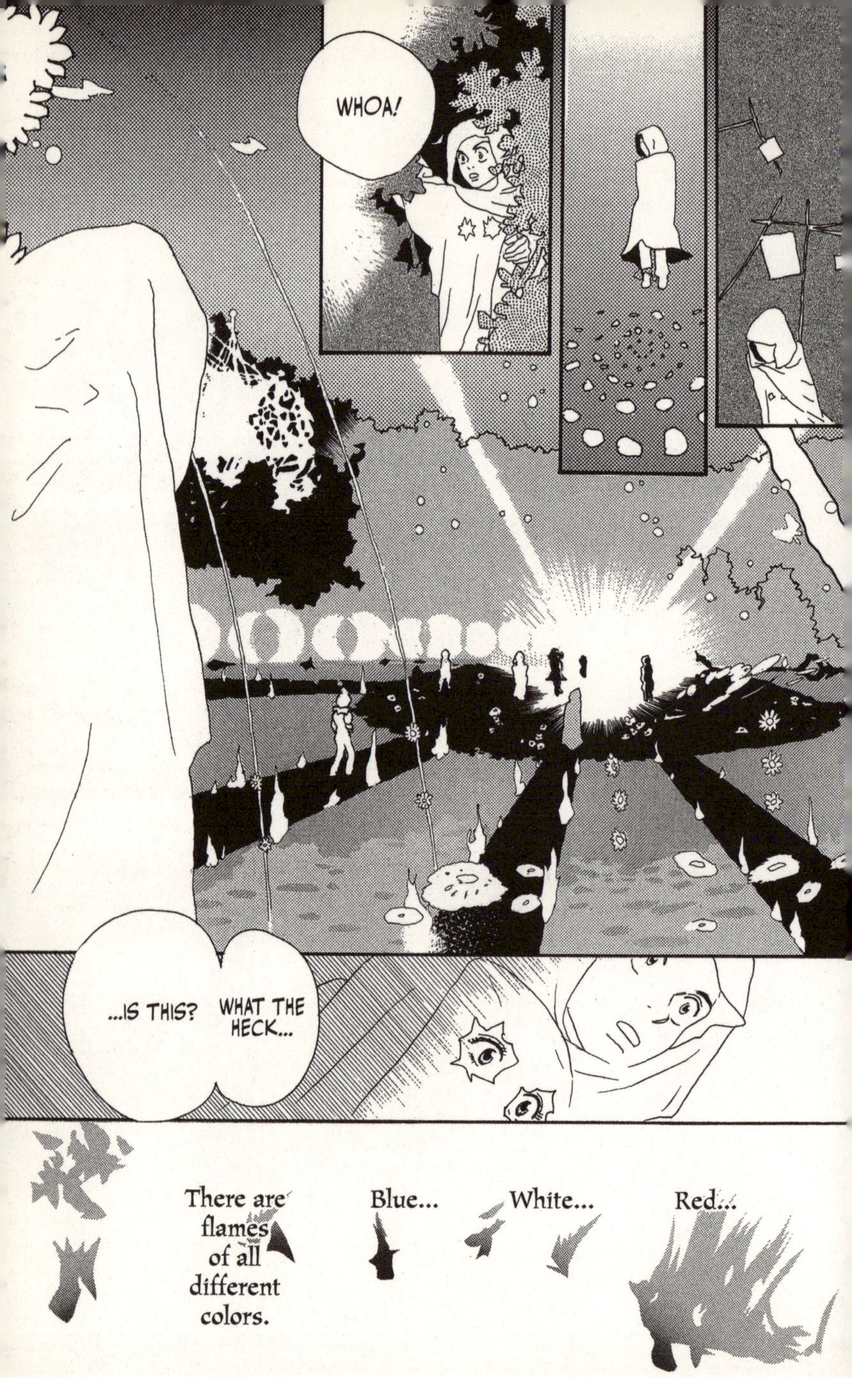
WHOA!
WHAT THE HECK...
...IS THIS?
Red...
White...
Blue...
There are flames of all different colors.

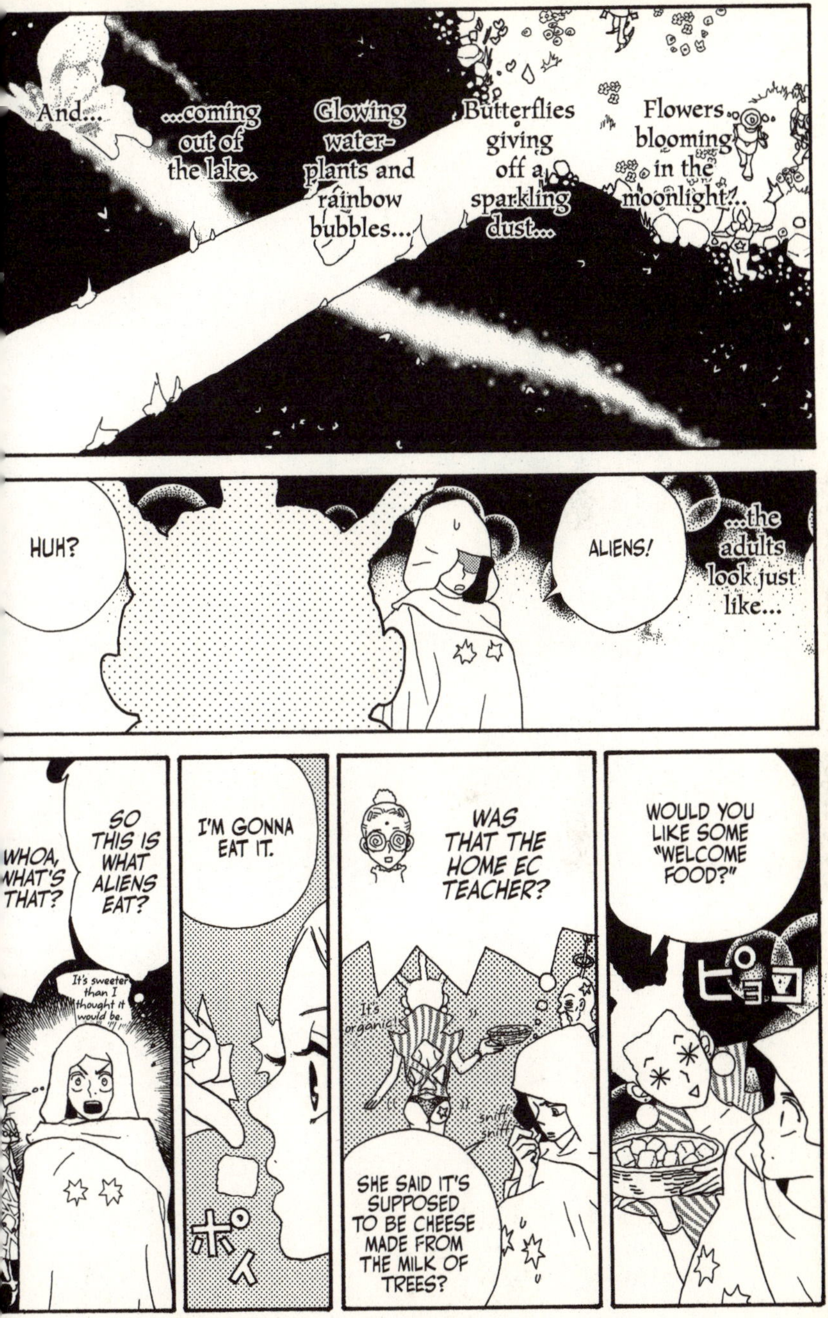
Flowers blooming in the moonlight...
Butterflies giving off a sparkling dust...
Glowing water-plants and rainbow bubbles...
...coming out of the lake.
And...
...the adults look just like...
ALIENS!
HUH?
WOULD YOU LIKE SOME "WELCOME FOOD?"
ピョコ
WAS THAT THE HOME EC TEACHER?
It's organic!
sniff sniff
SHE SAID IT'S SUPPOSED TO BE CHEESE MADE FROM THE MILK OF TREES?
I'M GONNA EAT IT.
ポイ
SO THIS IS WHAT ALIENS EAT?
WHOA, WHAT'S THAT?
It's sweeter than I thought it would be.

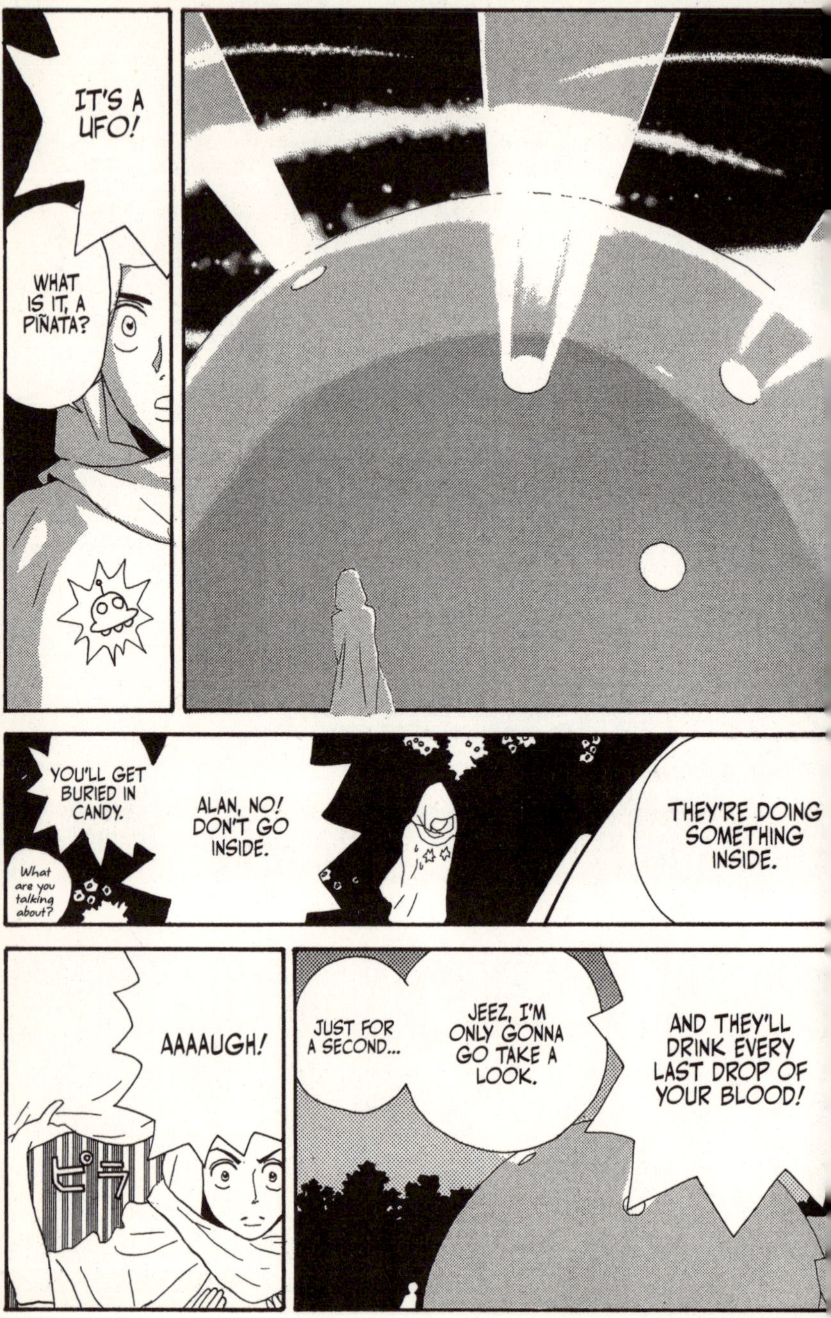
IT'S A UFO!
WHAT IS IT, A PIÑATA?
THEY'RE DOING SOMETHING INSIDE.
ALAN, NO! DON'T GO INSIDE.
YOU'LL GET BURIED IN CANDY.
What are you talking about?
AND THEY'LL DRINK EVERY LAST DROP OF YOUR BLOOD!
JEEZ, I'M ONLY GONNA GO TAKE A LOOK.
JUST FOR A SECOND...
AAAAUGH!
ピラ

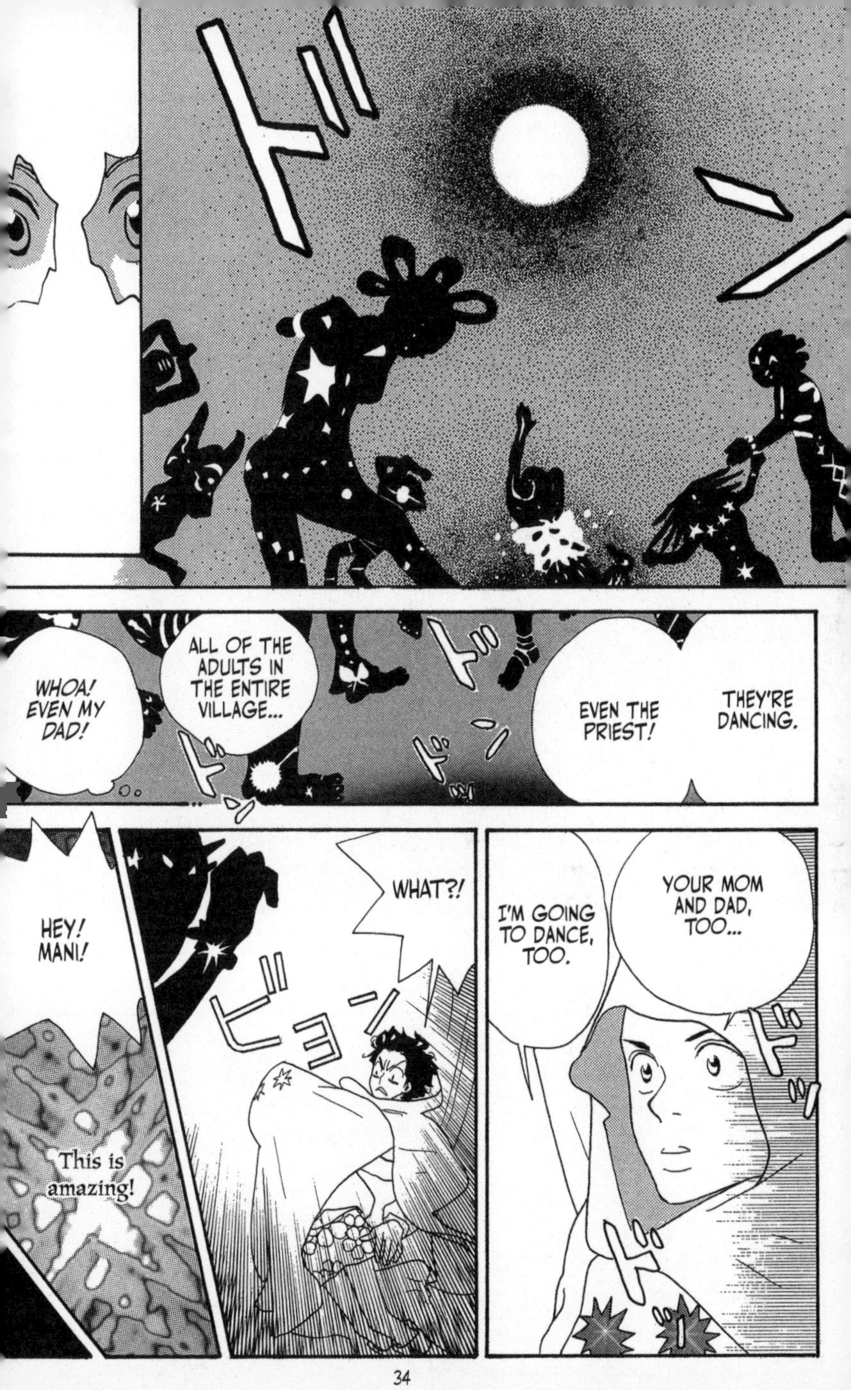
THEY'RE DANCING.
EVEN THE PRIEST!
ALL OF THE ADULTS IN THE ENTIRE VILLAGE...
WHOA! EVEN MY DAD!
YOUR MOM AND DAD, TOO...
I'M GOING TO DANCE, TOO.
WHAT?!
HEY! MANI!
This is amazing!

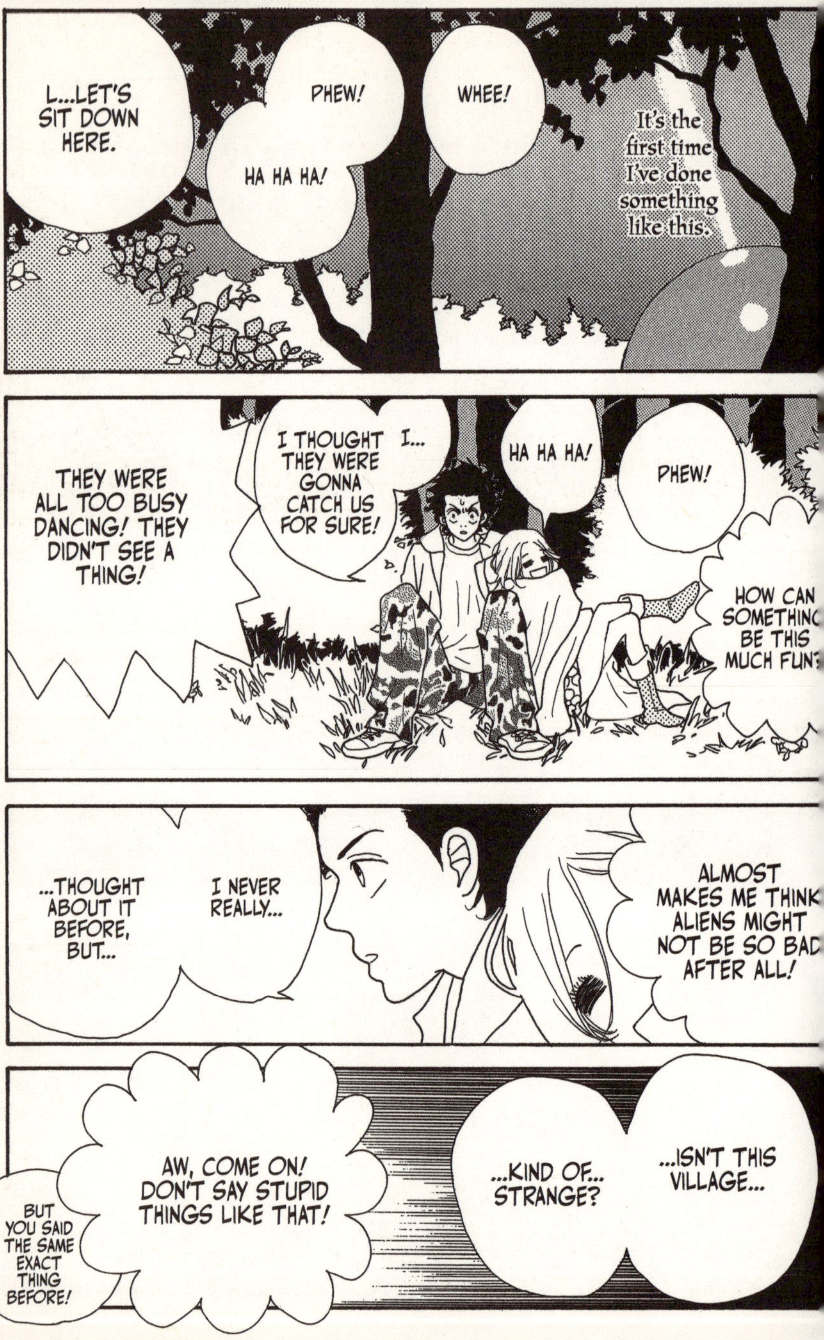
It's the first time I've done something like this.
WHEE!
PHEW!
HA HA HA!
L...LET'S SIT DOWN HERE.
PHEW!
HOW CAN SOMETHING BE THIS MUCH FUN?
HA HA HA!
I...
I THOUGHT THEY WERE GONNA CATCH US FOR SURE!
THEY WERE ALL TOO BUSY DANCING! THEY DIDN'T SEE A THING!
ALMOST MAKES ME THINK ALIENS MIGHT NOT BE SO BAD AFTER ALL!
I NEVER REALLY...
...THOUGHT ABOUT IT BEFORE, BUT...
...ISN'T THIS VILLAGE...
...KIND OF... STRANGE?
AW, COME ON! DON'T SAY STUPID THINGS LIKE THAT!
BUT YOU SAID THE SAME EXACT THING BEFORE!

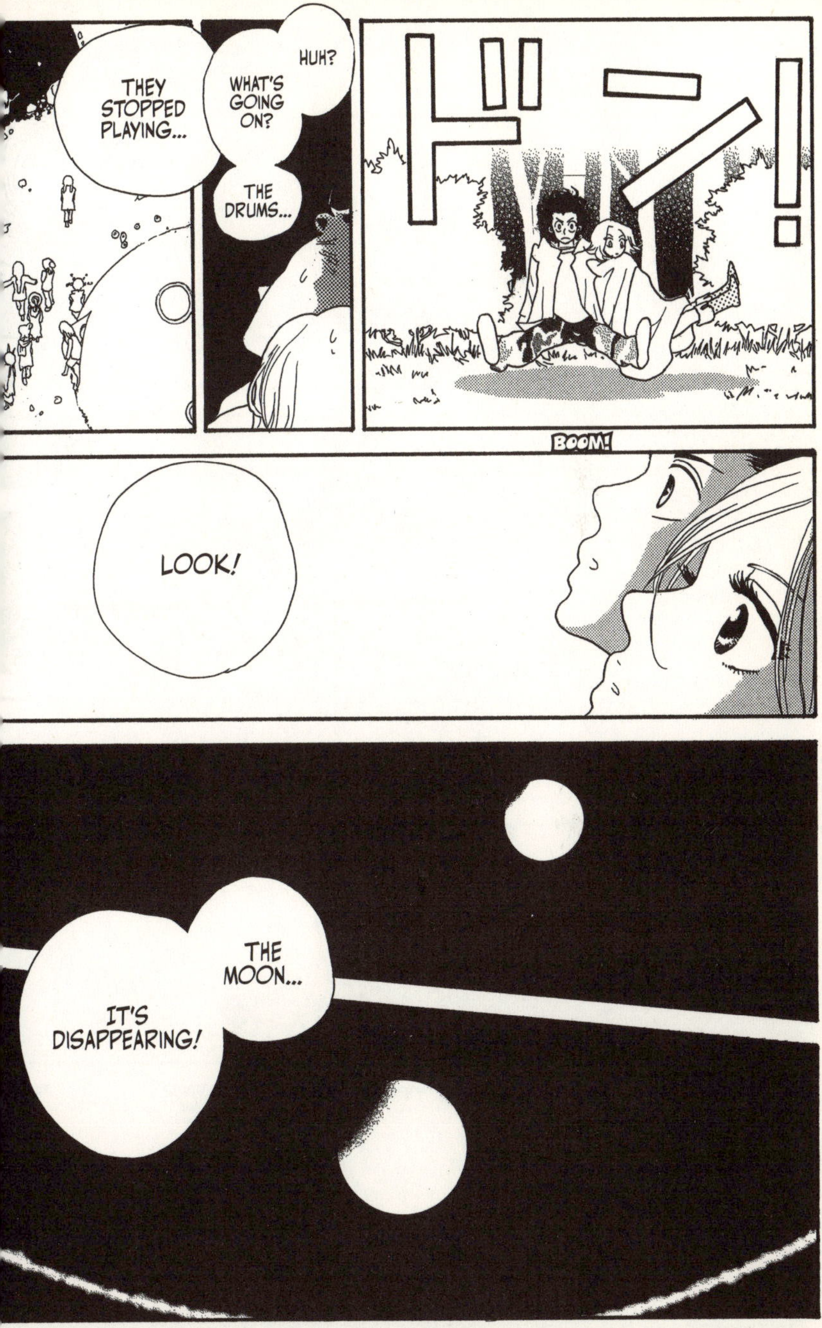

ドーン!
BOOM!
HUH?
WHAT'S GOING ON?
THE DRUMS...
THEY STOPPED PLAYING...
LOOK!
THE MOON...
IT'S DISAPPEARING!

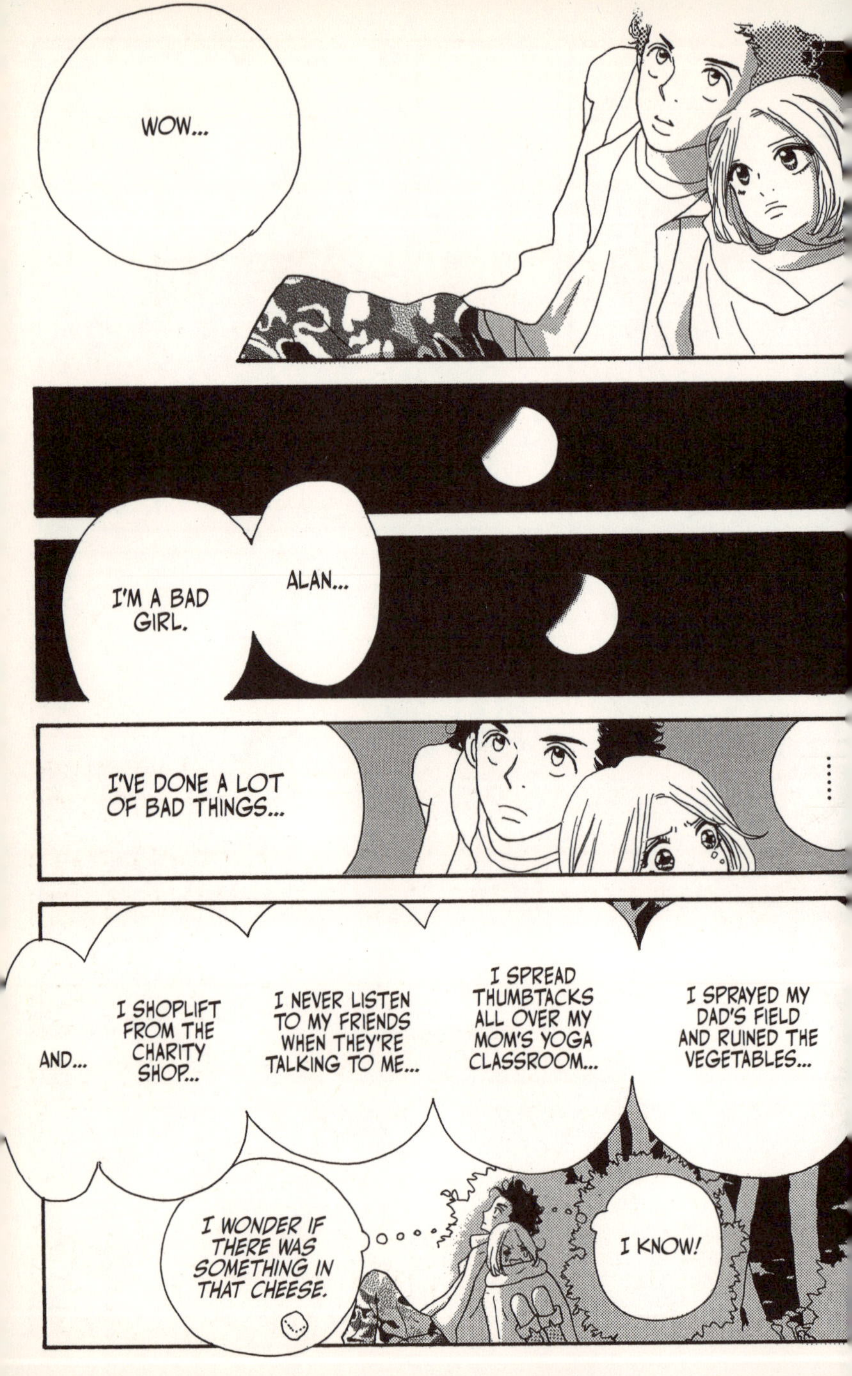
WOW...
ALAN...
I'M A BAD GIRL.
......
I'VE DONE A LOT OF BAD THINGS...
I SPRAYED MY DAD'S FIELD AND RUINED THE VEGETABLES...
I SPREAD THUMBTACKS ALL OVER MY MOM'S YOGA CLASSROOM...
I NEVER LISTEN TO MY FRIENDS WHEN THEY'RE TALKING TO ME...
I SHOPLIFT FROM THE CHARITY SHOP...
AND...
I KNOW!
I WONDER IF THERE WAS SOMETHING IN THAT CHEESE.

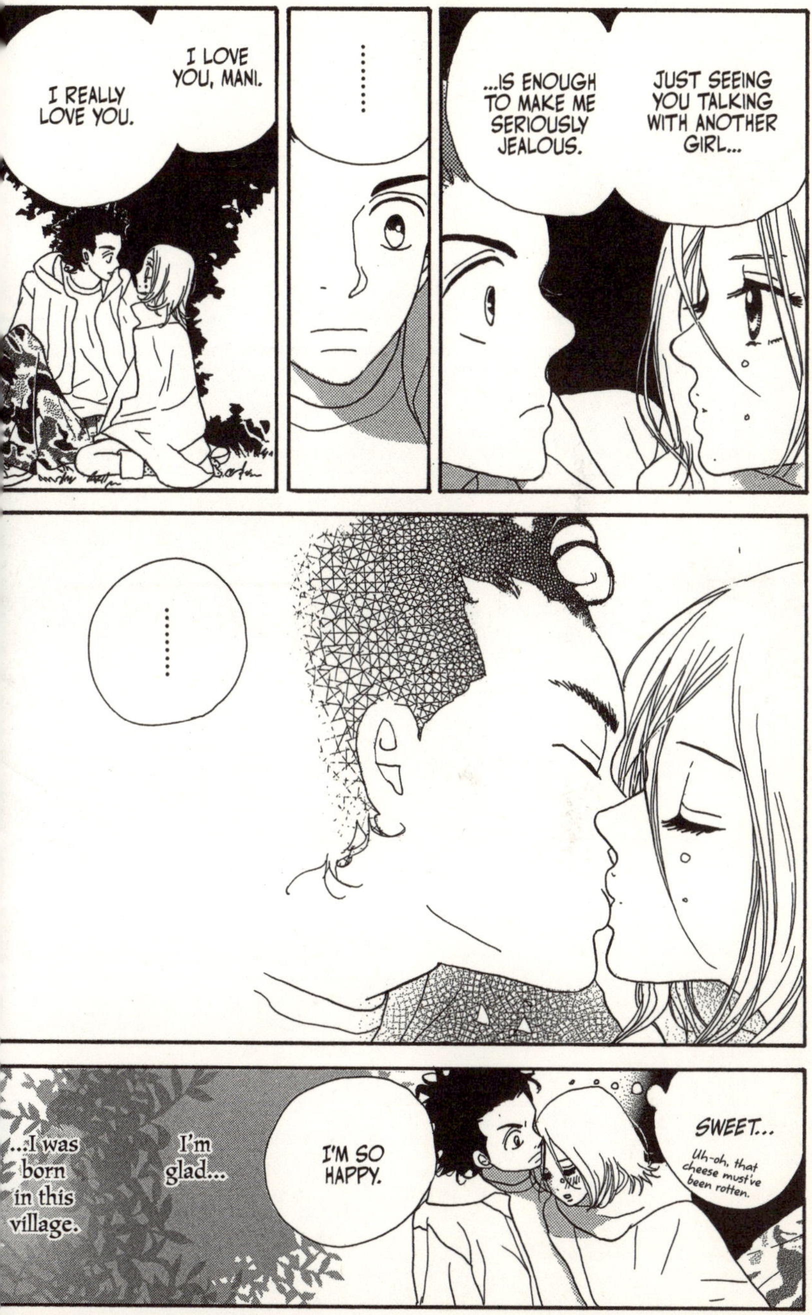
JUST SEEING YOU TALKING WITH ANOTHER GIRL...
...IS ENOUGH TO MAKE ME SERIOUSLY JEALOUS.
......
I LOVE YOU, MANI.
I REALLY LOVE YOU.
......
SWEET...
Uh-oh, that cheese must've been rotten.
I'M SO HAPPY.
I'm glad...
...I was born in this village.

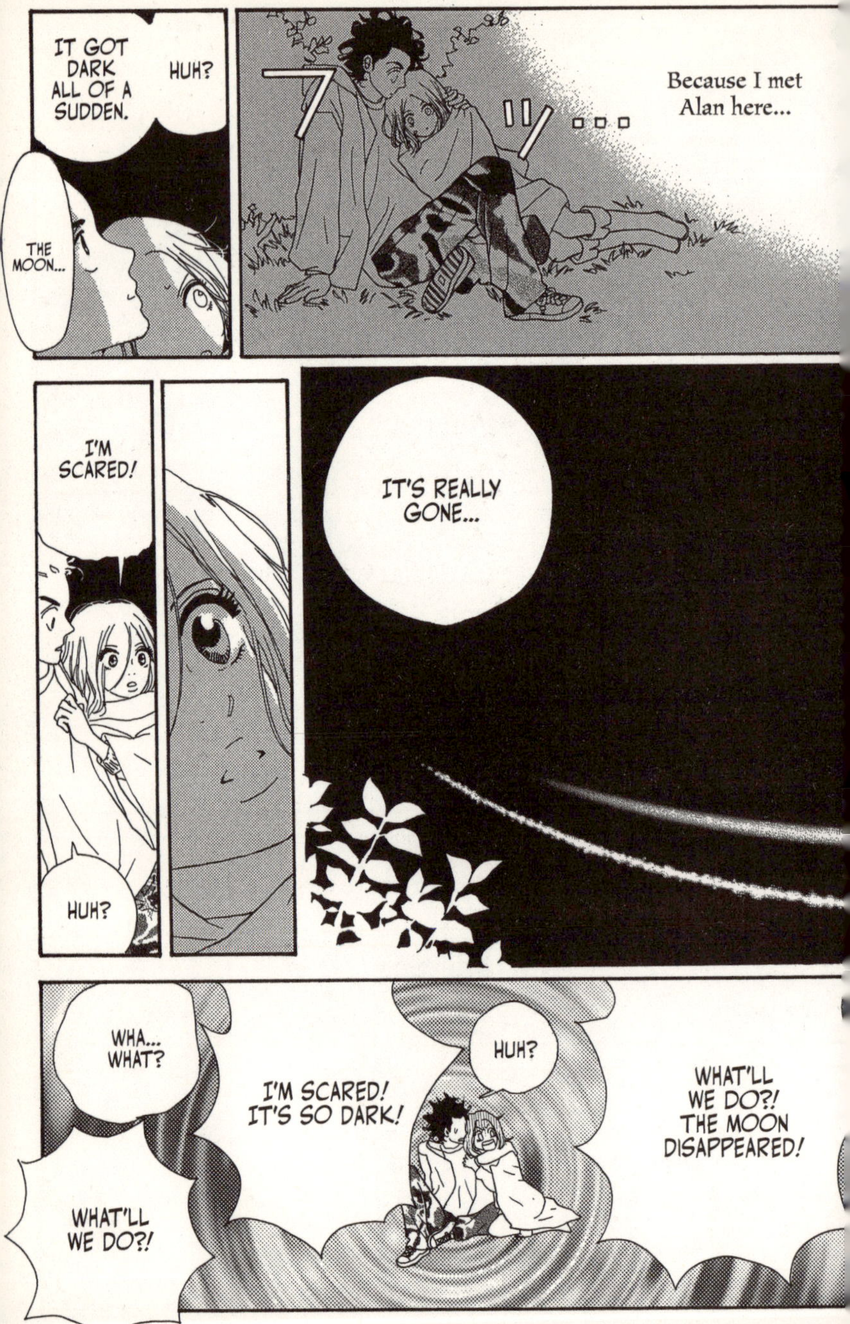
Because I met Alan here...
HUH?
IT GOT DARK ALL OF A SUDDEN.
THE MOON...
IT'S REALLY GONE...
I'M SCARED!
HUH?
WHAT'LL WE DO?! THE MOON DISAPPEARED!
HUH?
I'M SCARED! IT'S SO DARK!
WHA... WHAT?
WHAT'LL WE DO?!

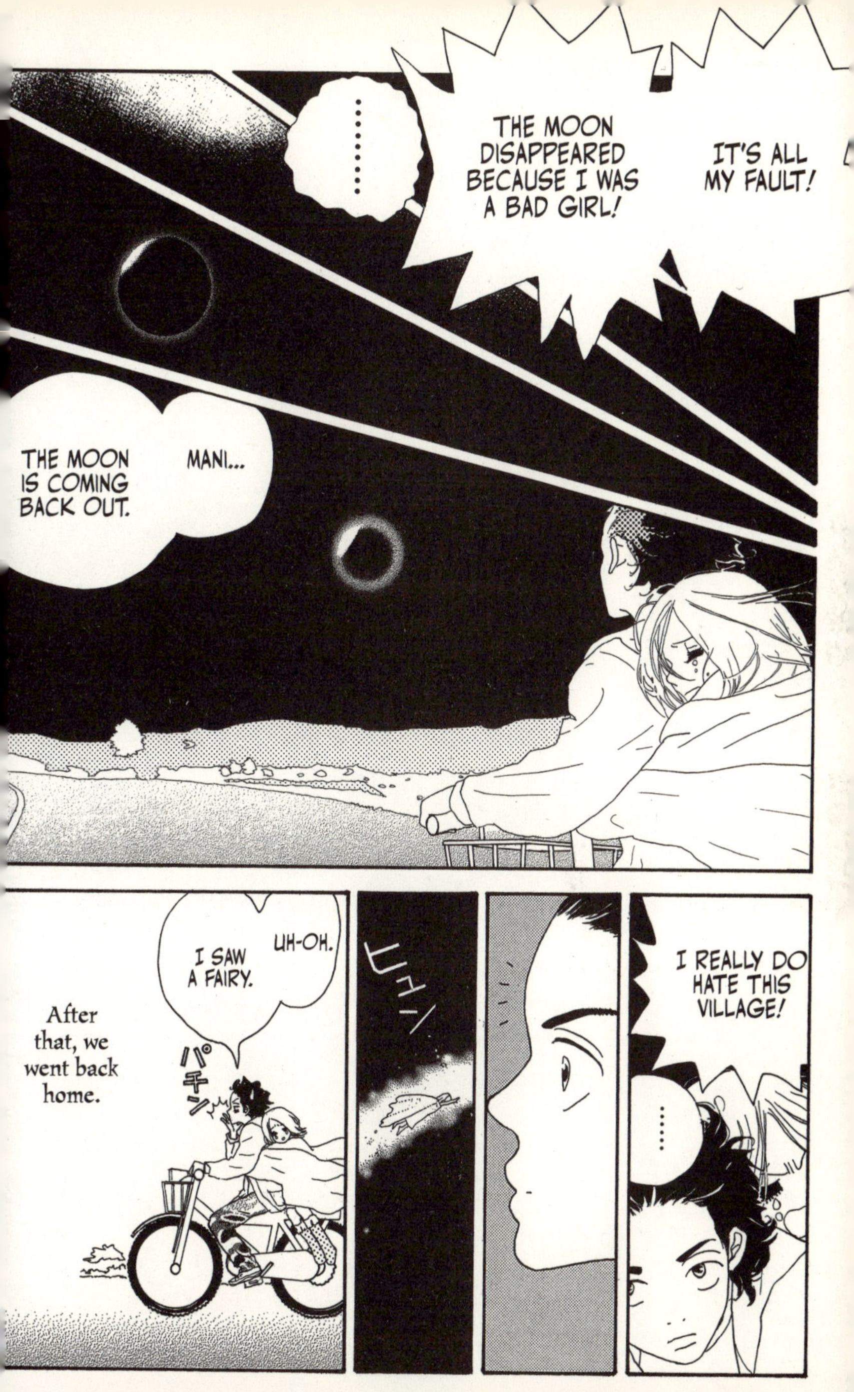
THE MOON DISAPPEARED BECAUSE I WAS A BAD GIRL!
IT'S ALL MY FAULT!
......
MANI...
THE MOON IS COMING BACK OUT.
I REALLY DO HATE THIS VILLAGE!
......
ヒュン
UH-OH.
I SAW A FAIRY.
パチン
After that, we went back home.

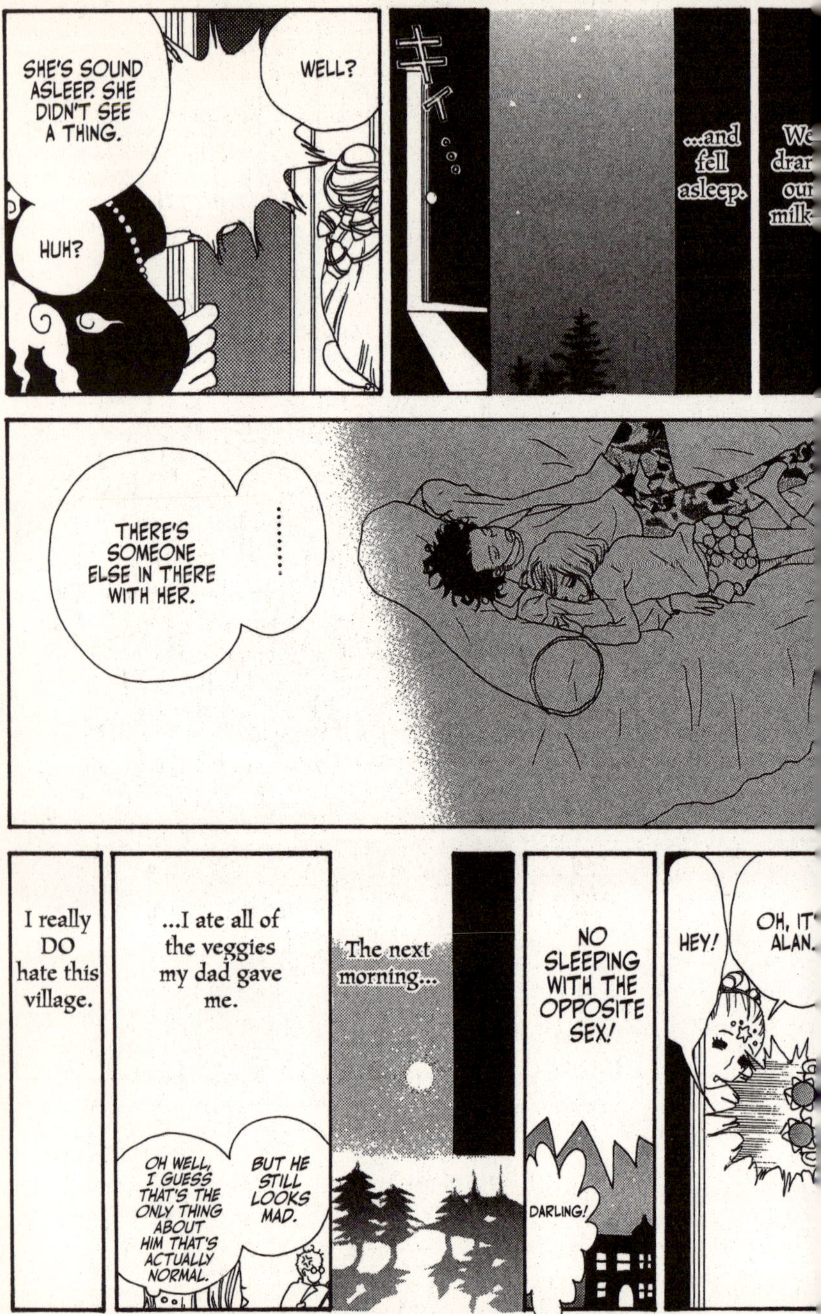

We dra our milk-
...and fell asleep.
キィ
WELL?
SHE'S SOUND ASLEEP. SHE DIDN'T SEE A THING.
HUH?
....
THERE'S SOMEONE ELSE IN THERE WITH HER.
OH, IT' ALAN.
HEY!
NO SLEEPING WITH THE OPPOSITE SEX!
DARLING!
The next morning...
...I ate all of the veggies my dad gave me.
BUT HE STILL LOOKS MAD.
OH WELL, I GUESS THAT'S THE ONLY THING ABOUT HIM THAT'S ACTUALLY NORMAL.
I really DO hate this village.

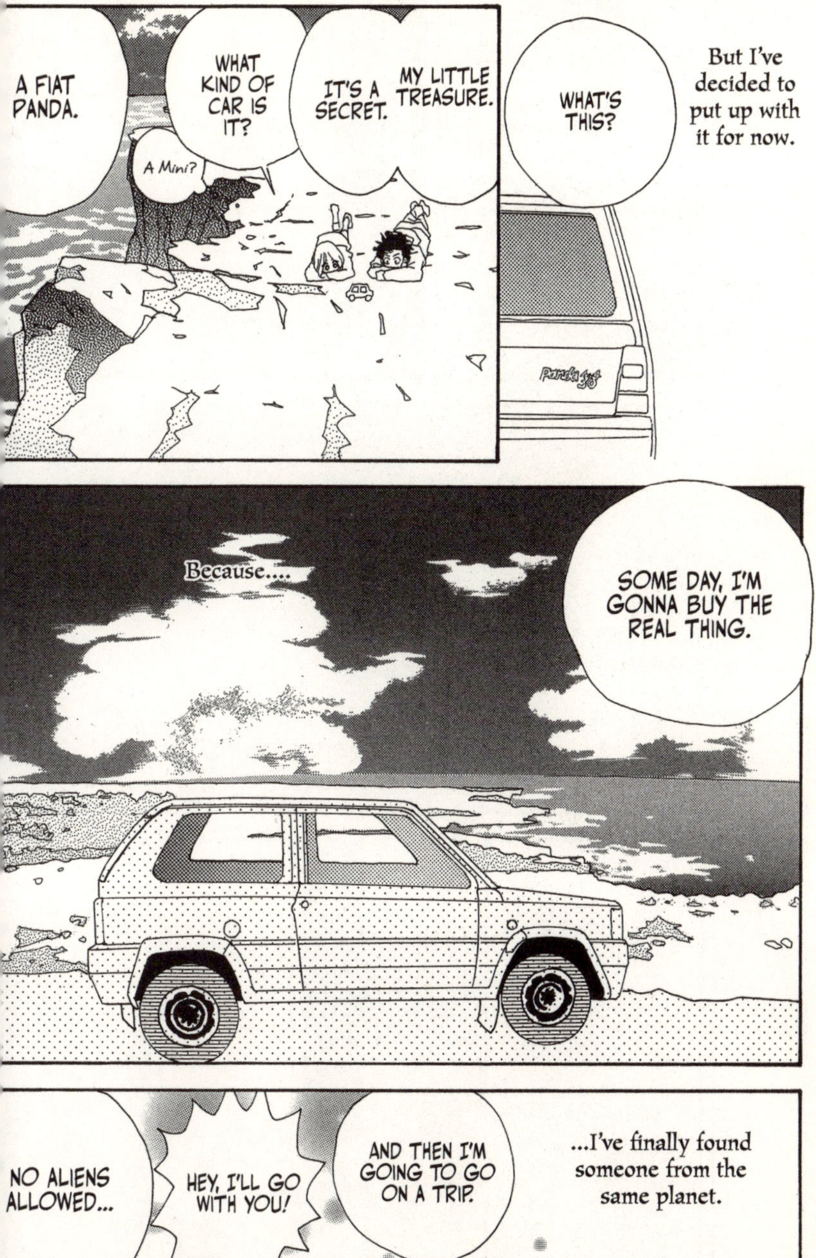

But I've decided to put up with it for now.
WHAT'S THIS?
MY LITTLE TREASURE.
IT'S A SECRET.
WHAT KIND OF CAR IS IT?
A Mini?
A FIAT PANDA.
SOME DAY, I'M GONNA BUY THE REAL THING.
Because....
...I've finally found someone from the same planet.
AND THEN I'M GOING TO GO ON A TRIP.
HEY, I'LL GO WITH YOU!
NO ALIENS ALLOWED...

The Laidback Person I Will Never Forget

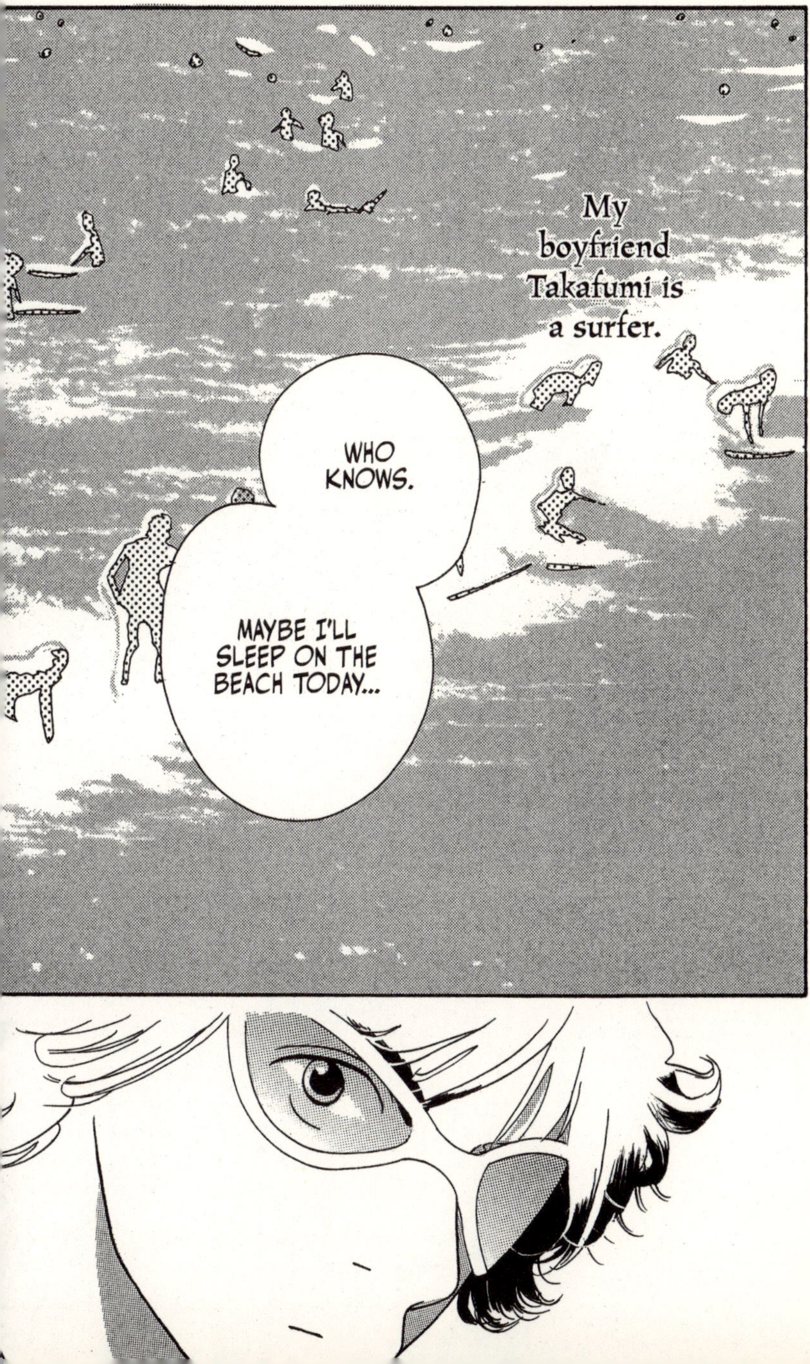
My boyfriend Takafumi is a surfer.
WHO KNOWS.
MAYBE I'LL SLEEP ON THE BEACH TODAY...

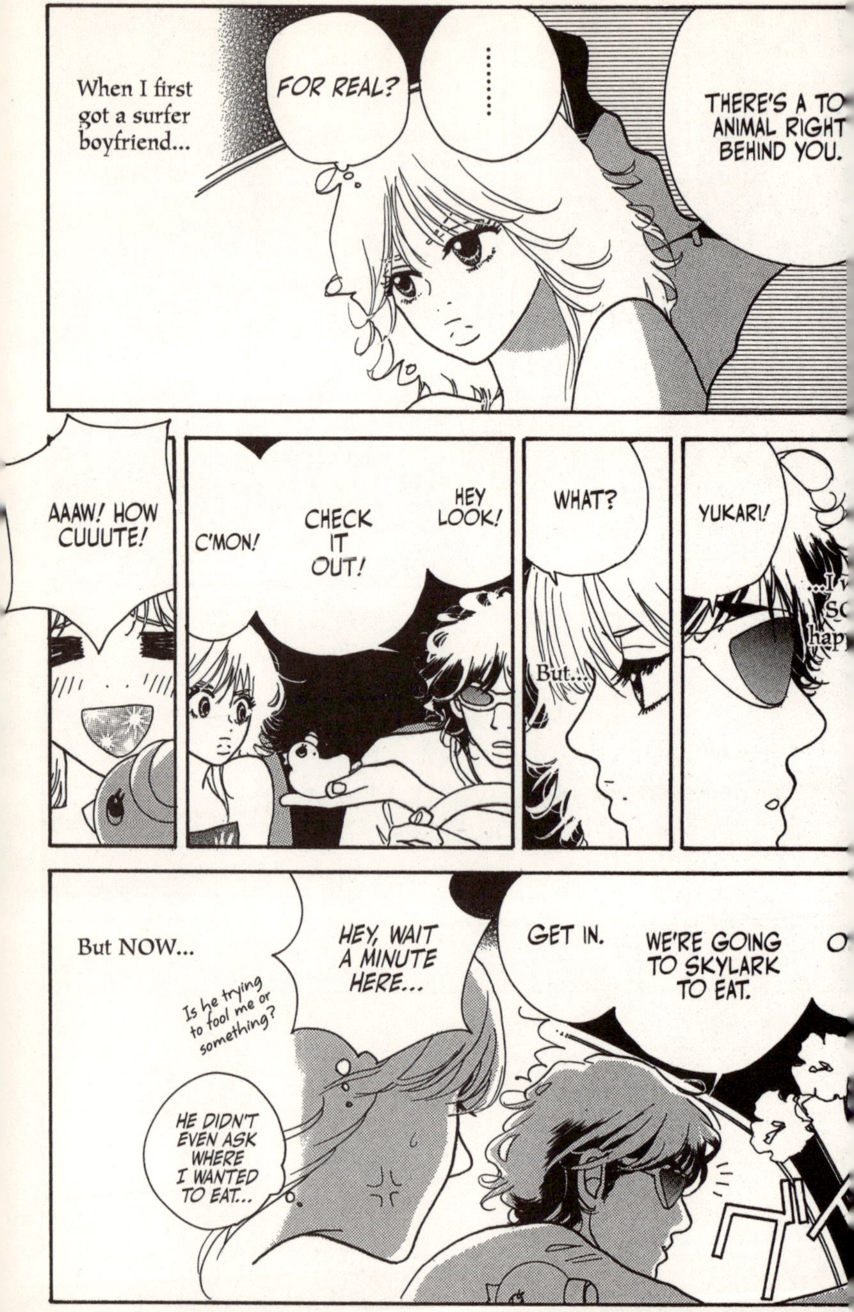
THERE'S A TO
ANIMAL RIGHT BEHIND YOU.
....
FOR REAL?
When I first got a surfer boyfriend...
YUKARI!
WHAT?
But...
HEY LOOK!
CHECK IT OUT!
C'MON!
AAAW! HOW CUUUTE!
WE'RE GOING TO SKYLARK TO EAT.
GET IN.
HEY, WAIT A MINUTE HERE...
Is he trying to fool me or something?
HE DIDN'T EVEN ASK WHERE I WANTED TO EAT...
But NOW...

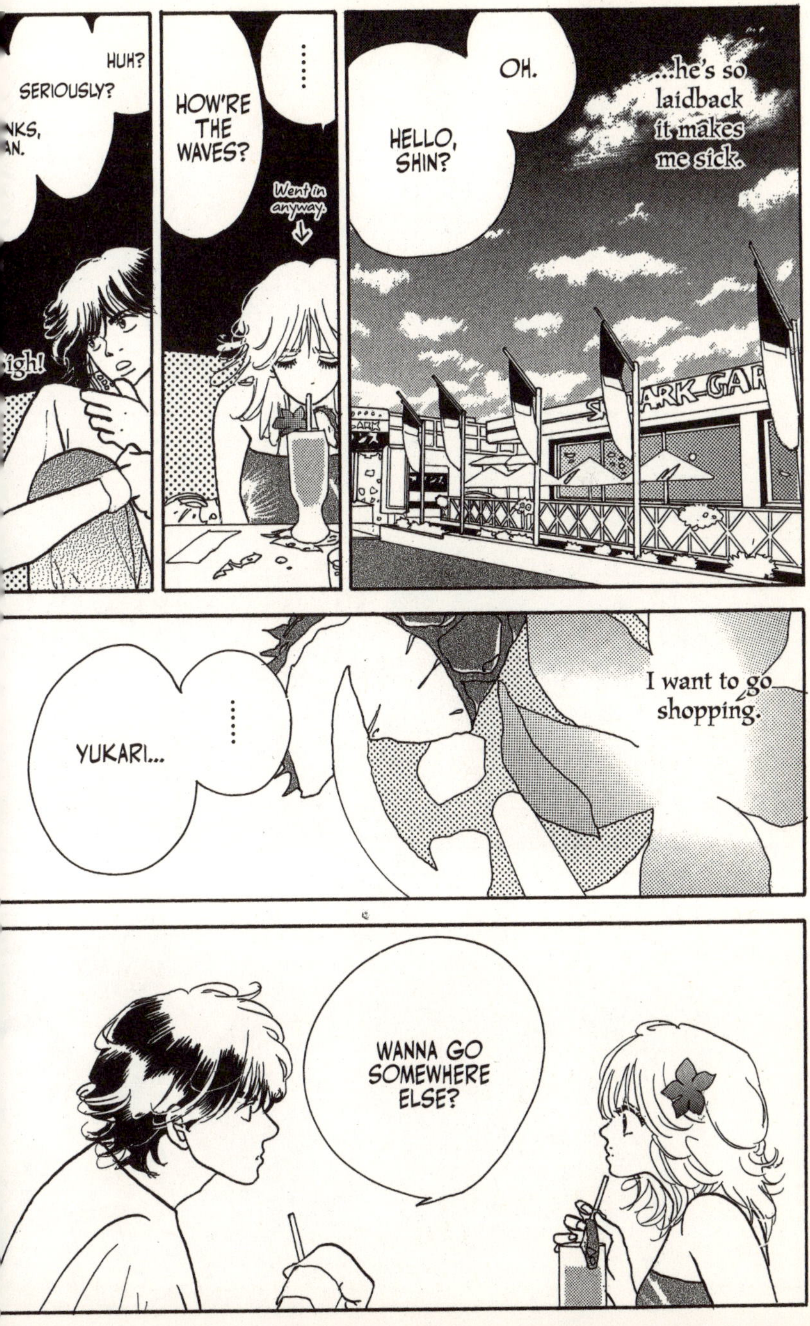
OH.
HELLO, SHIN?
...he's so laidback it makes me sick.
......
HOW'RE THE WAVES?
Went in anyway.
HUH?
SERIOUSLY?
I want to go shopping.
......
YUKARI...
WANNA GO SOMEWHERE ELSE?

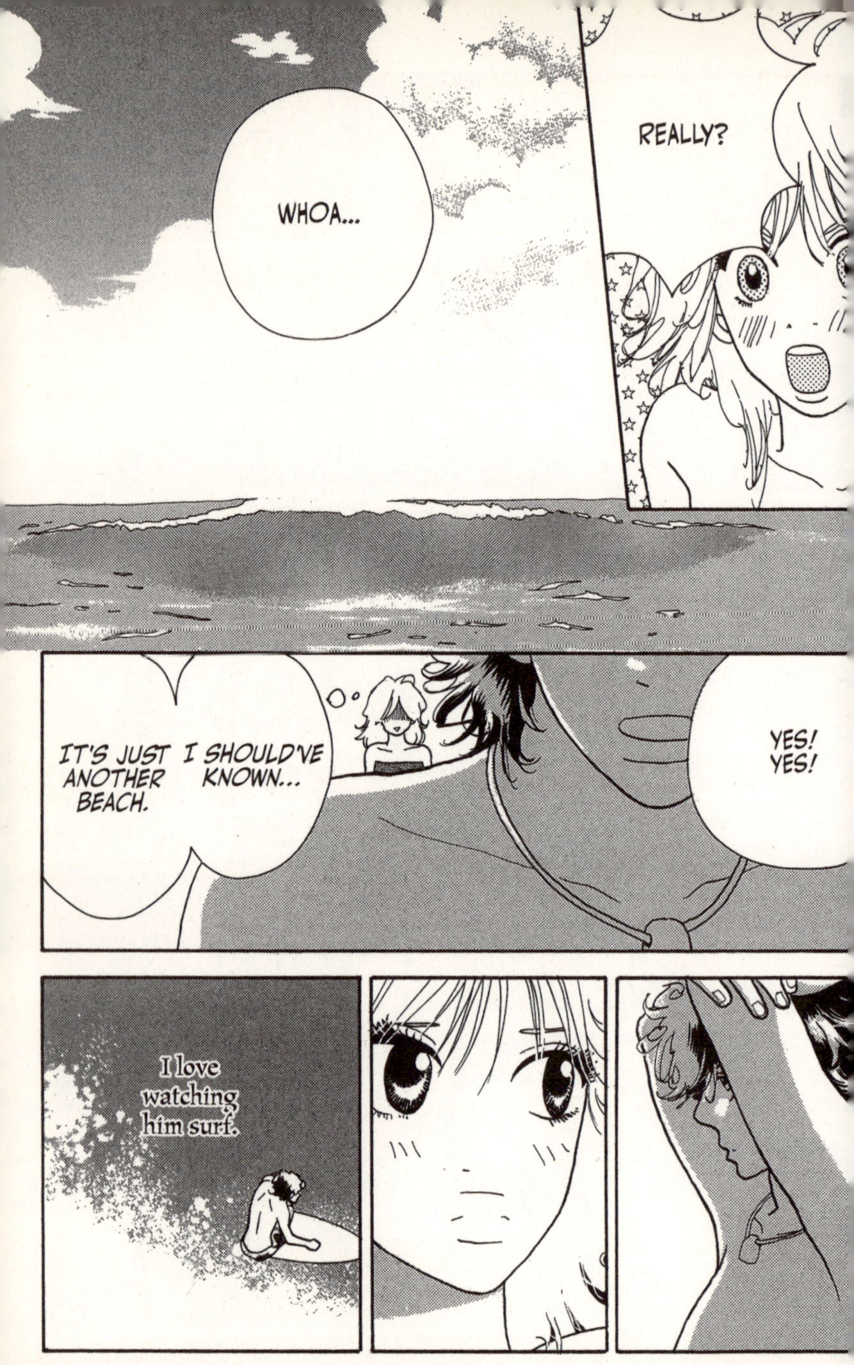
REALLY?
WHOA...
YES! YES!
IT'S JUST ANOTHER BEACH.
I SHOULD'VE KNOWN...
I love watching him surf.

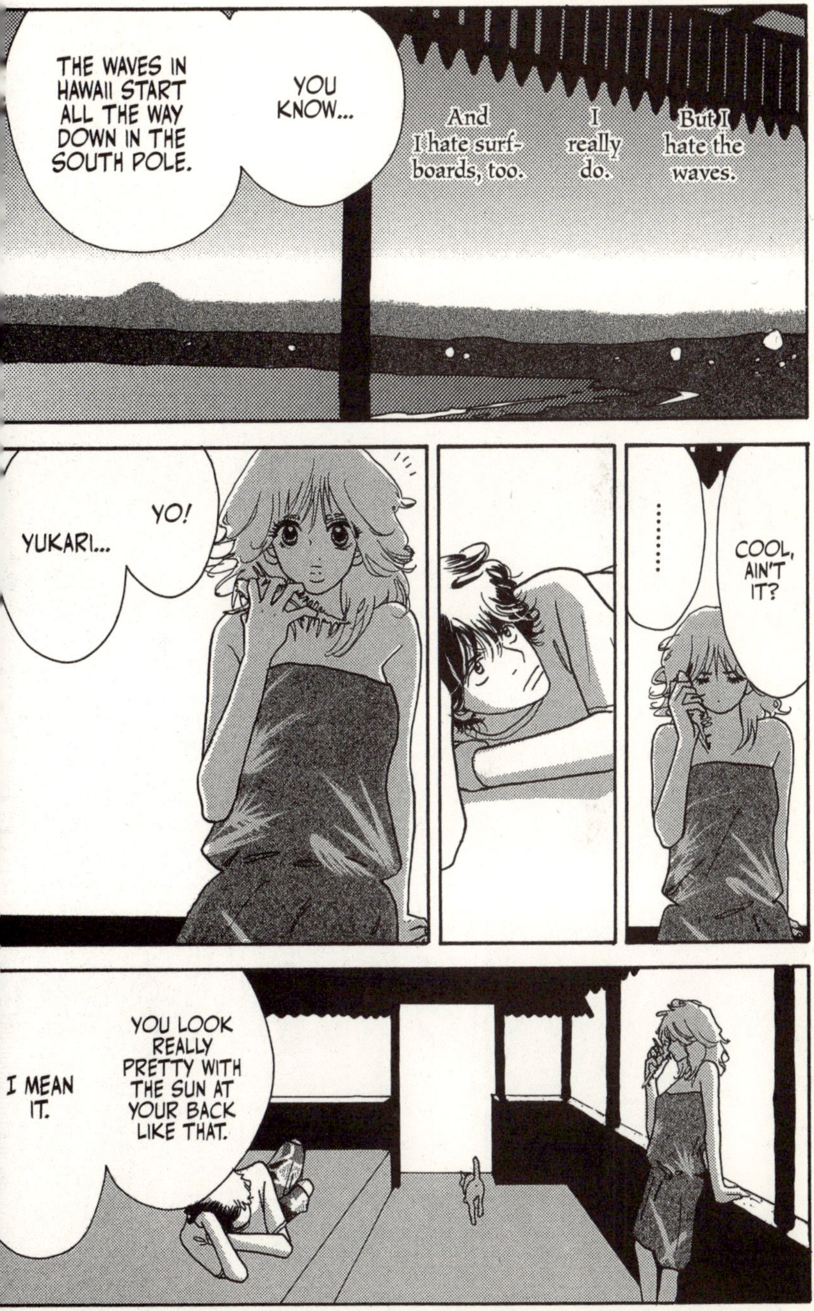
But I hate the waves.
I really do.
And I hate surfboards, too.
YOU KNOW...
THE WAVES IN HAWAII START ALL THE WAY DOWN IN THE SOUTH POLE.
COOL, AIN'T IT?
....
YO!
YUKARI...
YOU LOOK REALLY PRETTY WITH THE SUN AT YOUR BACK LIKE THAT.
I MEAN IT.

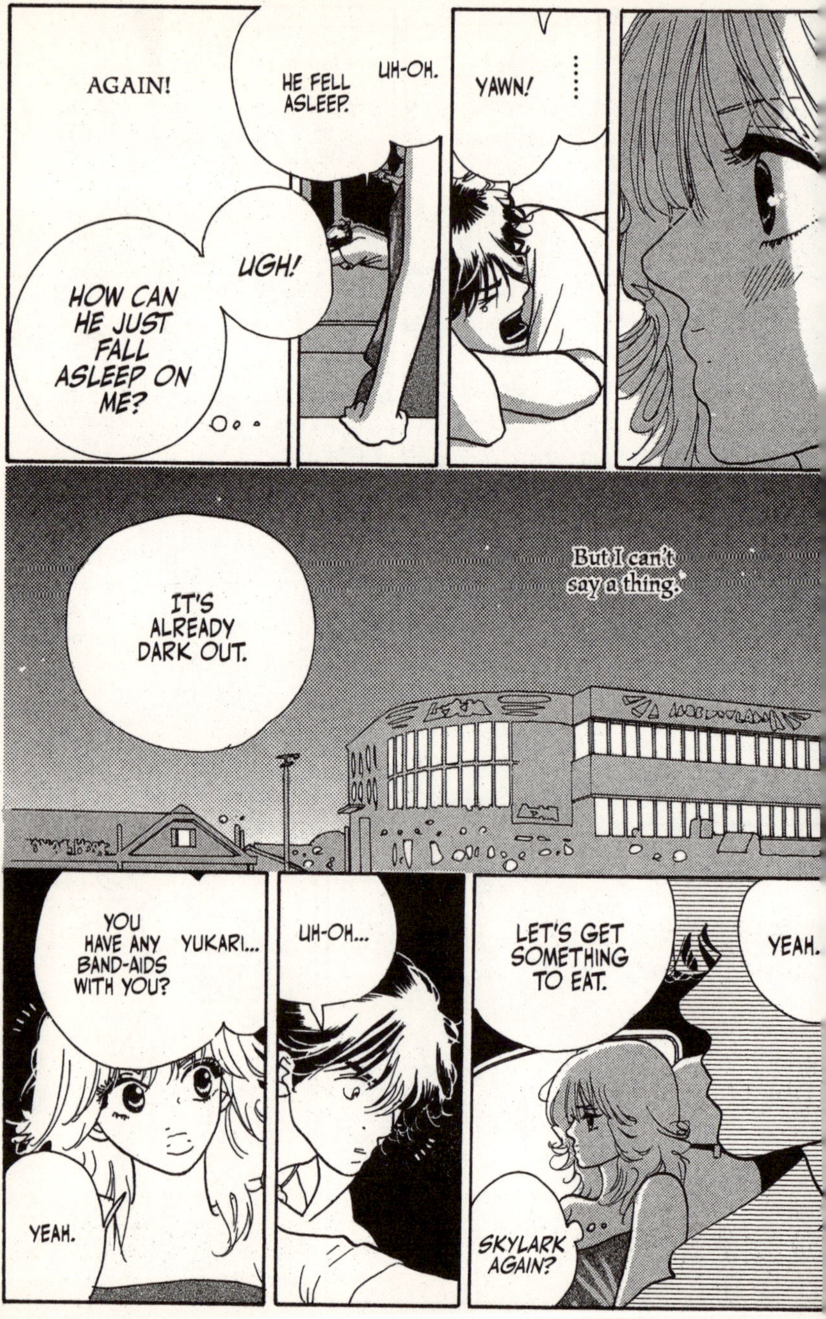
......
YAWN!
UH-OH.
HE FELL ASLEEP.
AGAIN!
UGH!
HOW CAN HE JUST FALL ASLEEP ON ME?
But I can't say a thing.
IT'S ALREADY DARK OUT.
YEAH.
LET'S GET SOMETHING TO EAT.
SKYLARK AGAIN?
UH-OH...
YUKARI...
YOU HAVE ANY BAND-AIDS WITH YOU?
YEAH.

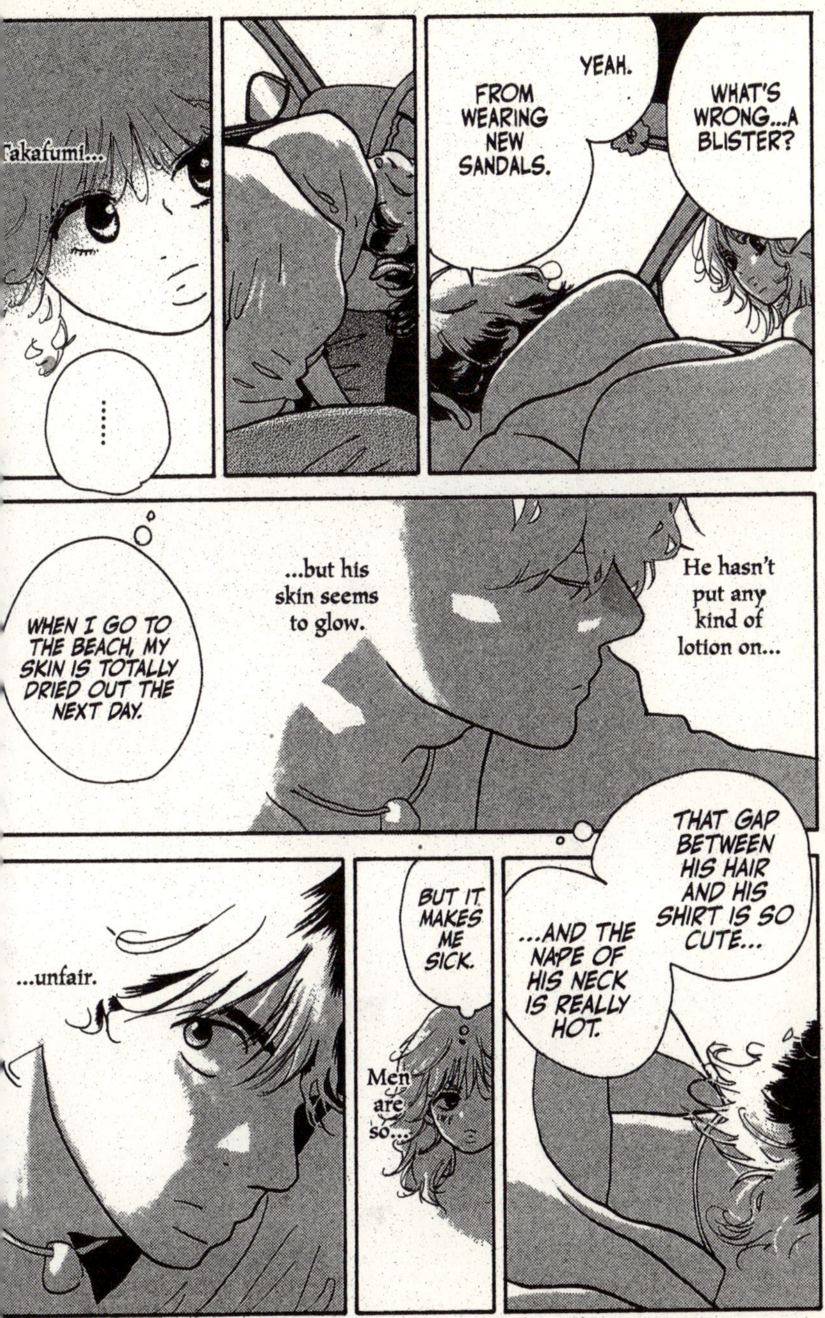

WHAT'S WRONG...A BLISTER?
YEAH.
FROM WEARING NEW SANDALS.
Takafumi...
......
He hasn't put any kind of lotion on...
...but his skin seems to glow.
WHEN I GO TO THE BEACH, MY SKIN IS TOTALLY DRIED OUT THE NEXT DAY.
THAT GAP BETWEEN HIS HAIR AND HIS SHIRT IS SO CUTE...
...AND THE NAPE OF HIS NECK IS REALLY HOT.
BUT IT MAKES ME SICK.
Men are so...
...unfair.

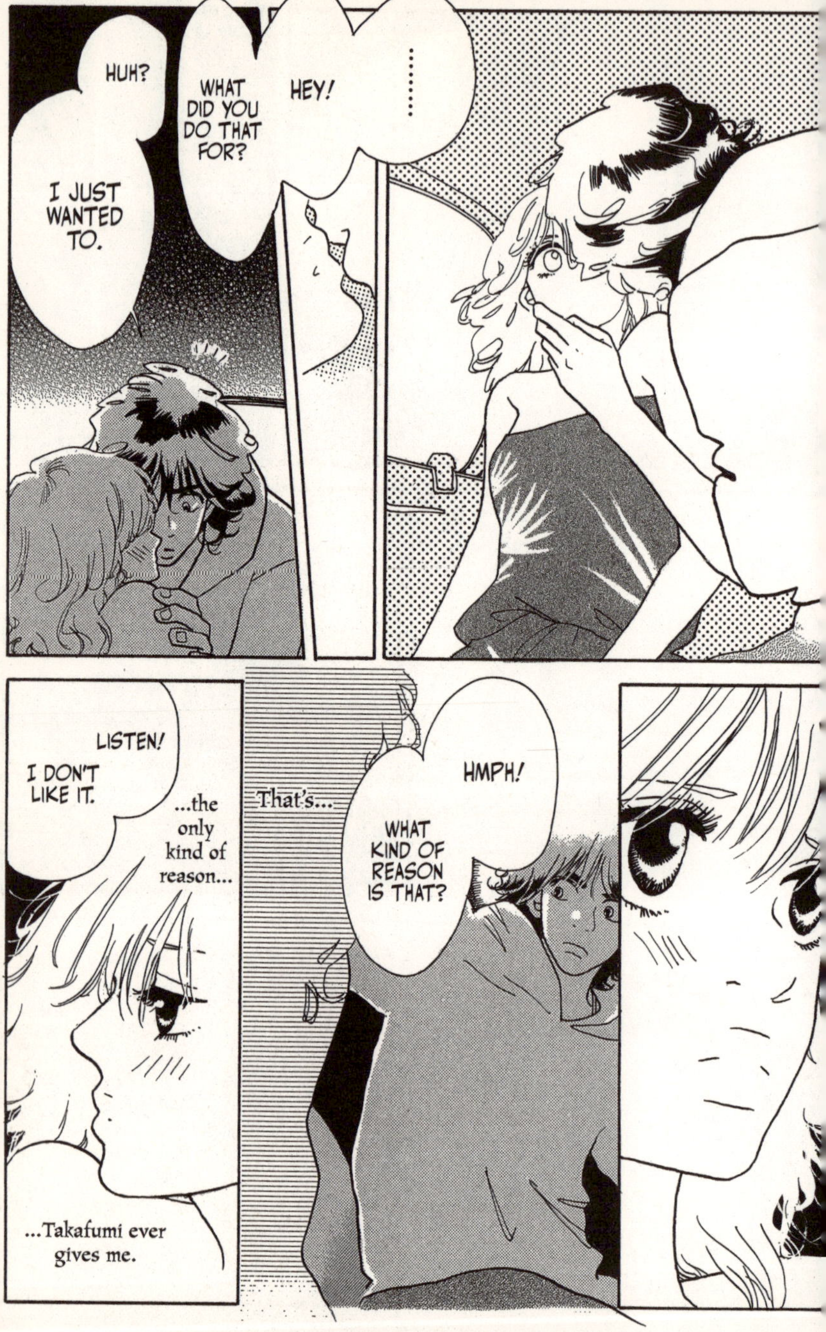
......
HEY!
WHAT DID YOU DO THAT FOR?
HUH?
I JUST WANTED TO.
HMPH!
WHAT KIND OF REASON IS THAT?
That's...
LISTEN!
I DON'T LIKE IT.
...the only kind of reason...
...Takafumi ever gives me.

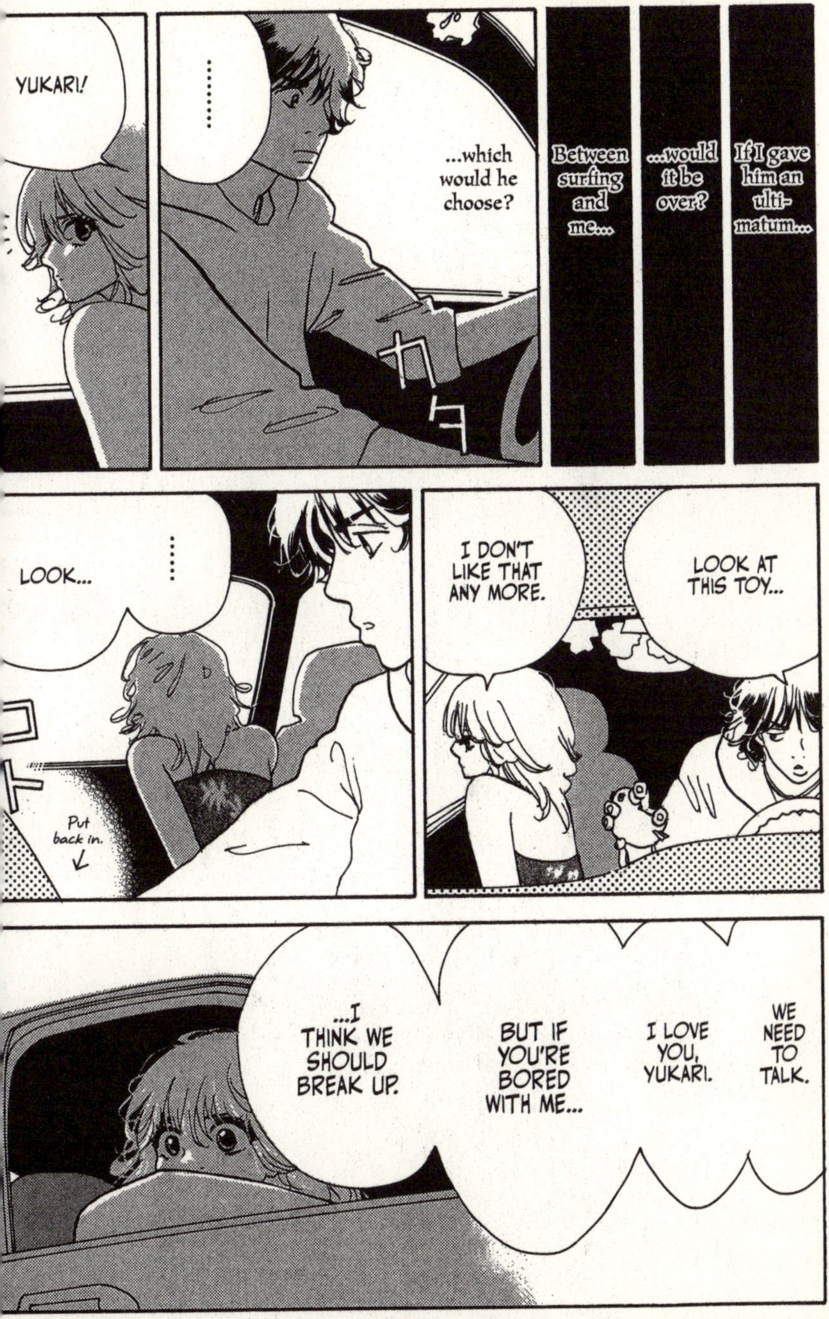
If I gave him an ultimatum...
...would it be over?
Between surfing and me...
...which would he choose?
......
YUKARI!
LOOK AT THIS TOY...
I DON'T LIKE THAT ANY MORE.
......
LOOK...
Put back in.
WE NEED TO TALK.
I LOVE YOU, YUKARI.
BUT IF YOU'RE BORED WITH ME...
...I THINK WE SHOULD BREAK UP.

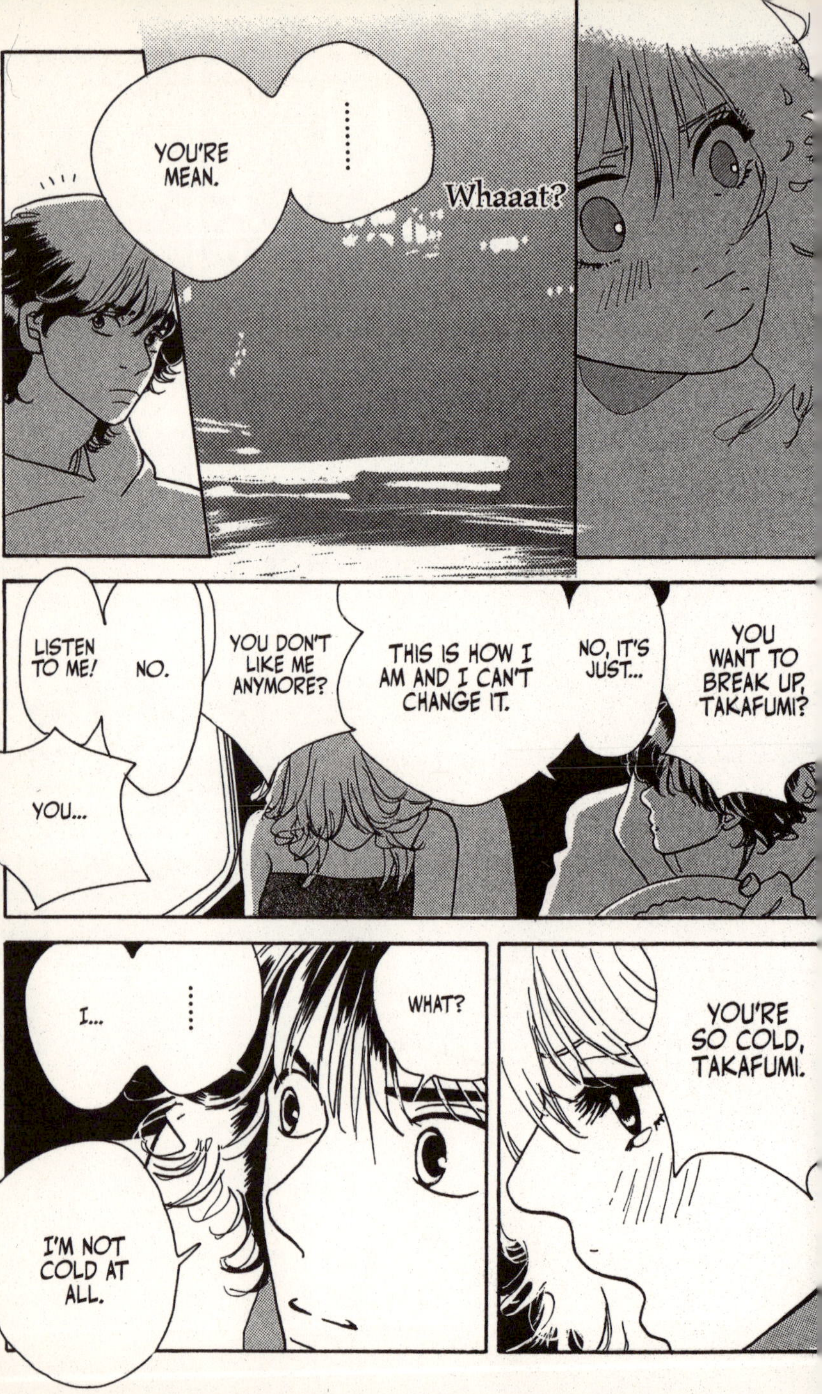
Whaaat?
......
YOU'RE MEAN.
YOU WANT TO BREAK UP, TAKAFUMI?
NO, IT'S JUST...
THIS IS HOW I AM AND I CAN'T CHANGE IT.
YOU DON'T LIKE ME ANYMORE?
NO.
LISTEN TO ME!
YOU...
YOU'RE SO COLD, TAKAFUMI.
WHAT?
......
I...
I'M NOT COLD AT ALL.

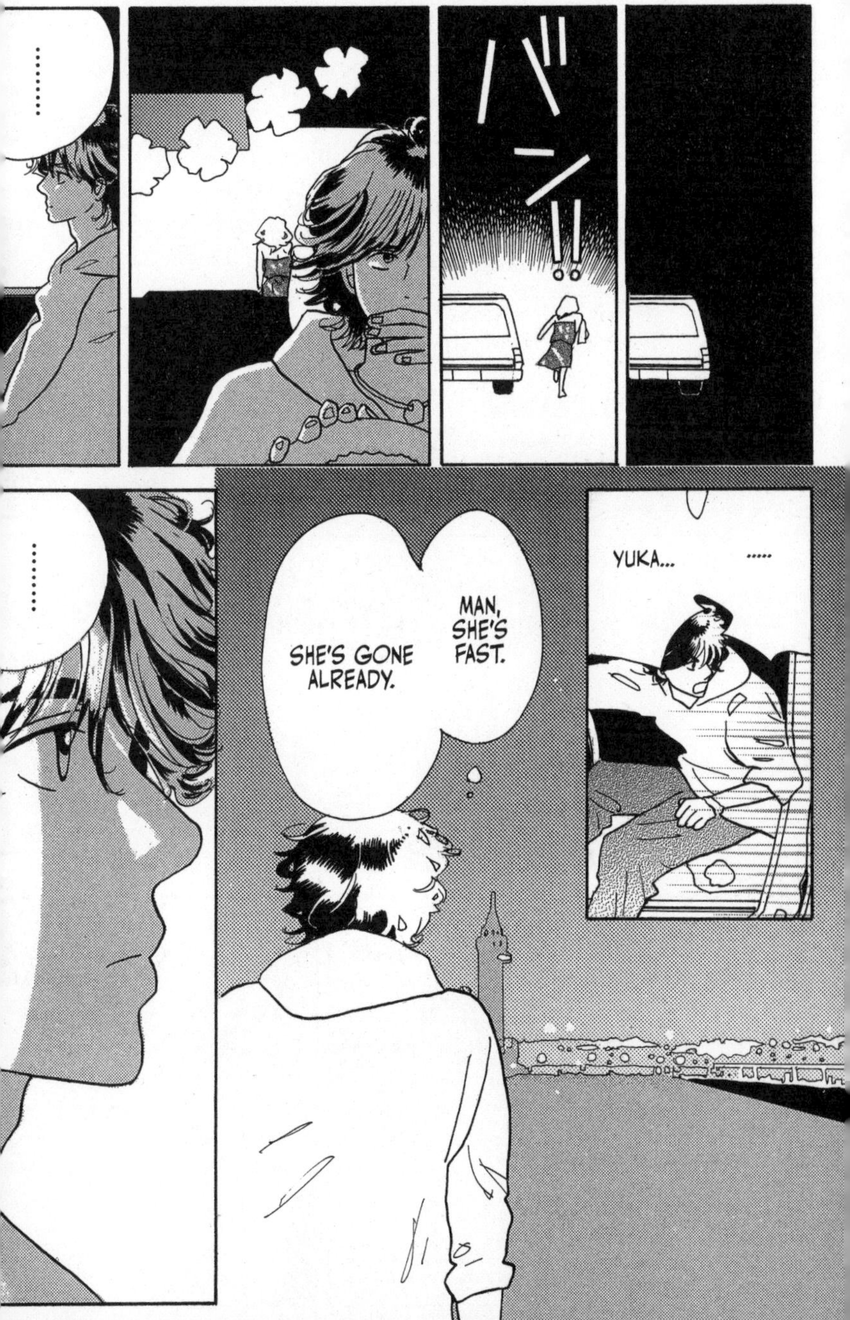
バーン!!
......
.....
YUKA...
MAN, SHE'S FAST.
SHE'S GONE ALREADY.
......

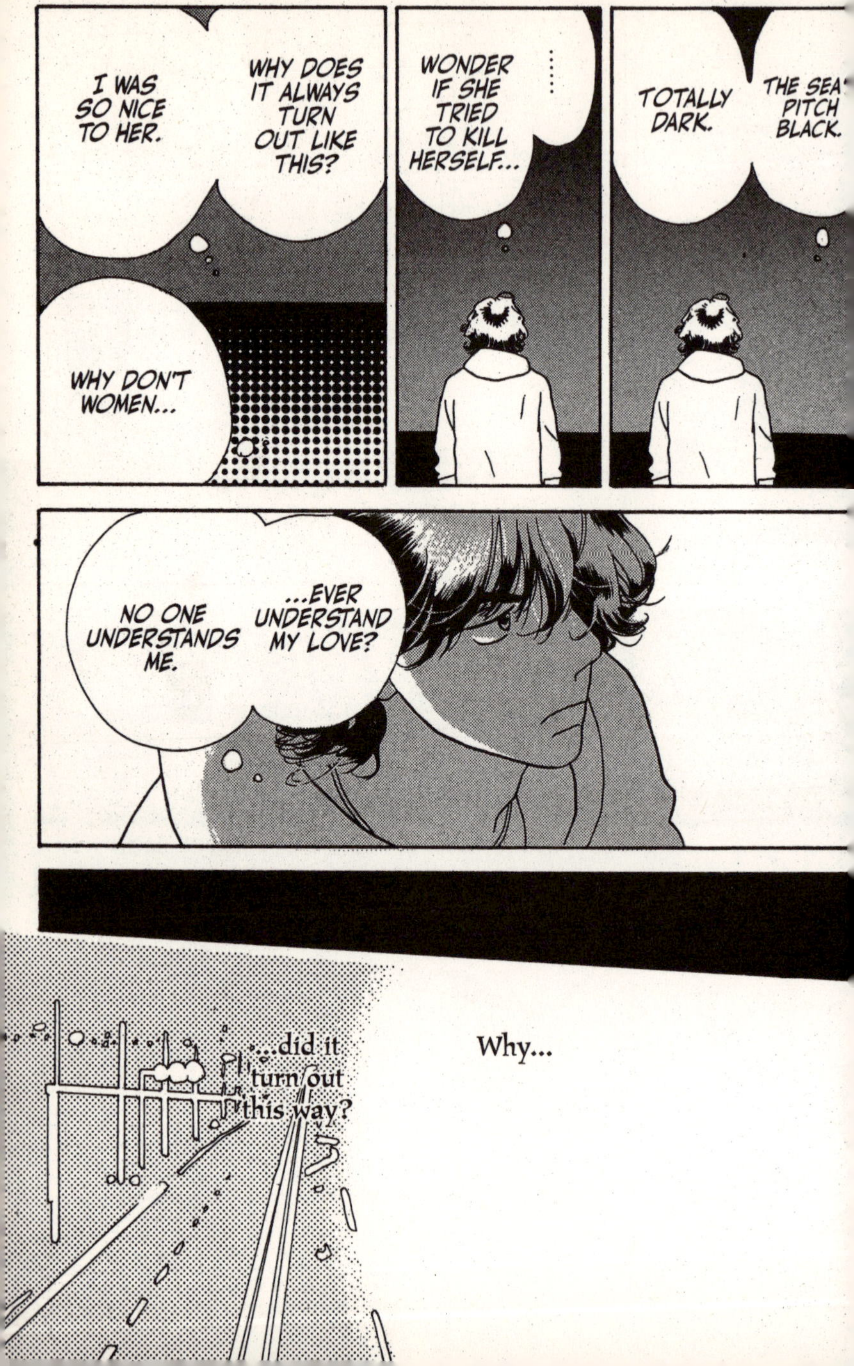

THE SEA' PITCH BLACK.
TOTALLY DARK.
......
WONDER IF SHE TRIED TO KILL HERSELF...
WHY DOES IT ALWAYS TURN OUT LIKE THIS?
I WAS SO NICE TO HER.
WHY DON'T WOMEN...
...EVER UNDERSTAND MY LOVE?
NO ONE UNDERSTANDS ME.
Why...
...did it turn out this way?

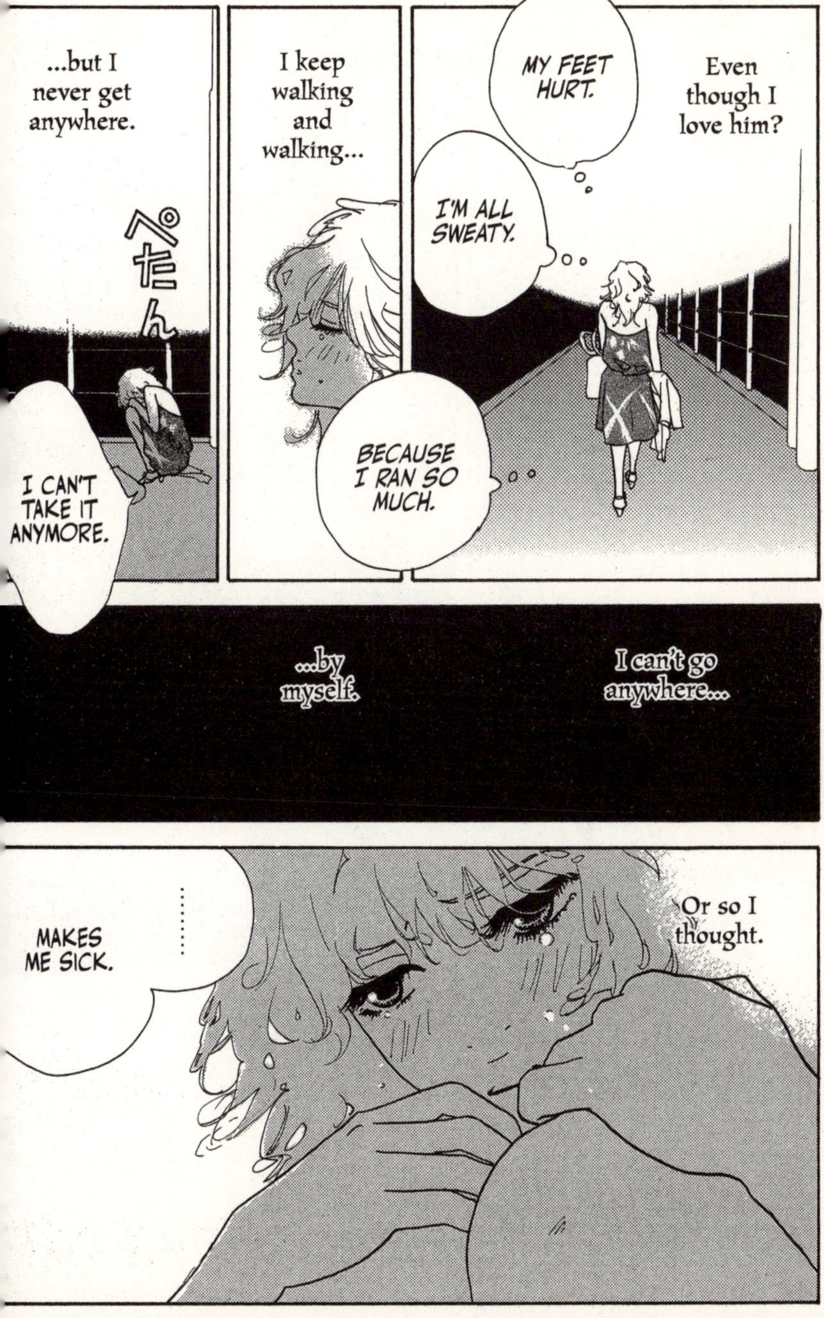
Even though I love him?
MY FEET HURT.
I'M ALL SWEATY.
BECAUSE I RAN SO MUCH.
I keep walking and walking...
...but I never get anywhere.
ぺたん
I CAN'T TAKE IT ANYMORE.
I can't go anywhere...
...by myself.
Or so I thought.
......
MAKES ME SICK.

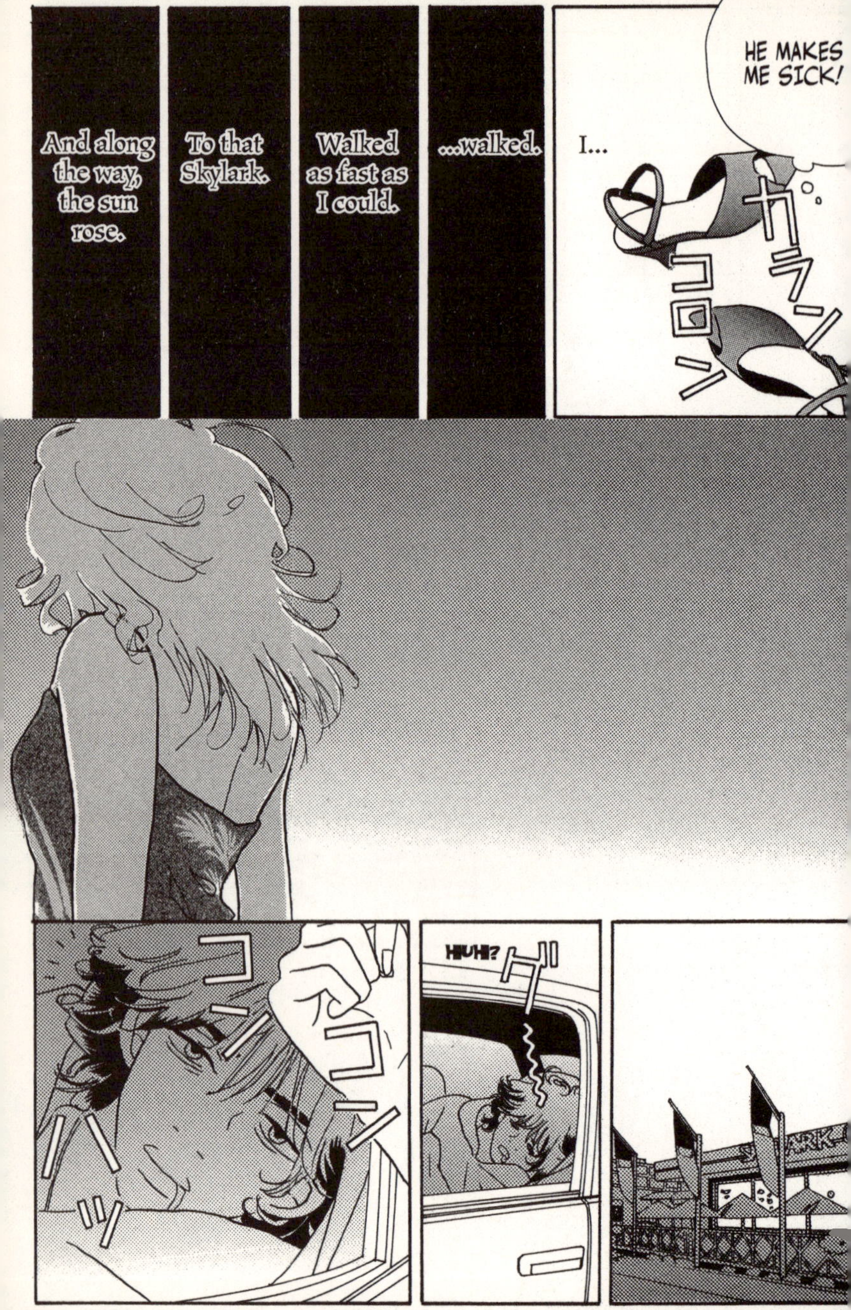
HE MAKES ME SICK!
I...
カラーン
コロン
...walked.
Walked as fast as I could.
To that Skylark.
And along the way, the sun rose.
HUH?

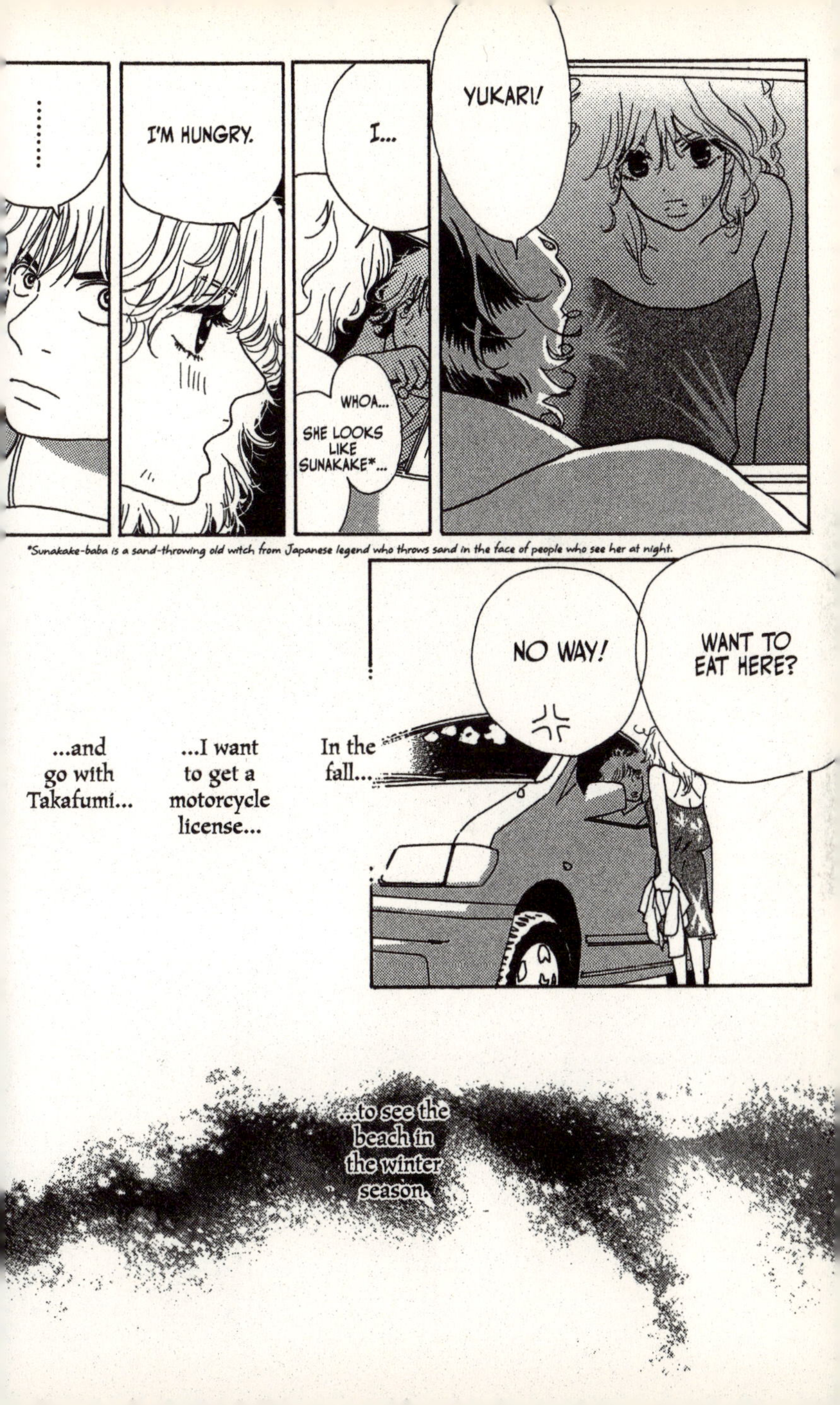
YUKARI!
I...
WHOA... SHE LOOKS LIKE SUNAKAKE*...
I'M HUNGRY.
....
WANT TO EAT HERE?
NO WAY!
In the fall...
...I want to get a motorcycle license...
...and go with Takafumi...
...to see the beach in the winter season.

*Sunakake-baba is a sand-throwing old witch from Japanese legend who throws sand in the face of people who see her at night.

Club Hurricane
Adventure 1

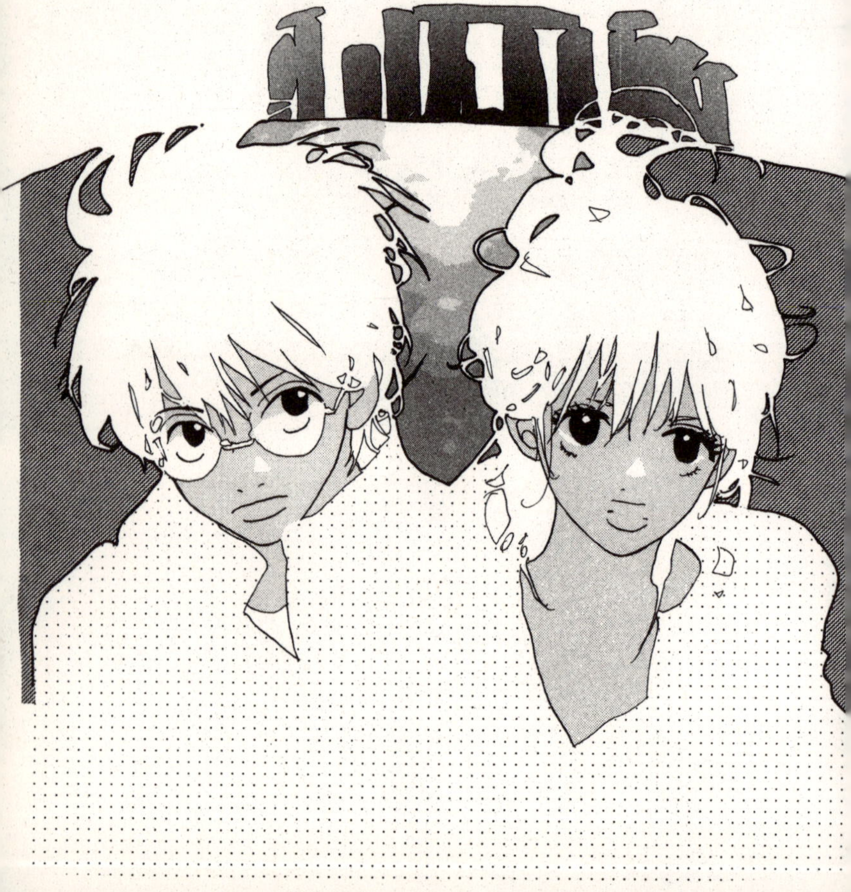

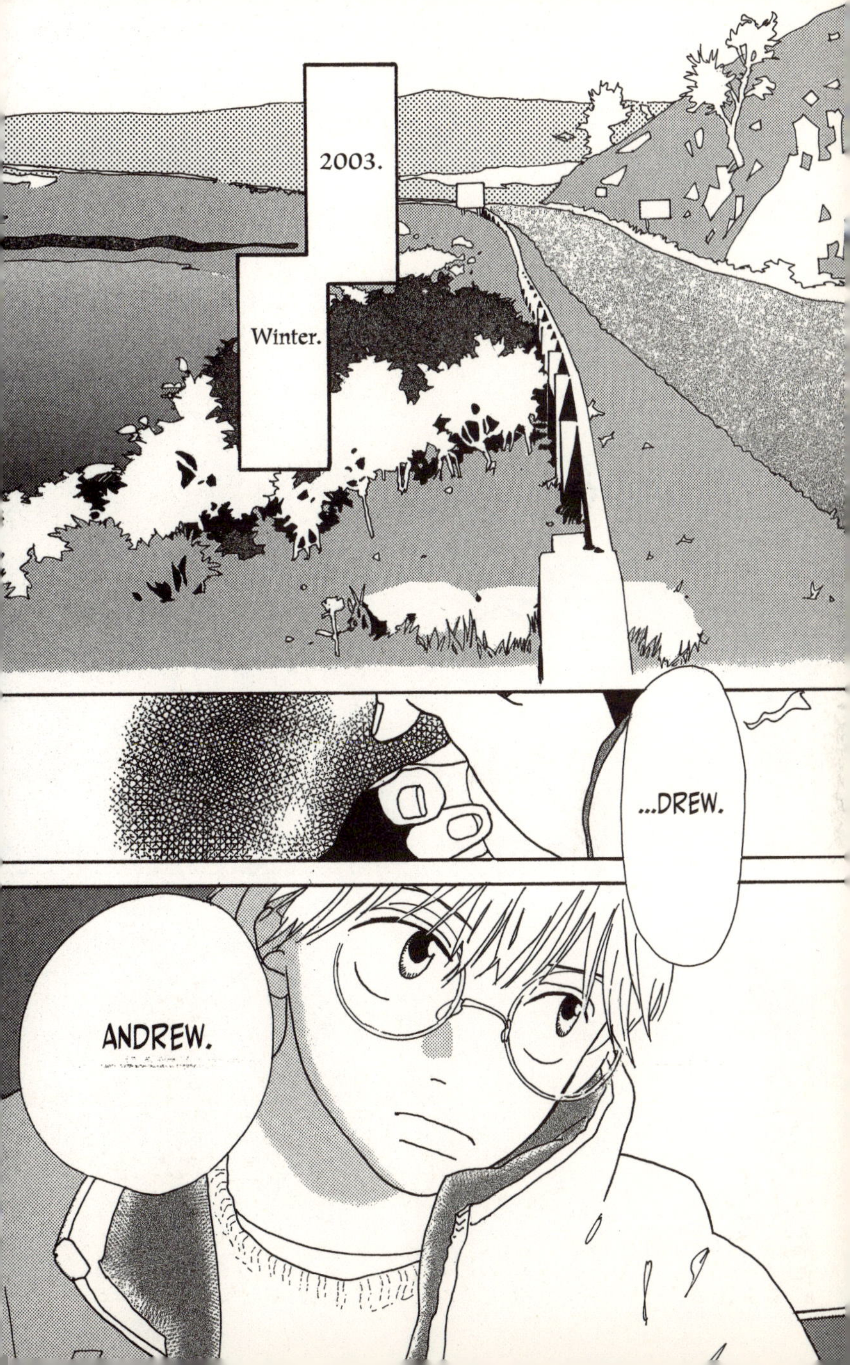
2003.
Winter.
...DREW.
ANDREW.

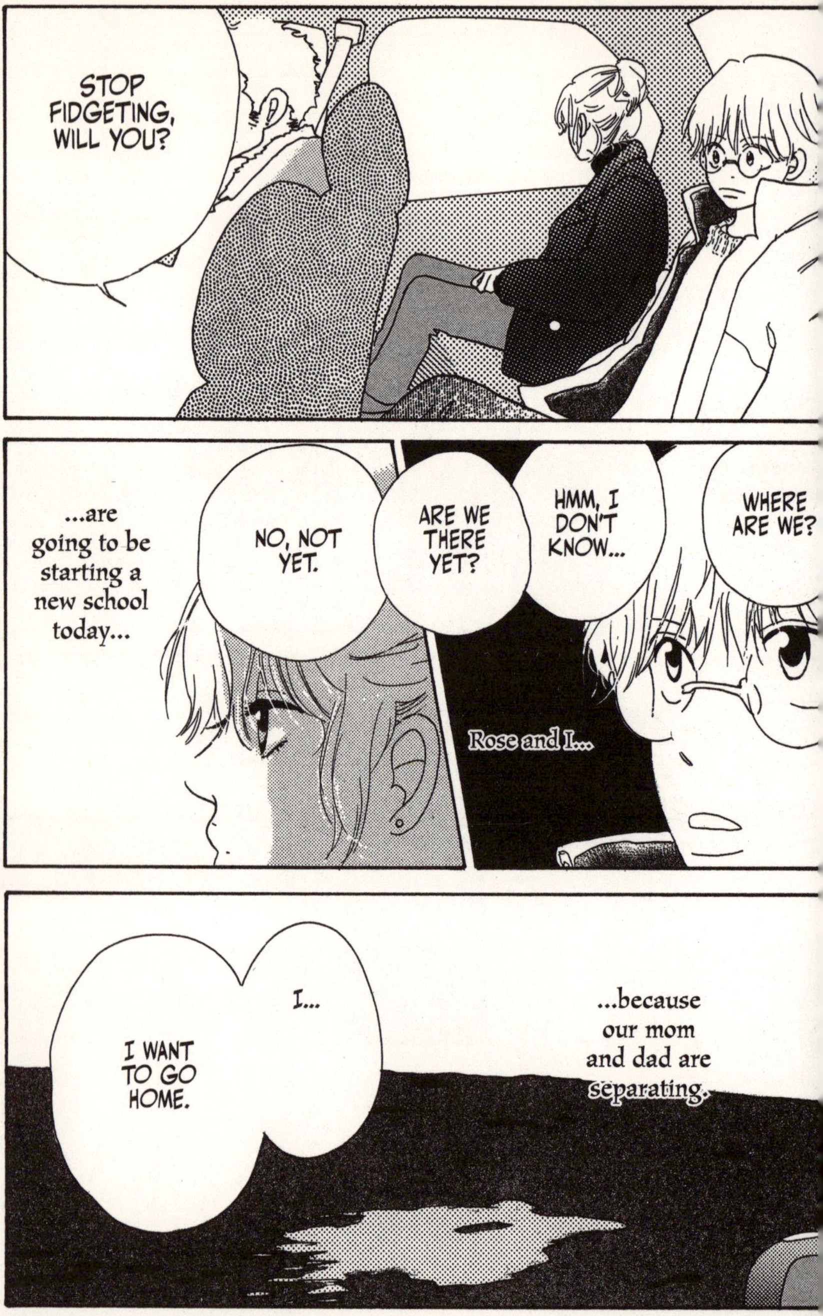

STOP FIDGETING, WILL YOU?
WHERE ARE WE?
HMM, I DON'T KNOW...
Rose and I...
ARE WE THERE YET?
NO, NOT YET.
...are going to be starting a new school today...
...because our mom and dad are separating.
I...
I WANT TO GO HOME.

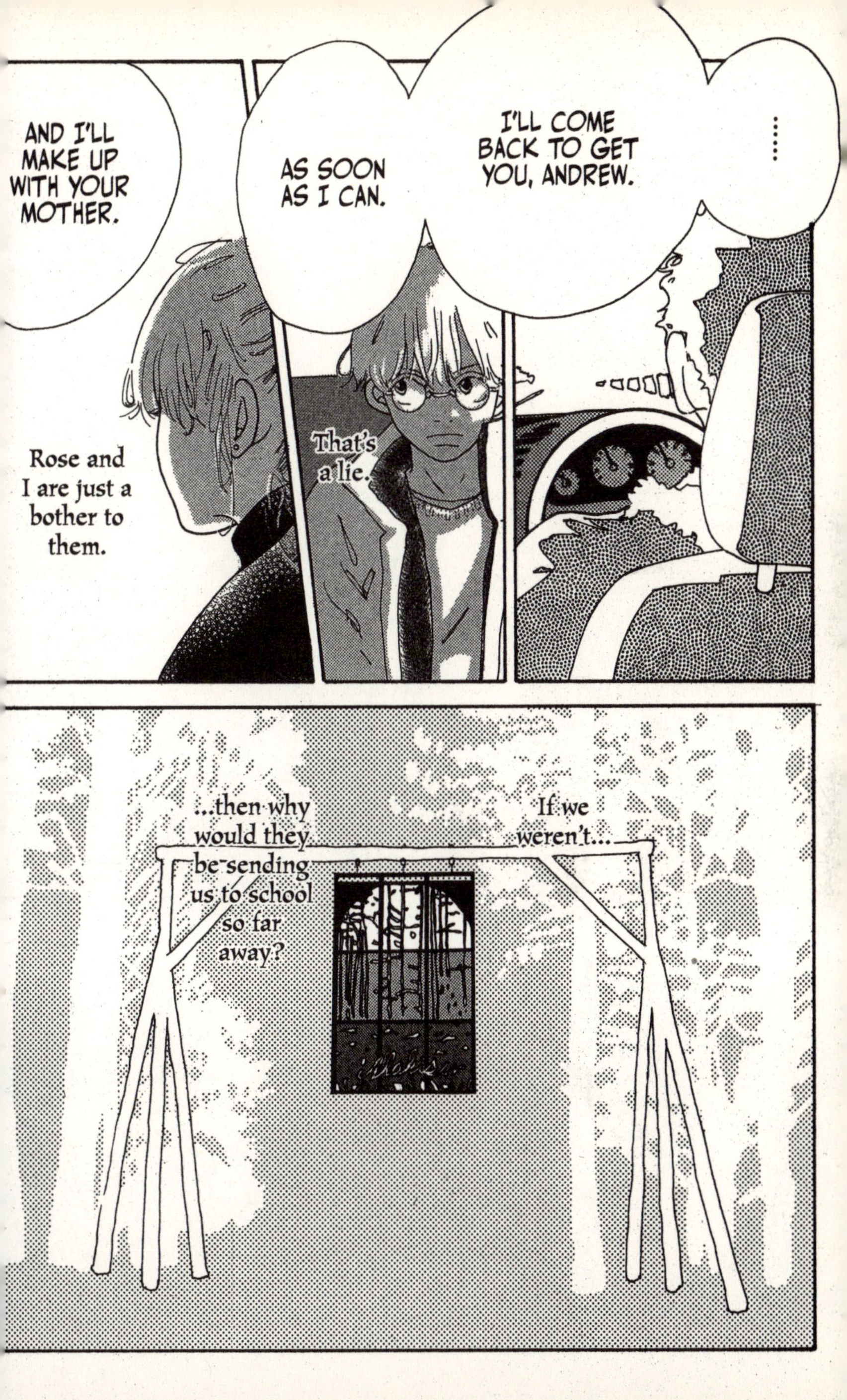
......
I'LL COME BACK TO GET YOU, ANDREW.
AS SOON AS I CAN.
That's a lie.
AND I'LL MAKE UP WITH YOUR MOTHER.
Rose and I are just a bother to them.
If we weren't...
...then why would they be sending us to school so far away?

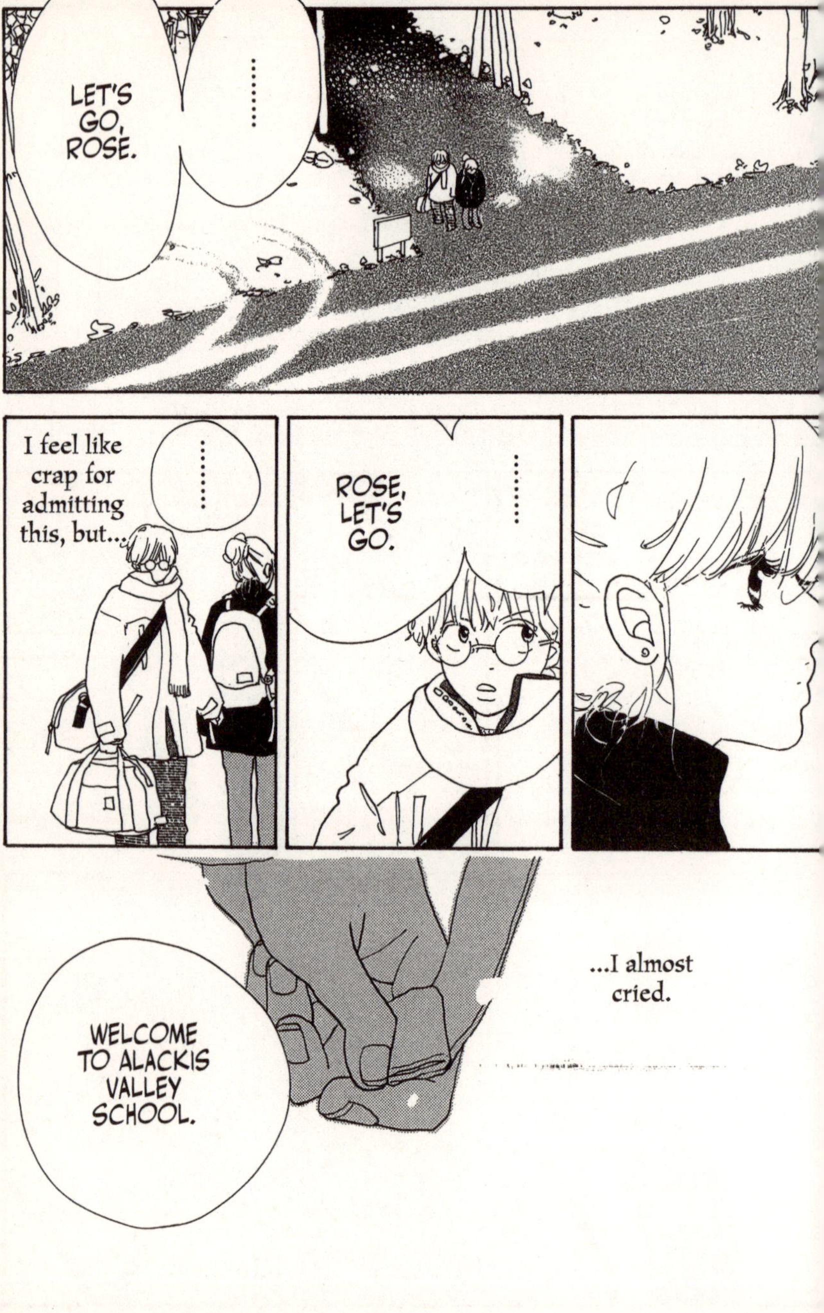
....
LET'S GO, ROSE.
....
I feel like crap for admitting this, but...
....
ROSE, LET'S GO.
...I almost cried.
WELCOME TO ALACKIS VALLEY SCHOOL.

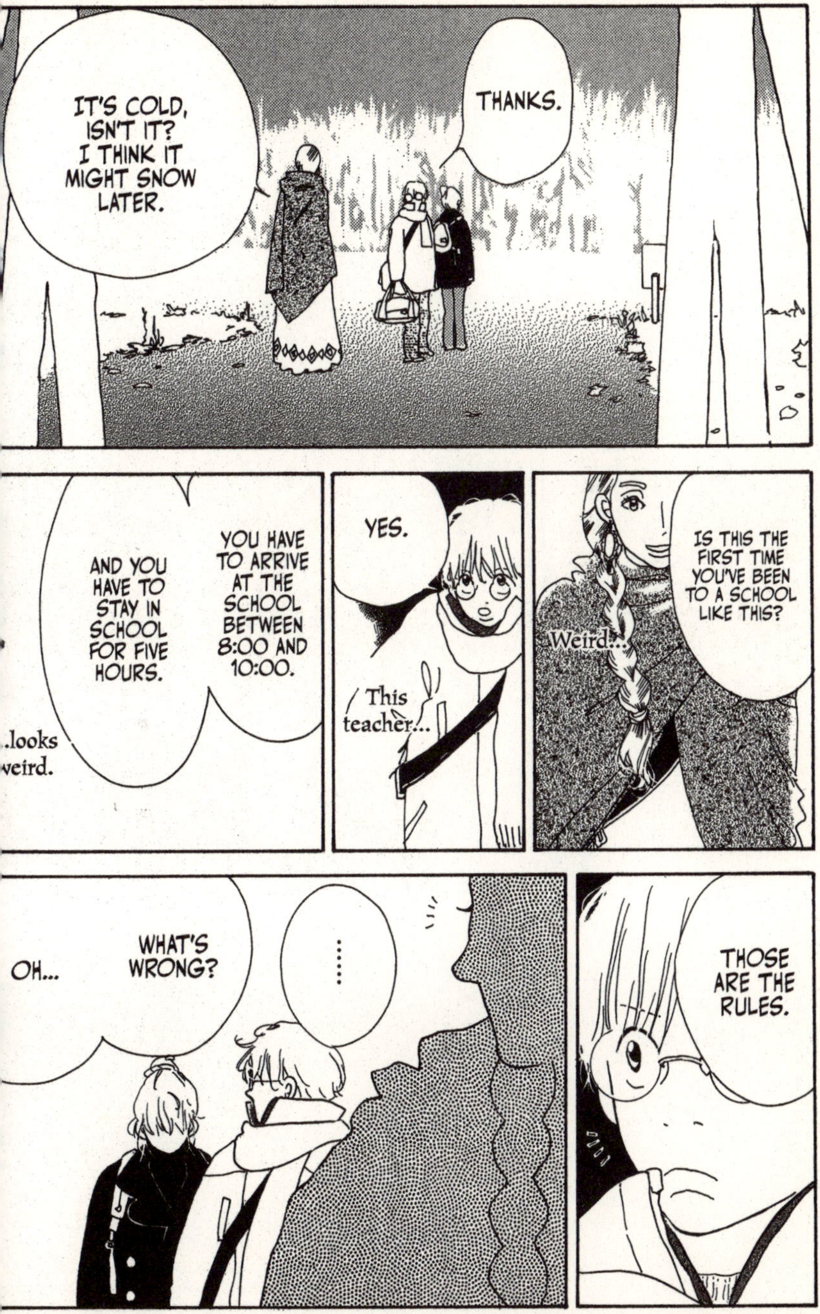

THANKS.
IT'S COLD, ISN'T IT? I THINK IT MIGHT SNOW LATER.
IS THIS THE FIRST TIME YOU'VE BEEN TO A SCHOOL LIKE THIS?
Weird...
YES.
This teacher...
YOU HAVE TO ARRIVE AT THE SCHOOL BETWEEN 8:00 AND 10:00.
AND YOU HAVE TO STAY IN SCHOOL FOR FIVE HOURS.
.looks weird.
THOSE ARE THE RULES.
......
WHAT'S WRONG?
OH...

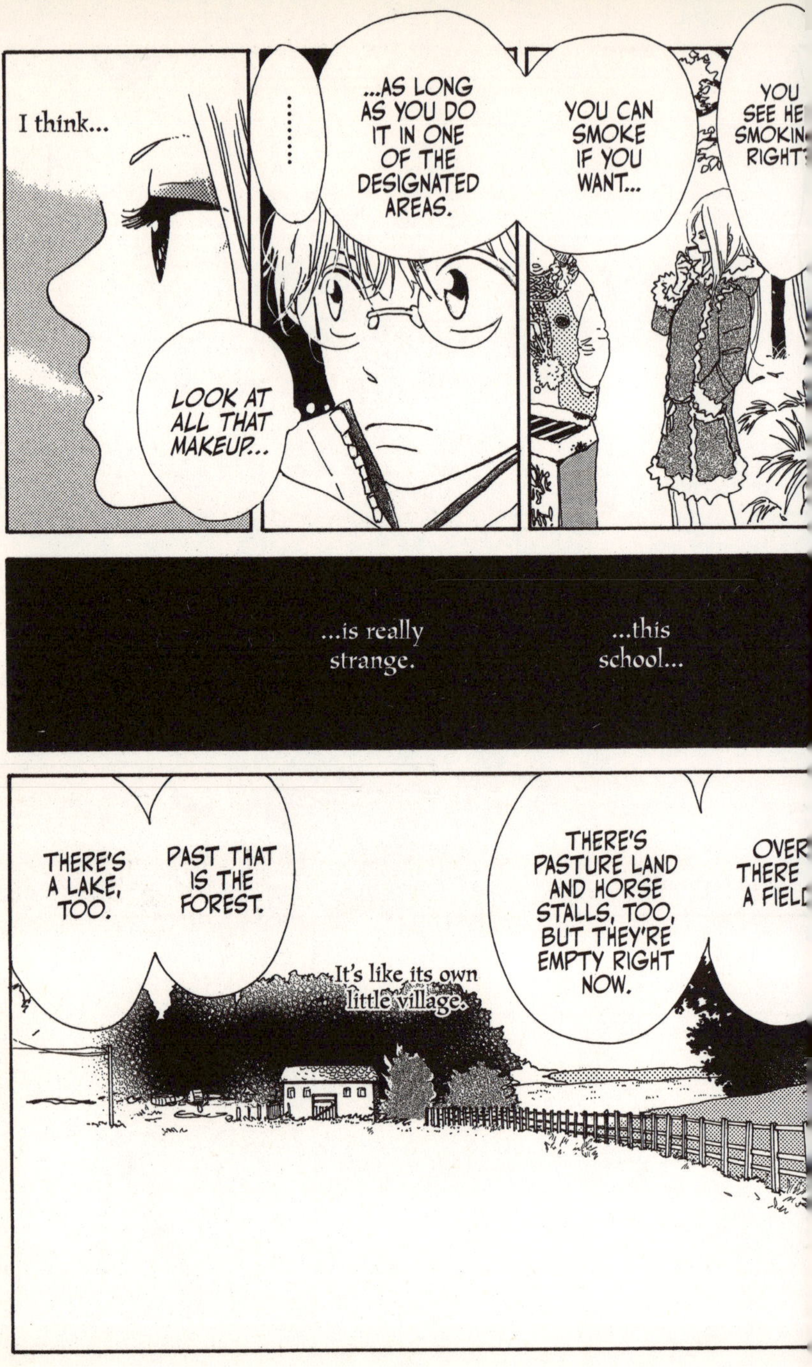

YOU SEE HE SMOKIN RIGHT
YOU CAN SMOKE IF YOU WANT...
...AS LONG AS YOU DO IT IN ONE OF THE DESIGNATED AREAS.
....
I think...
LOOK AT ALL THAT MAKEUP...
...this school...
...is really strange.
OVER THERE A FIEL
THERE'S PASTURE LAND AND HORSE STALLS, TOO, BUT THEY'RE EMPTY RIGHT NOW.
It's like its own little village.
PAST THAT IS THE FOREST.
THERE'S A LAKE, TOO.

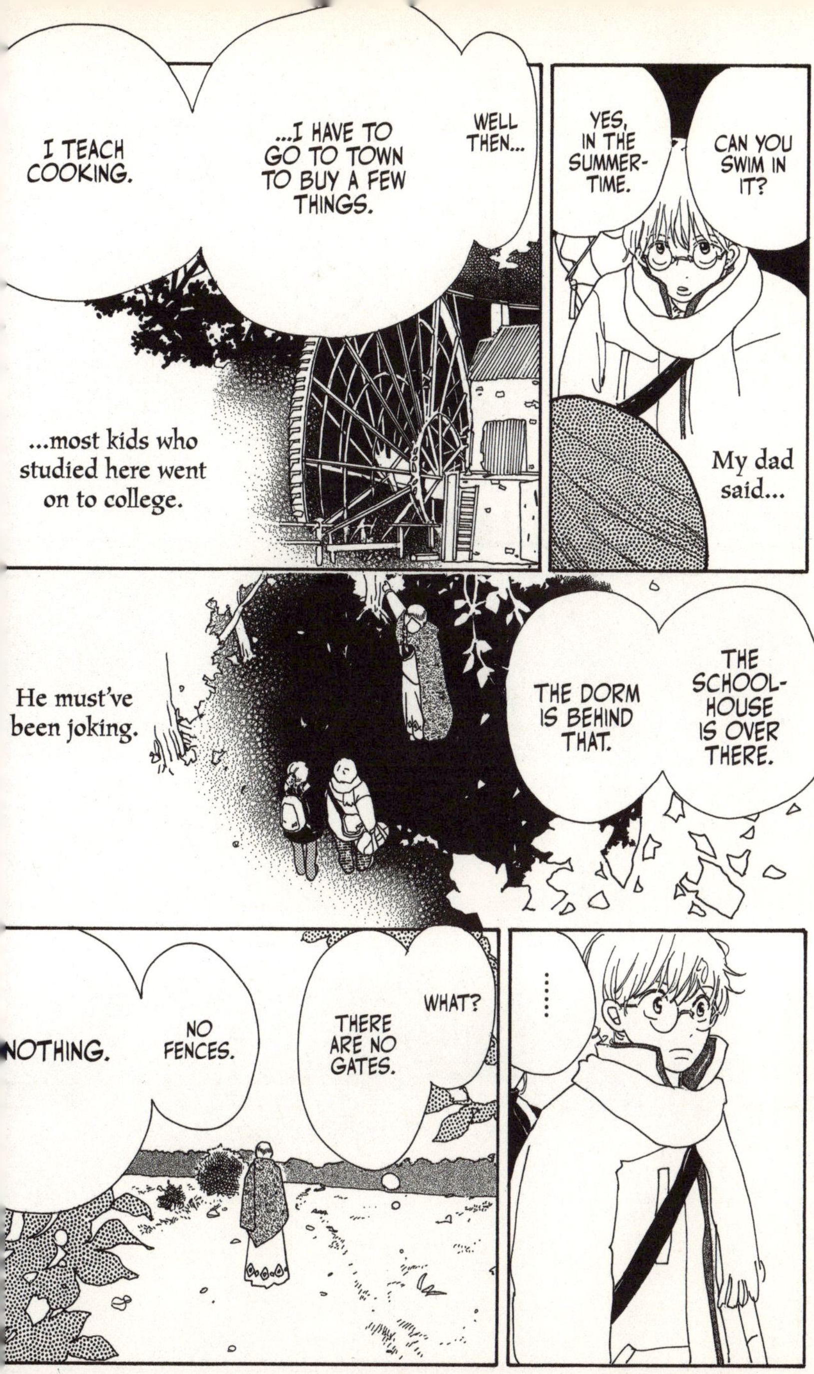
CAN YOU SWIM IN IT?
YES, IN THE SUMMER-TIME.
My dad said...
WELL THEN...
...I HAVE TO GO TO TOWN TO BUY A FEW THINGS.
I TEACH COOKING.
...most kids who studied here went on to college.
THE SCHOOL-HOUSE IS OVER THERE.
THE DORM IS BEHIND THAT.
He must've been joking.
......
WHAT?
THERE ARE NO GATES.
NO FENCES.
NOTHING.

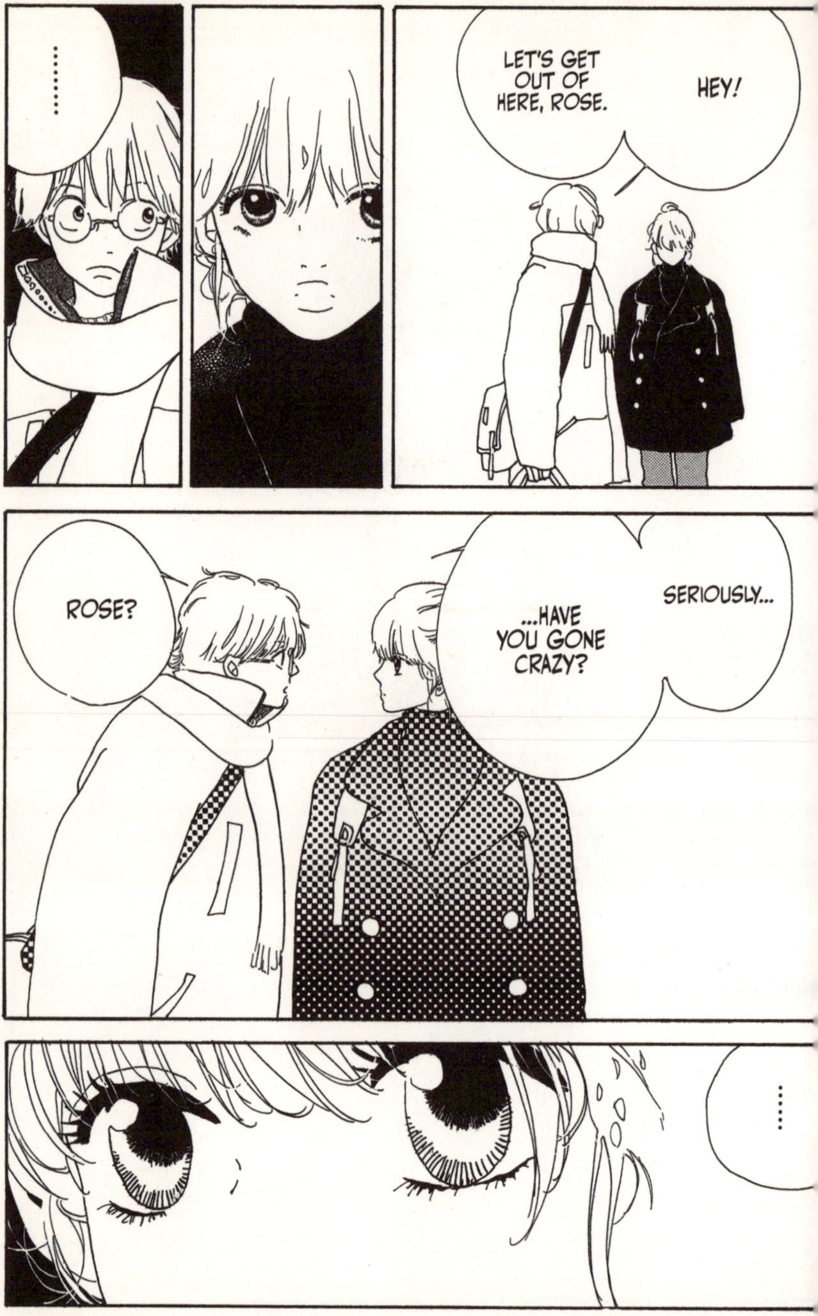
HEY!
LET'S GET OUT OF HERE, ROSE.
……
SERIOUSLY...
...HAVE YOU GONE CRAZY?
ROSE?
……

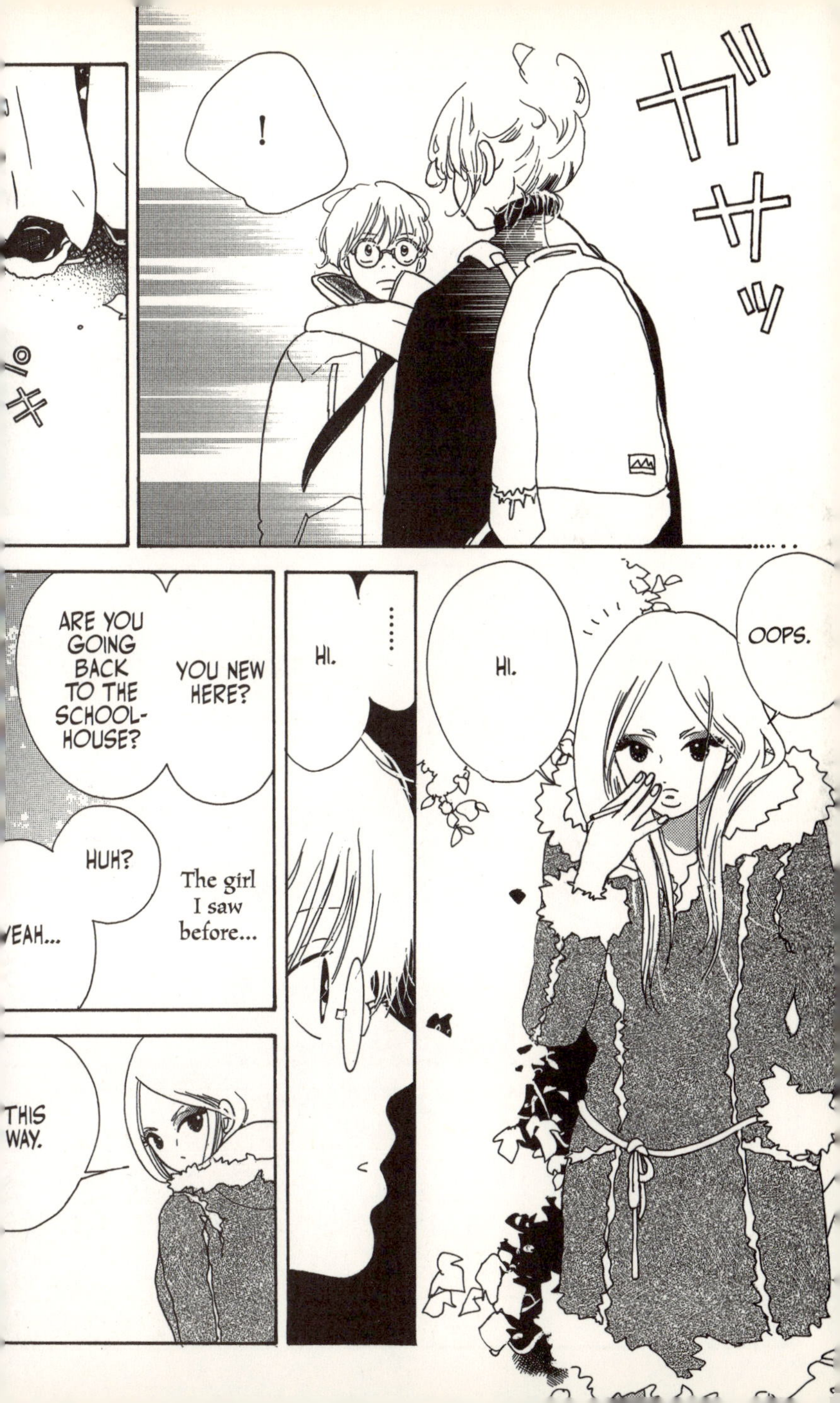
ガサッ
!
ポキ
OOPS.
HI.
......
HI.
YOU NEW HERE?
ARE YOU GOING BACK TO THE SCHOOL-HOUSE?
HUH?
The girl I saw before...
EAH...
THIS WAY.

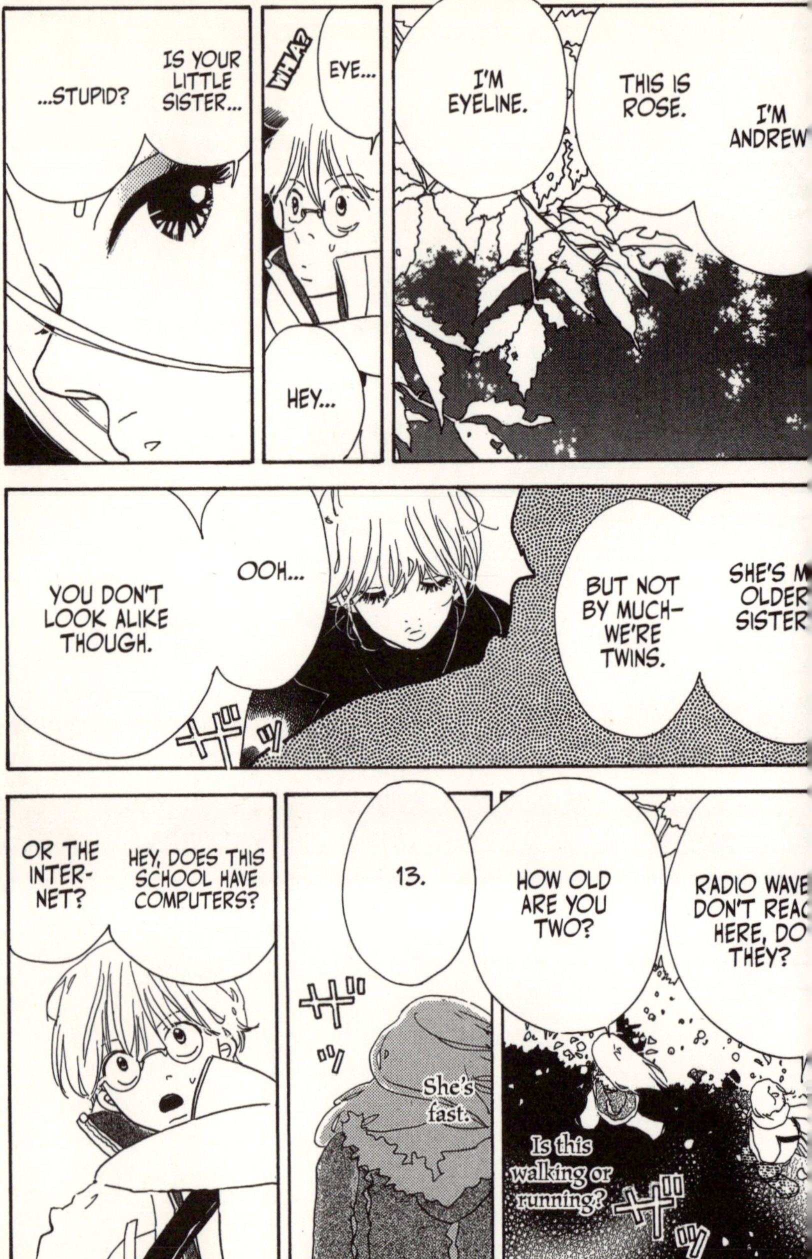
I'M ANDREW
THIS IS ROSE.
I'M EYELINE.
WHA?
EYE...
HEY...
IS YOUR LITTLE SISTER...
...STUPID?
SHE'S M OLDER SISTER
BUT NOT BY MUCH— WE'RE TWINS.
OOH...
YOU DON'T LOOK ALIKE THOUGH.
ザッ
RADIO WAVE DON'T REAC HERE, DO THEY?
HOW OLD ARE YOU TWO?
Is this walking or running?
ザッ
13.
ザッ
She's fast.
HEY, DOES THIS SCHOOL HAVE COMPUTERS?
OR THE INTER-NET?

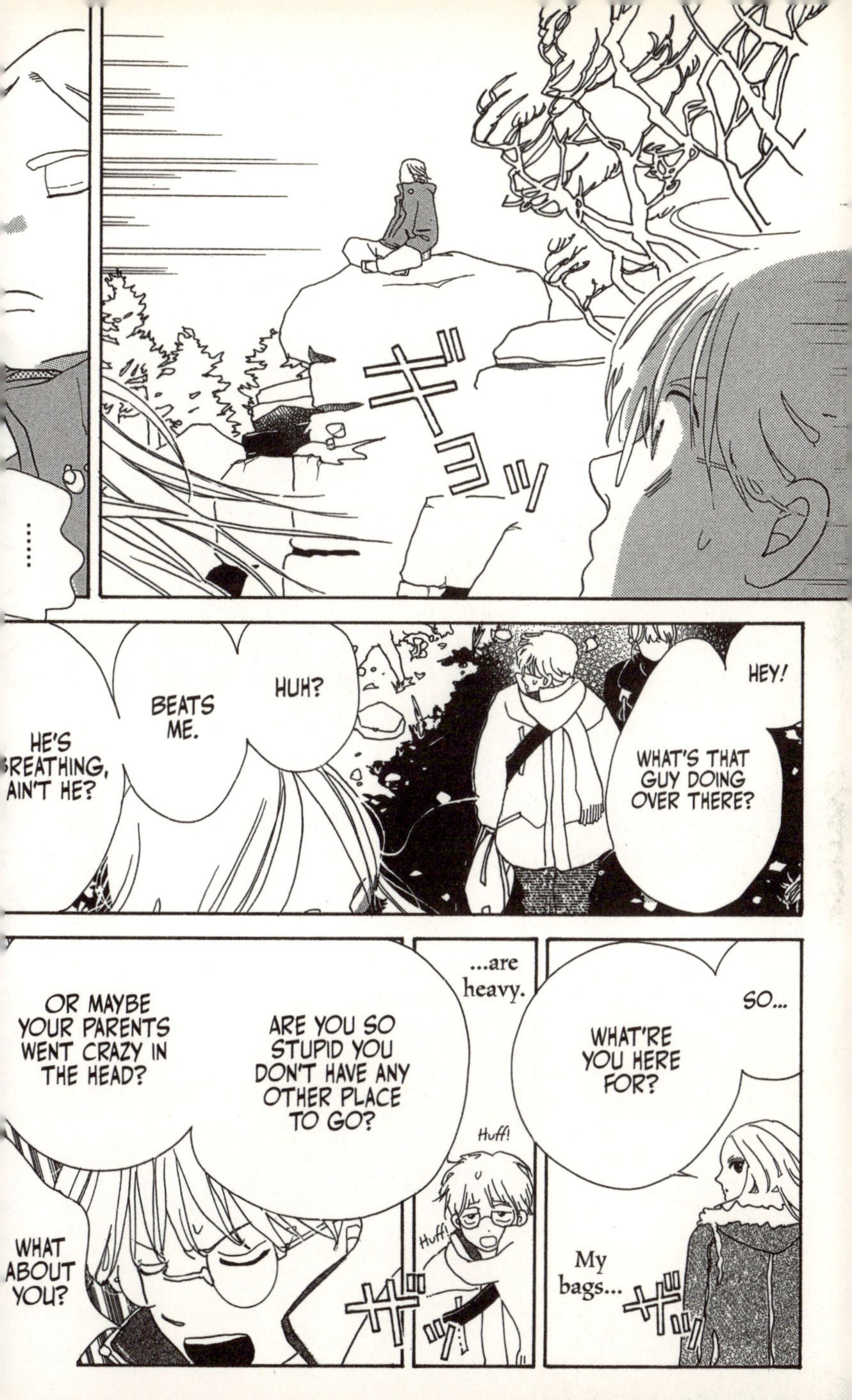
ギョッ
......
HEY!
WHAT'S THAT GUY DOING OVER THERE?
HUH?
BEATS ME.
HE'S BREATHING, AIN'T HE?
SO...
WHAT'RE YOU HERE FOR?
My bags...
ザッ
...are heavy.
Huff!
Huff!
ザッ
ARE YOU SO STUPID YOU DON'T HAVE ANY OTHER PLACE TO GO?
OR MAYBE YOUR PARENTS WENT CRAZY IN THE HEAD?
WHAT ABOUT YOU?

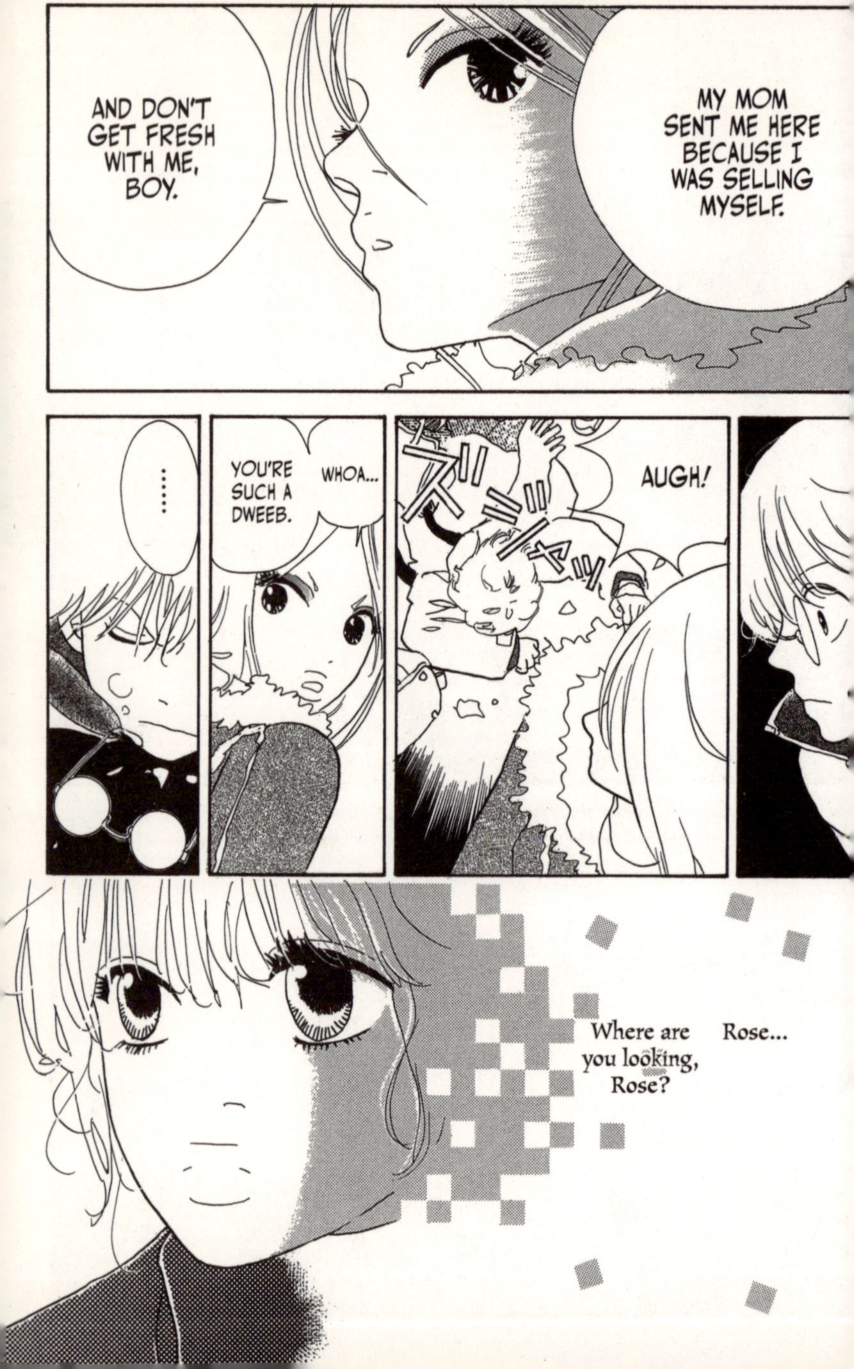
MY MOM SENT ME HERE BECAUSE I WAS SELLING MYSELF.
AND DON'T GET FRESH WITH ME, BOY.
AUGH!
WHOA...
YOU'RE SUCH A DWEEB.
......
Rose...
Where are you looking, Rose?

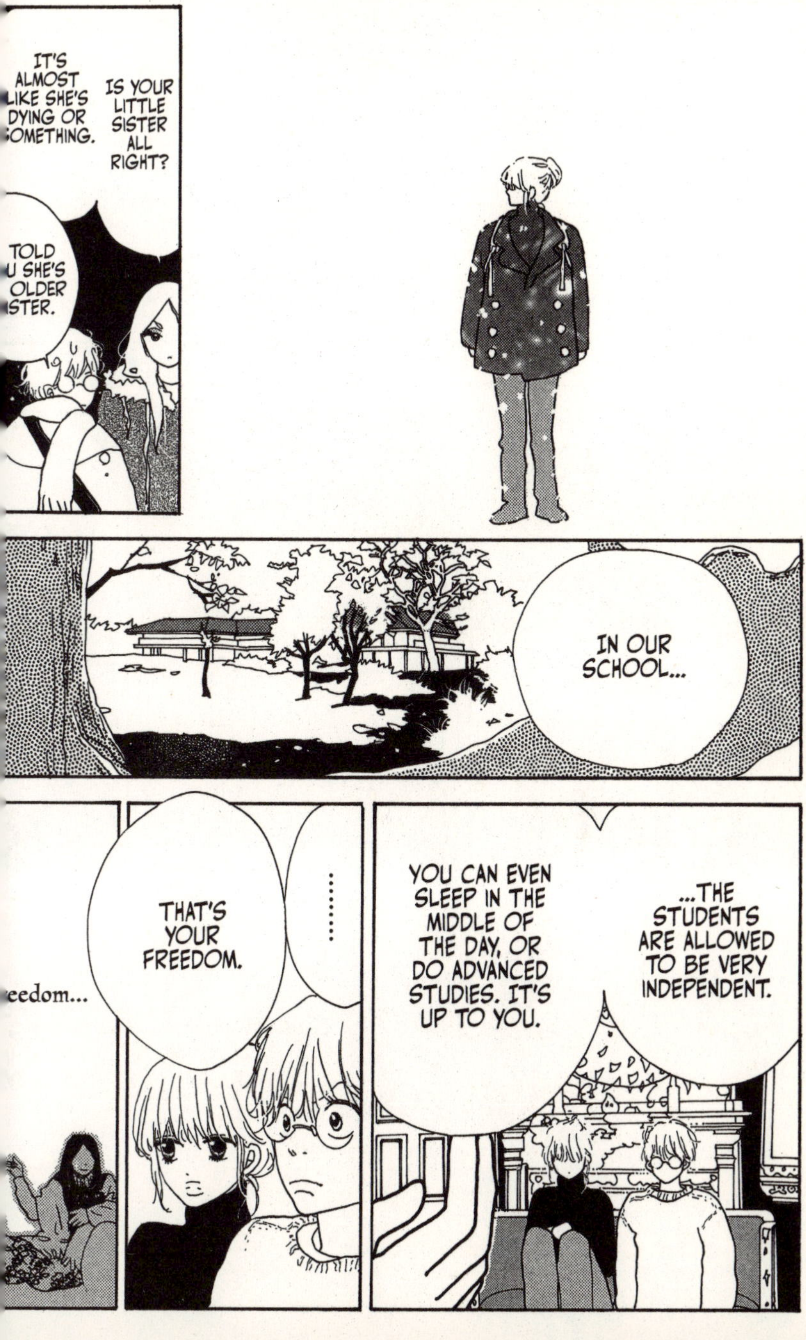
IS YOUR LITTLE SISTER ALL RIGHT?
IT'S ALMOST LIKE SHE'S DYING OR OMETHING.
TOLD U SHE'S OLDER STER.
IN OUR SCHOOL...
...THE STUDENTS ARE ALLOWED TO BE VERY INDEPENDENT.
YOU CAN EVEN SLEEP IN THE MIDDLE OF THE DAY, OR DO ADVANCED STUDIES. IT'S UP TO YOU.
....
THAT'S YOUR FREEDOM.
eedom...

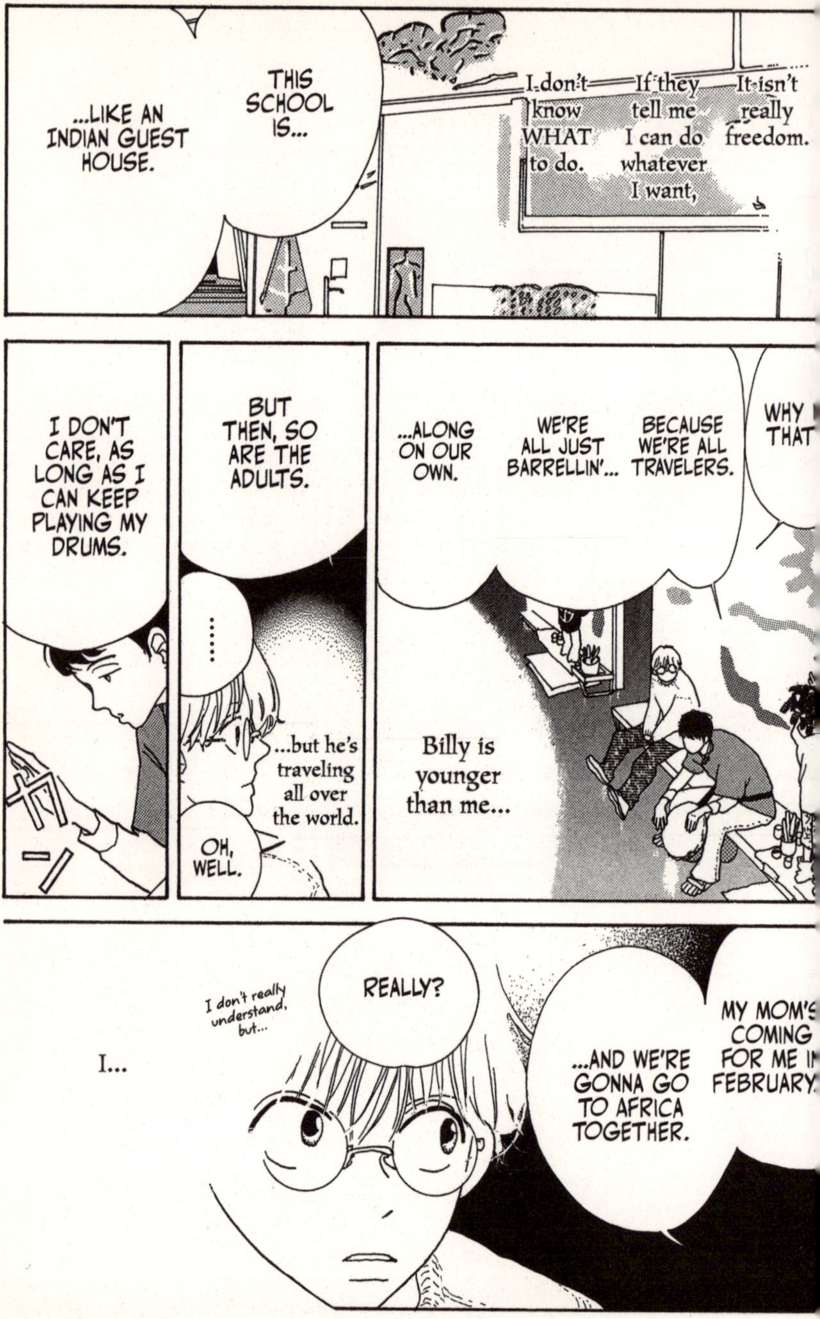
THIS SCHOOL IS...
...LIKE AN INDIAN GUEST HOUSE.
It isn't really freedom.
If they tell me I can do whatever I want,
I don't know WHAT to do.
WHY THAT
BECAUSE WE'RE ALL TRAVELERS.
WE'RE ALL JUST BARRELLIN'...
...ALONG ON OUR OWN.
Billy is younger than me...
...but he's traveling all over the world.
BUT THEN, SO ARE THE ADULTS.
......
OH, WELL.
I DON'T CARE, AS LONG AS I CAN KEEP PLAYING MY DRUMS.
MY MOM'S COMING FOR ME IN FEBRUARY.
...AND WE'RE GONNA GO TO AFRICA TOGETHER.
REALLY?
I don't really understand, but...
I...

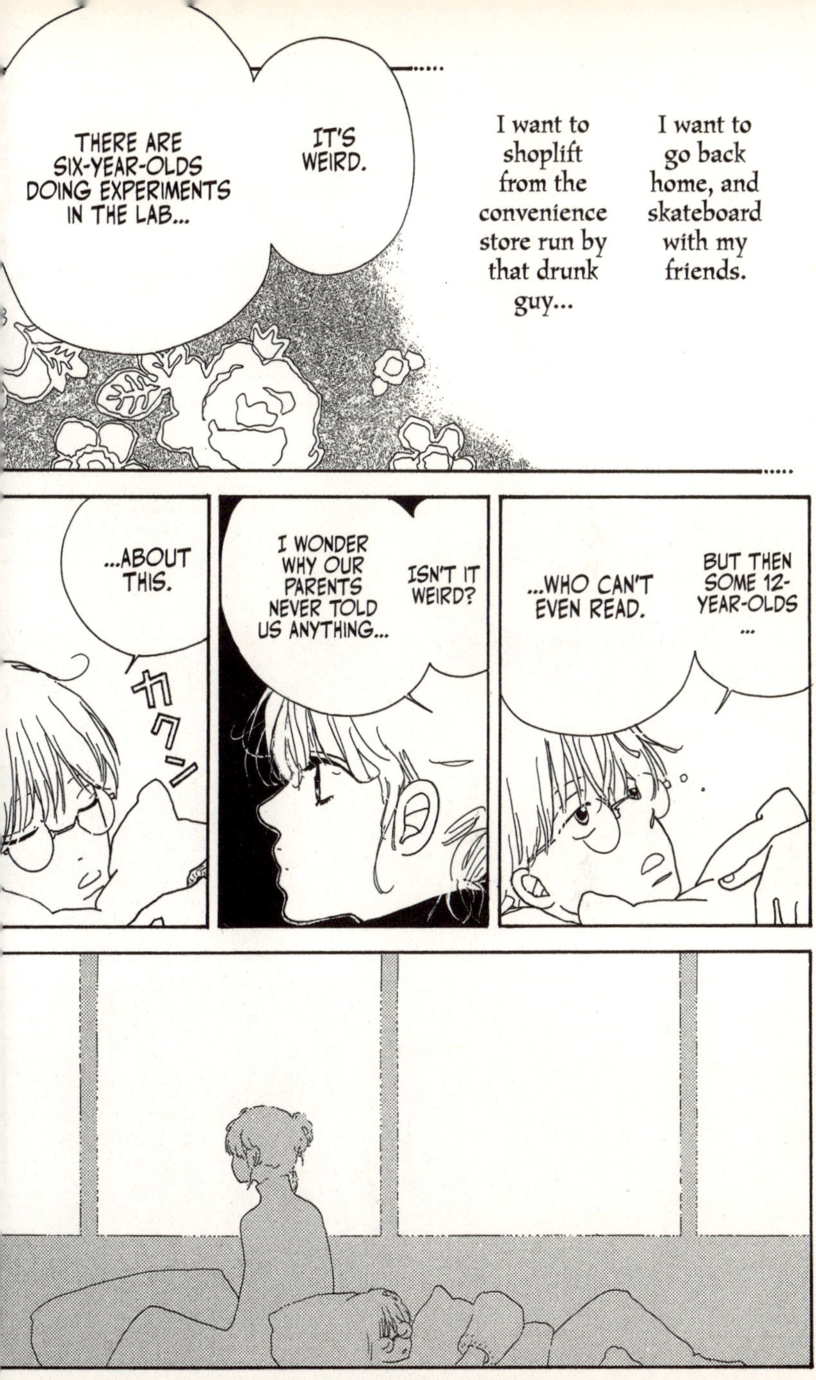

I want to go back home, and skateboard with my friends.
I want to shoplift from the convenience store run by that drunk guy...
IT'S WEIRD.
THERE ARE SIX-YEAR-OLDS DOING EXPERIMENTS IN THE LAB...
BUT THEN SOME 12-YEAR-OLDS ...
...WHO CAN'T EVEN READ.
ISN'T IT WEIRD?
I WONDER WHY OUR PARENTS NEVER TOLD US ANYTHING...
...ABOUT THIS.
カクン

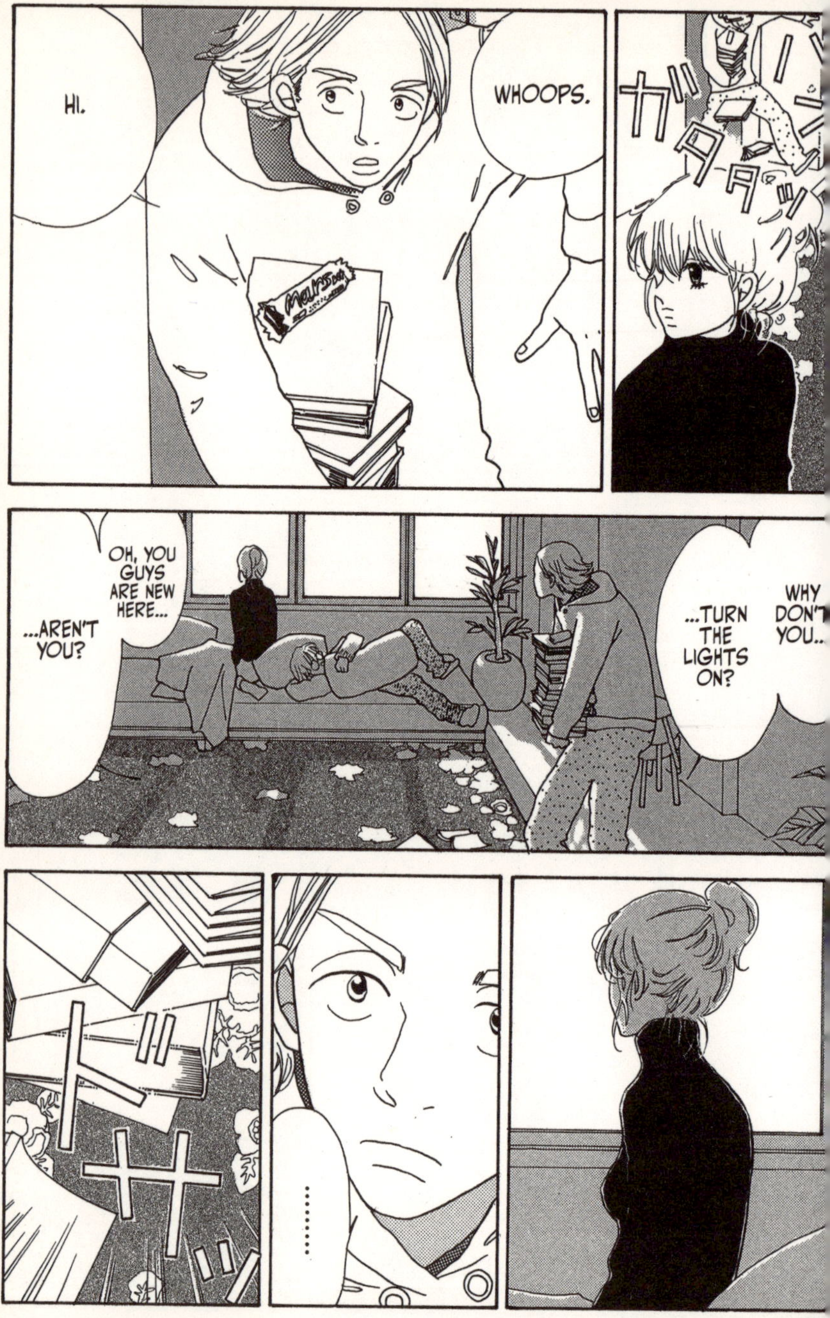
WHOOPS.
HI.
WHY DON'T YOU...
...TURN THE LIGHTS ON?
OH, YOU GUYS ARE NEW HERE...
...AREN'T YOU?
......

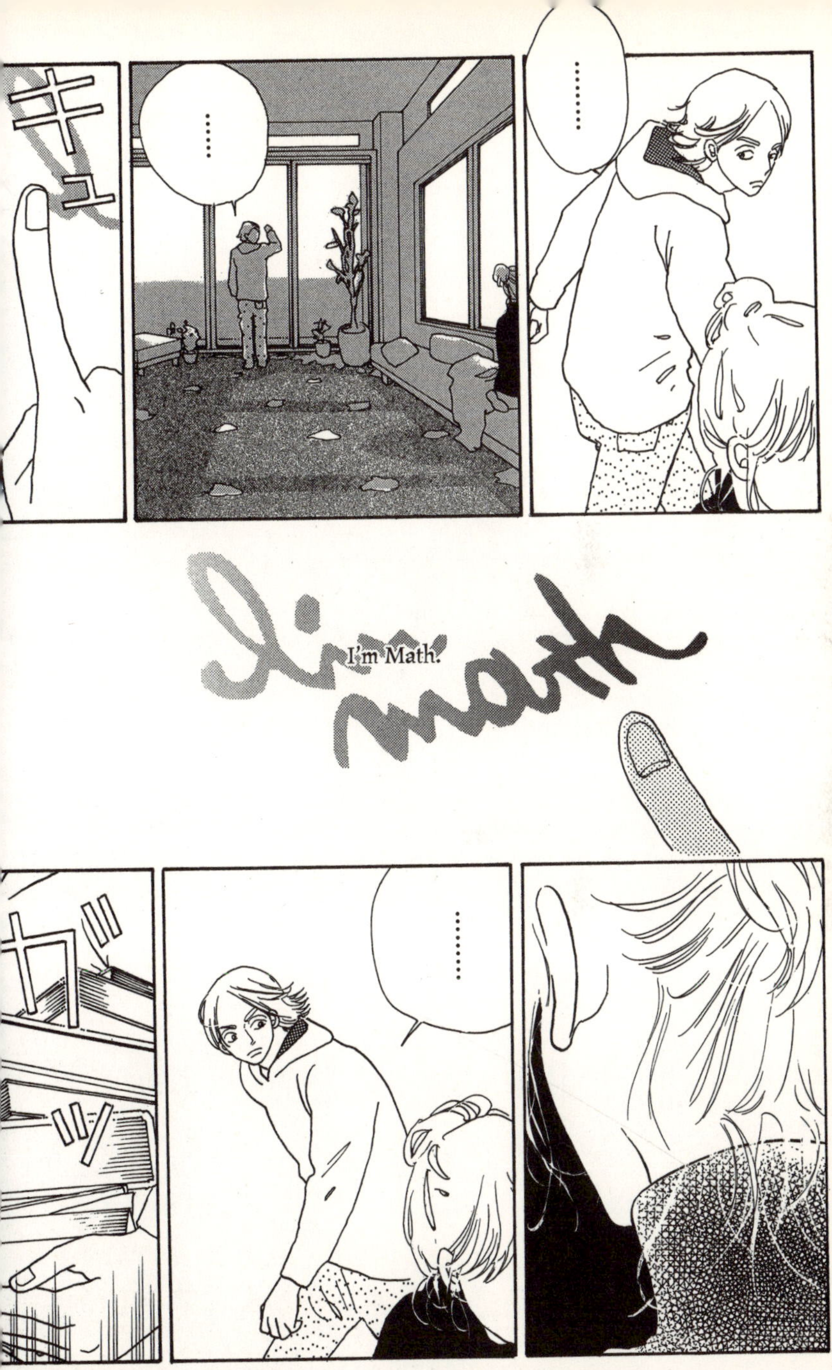
....
......
キュ
I'm math
I'm Math.
....

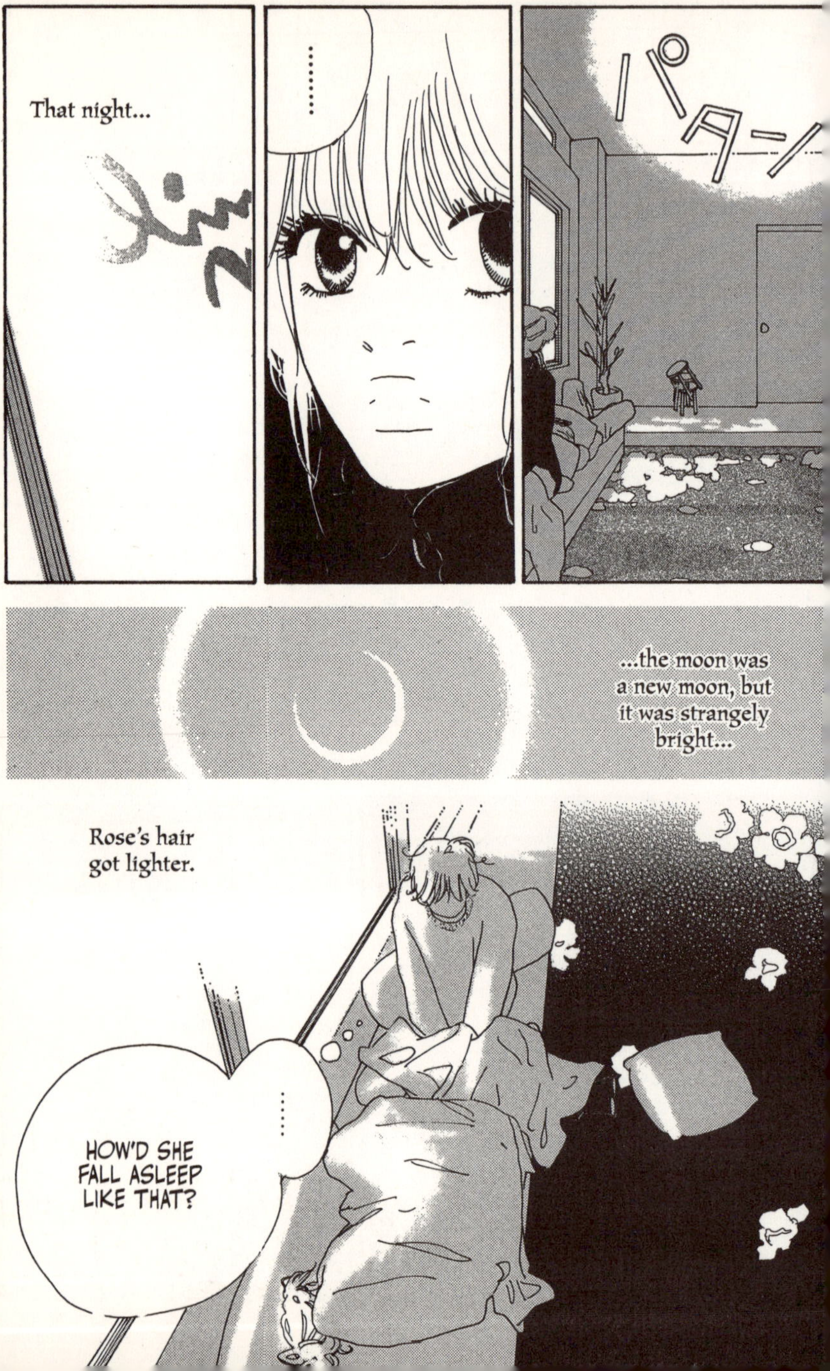

パターン
......
That night...
...the moon was a new moon, but it was strangely bright...
Rose's hair got lighter.
......
HOW'D SHE FALL ASLEEP LIKE THAT?

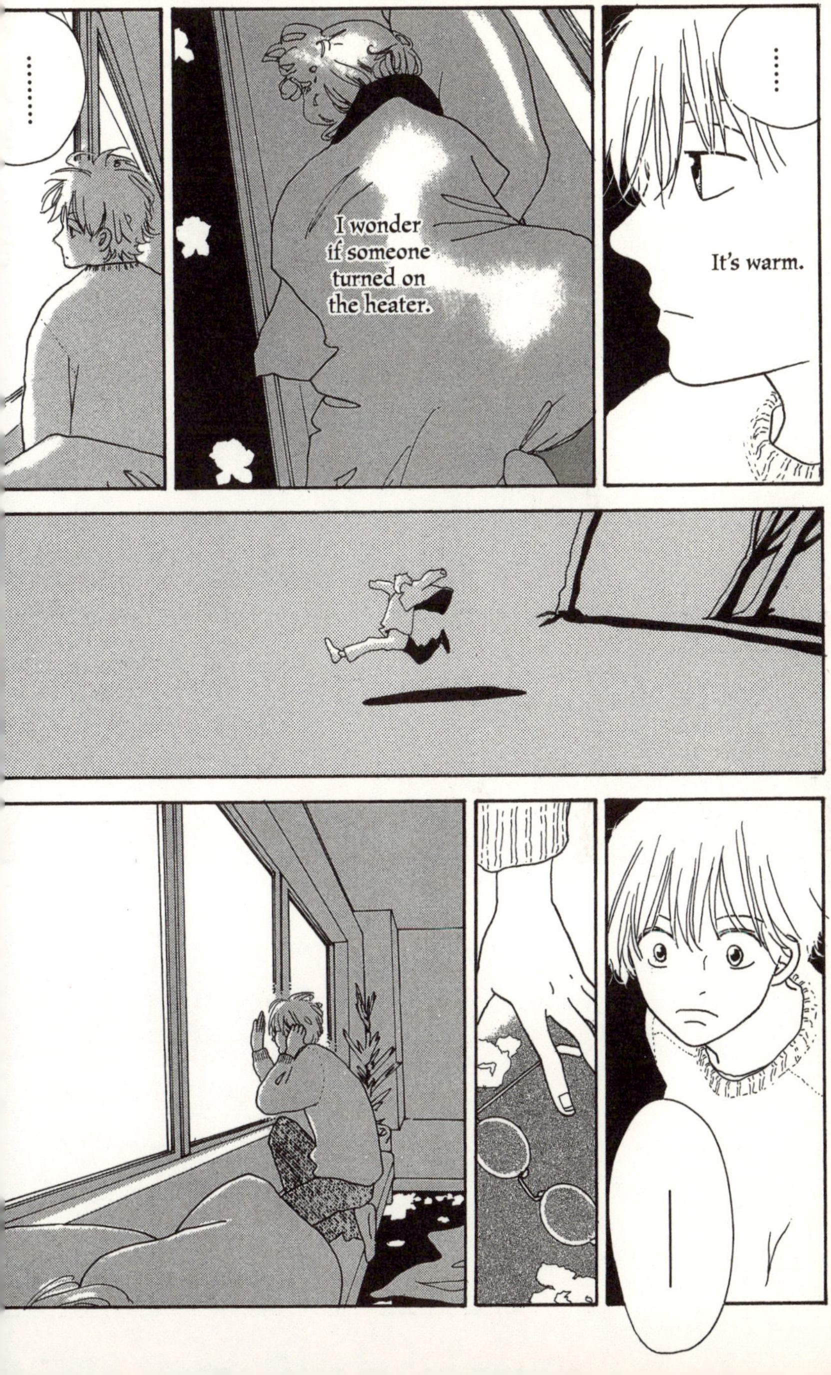
……
It's warm.
I wonder if someone turned on the heater.
……

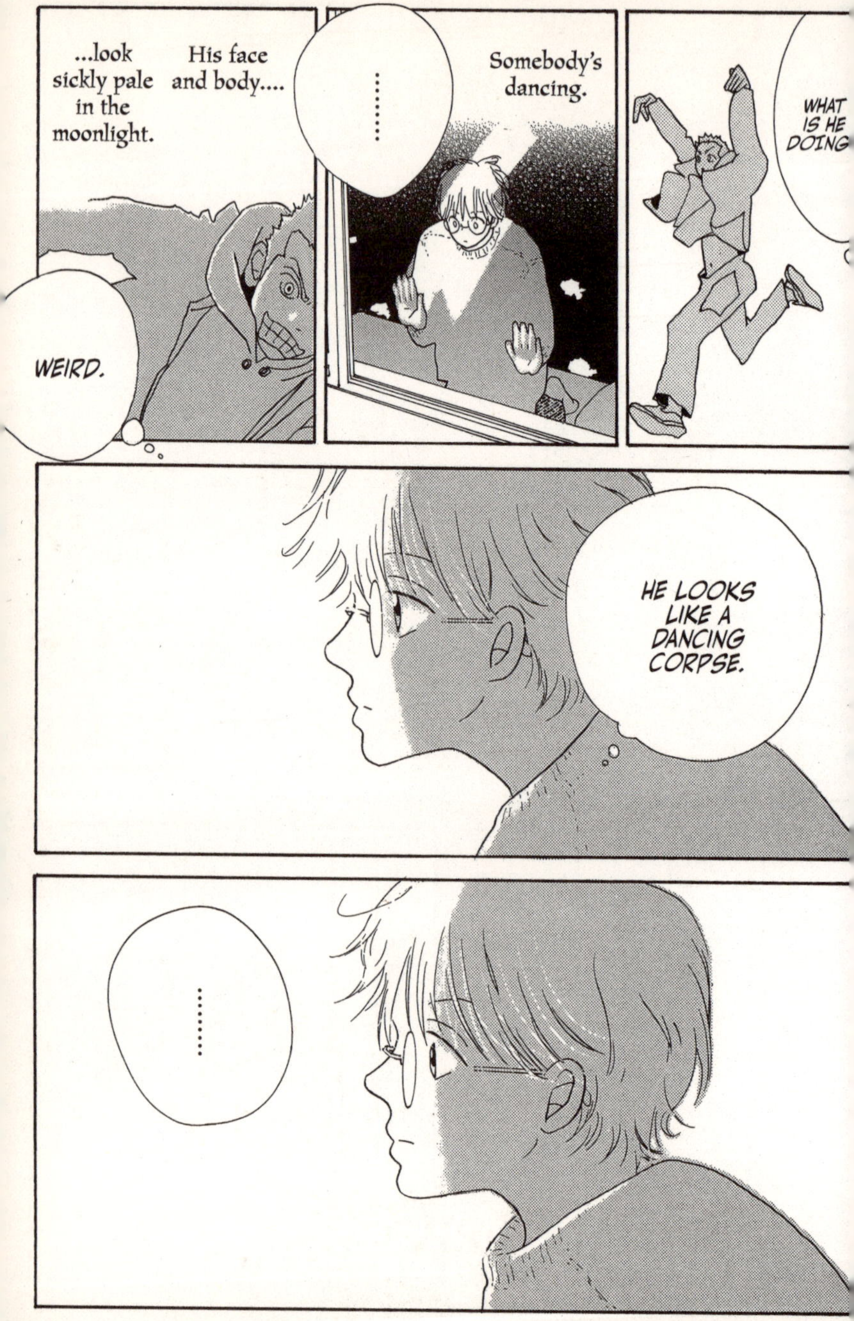
WHAT IS HE DOING
Somebody's dancing.
....
His face and body....
...look sickly pale in the moonlight.
WEIRD.
HE LOOKS LIKE A DANCING CORPSE.
....

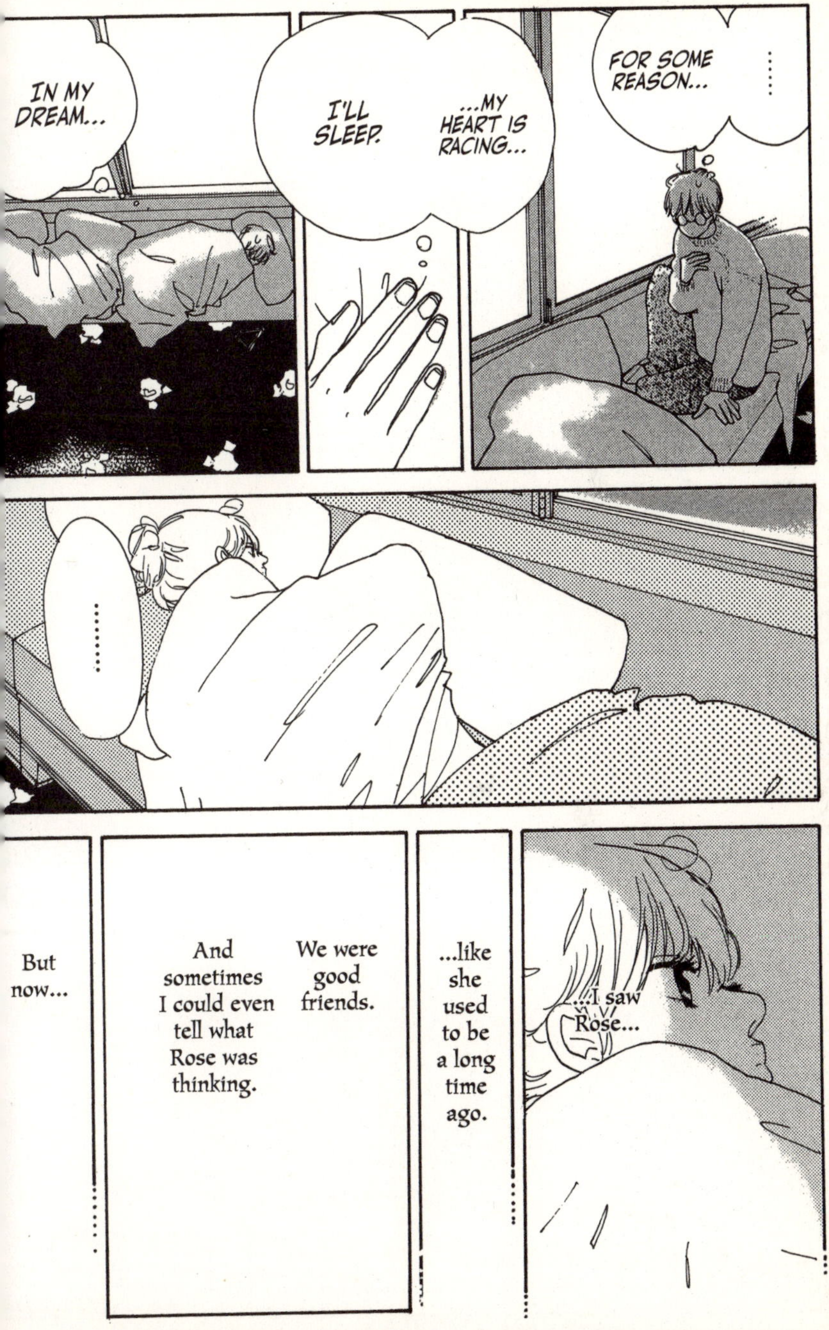
......
FOR SOME REASON...
...MY HEART IS RACING...
I'LL SLEEP.
IN MY DREAM...
......
...I saw Rose...
...like she used to be a long time ago.
We were good friends.
And sometimes I could even tell what Rose was thinking.
But now...

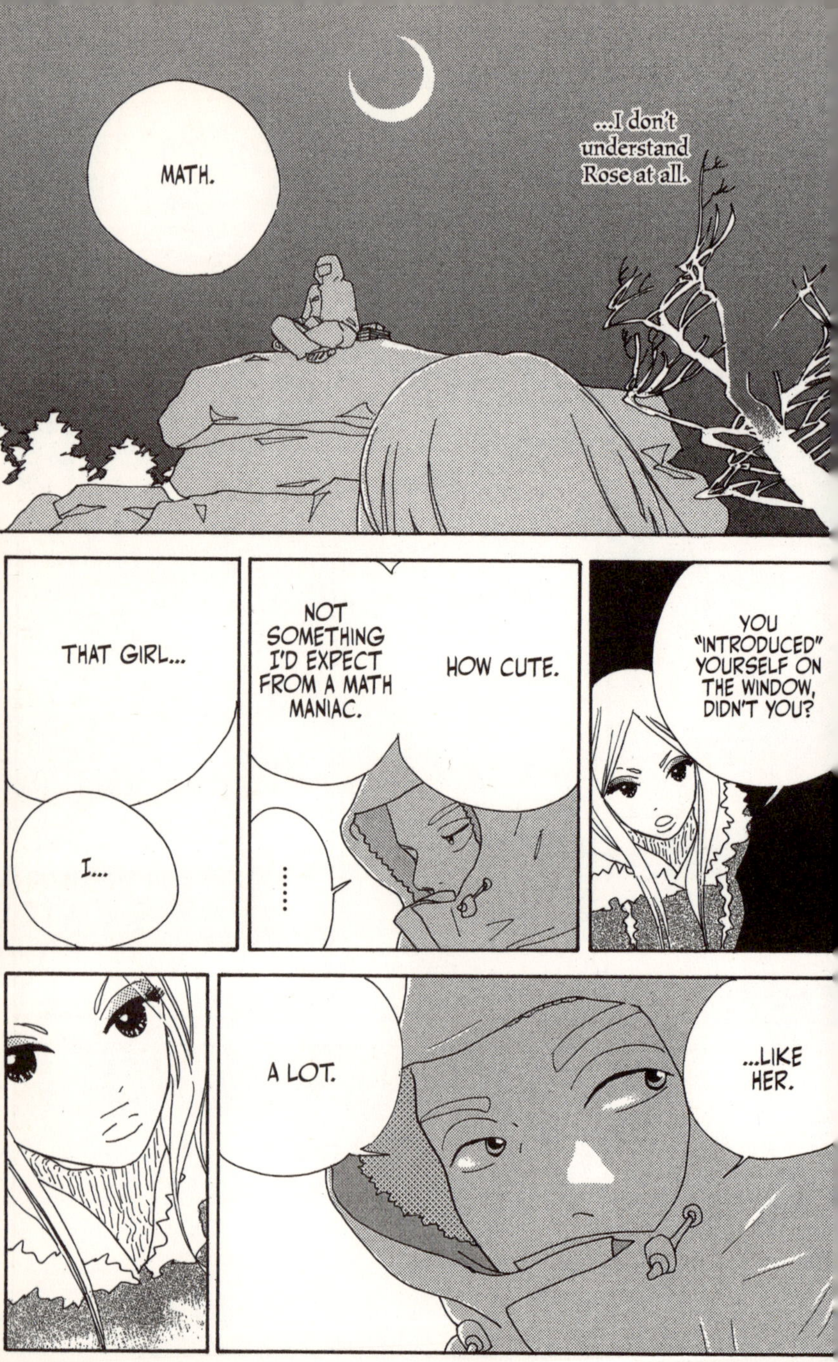
...I don't understand Rose at all.
MATH.
YOU "INTRODUCED" YOURSELF ON THE WINDOW, DIDN'T YOU?
HOW CUTE.
NOT SOMETHING I'D EXPECT FROM A MATH MANIAC.
......
THAT GIRL...
I...
...LIKE HER.
A LOT.

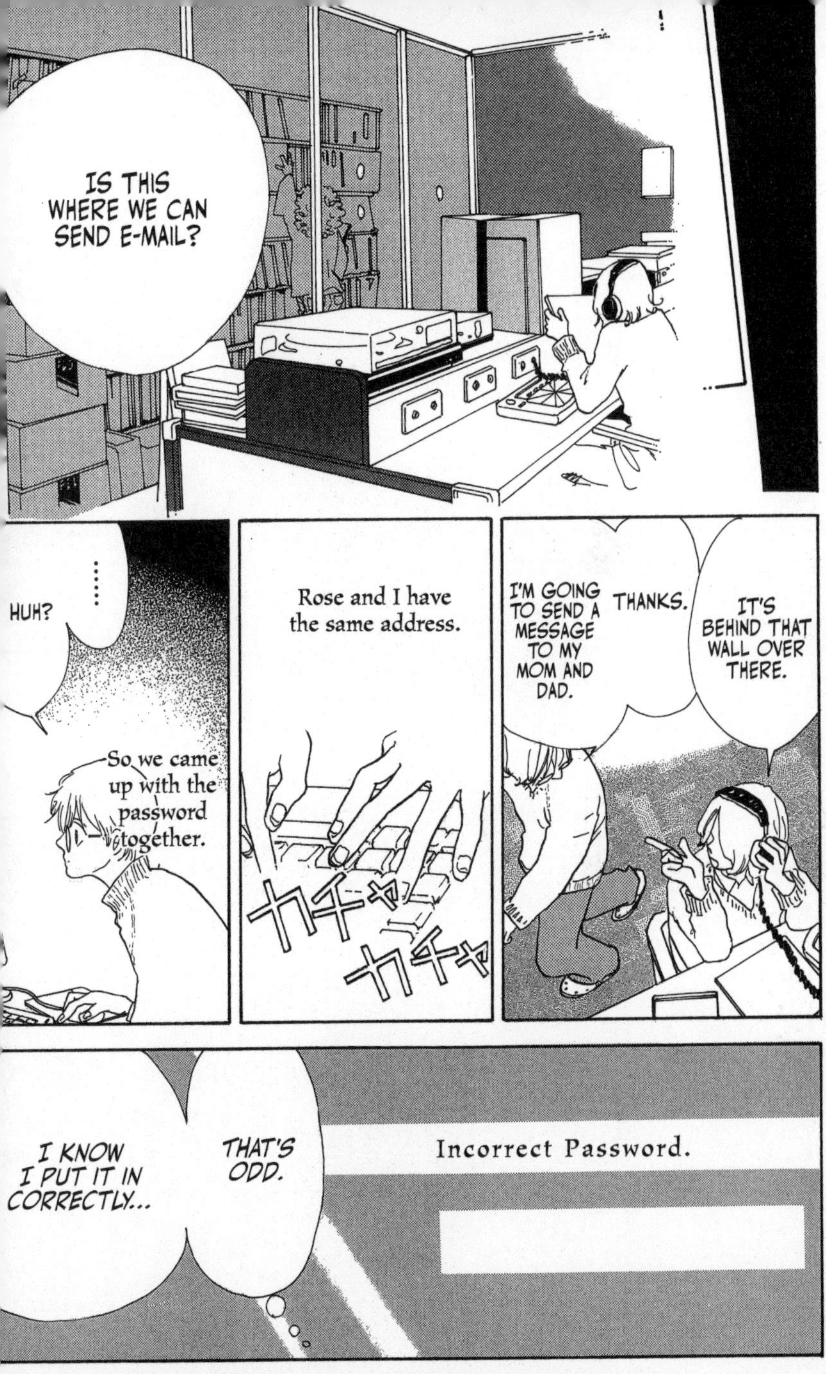
IS THIS WHERE WE CAN SEND E-MAIL?
IT'S BEHIND THAT WALL OVER THERE.
THANKS.
I'M GOING TO SEND A MESSAGE TO MY MOM AND DAD.
Rose and I have the same address.
カチャ
カチャ
......
HUH?
So we came up with the password together.
Incorrect Password.
THAT'S ODD.
I KNOW I PUT IT IN CORRECTLY...

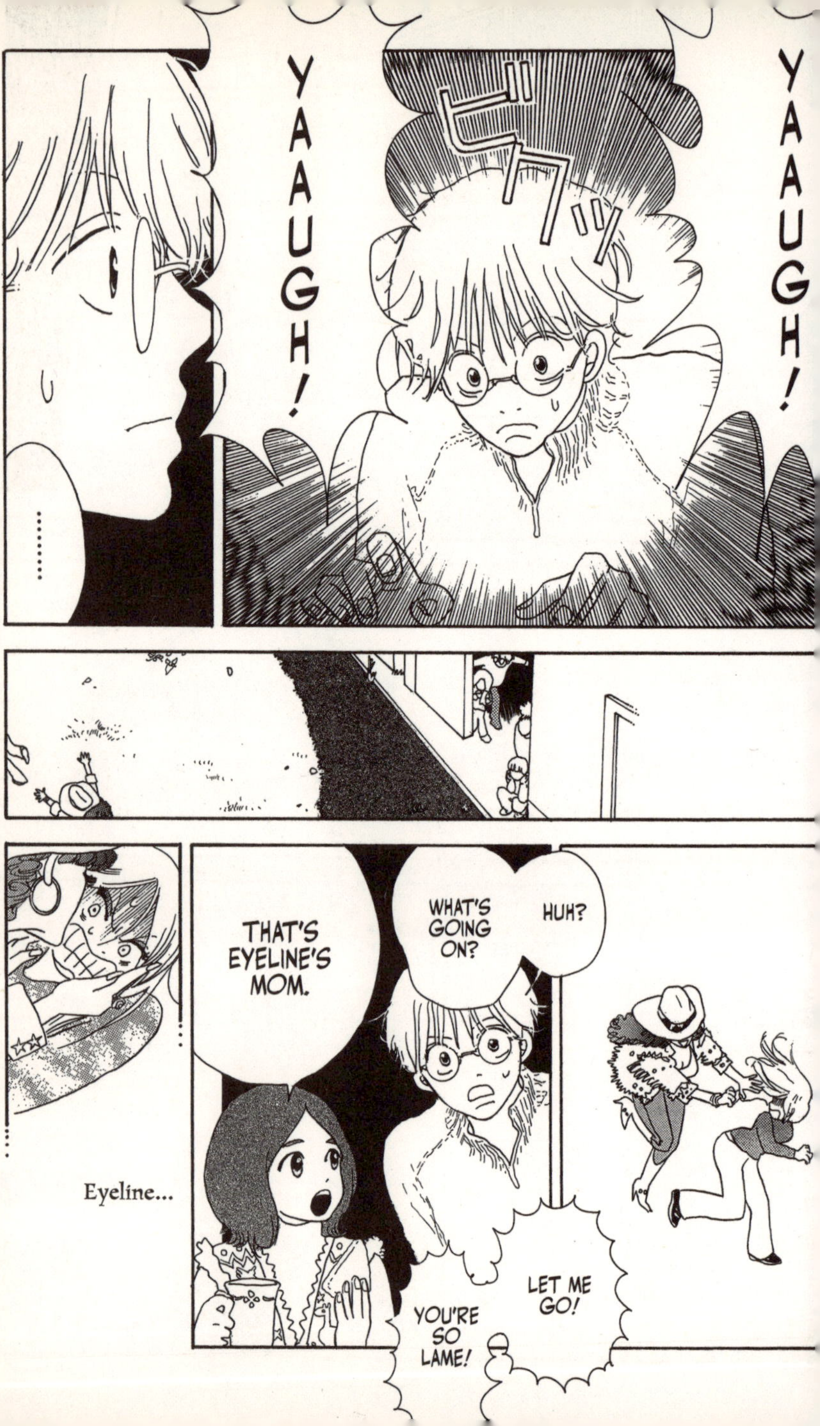
YAAUGH!
ビクッ
YAAUGH!
....
HUH?
WHAT'S GOING ON?
LET ME GO!
YOU'RE SO LAME!
THAT'S EYELINE'S MOM.
......
Eyeline...

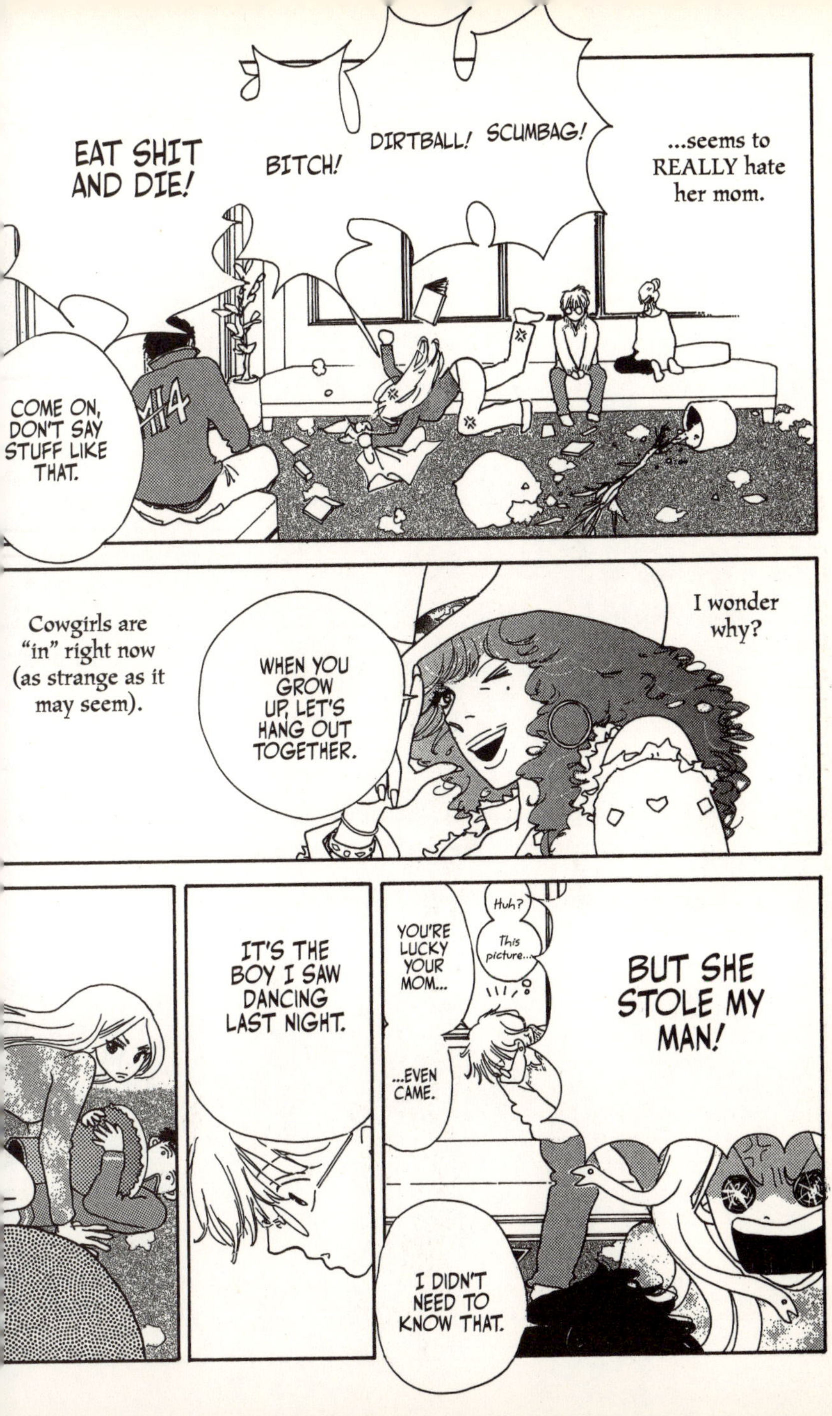
...seems to REALLY hate her mom.
DIRTBALL! SCUMBAG!
BITCH!
EAT SHIT AND DIE!
COME ON, DON'T SAY STUFF LIKE THAT.
I wonder why?
WHEN YOU GROW UP, LET'S HANG OUT TOGETHER.
Cowgirls are "in" right now (as strange as it may seem).
BUT SHE STOLE MY MAN!
Huh?
This picture...
YOU'RE LUCKY YOUR MOM...
...EVEN CAME.
I DIDN'T NEED TO KNOW THAT.
IT'S THE BOY I SAW DANCING LAST NIGHT.

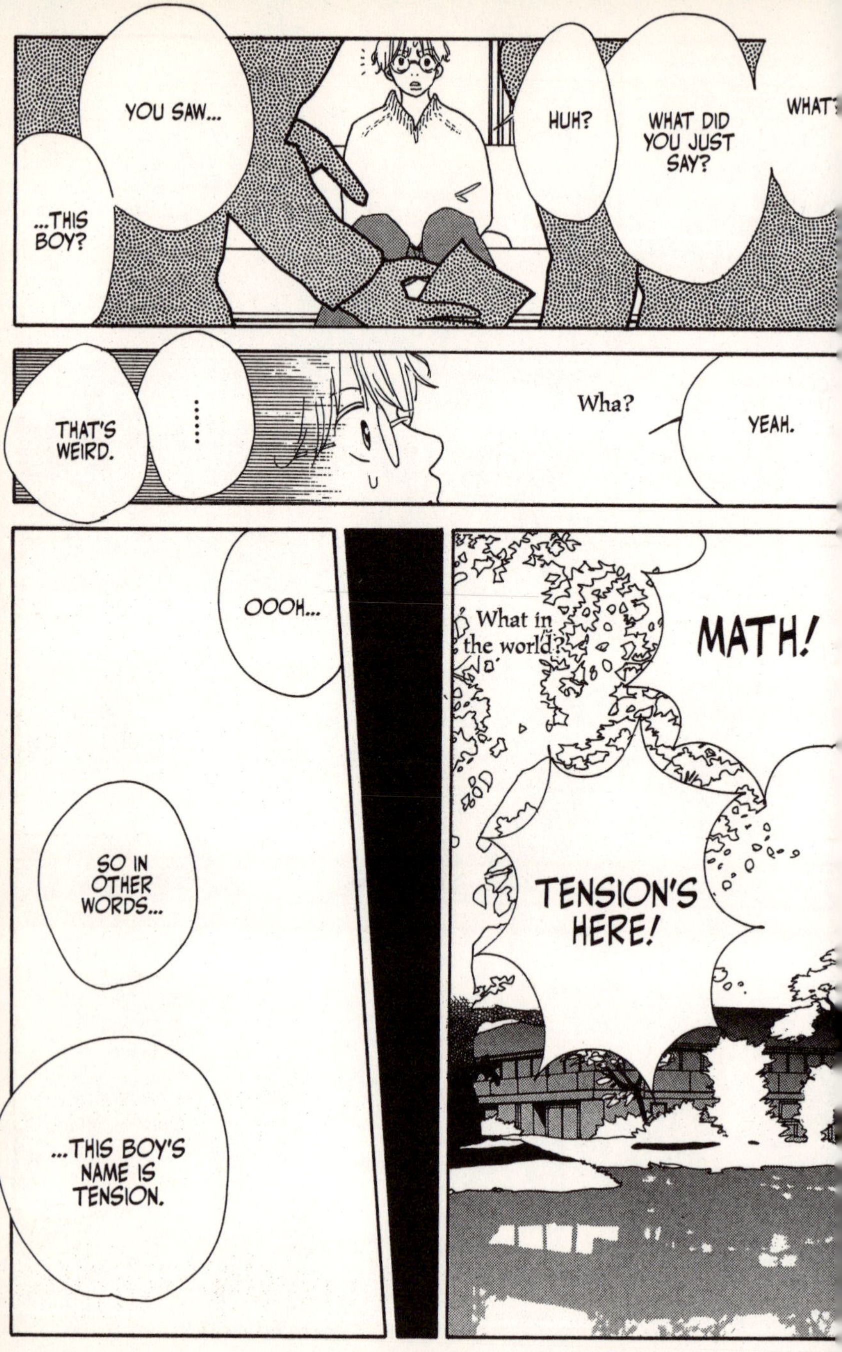
WHAT'
WHAT DID YOU JUST SAY?
HUH?
YOU SAW...
...THIS BOY?
YEAH.
Wha?
......
THAT'S WEIRD.
MATH!
What in the world?
TENSION'S HERE!
OOOH...
SO IN OTHER WORDS...
...THIS BOY'S NAME IS TENSION.

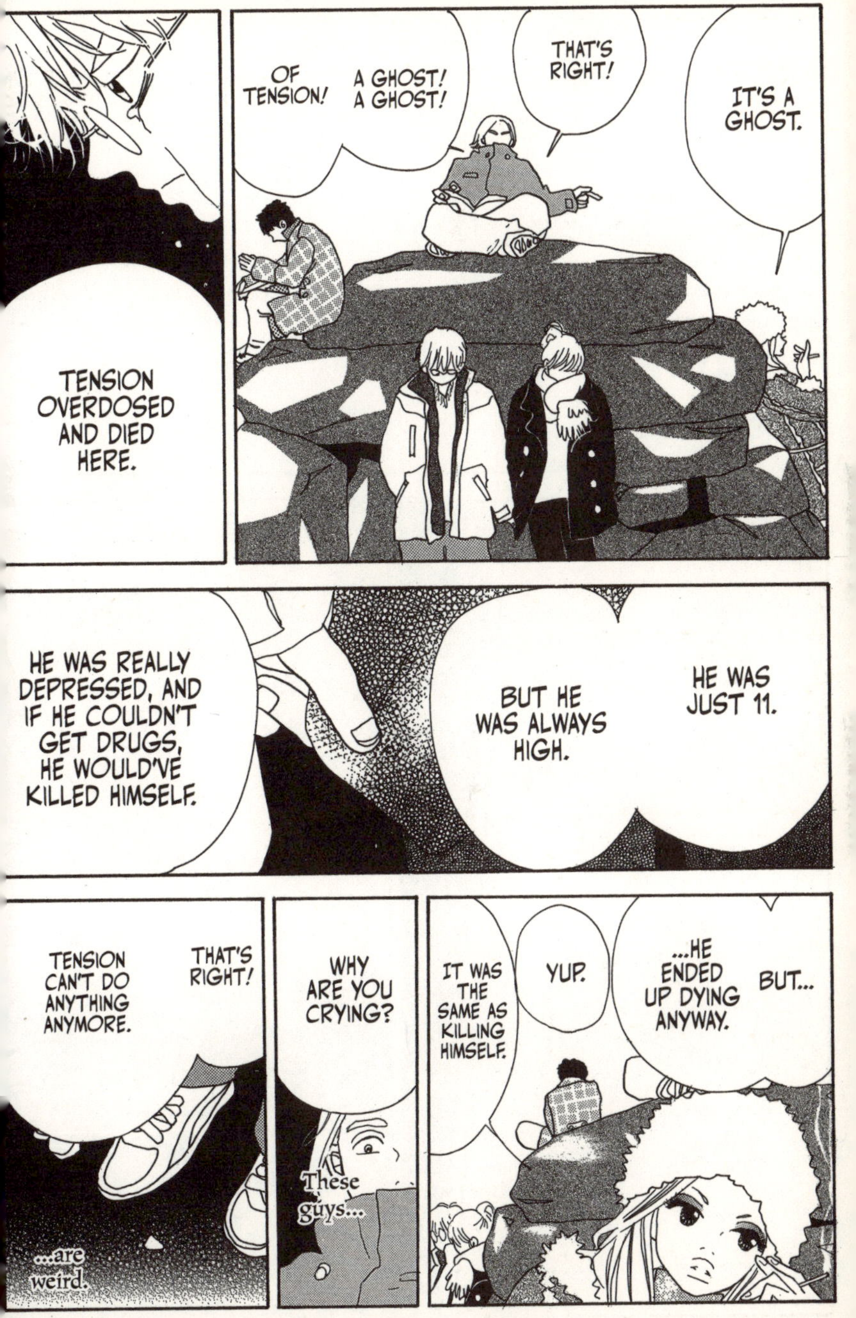
IT'S A GHOST.
THAT'S RIGHT!
A GHOST! A GHOST!
OF TENSION!
TENSION OVERDOSED AND DIED HERE.
HE WAS JUST 11.
BUT HE WAS ALWAYS HIGH.
HE WAS REALLY DEPRESSED, AND IF HE COULDN'T GET DRUGS, HE WOULD'VE KILLED HIMSELF.
BUT...
...HE ENDED UP DYING ANYWAY.
YUP.
IT WAS THE SAME AS KILLING HIMSELF.
WHY ARE YOU CRYING?
These guys...
THAT'S RIGHT!
TENSION CAN'T DO ANYTHING ANYMORE.
...are weird.

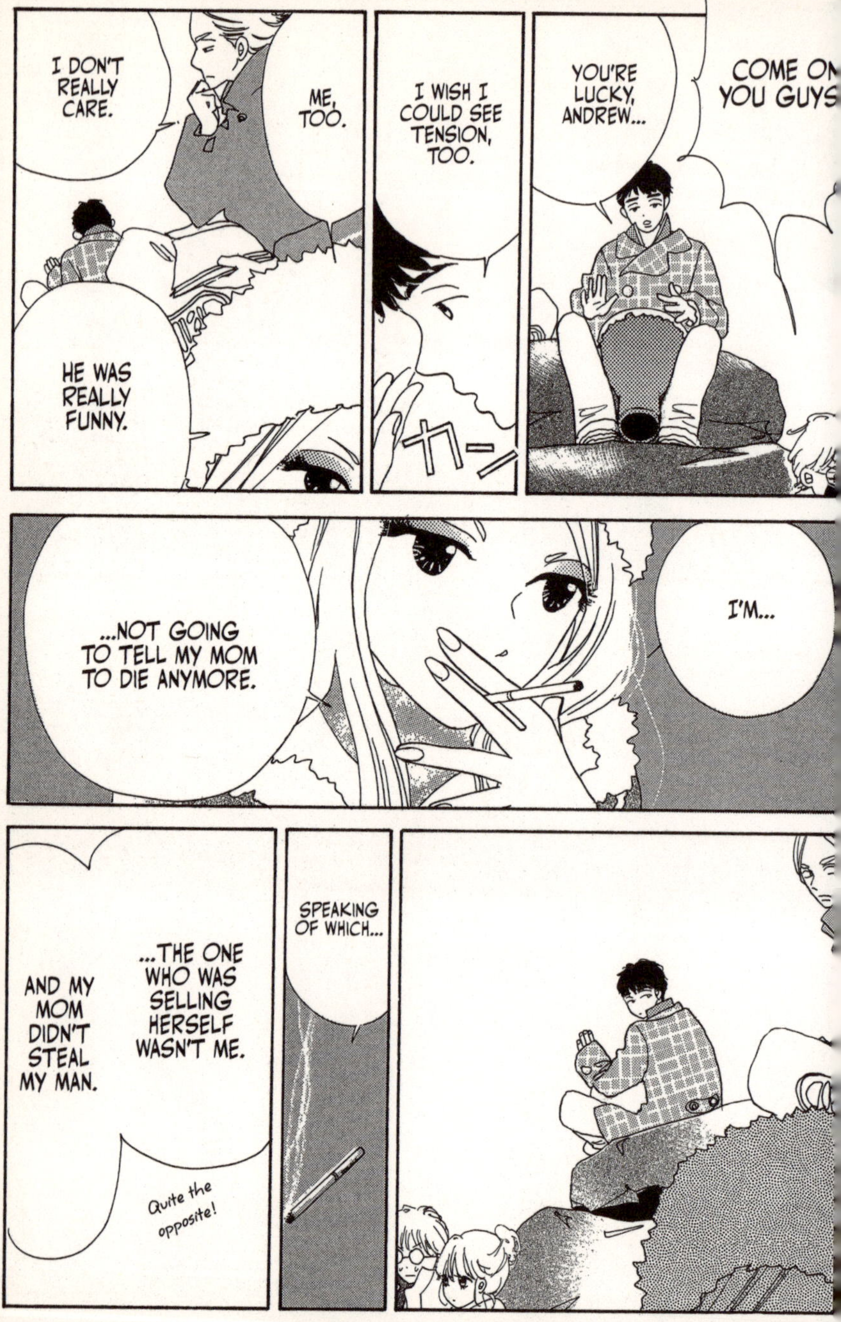
COME ON YOU GUYS
YOU'RE LUCKY, ANDREW...
I WISH I COULD SEE TENSION, TOO.
カーン
ME, TOO.
I DON'T REALLY CARE.
HE WAS REALLY FUNNY.
I'M...
...NOT GOING TO TELL MY MOM TO DIE ANYMORE.
SPEAKING OF WHICH...
...THE ONE WHO WAS SELLING HERSELF WASN'T ME.
AND MY MOM DIDN'T STEAL MY MAN.
Quite the opposite!

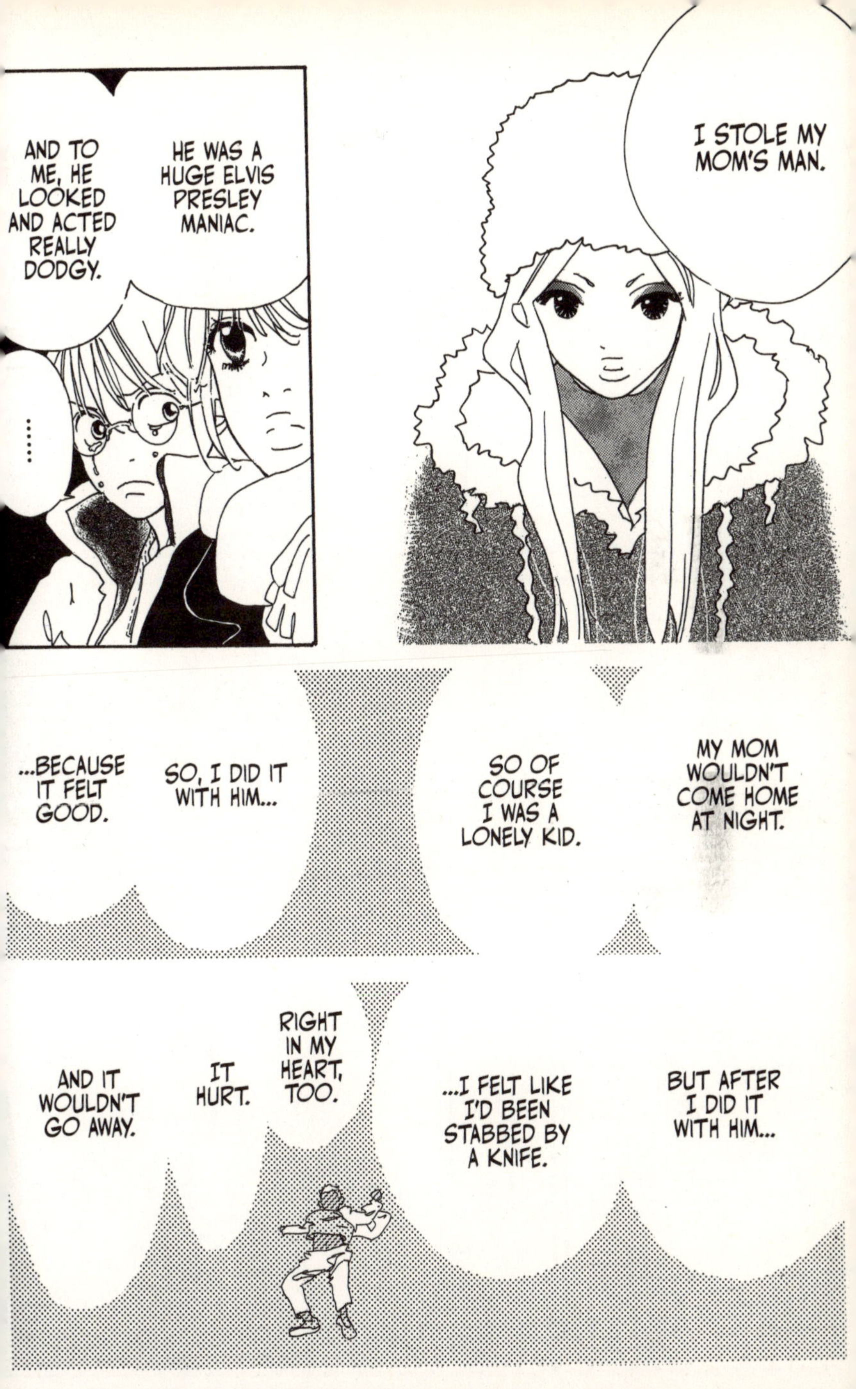
I STOLE MY MOM'S MAN.
HE WAS A HUGE ELVIS PRESLEY MANIAC.
AND TO ME, HE LOOKED AND ACTED REALLY DODGY.
......
MY MOM WOULDN'T COME HOME AT NIGHT.
SO OF COURSE I WAS A LONELY KID.
SO, I DID IT WITH HIM...
...BECAUSE IT FELT GOOD.
BUT AFTER I DID IT WITH HIM...
...I FELT LIKE I'D BEEN STABBED BY A KNIFE.
RIGHT IN MY HEART, TOO.
IT HURT.
AND IT WOULDN'T GO AWAY.

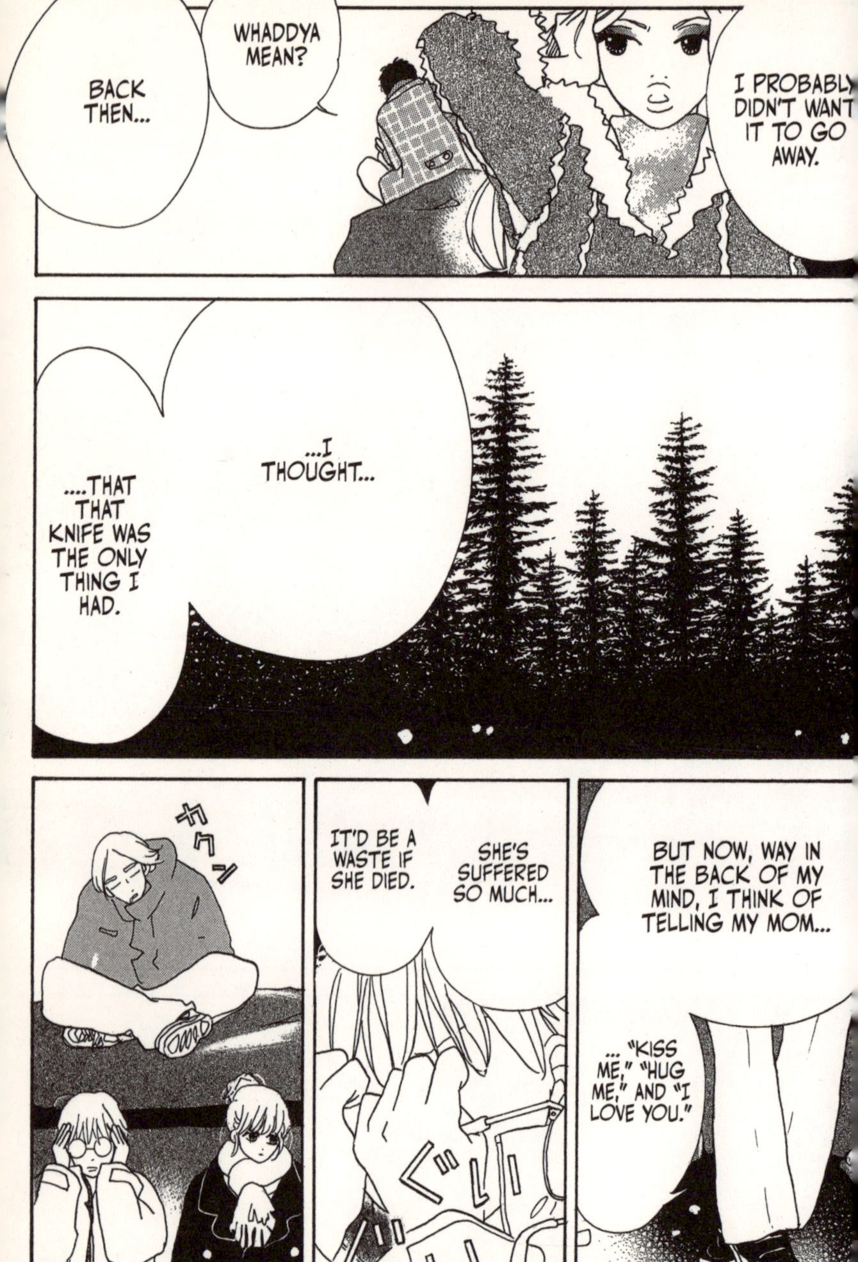
I PROBABLY DIDN'T WANT IT TO GO AWAY.
WHADDYA MEAN?
BACK THEN...
...I THOUGHT...
....THAT THAT KNIFE WAS THE ONLY THING I HAD.
BUT NOW, WAY IN THE BACK OF MY MIND, I THINK OF TELLING MY MOM...
... "KISS ME," "HUG ME," AND "I LOVE YOU."
SHE'S SUFFERED SO MUCH...
IT'D BE A WASTE IF SHE DIED.

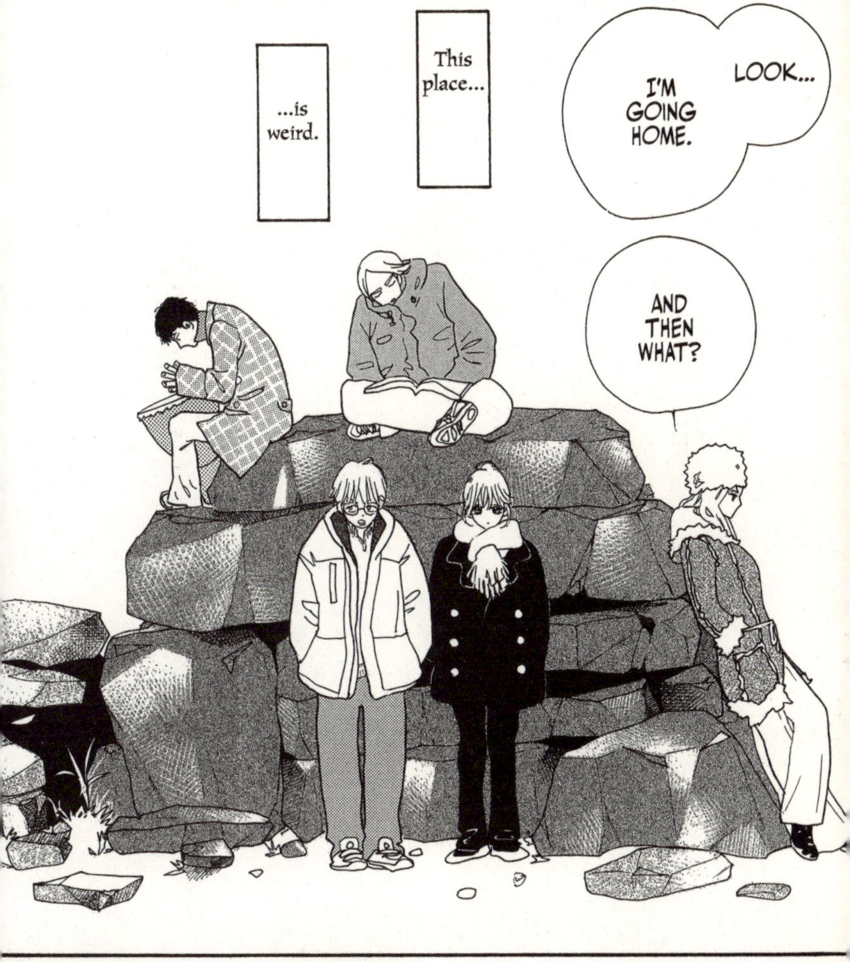
LOOK...
I'M GOING HOME.
This place...
...is weird.
AND THEN WHAT?

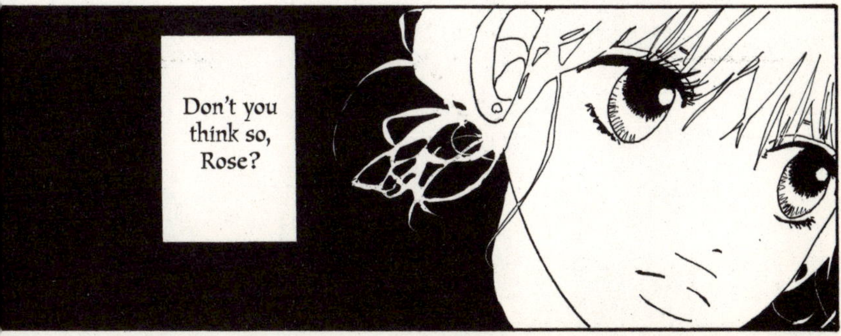
Don't you think so, Rose?

Club Hurricane Adventure 2

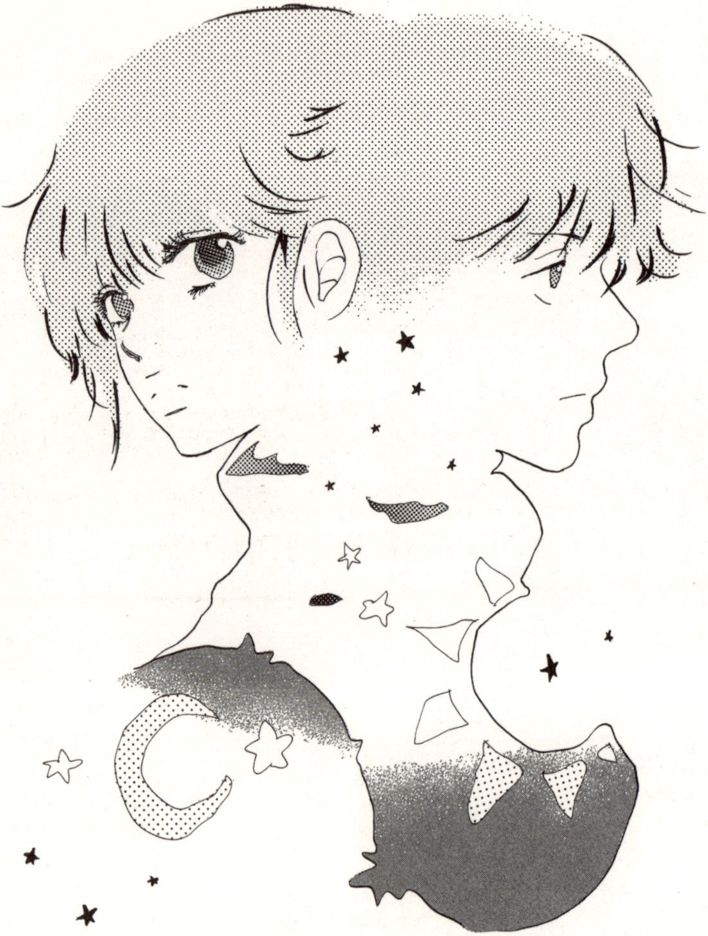

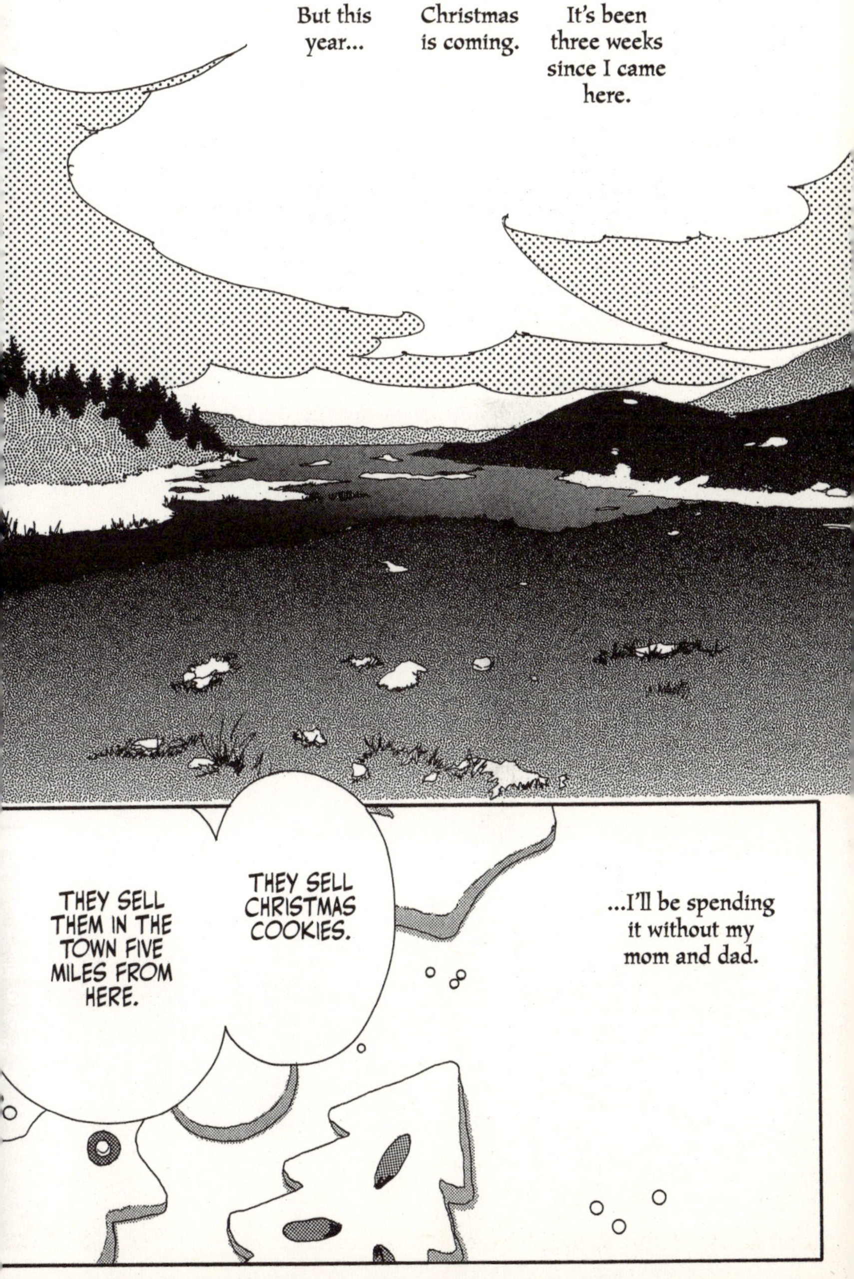
It's been three weeks since I came here.
Christmas is coming.
But this year...
...I'll be spending it without my mom and dad.
THEY SELL CHRISTMAS COOKIES.
THEY SELL THEM IN THE TOWN FIVE MILES FROM HERE.

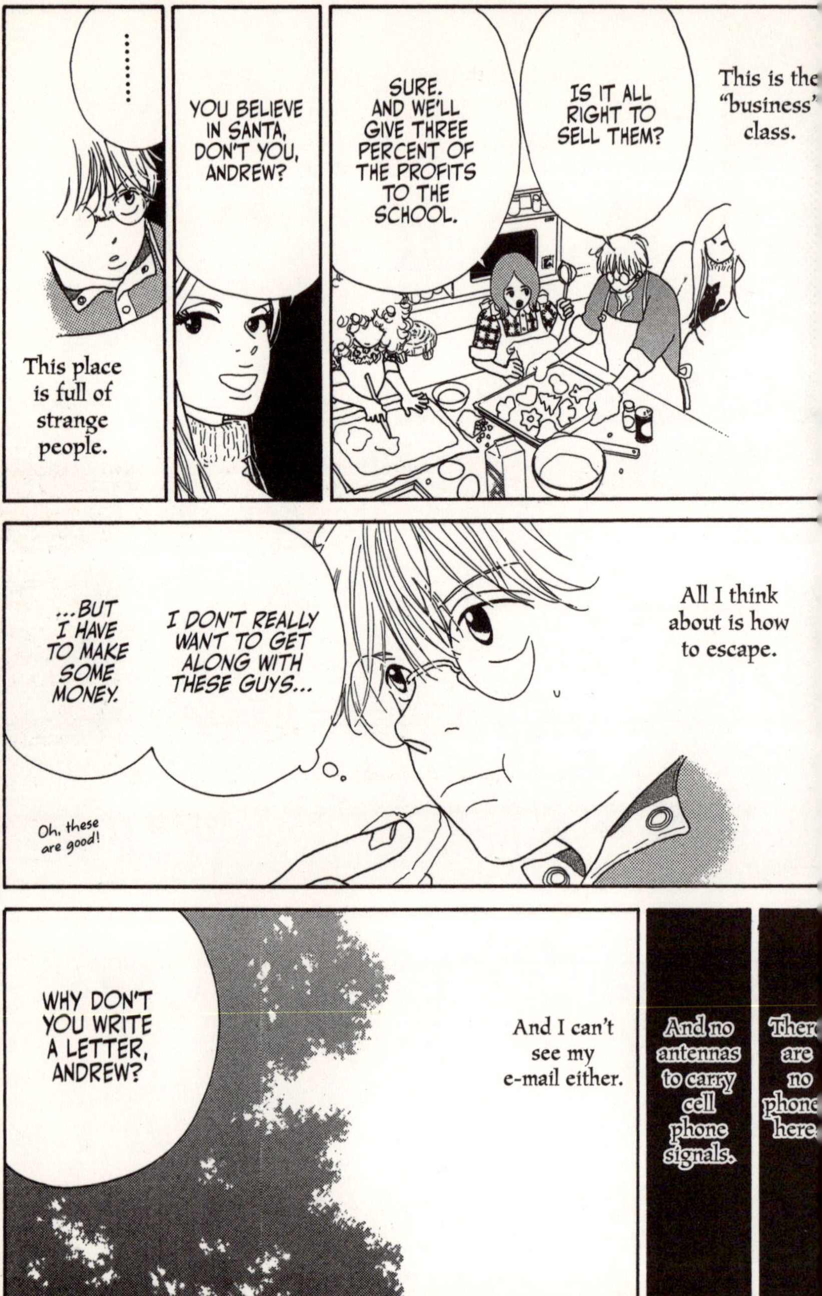
This is the "business" class.
IS IT ALL RIGHT TO SELL THEM?
SURE. AND WE'LL GIVE THREE PERCENT OF THE PROFITS TO THE SCHOOL.
YOU BELIEVE IN SANTA, DON'T YOU, ANDREW?
....
This place is full of strange people.
All I think about is how to escape.
I DON'T REALLY WANT TO GET ALONG WITH THESE GUYS...
...BUT I HAVE TO MAKE SOME MONEY.
Oh, these are good!
Ther are no phone here.
And no antennas to carry cell phone signals.
And I can't see my e-mail either.
WHY DON'T YOU WRITE A LETTER, ANDREW?

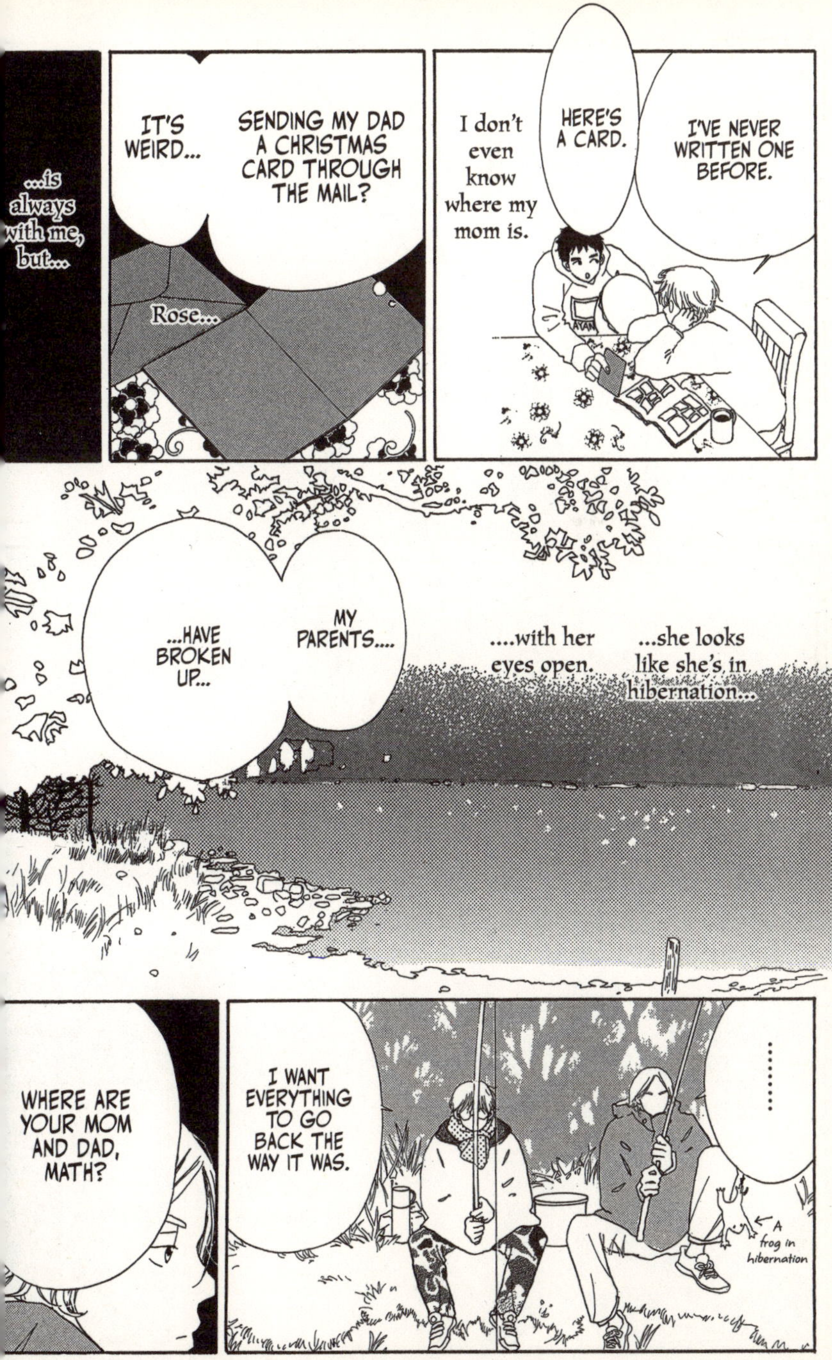
I'VE NEVER WRITTEN ONE BEFORE.
HERE'S A CARD.
I don't even know where my mom is.
SENDING MY DAD A CHRISTMAS CARD THROUGH THE MAIL?
IT'S WEIRD...
Rose...
...is always with me, but...
...she looks like she's in hibernation...
....with her eyes open.
MY PARENTS....
...HAVE BROKEN UP...
....
← A frog in hibernation
I WANT EVERYTHING TO GO BACK THE WAY IT WAS.
WHERE ARE YOUR MOM AND DAD, MATH?

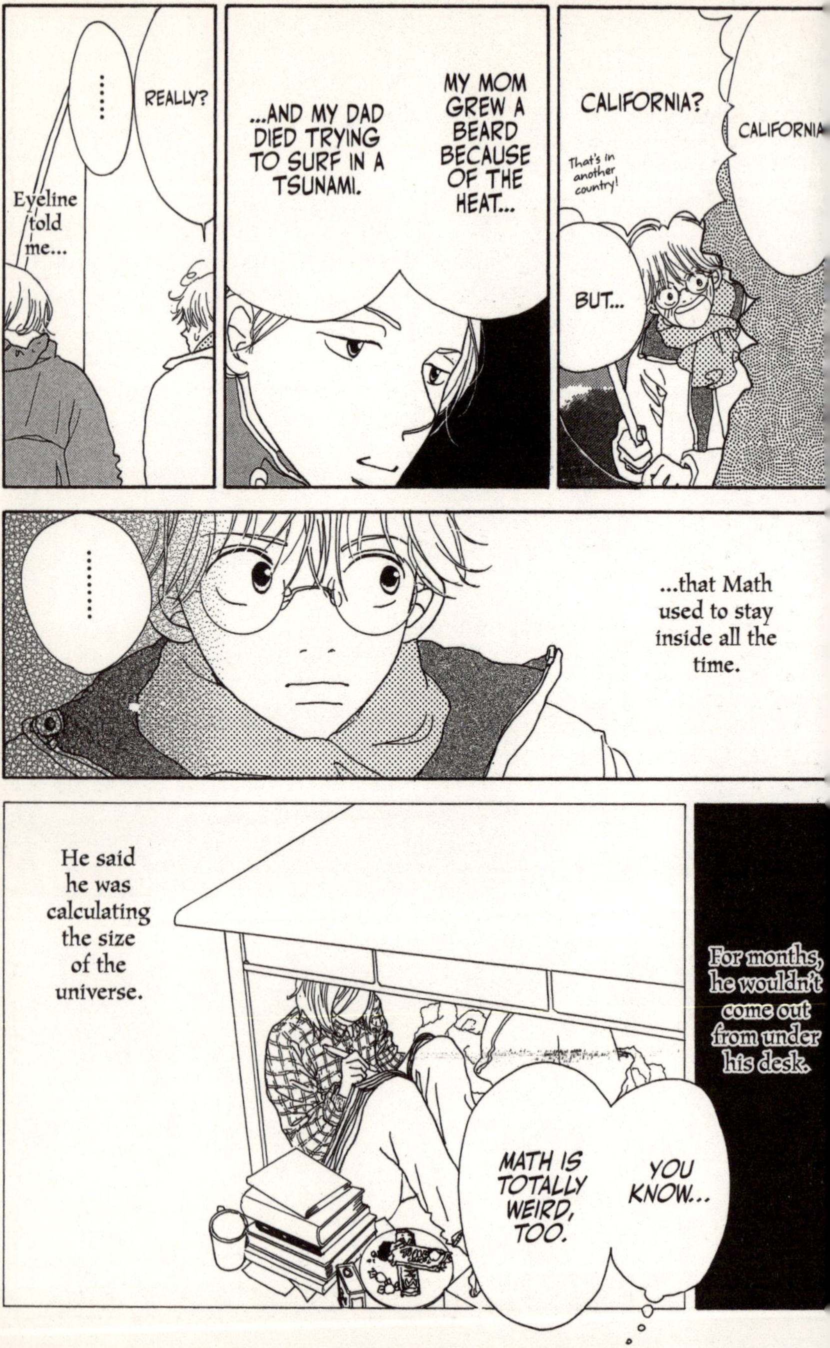
CALIFORNIA
CALIFORNIA?
That's in another country!
BUT...
MY MOM GREW A BEARD BECAUSE OF THE HEAT...
...AND MY DAD DIED TRYING TO SURF IN A TSUNAMI.
REALLY?
......
Eyeline told me...
...that Math used to stay inside all the time.
....
For months, he wouldn't come out from under his desk.
YOU KNOW...
MATH IS TOTALLY WEIRD, TOO.
He said he was calculating the size of the universe.

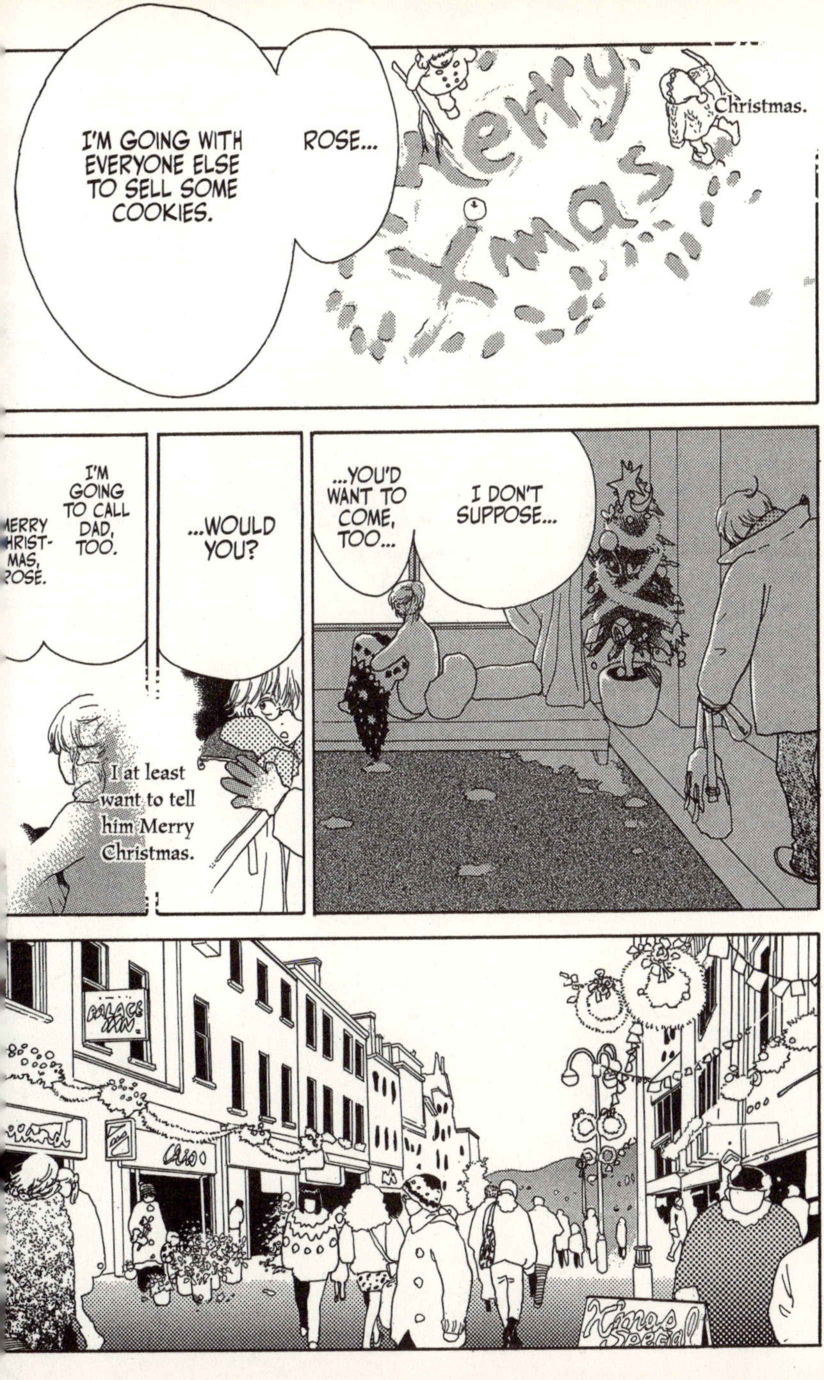
Merry Xmas
Christmas.
ROSE...
I'M GOING WITH EVERYONE ELSE TO SELL SOME COOKIES.
I DON'T SUPPOSE...
...YOU'D WANT TO COME, TOO...
...WOULD YOU?
I'M GOING TO CALL DAD, TOO.
ERRY HRIST- MAS, OSE.
I at least want to tell him Merry Christmas.
PALACE INN
Xmas Special

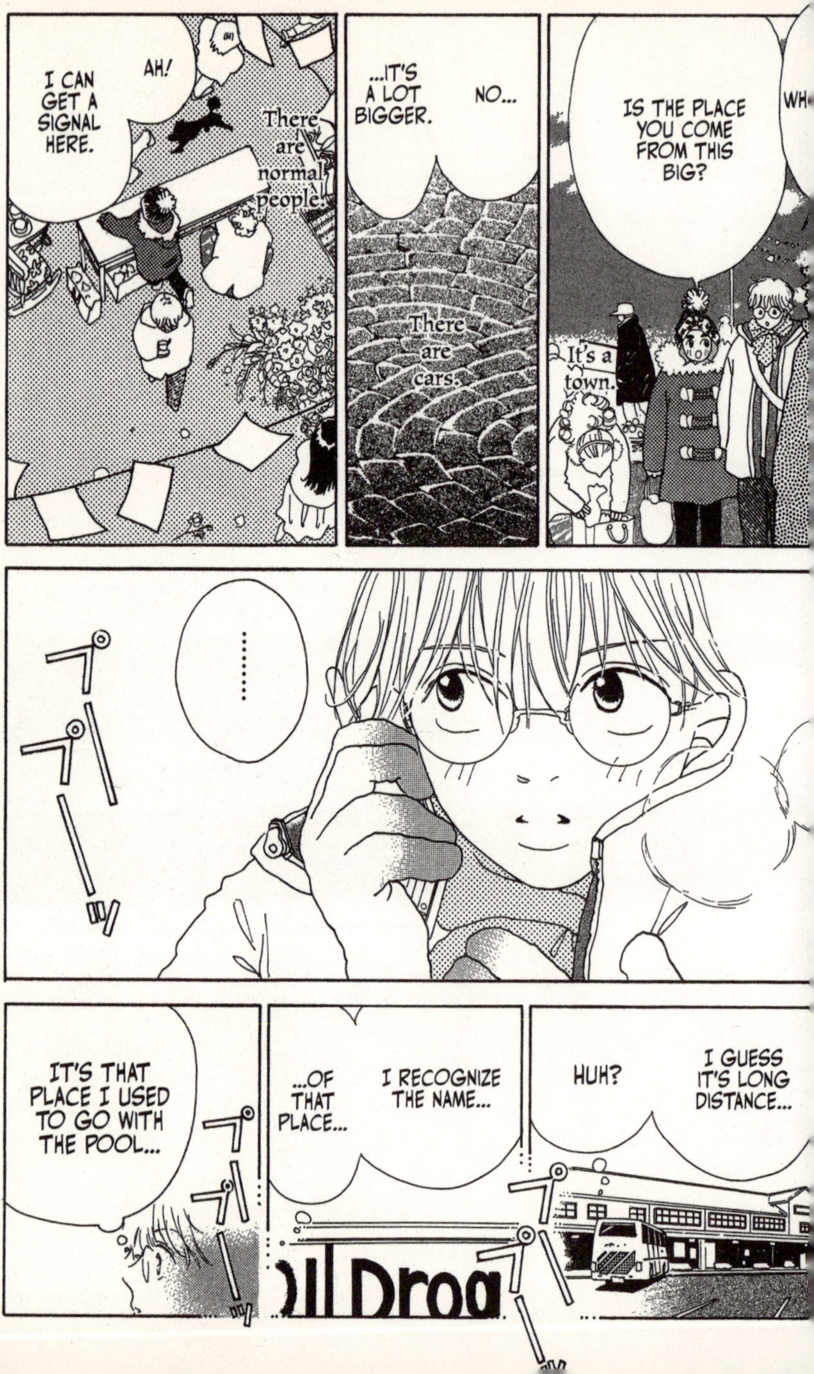
WH
IS THE PLACE YOU COME FROM THIS BIG?
It's a town.
NO...
...IT'S A LOT BIGGER.
There are cars.
AH!
I CAN GET A SIGNAL HERE.
There are normal people.
......
I GUESS IT'S LONG DISTANCE...
HUH?
I RECOGNIZE THE NAME...
...OF THAT PLACE...
IT'S THAT PLACE I USED TO GO WITH THE POOL...

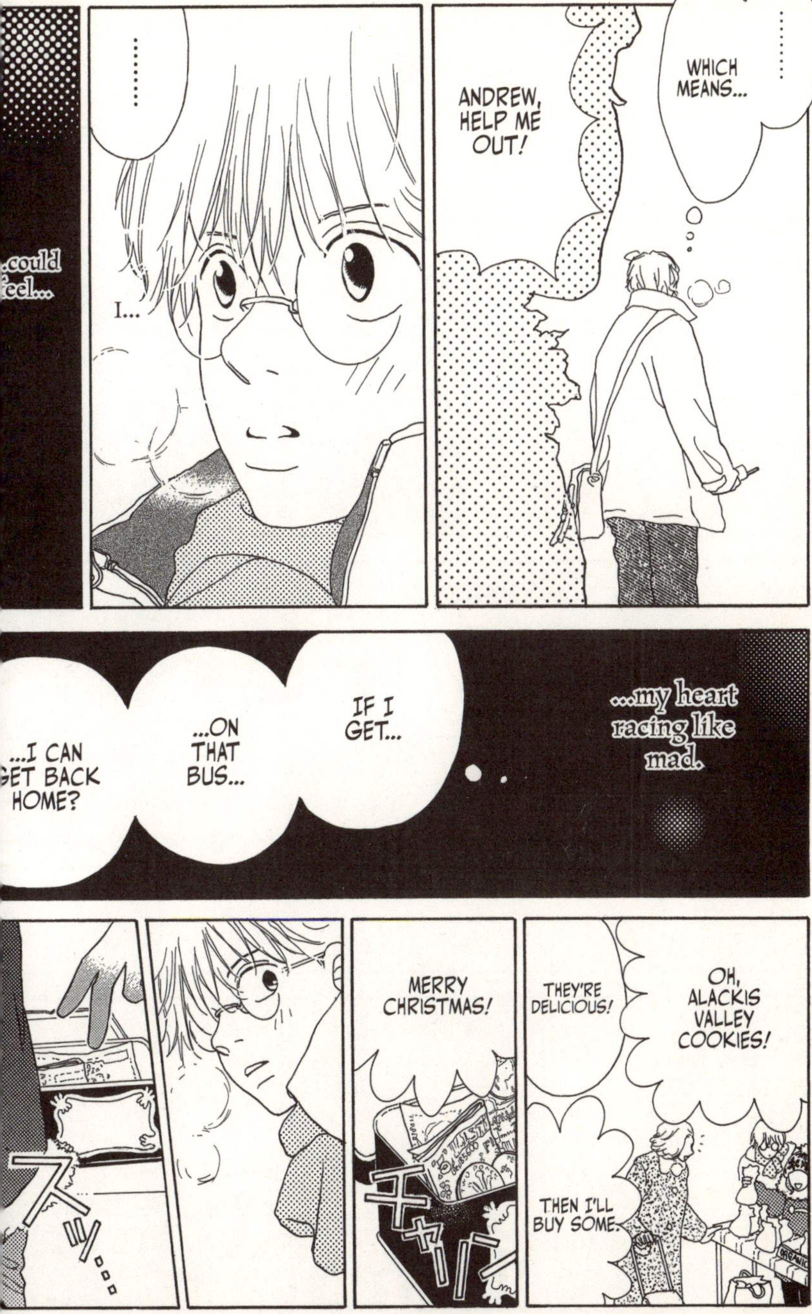
......
WHICH MEANS...
ANDREW, HELP ME OUT!
......
I...
.could feel...
...my heart racing like mad.
IF I GET...
...ON THAT BUS...
...I CAN GET BACK HOME?
OH, ALACKIS VALLEY COOKIES!
THEY'RE DELICIOUS!
THEN I'LL BUY SOME.
MERRY CHRISTMAS!
スッ...

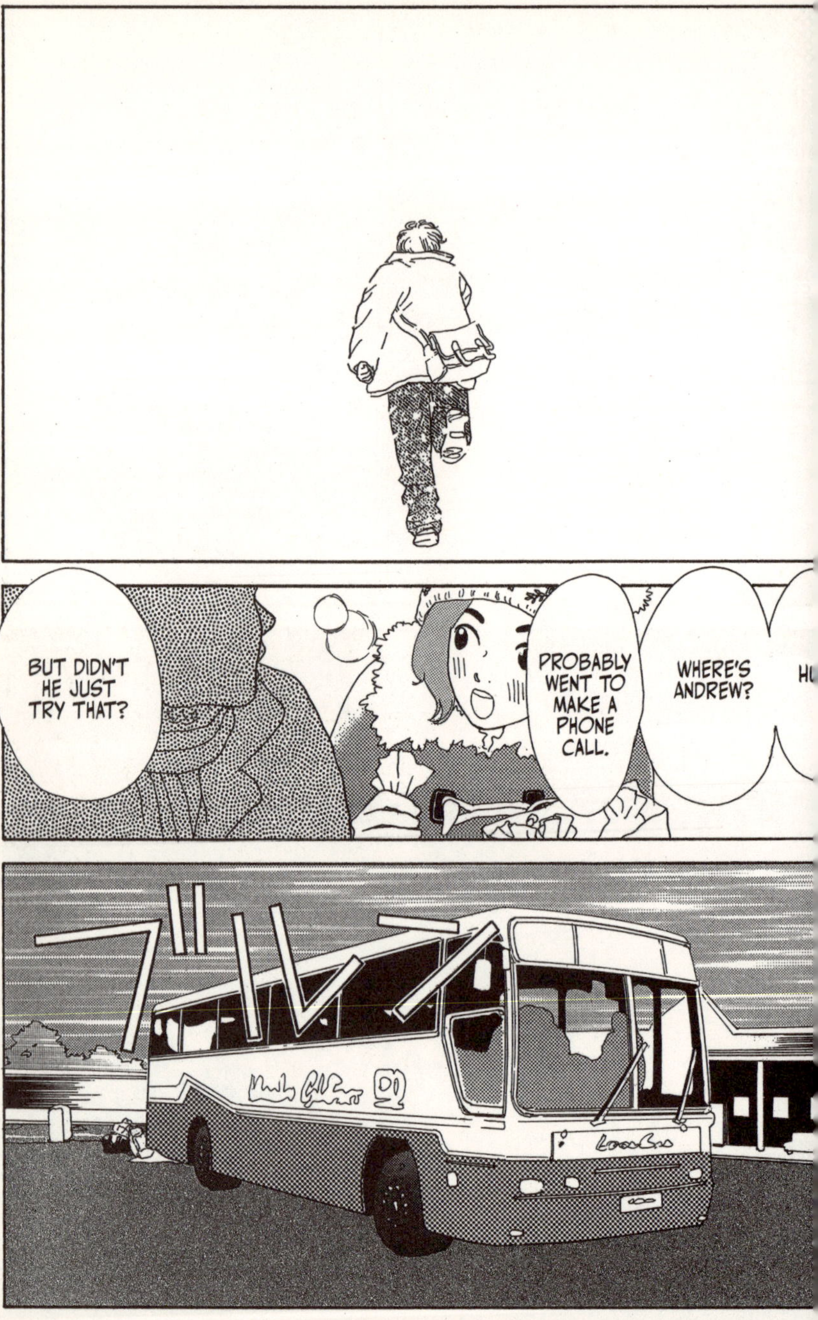
WHERE'S ANDREW?
PROBABLY WENT TO MAKE A PHONE CALL.
BUT DIDN'T HE JUST TRY THAT?
ブルン

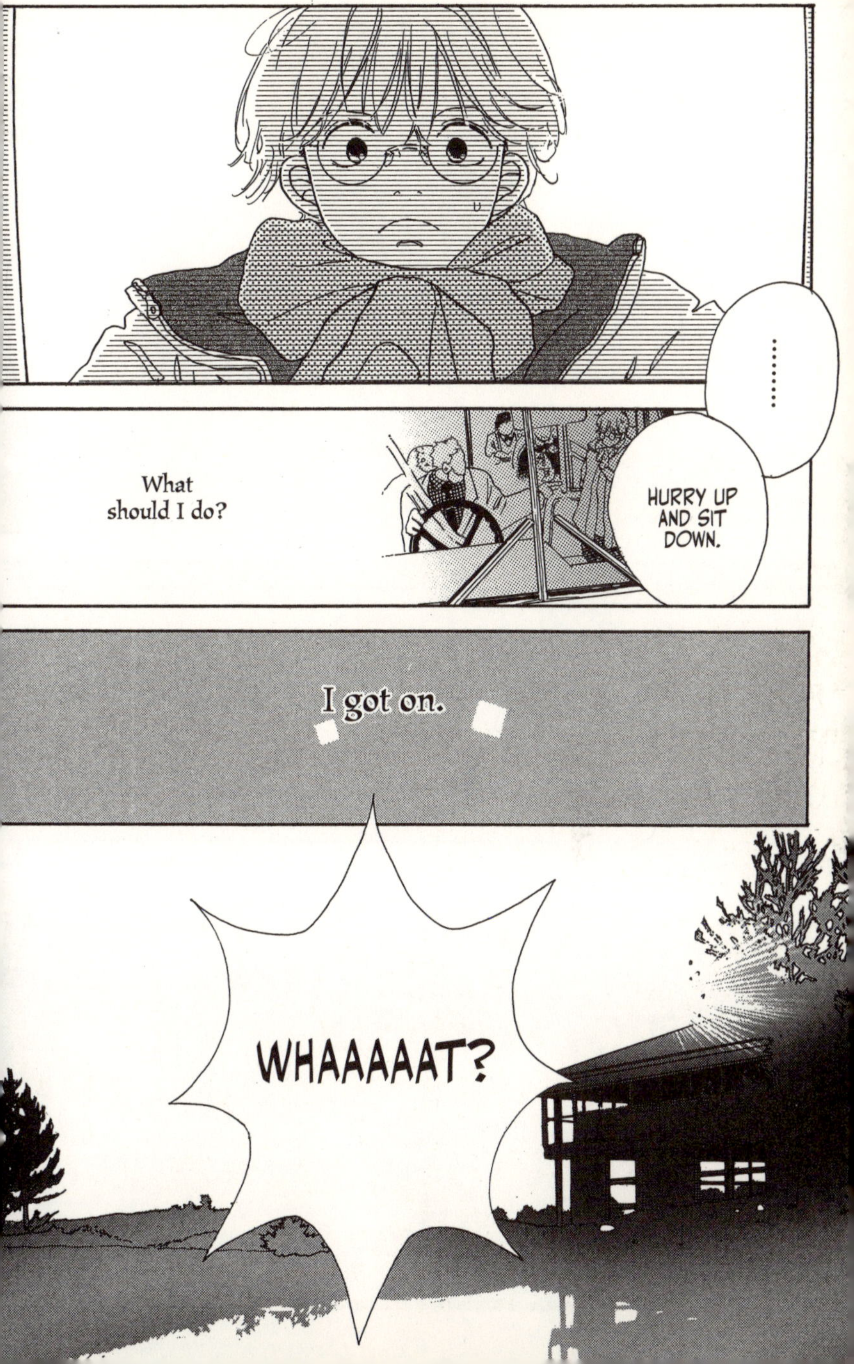
....
HURRY UP AND SIT DOWN.
What should I do?
I got on.
WHAAAAAT?

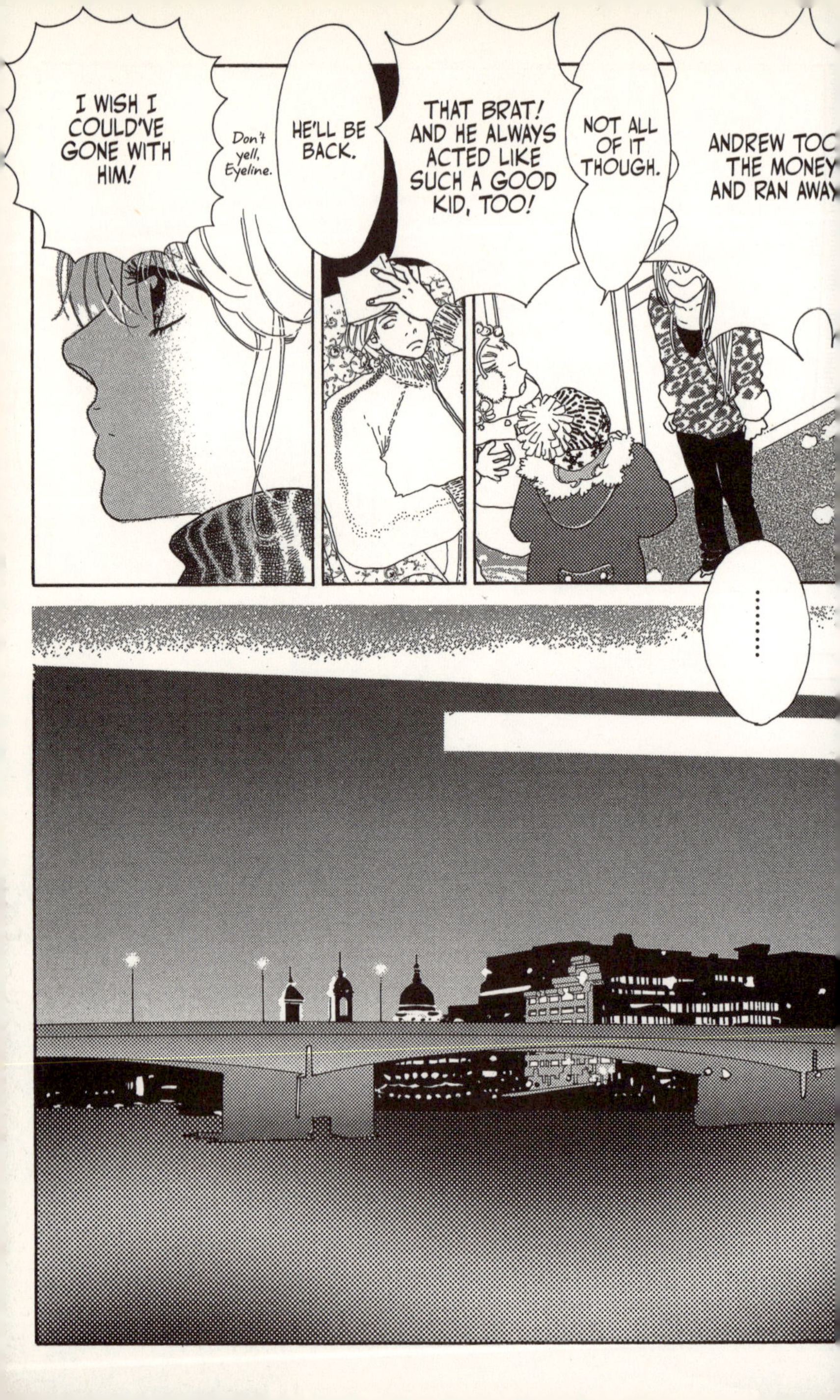
ANDREW TOC THE MONEY AND RAN AWAY
NOT ALL OF IT THOUGH.
THAT BRAT! AND HE ALWAYS ACTED LIKE SUCH A GOOD KID, TOO!
HE'LL BE BACK.
Don't yell, Eyeline.
I WISH I COULD'VE GONE WITH HIM!
....

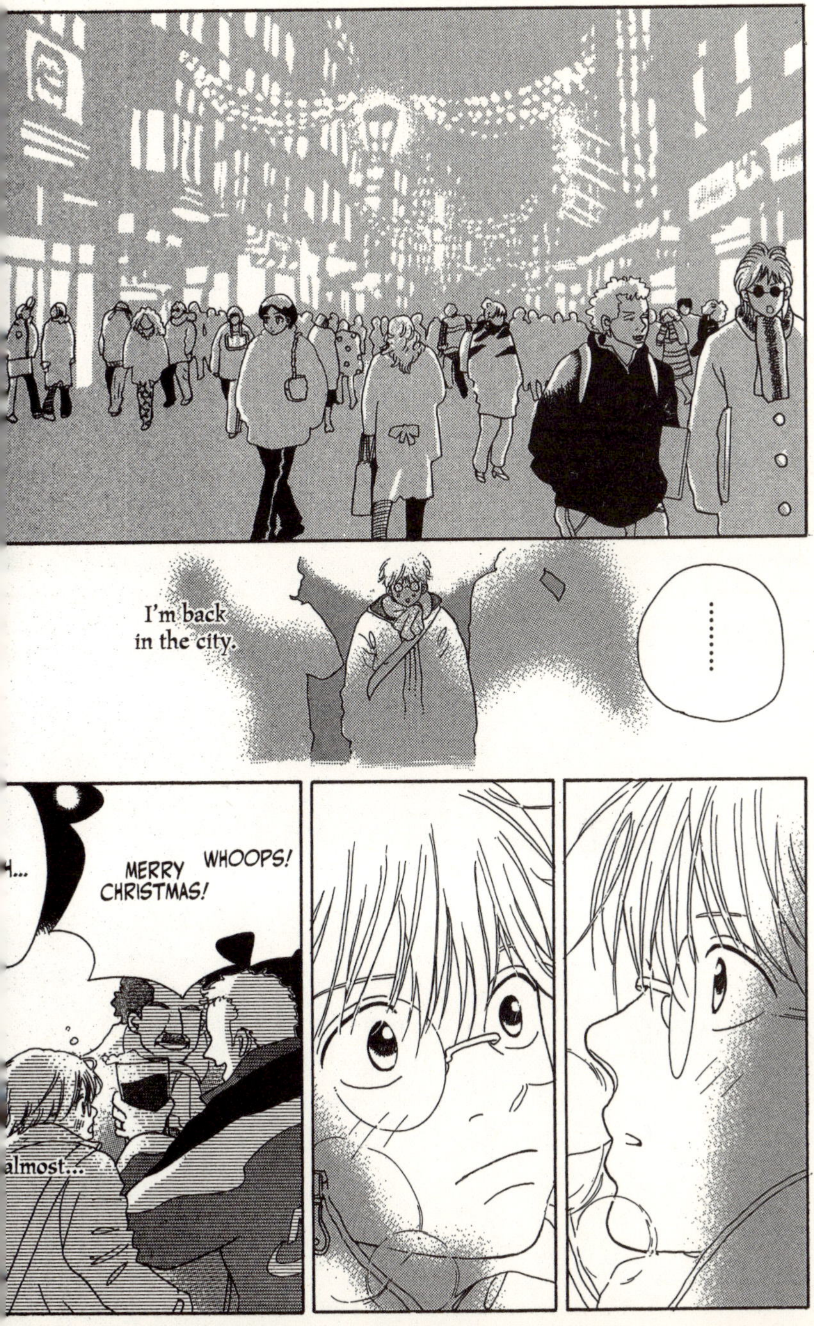
....
I'm back in the city.
WHOOPS!
MERRY CHRISTMAS!
almost...

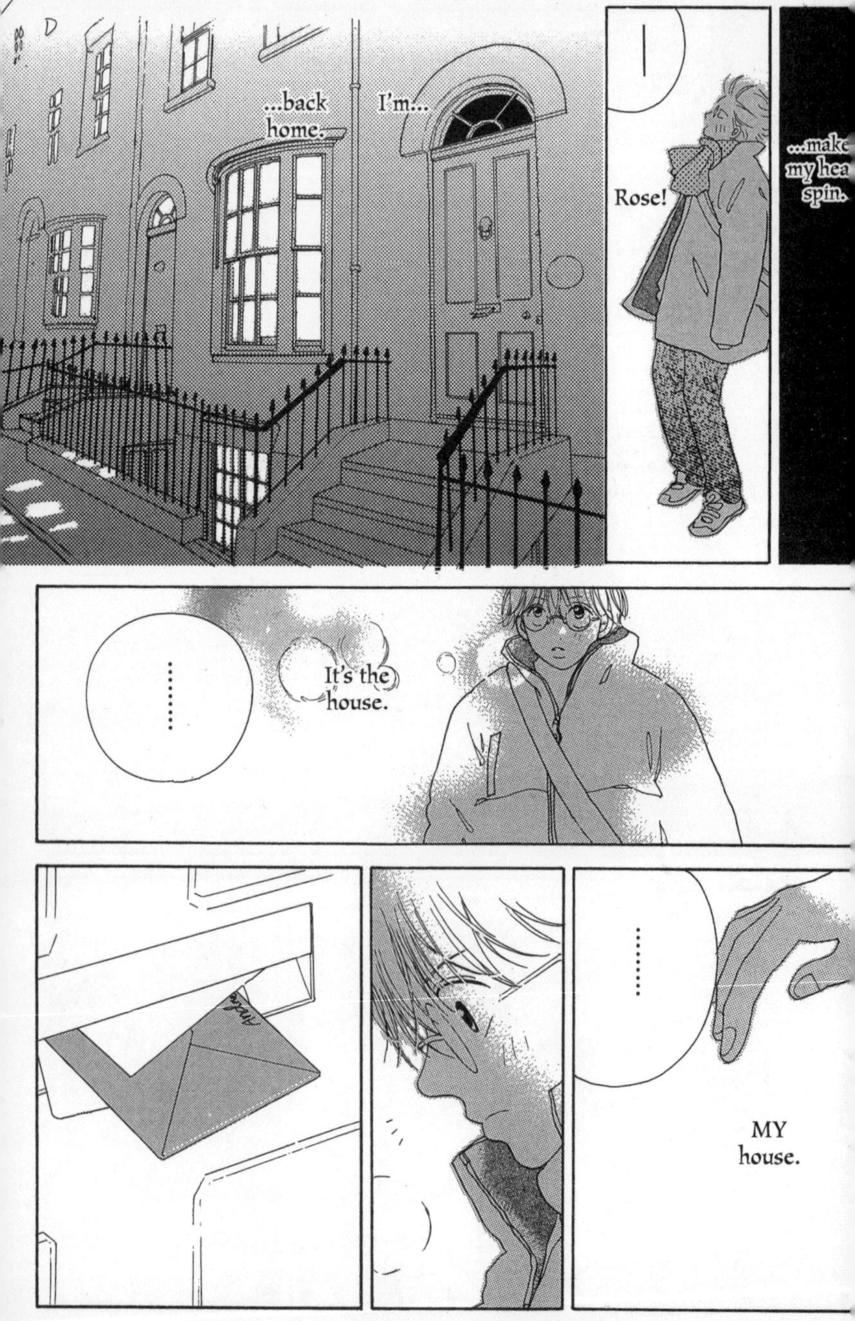

...make
my hea
spin.
Rose!
I'm...
...back
home.
It's the
house.
......
......
MY
house.

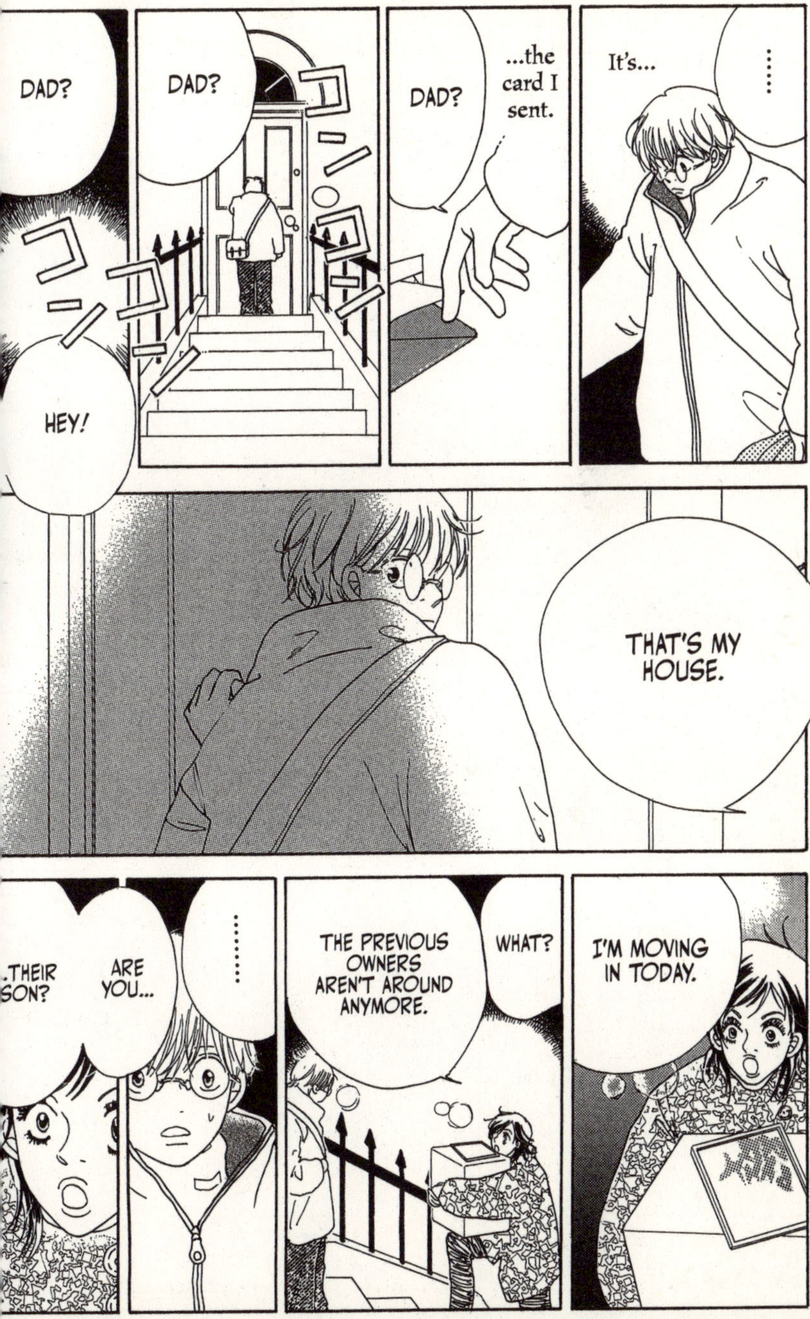
......
It's...
...the card I sent.
DAD?
DAD?
DAD?
HEY!
THAT'S MY HOUSE.
I'M MOVING IN TODAY.
WHAT?
THE PREVIOUS OWNERS AREN'T AROUND ANYMORE.
......
ARE YOU...
.THEIR SON?

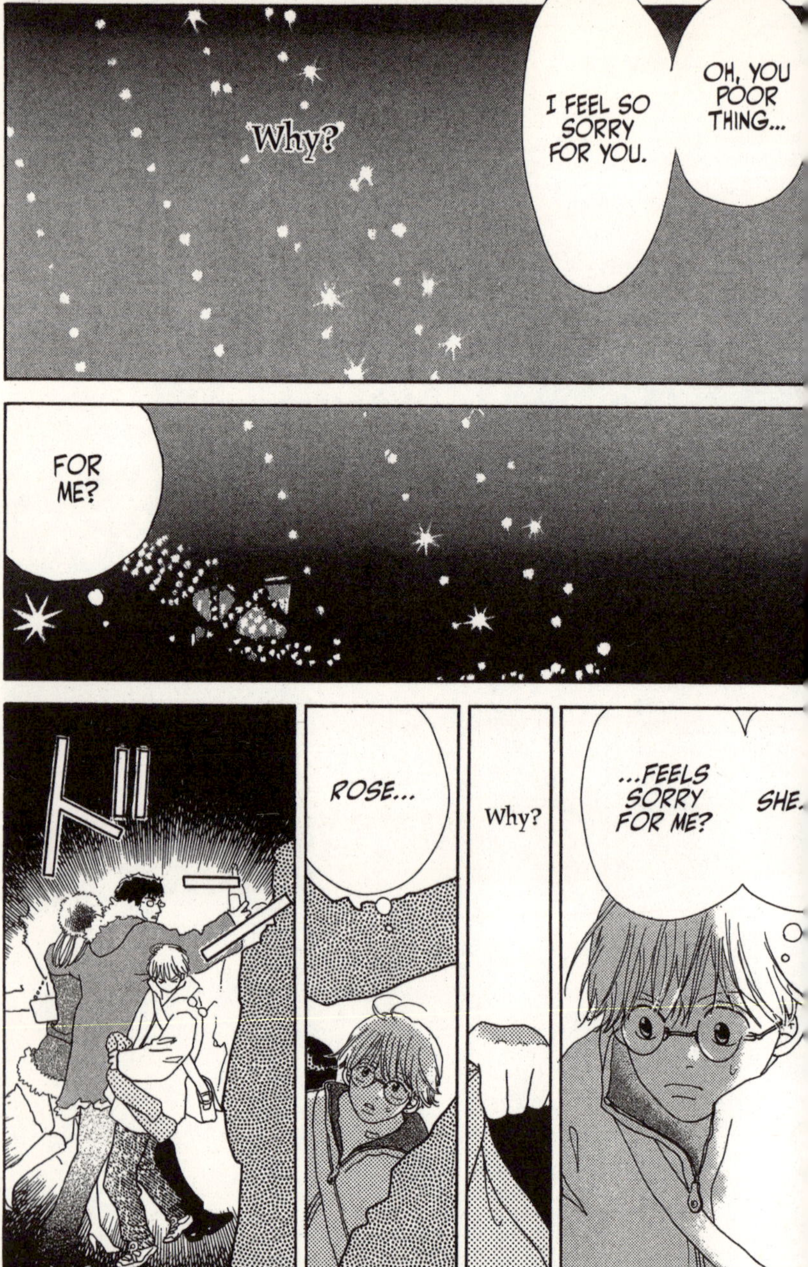
OH, YOU POOR THING...
I FEEL SO SORRY FOR YOU.
Why?
FOR ME?
SHE.
...FEELS SORRY FOR ME?
Why?
ROSE...

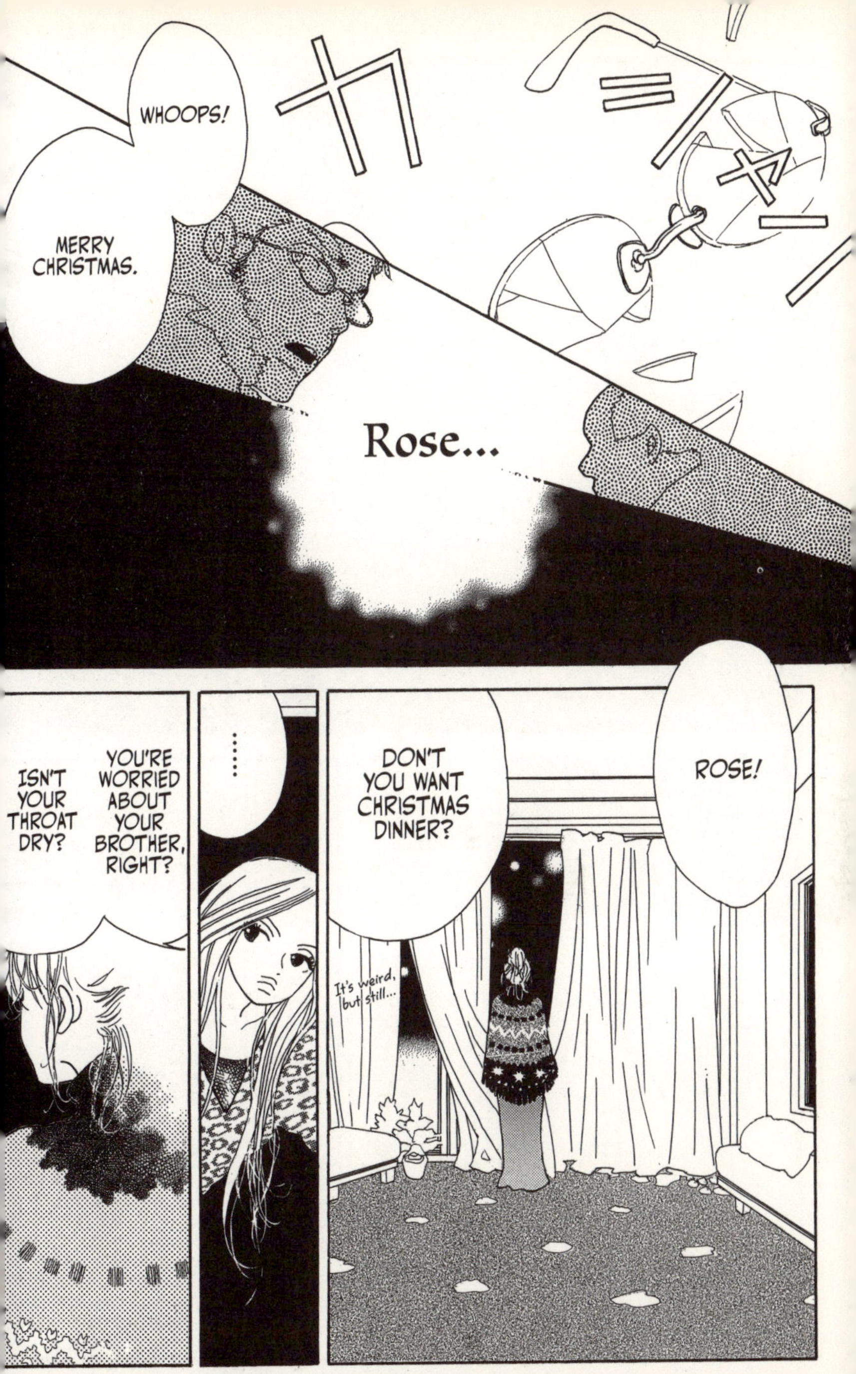
WHOOPS!
MERRY CHRISTMAS.
Rose...
ROSE!
DON'T YOU WANT CHRISTMAS DINNER?
It's weird, but still...
......
YOU'RE WORRIED ABOUT YOUR BROTHER, RIGHT?
ISN'T YOUR THROAT DRY?

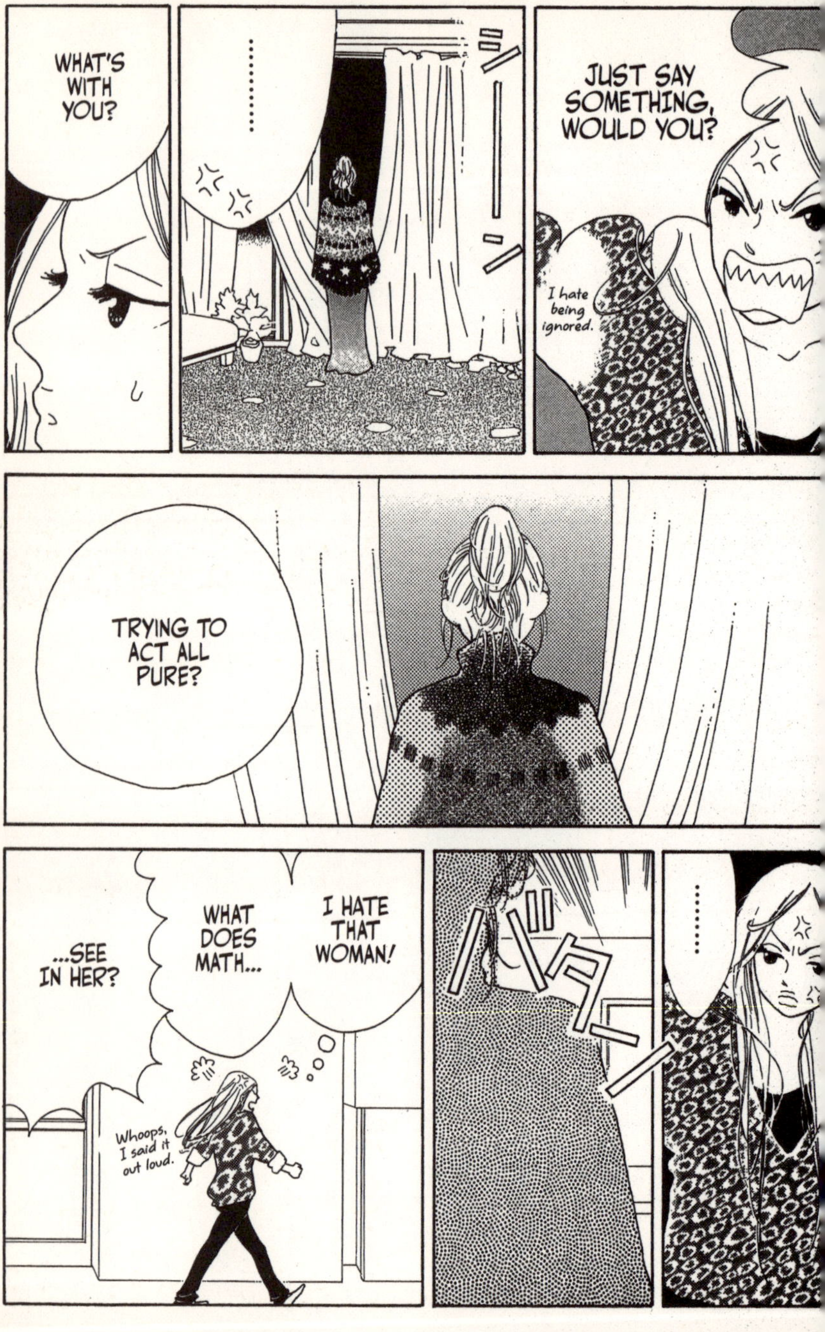
JUST SAY SOMETHING, WOULD YOU?
I hate being ignored.
....
WHAT'S WITH YOU?
TRYING TO ACT ALL PURE?
......
I HATE THAT WOMAN!
WHAT DOES MATH...
...SEE IN HER?
Whoops, I said it out loud.

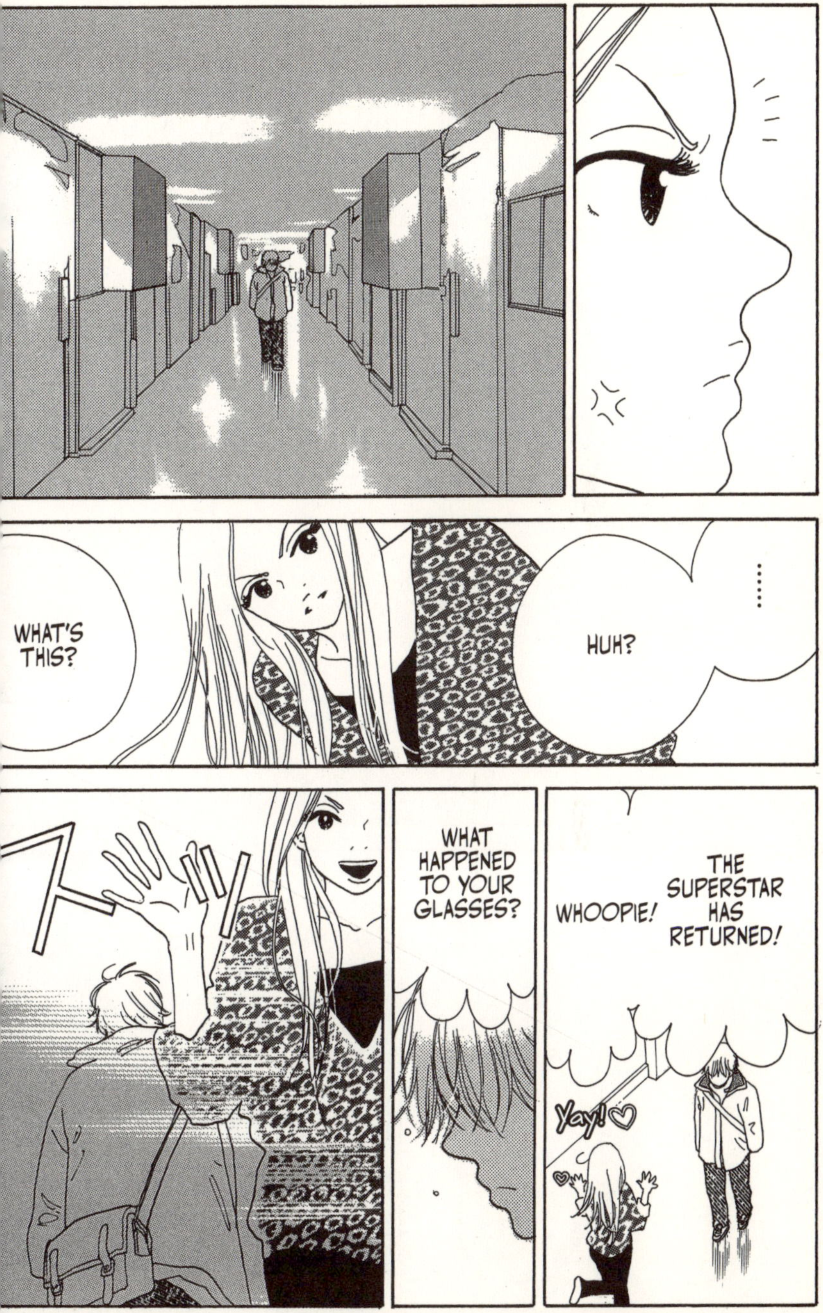
......
HUH?
WHAT'S THIS?
THE SUPERSTAR HAS RETURNED!
WHOOPIE!
Yay!♡
WHAT HAPPENED TO YOUR GLASSES?

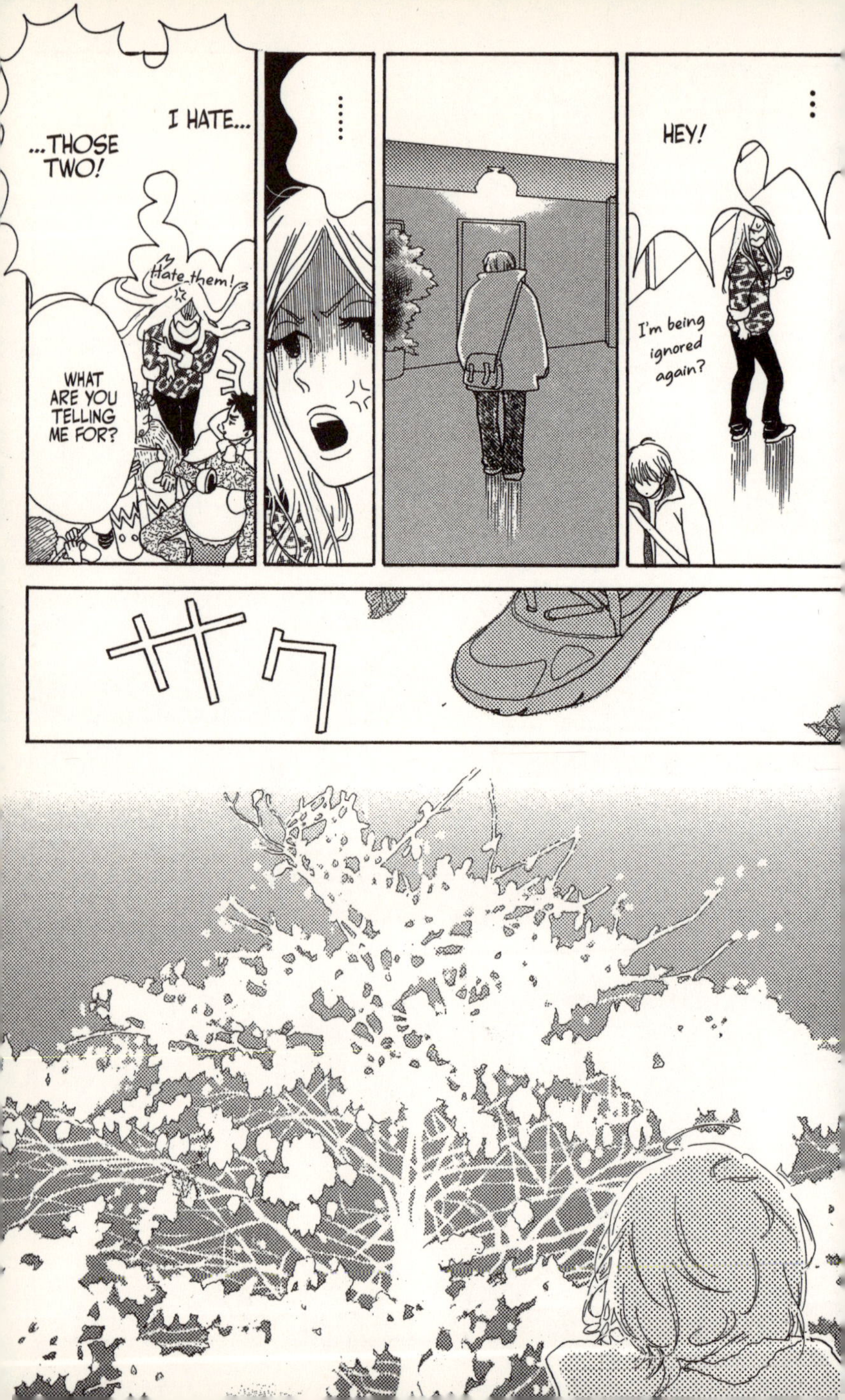
...
HEY!
I'm being ignored again?
......
I HATE...
...THOSE TWO!
Hate them!
WHAT ARE YOU TELLING ME FOR?
サク

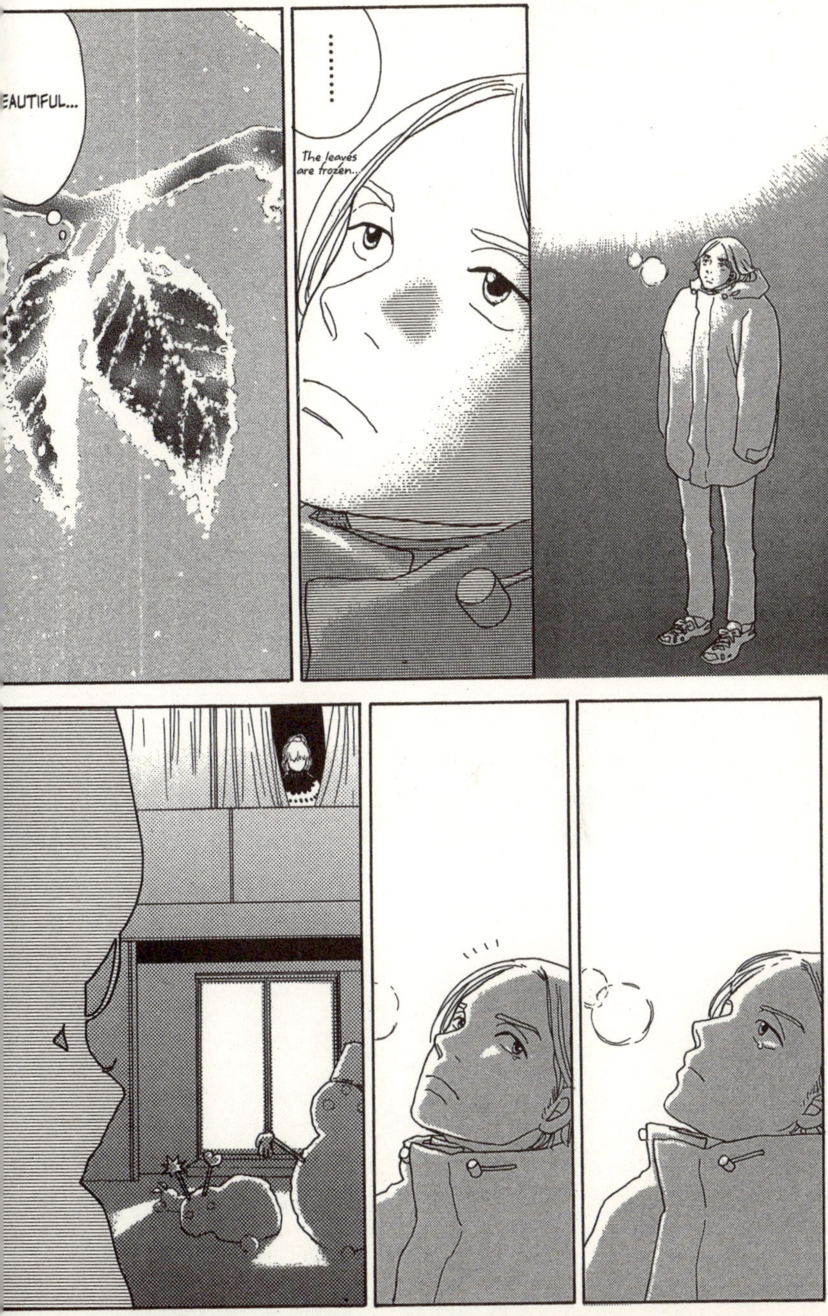
....
The leaves are frozen...
EAUTIFUL...

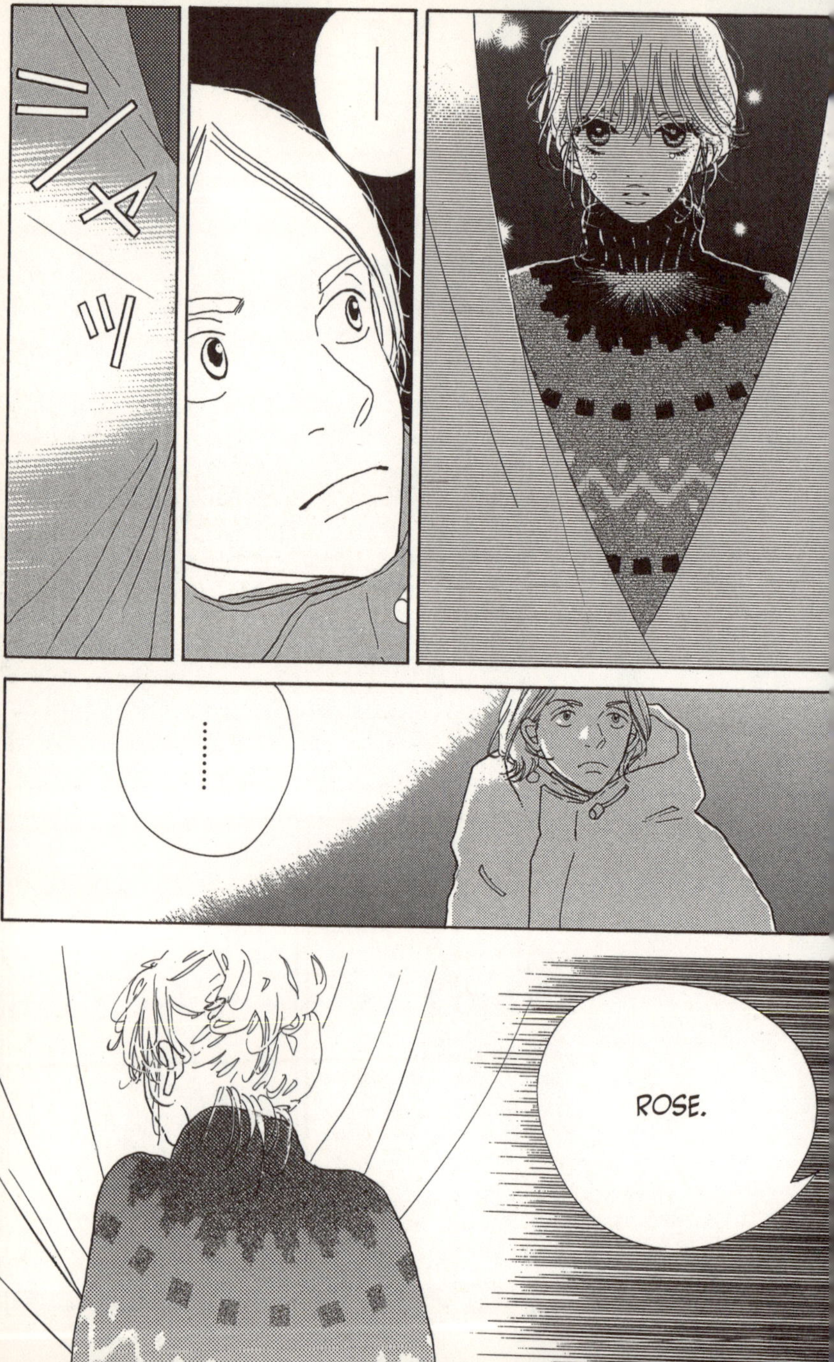
—
......
ROSE.

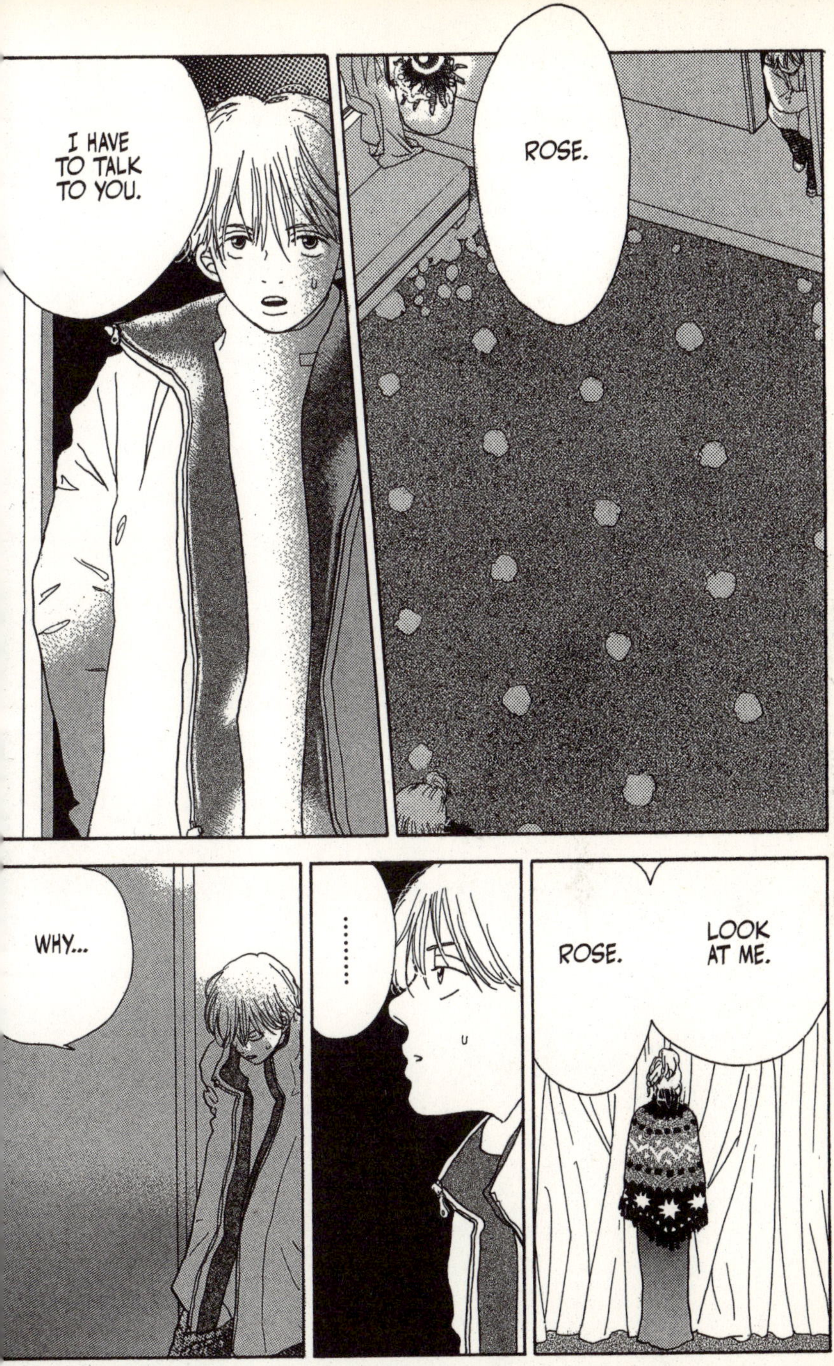
ROSE.
I HAVE TO TALK TO YOU.
ROSE. LOOK AT ME.
....
WHY...

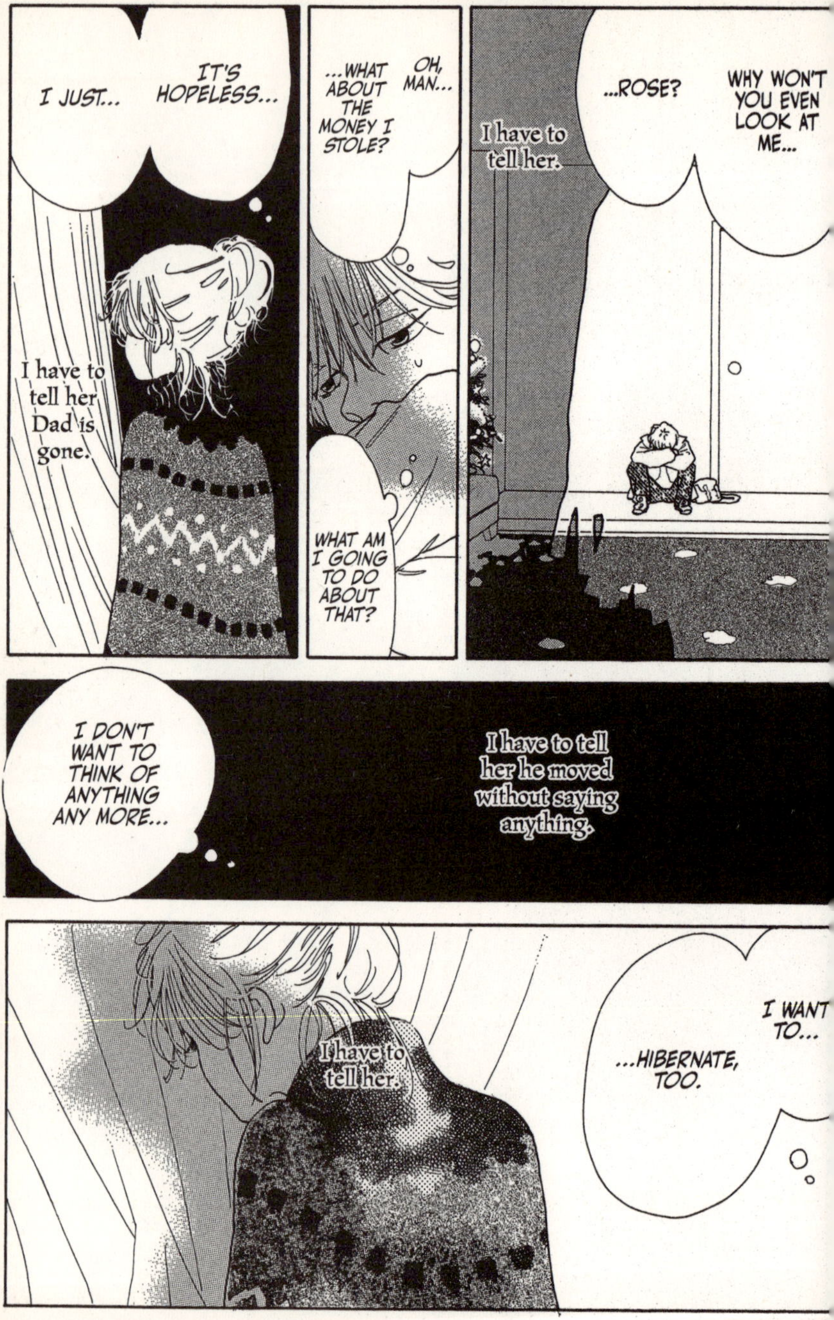
WHY WON'T YOU EVEN LOOK AT ME...
...ROSE?
I have to tell her.
OH, MAN...
...WHAT ABOUT THE MONEY I STOLE?
WHAT AM I GOING TO DO ABOUT THAT?
IT'S HOPELESS...
I JUST...
I have to tell her Dad is gone.
I have to tell her he moved without saying anything.
I DON'T WANT TO THINK OF ANYTHING ANY MORE...
I WANT TO...
...HIBERNATE, TOO.
I have to tell her.

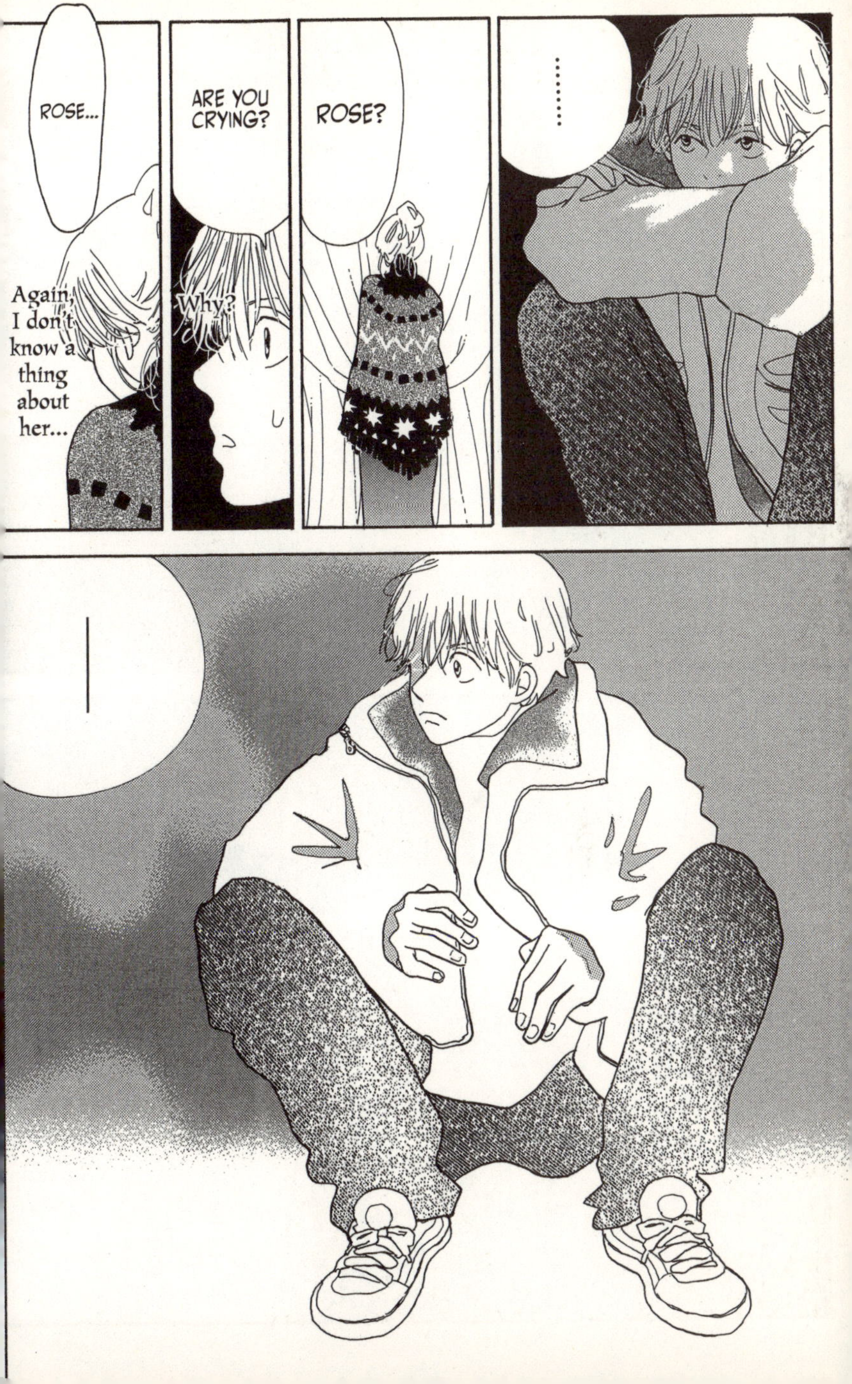

......
ROSE?
ARE YOU CRYING?
Why?
ROSE...
Again, I don't know a thing about her...

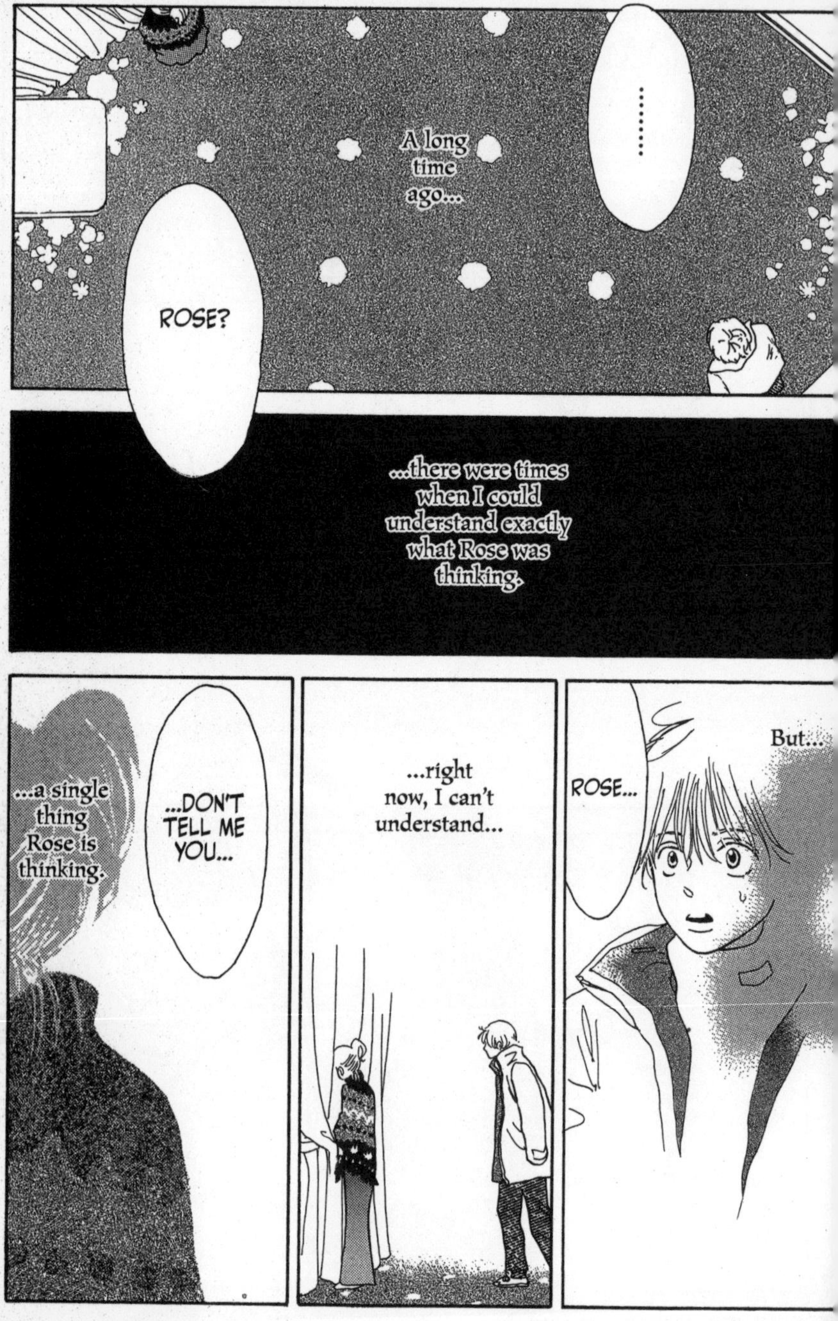
......
A long time ago...
ROSE?
...there were times when I could understand exactly what Rose was thinking.
But...
ROSE...
...right now, I can't understand...
...DON'T TELL ME YOU...
...a single thing Rose is thinking.

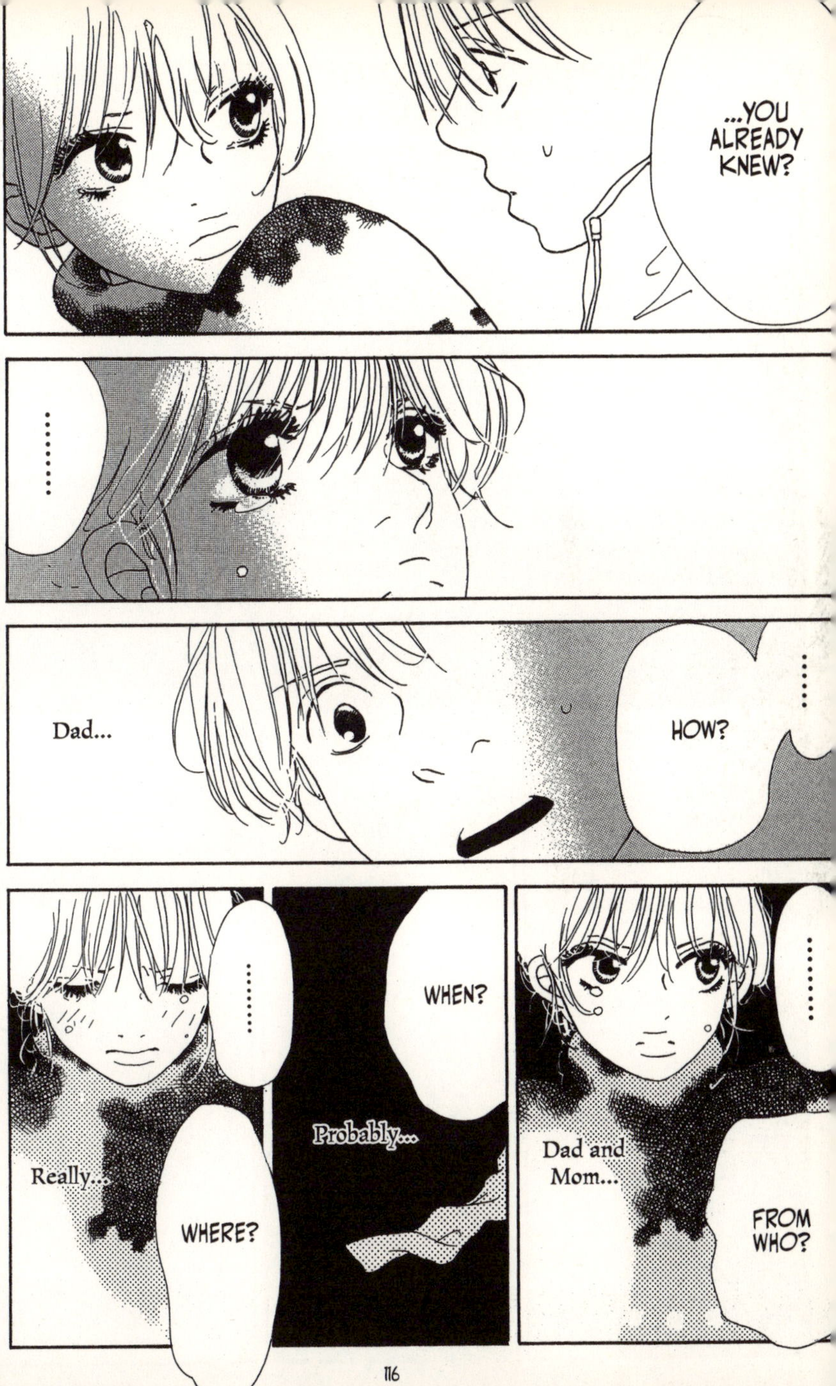
...YOU ALREADY KNEW?
....
......
HOW?
Dad...
....
FROM WHO?
Dad and Mom...
WHEN?
Probably...
....
Really...
WHERE?

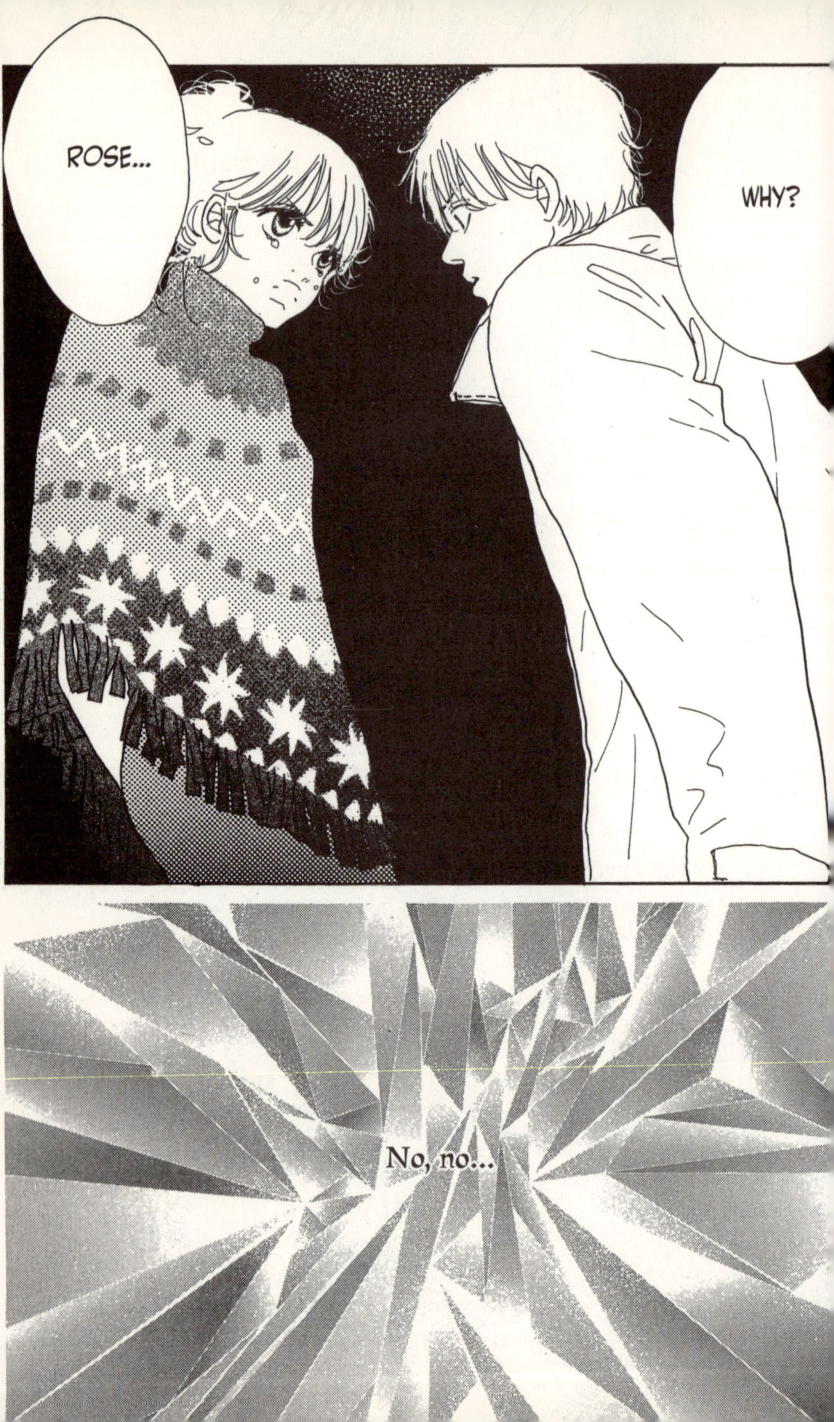
WHY?
ROSE...
No, no...

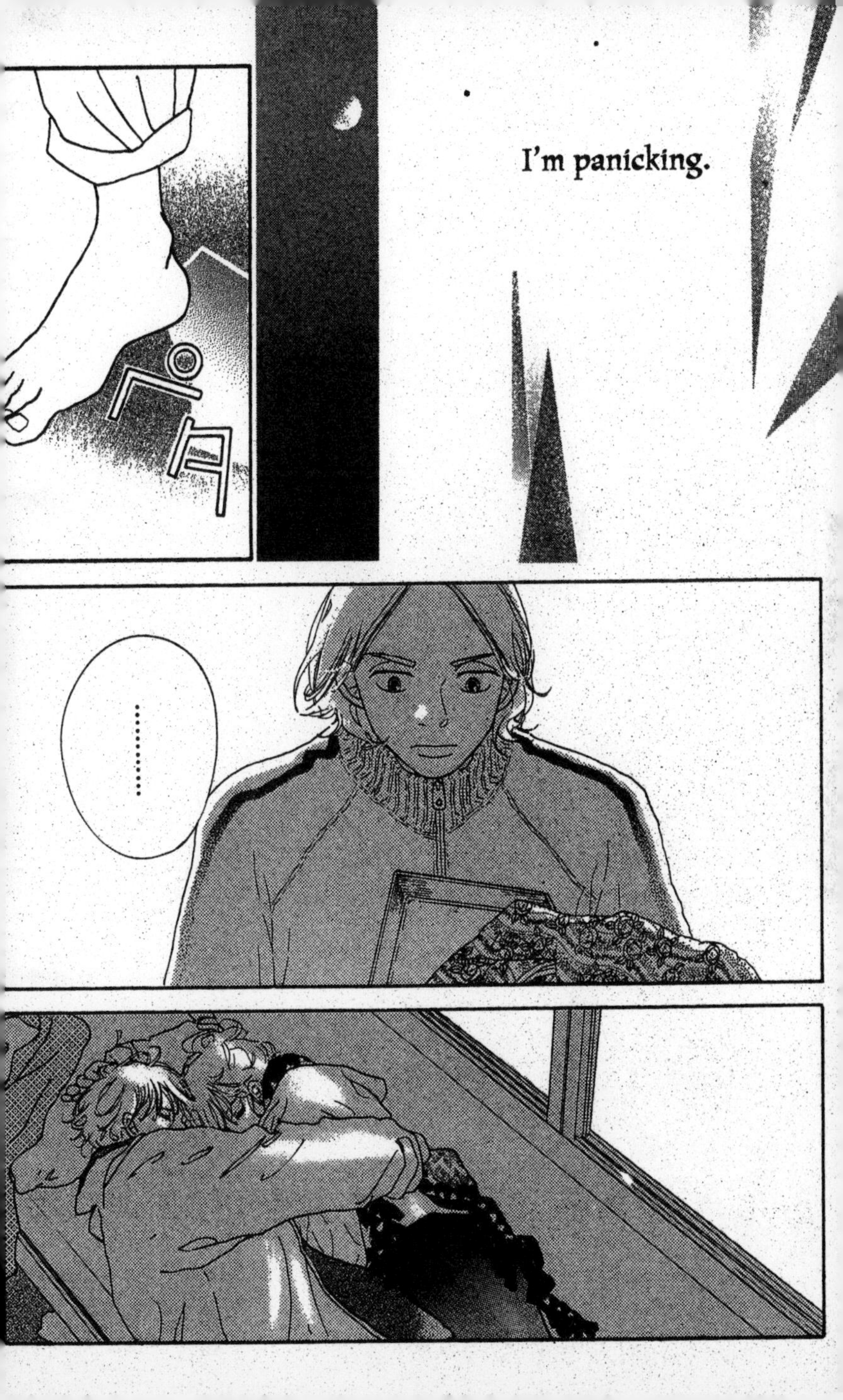
I'm panicking.
....

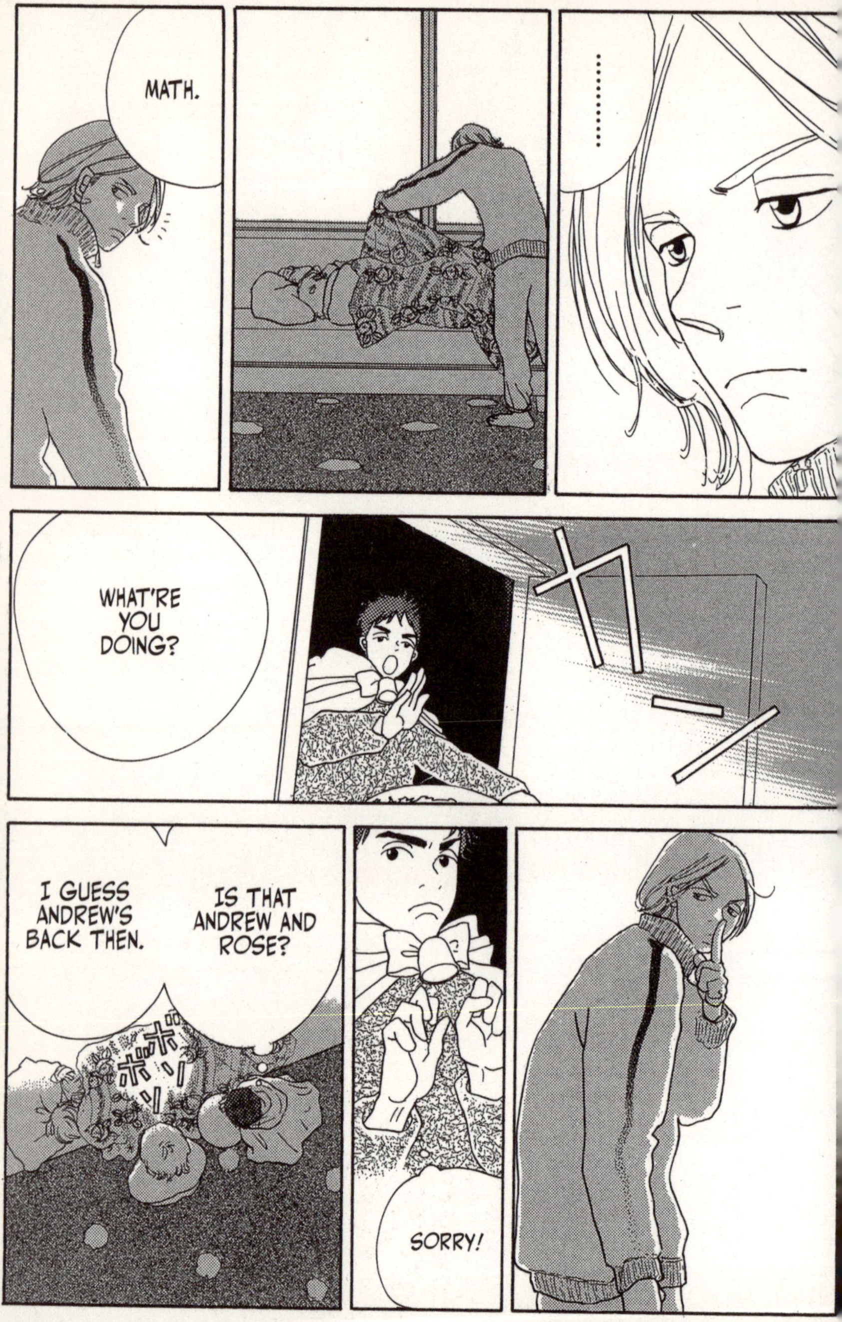
......
MATH.
WHAT'RE YOU DOING?
SORRY!
IS THAT ANDREW AND ROSE?
I GUESS ANDREW'S BACK THEN.

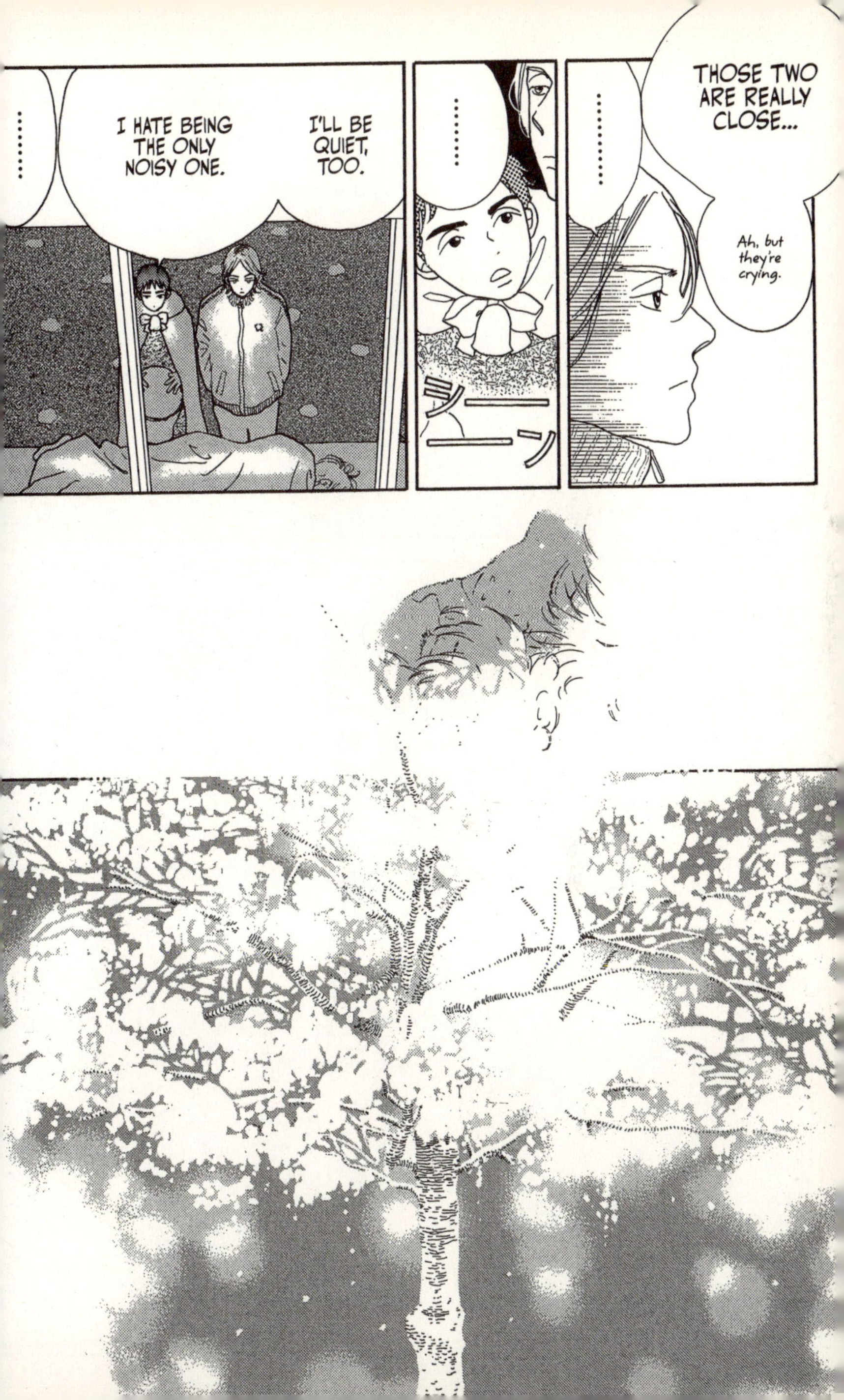
THOSE TWO ARE REALLY CLOSE...
Ah, but they're crying.
....
....
シーーーン
I'LL BE QUIET, TOO.
I HATE BEING THE ONLY NOISY ONE.
....

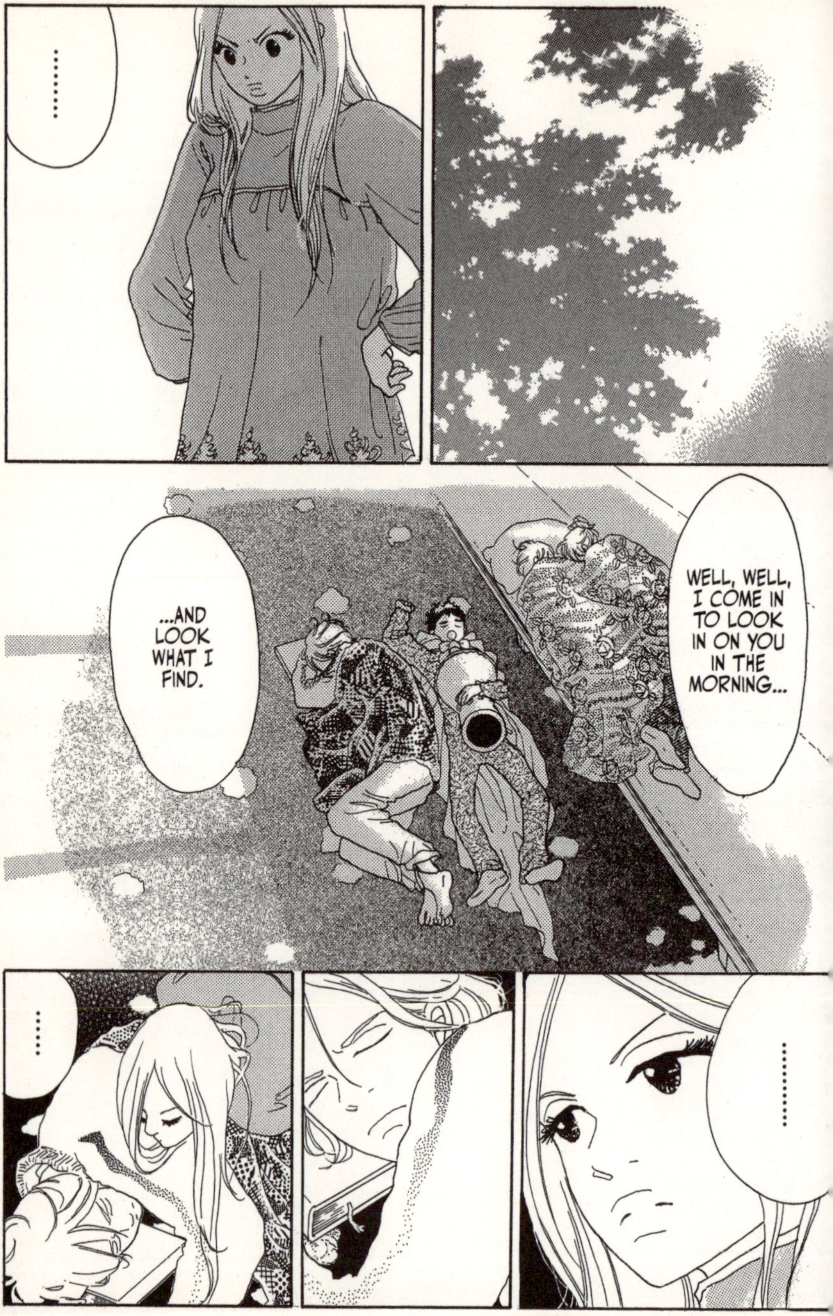
......
WELL, WELL, I COME IN TO LOOK IN ON YOU IN THE MORNING...
...AND LOOK WHAT I FIND.
....
......

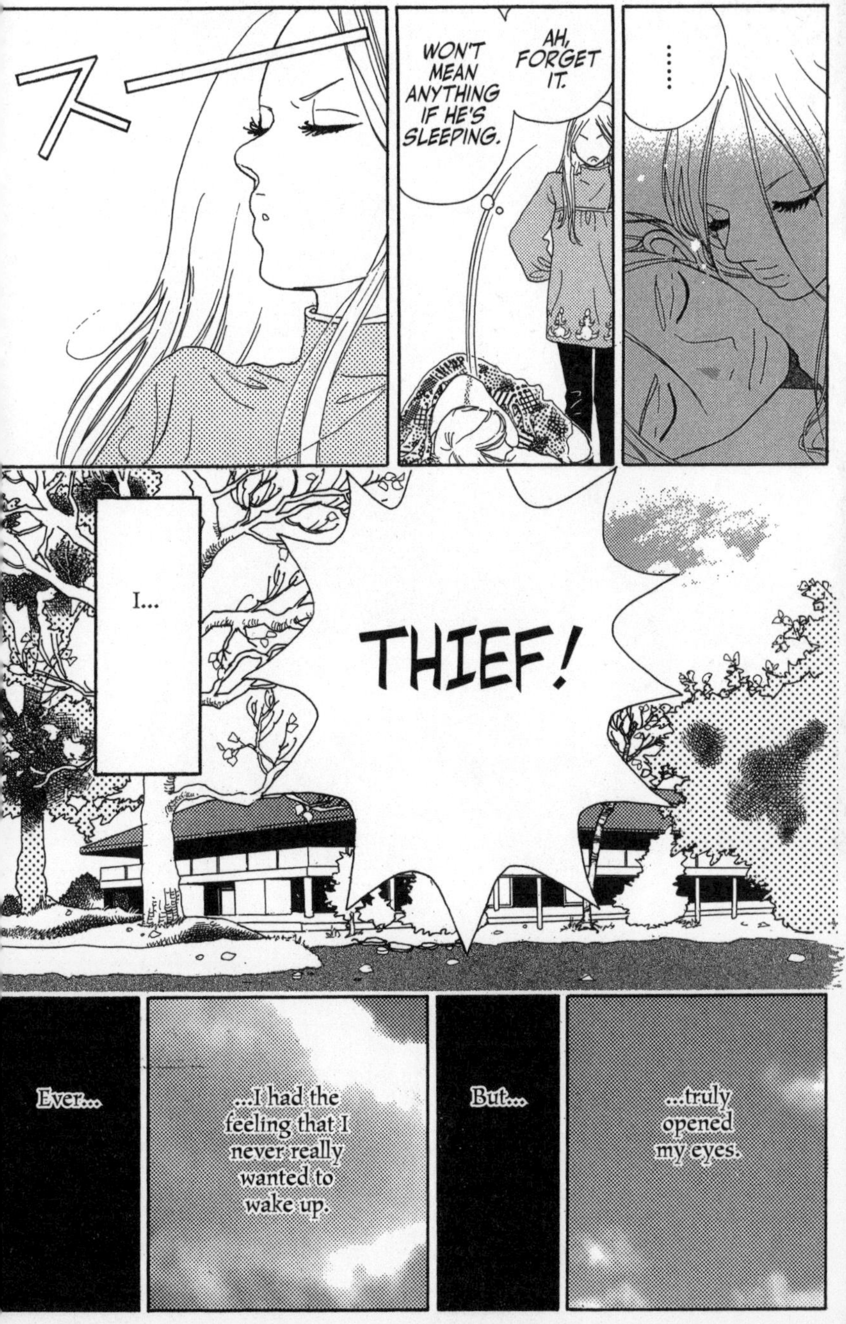
......
AH, FORGET IT.
WON'T MEAN ANYTHING IF HE'S SLEEPING.
スー
THIEF!
I...
...truly opened my eyes.
But...
...I had the feeling that I never really wanted to wake up.
Ever...

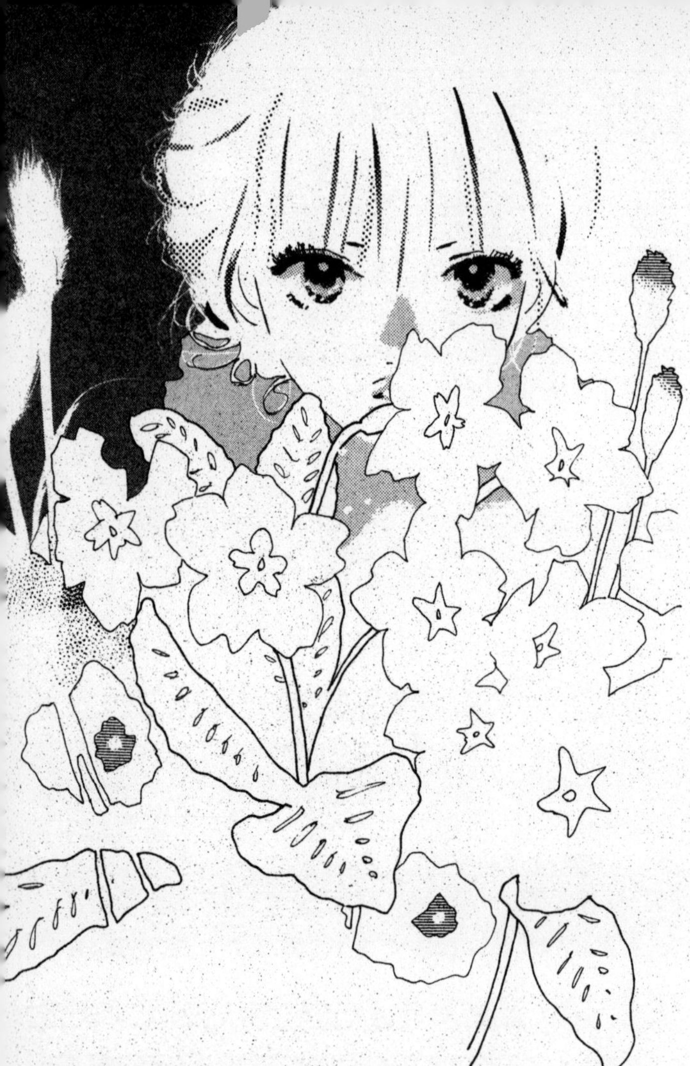

Club Hurricane
Adventure 3

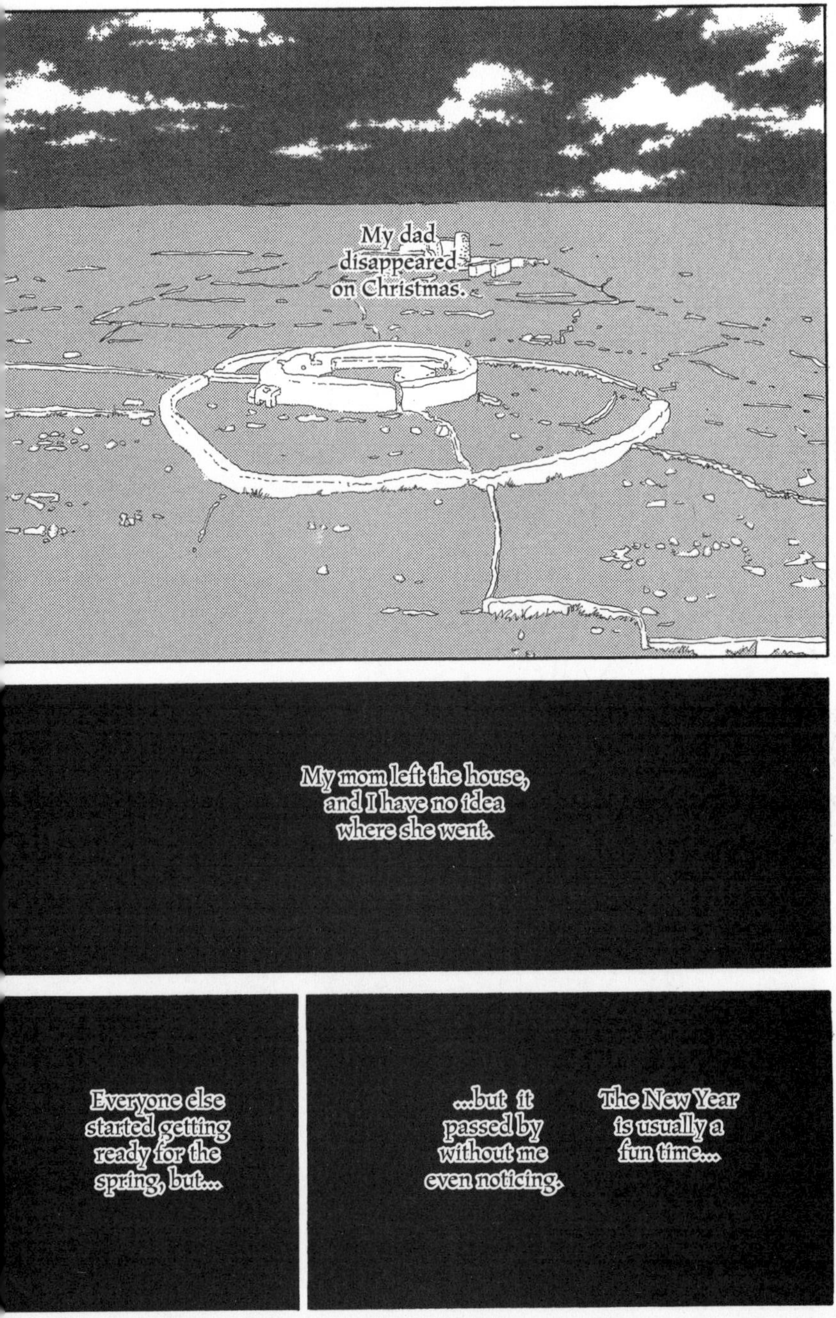
My dad disappeared on Christmas.
My mom left the house, and I have no idea where she went.
The New Year is usually a fun time...
...but it passed by without me even noticing.
Everyone else started getting ready for the spring, but...

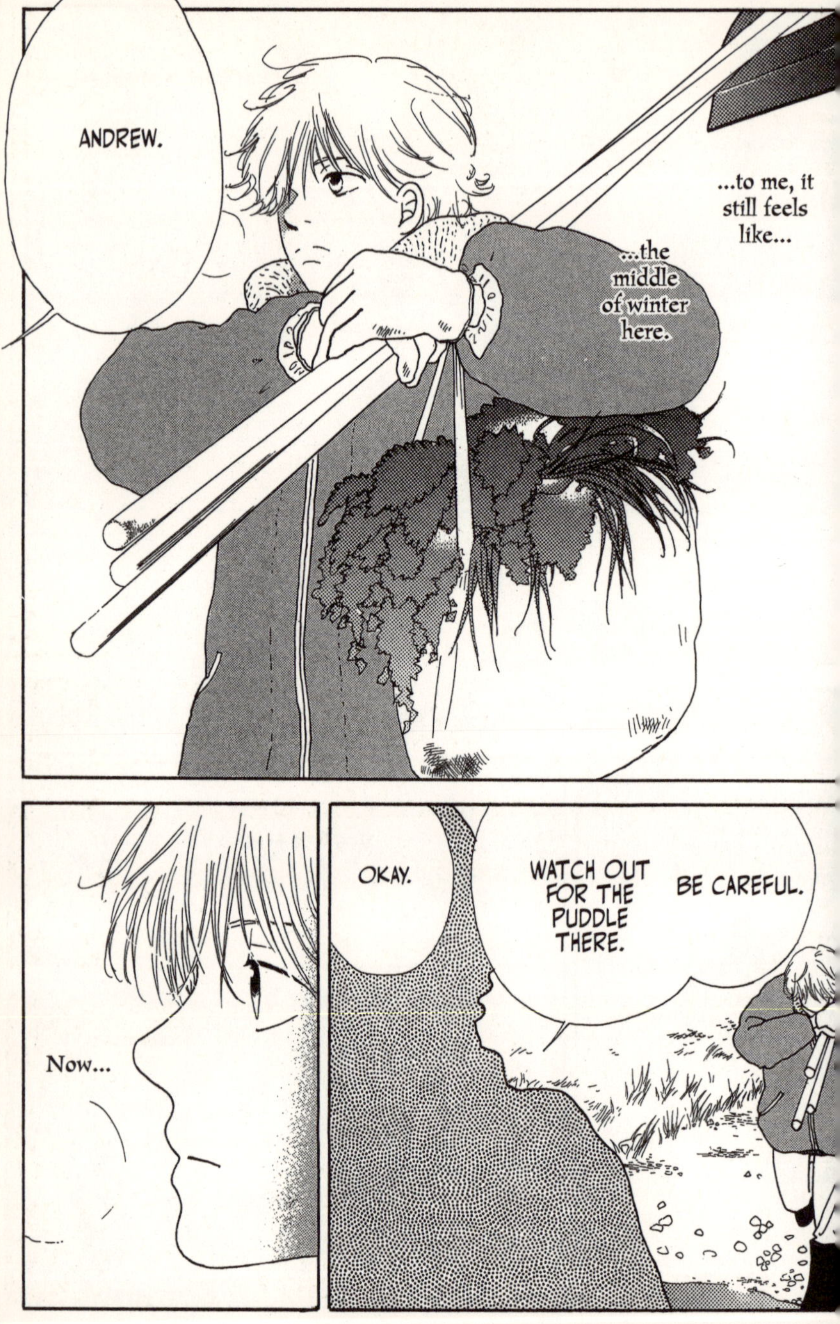
...to me, it still feels like...
...the middle of winter here.
ANDREW.
BE CAREFUL.
WATCH OUT FOR THE PUDDLE THERE.
OKAY.
Now...

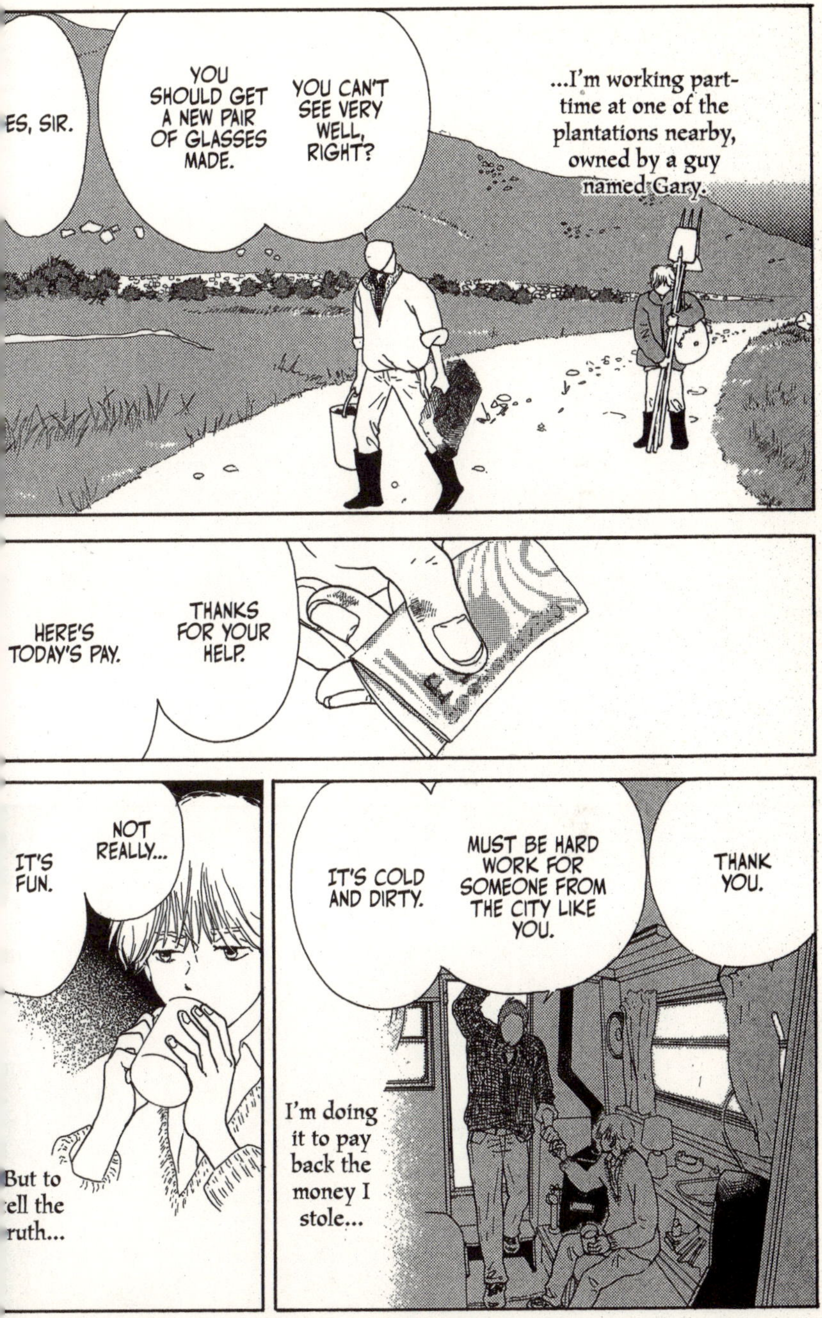
...I'm working part-time at one of the plantations nearby, owned by a guy named Gary.
YOU CAN'T SEE VERY WELL, RIGHT?
YOU SHOULD GET A NEW PAIR OF GLASSES MADE.
ES, SIR.
THANKS FOR YOUR HELP.
HERE'S TODAY'S PAY.
THANK YOU.
MUST BE HARD WORK FOR SOMEONE FROM THE CITY LIKE YOU.
IT'S COLD AND DIRTY.
I'm doing it to pay back the money I stole...
NOT REALLY...
IT'S FUN.
But to ell the ruth...

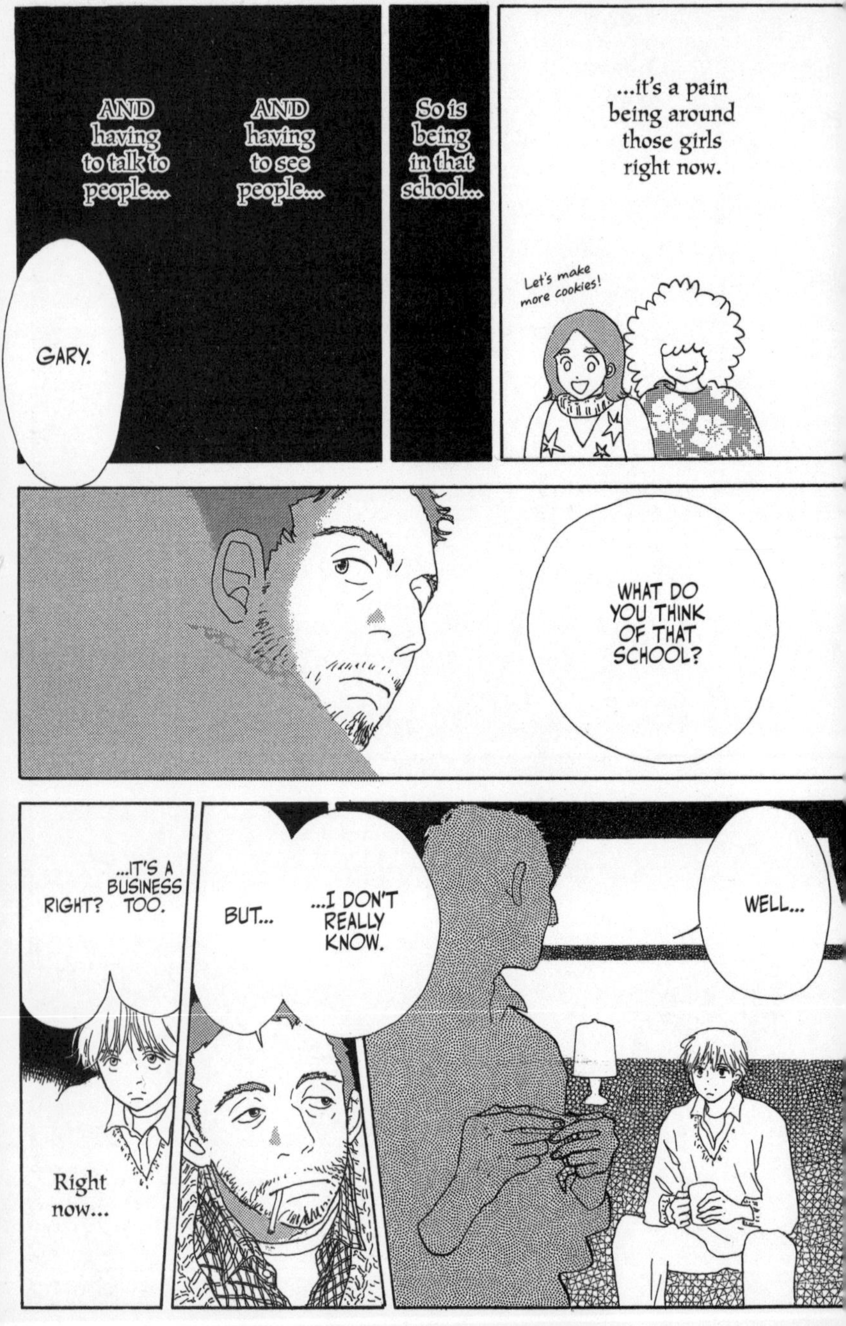
...it's a pain being around those girls right now.
Let's make more cookies!
So is being in that school...
AND having to see people...
AND having to talk to people...
GARY.
WHAT DO YOU THINK OF THAT SCHOOL?
WELL...
...I DON'T REALLY KNOW.
BUT...
...IT'S A BUSINESS TOO.
RIGHT?
Right now...

...it's the only place...

...I have to go.

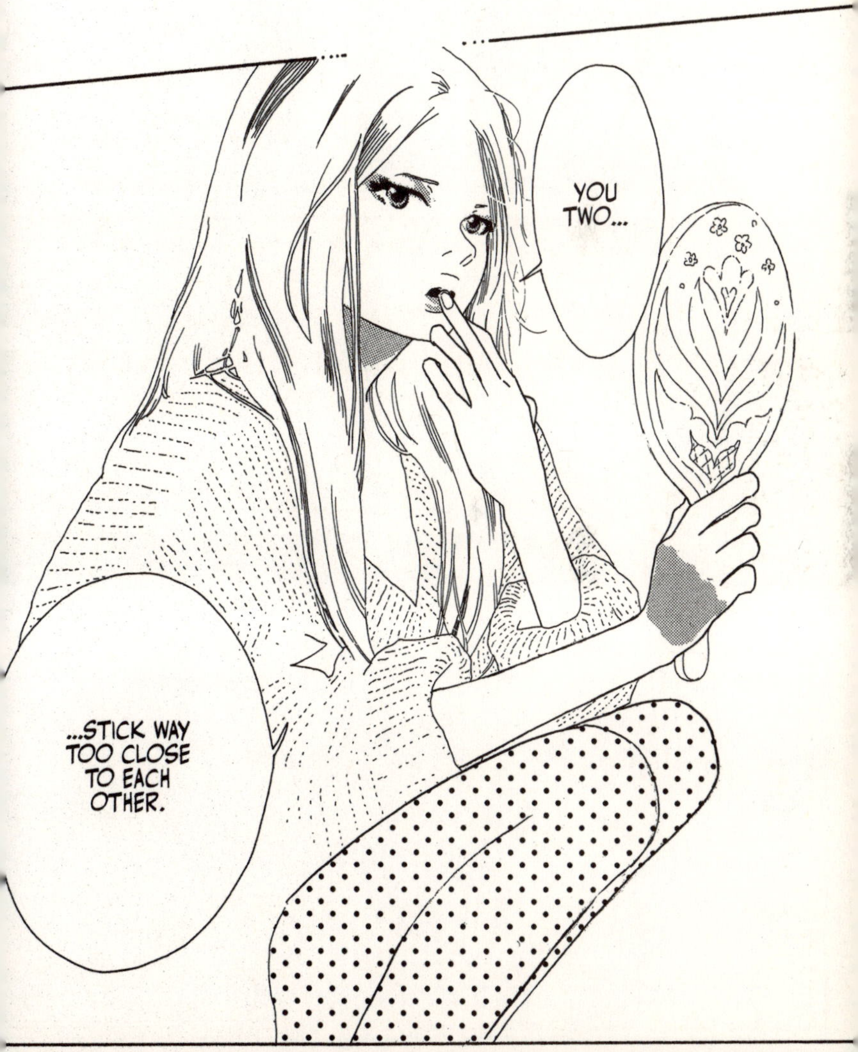
YOU TWO...
...STICK WAY TOO CLOSE TO EACH OTHER.

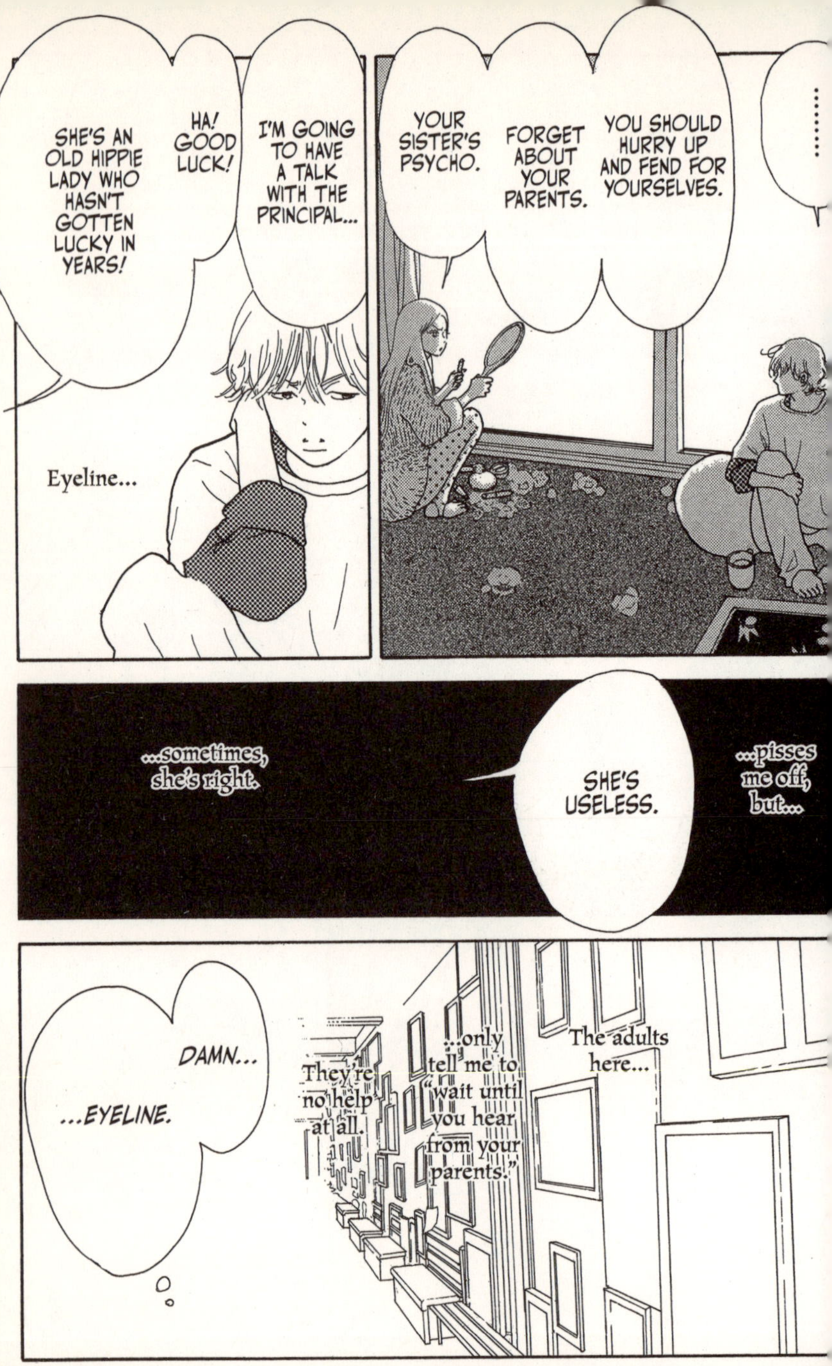
......
YOU SHOULD HURRY UP AND FEND FOR YOURSELVES.
FORGET ABOUT YOUR PARENTS.
YOUR SISTER'S PSYCHO.
I'M GOING TO HAVE A TALK WITH THE PRINCIPAL...
HA! GOOD LUCK!
SHE'S AN OLD HIPPIE LADY WHO HASN'T GOTTEN LUCKY IN YEARS!
Eyeline...
...pisses me off, but...
SHE'S USELESS.
...sometimes, she's right.
The adults here...
...only tell me to "wait until you hear from your parents."
They're no help at all.
DAMN...
...EYELINE.

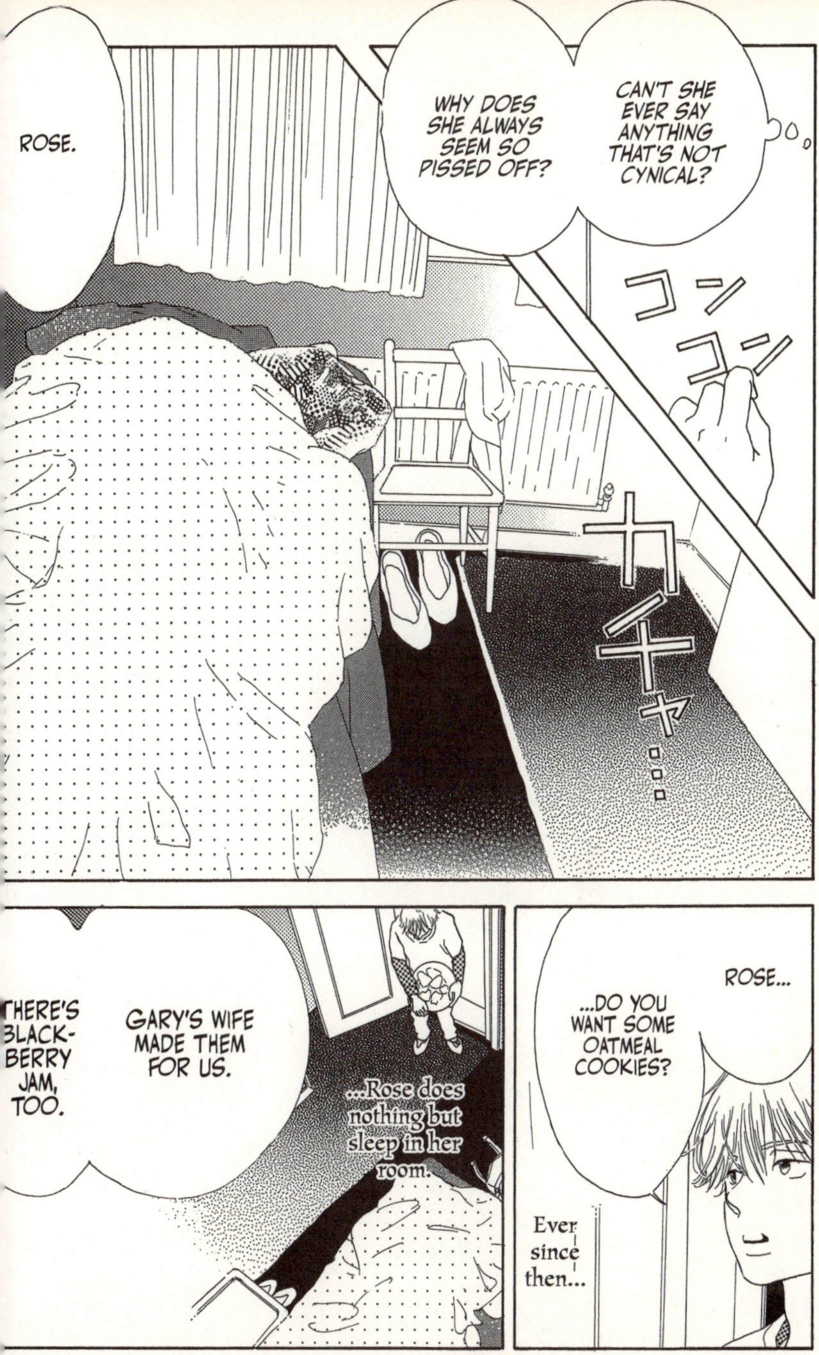
CAN'T SHE EVER SAY ANYTHING THAT'S NOT CYNICAL?
WHY DOES SHE ALWAYS SEEM SO PISSED OFF?
コン コン
カチャ…
ROSE.
ROSE...
...DO YOU WANT SOME OATMEAL COOKIES?
Ever since then...
...Rose does nothing but sleep in her room.
GARY'S WIFE MADE THEM FOR US.
THERE'S BLACKBERRY JAM, TOO.

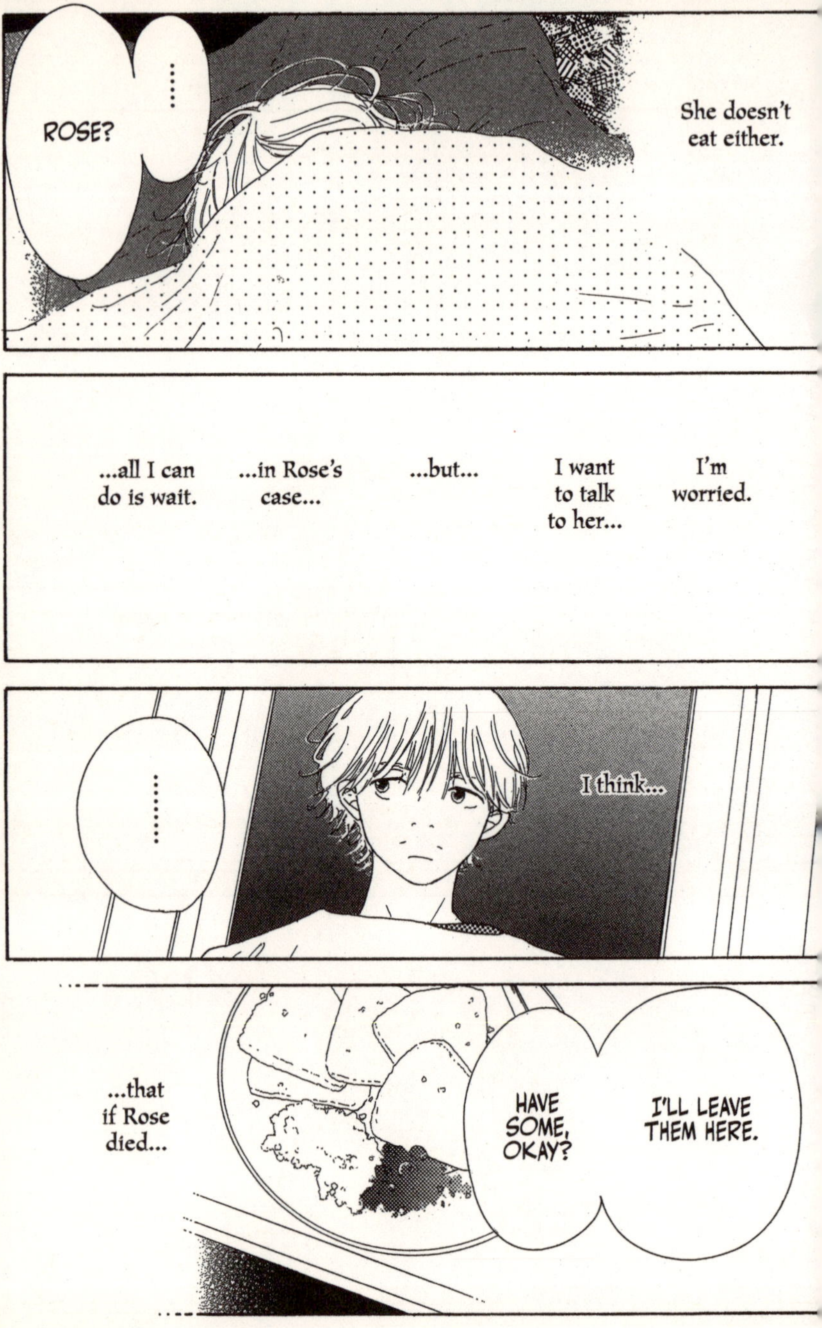
She doesn't eat either.
......
ROSE?
I'm worried.
I want to talk to her...
...but...
...in Rose's case...
...all I can do is wait.
I think...
....
I'LL LEAVE THEM HERE.
HAVE SOME, OKAY?
...that if Rose died...

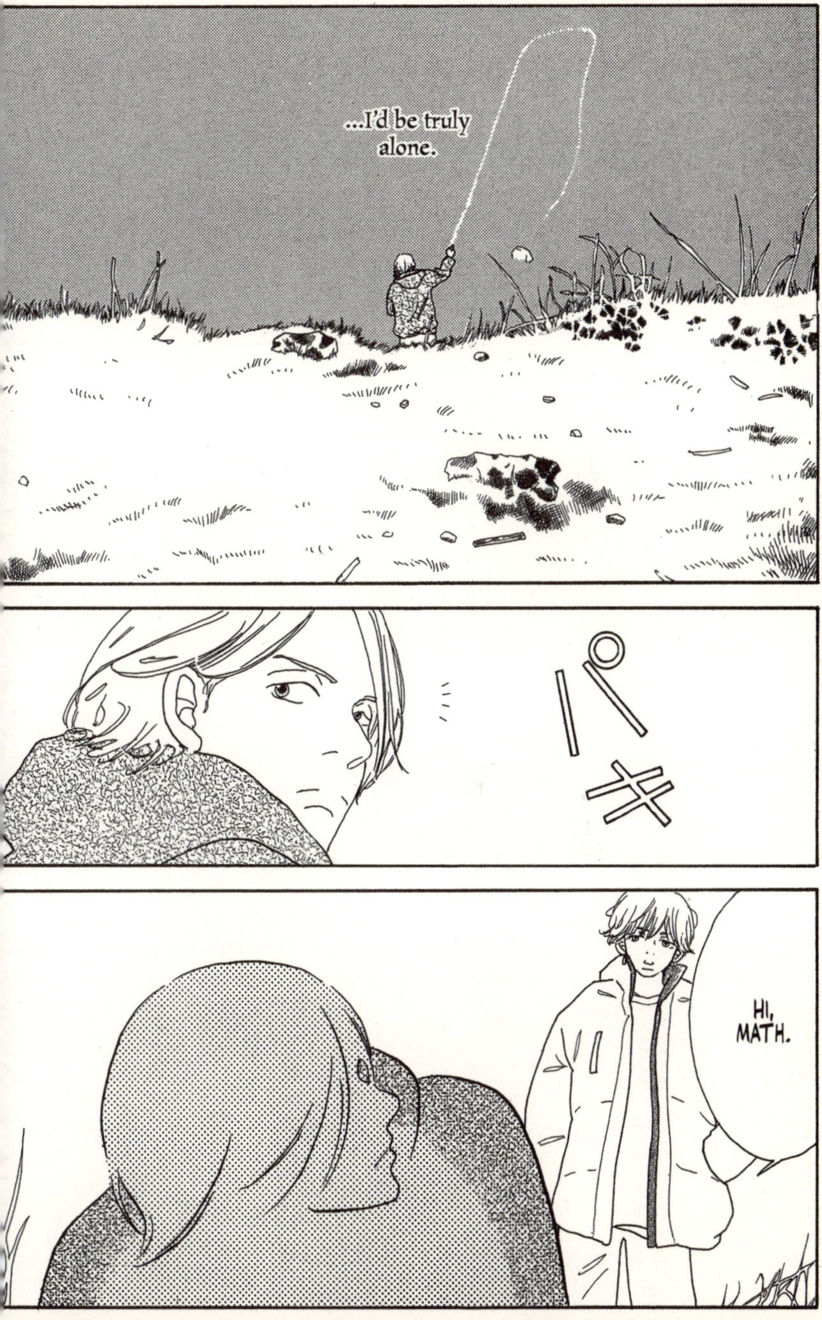
...I'd be truly alone.
パキ
HI, MATH.

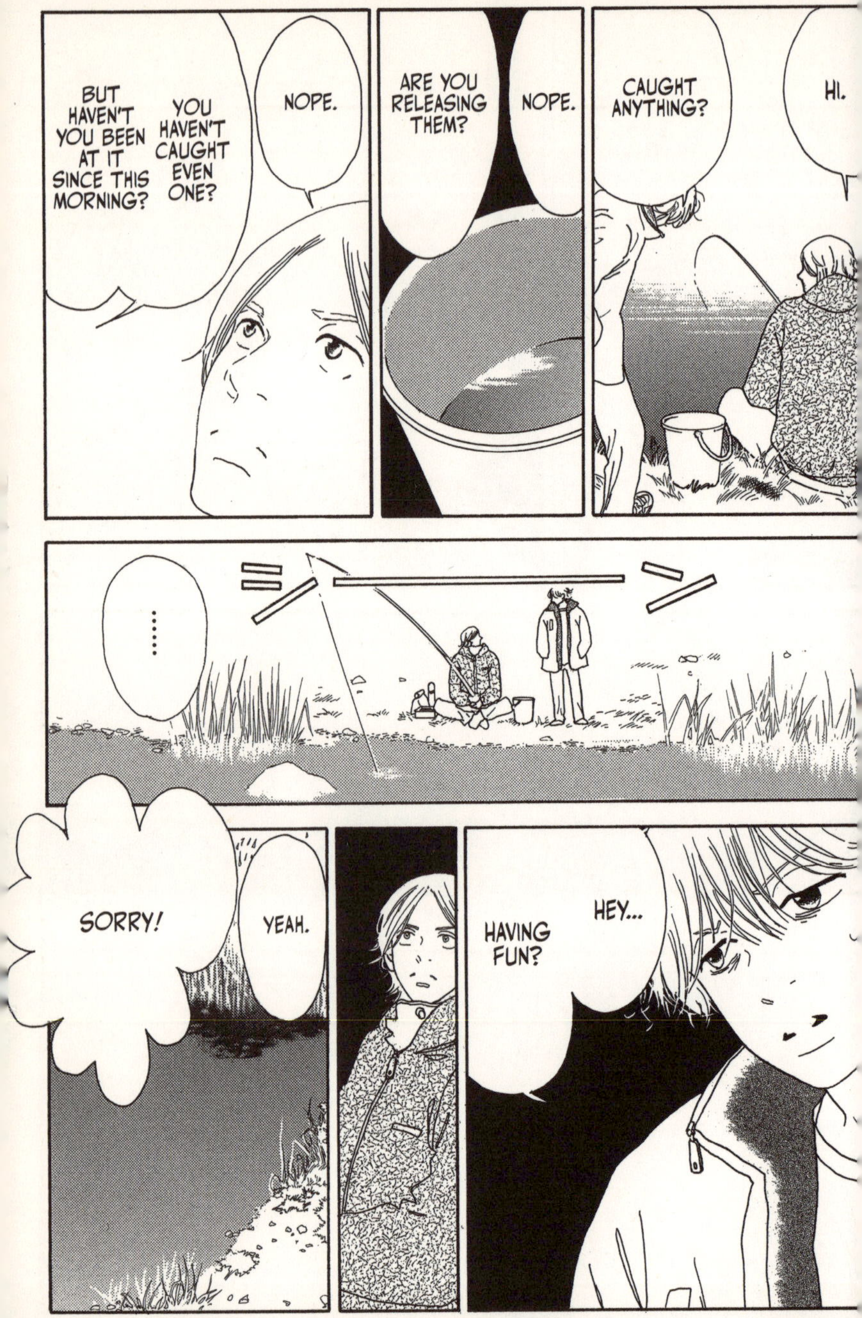
HI.
CAUGHT ANYTHING?
NOPE.
ARE YOU RELEASING THEM?
NOPE.
YOU HAVEN'T CAUGHT EVEN ONE?
BUT HAVEN'T YOU BEEN AT IT SINCE THIS MORNING?
......
HEY...
HAVING FUN?
YEAH.
SORRY!

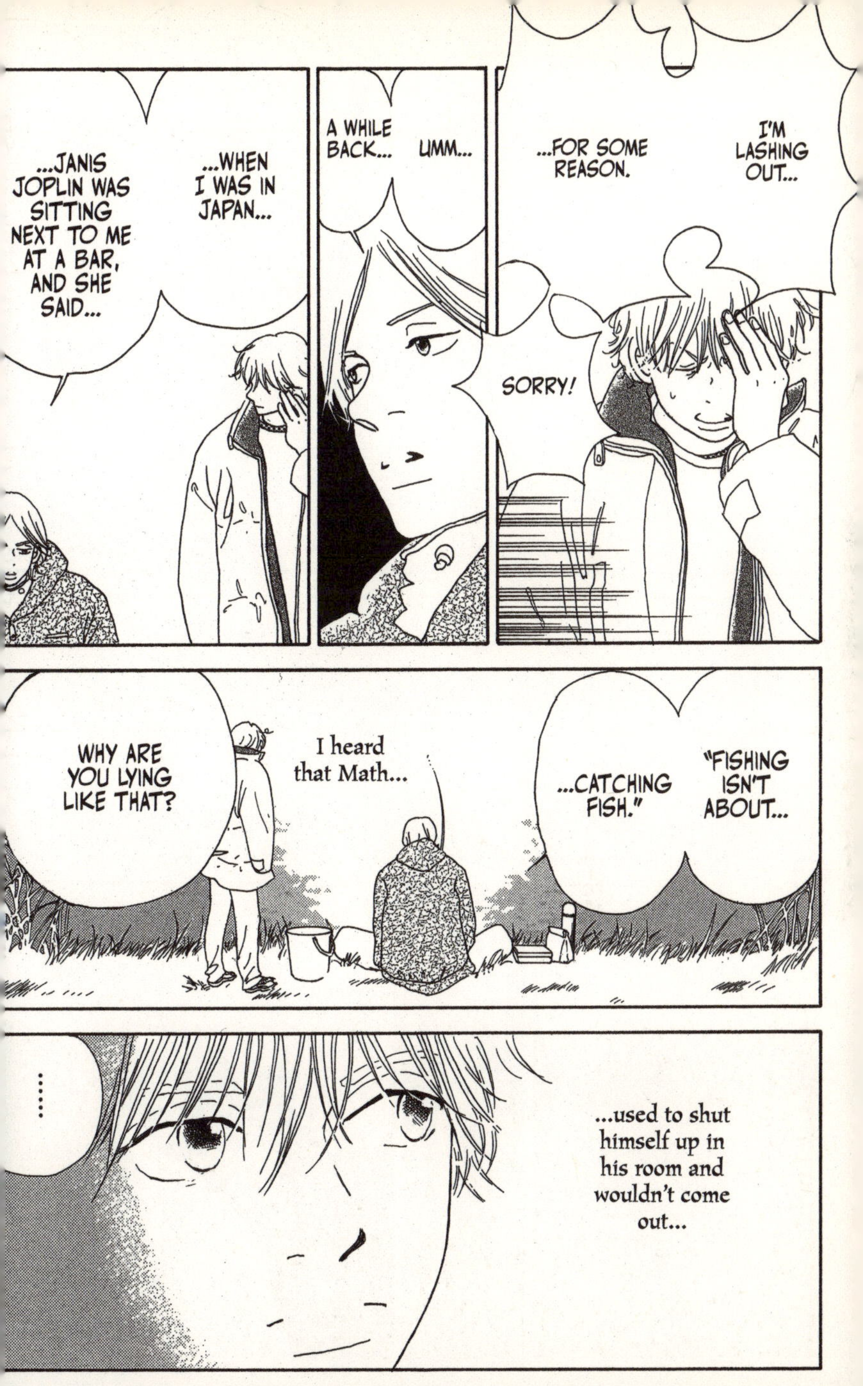
I'M LASHING OUT...
...FOR SOME REASON.
SORRY!
UMM...
A WHILE BACK...
...WHEN I WAS IN JAPAN...
...JANIS JOPLIN WAS SITTING NEXT TO ME AT A BAR, AND SHE SAID...
"FISHING ISN'T ABOUT...
...CATCHING FISH."
I heard that Math...
WHY ARE YOU LYING LIKE THAT?
...used to shut himself up in his room and wouldn't come out...
......

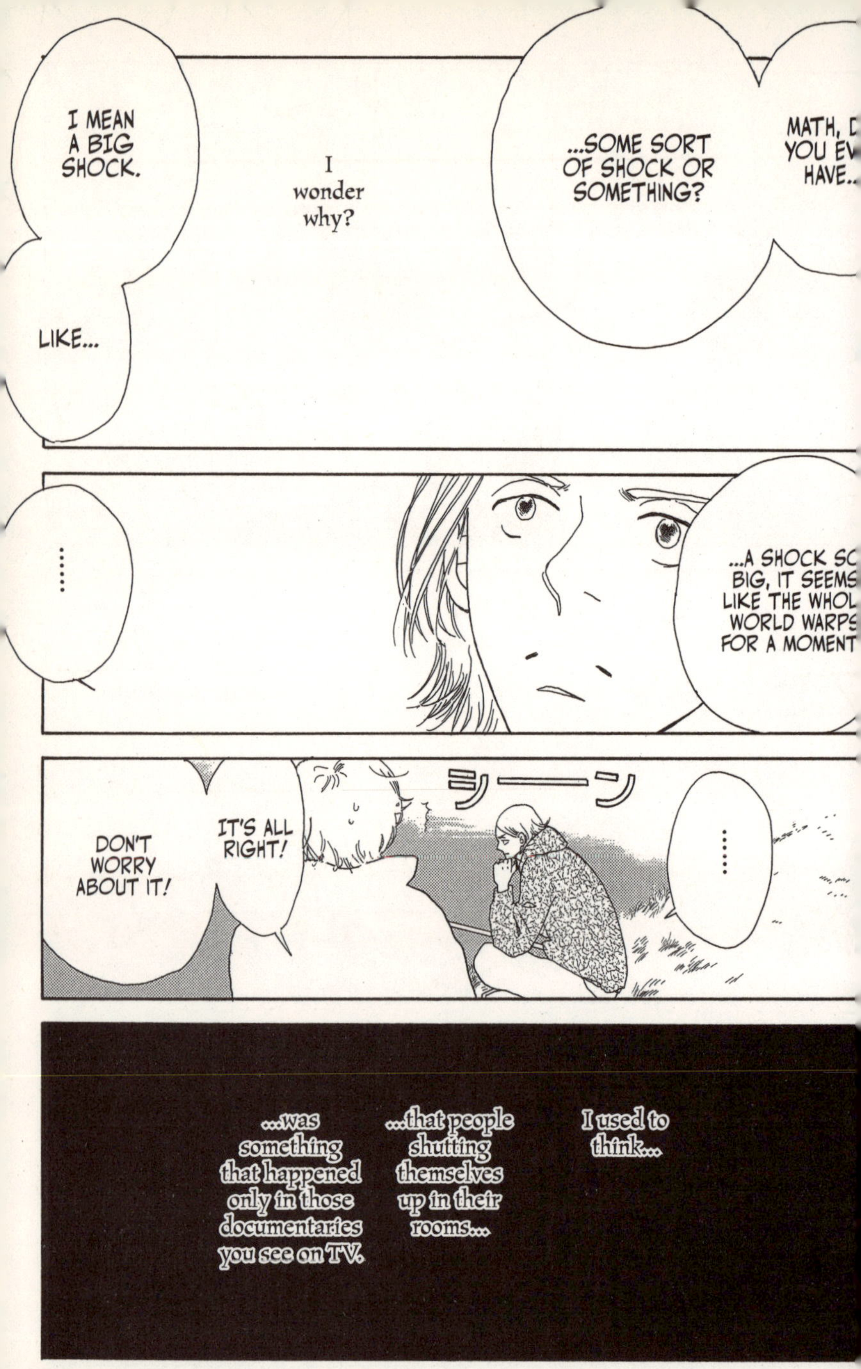
MATH, D YOU EV HAVE...
...SOME SORT OF SHOCK OR SOMETHING?
I wonder why?
I MEAN A BIG SHOCK.
LIKE...
...A SHOCK SC BIG, IT SEEMS LIKE THE WHOL WORLD WARPS FOR A MOMENT
......
......
シーン
IT'S ALL RIGHT!
DON'T WORRY ABOUT IT!
I used to think...
...that people shutting themselves up in their rooms...
...was something that happened only in those documentaries you see on TV.

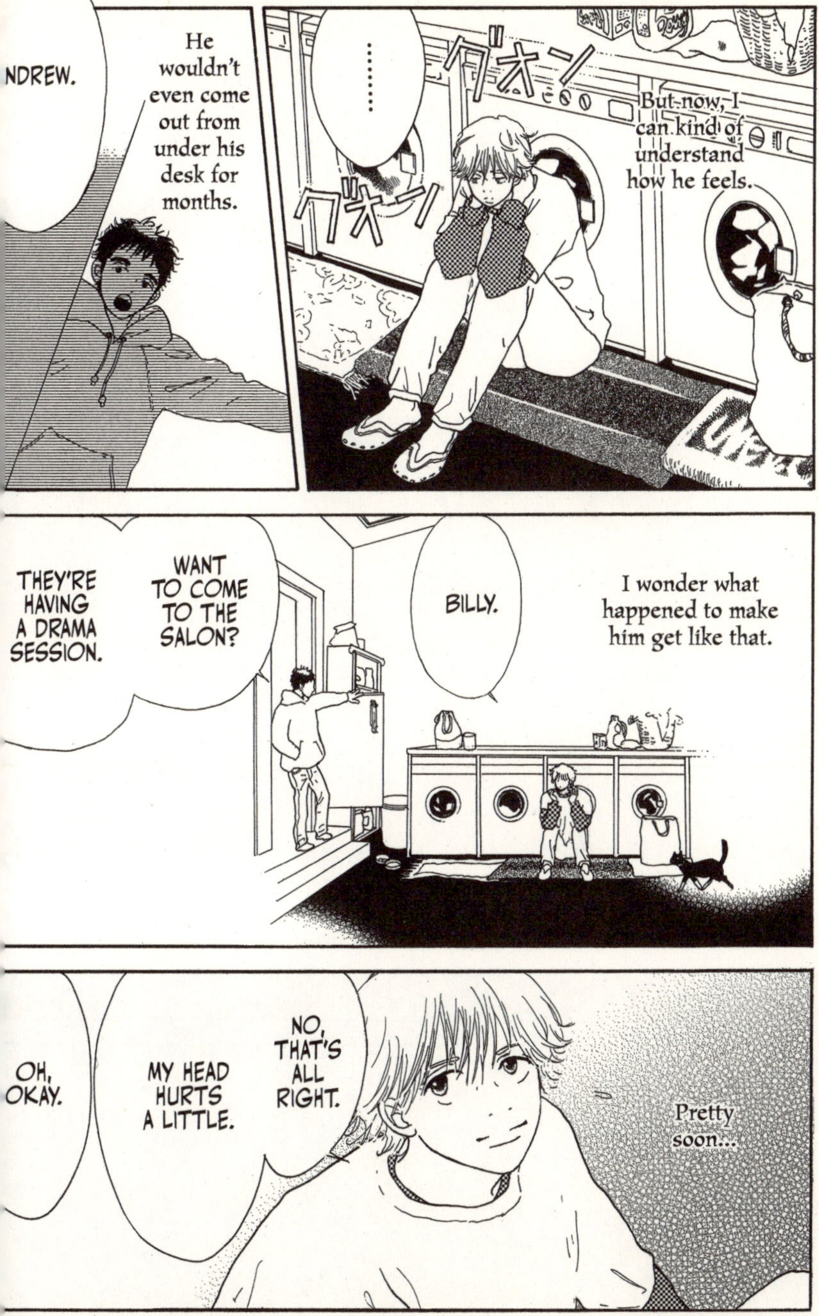
But now, I can kind of understand how he feels.
グオーン
……
グオーン
He wouldn't even come out from under his desk for months.
NDREW.
I wonder what happened to make him get like that.
BILLY.
WANT TO COME TO THE SALON?
THEY'RE HAVING A DRAMA SESSION.
Pretty soon...
NO, THAT'S ALL RIGHT.
MY HEAD HURTS A LITTLE.
OH, OKAY.

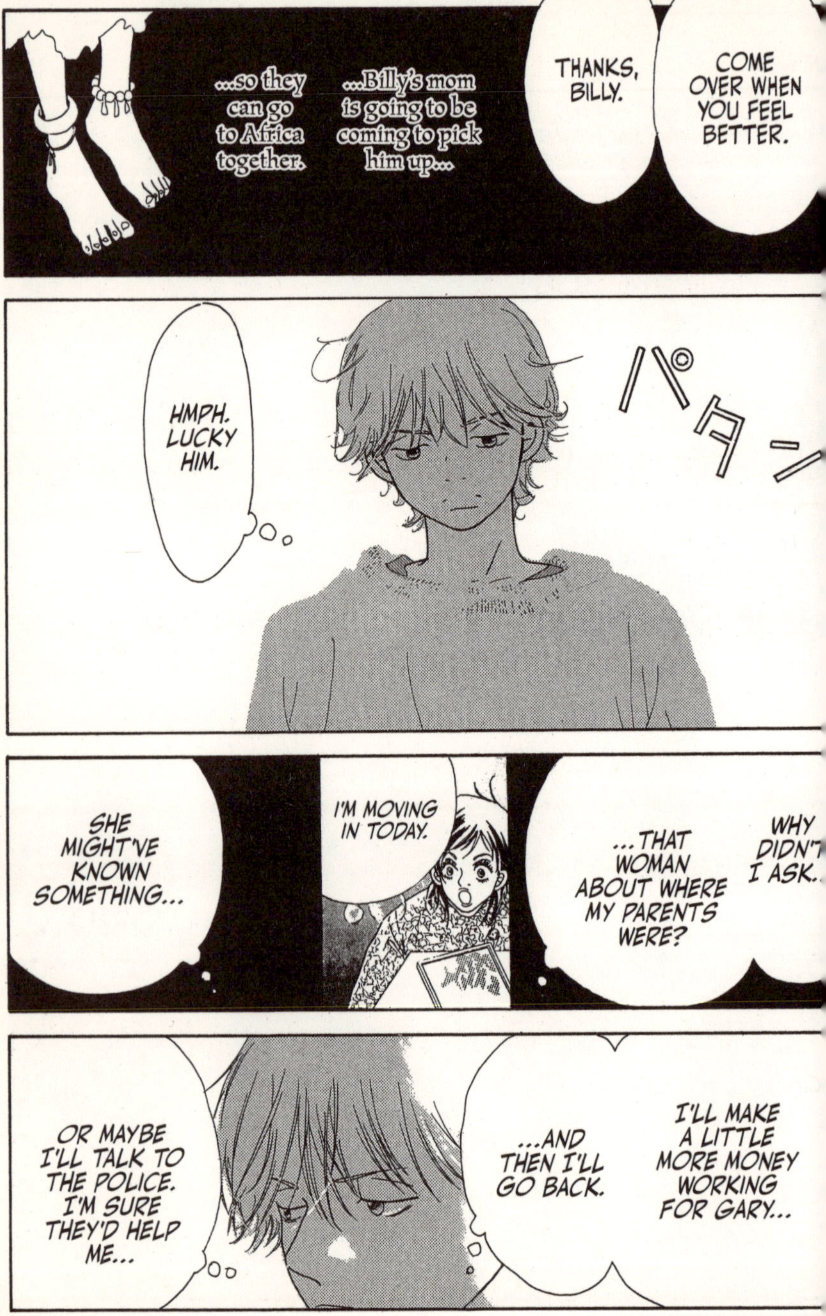
COME OVER WHEN YOU FEEL BETTER.
THANKS, BILLY.
...Billy's mom is going to be coming to pick him up...
...so they can go to Africa together.
パターン
HMPH. LUCKY HIM.
WHY DIDN'T I ASK...
...THAT WOMAN ABOUT WHERE MY PARENTS WERE?
I'M MOVING IN TODAY.
SHE MIGHT'VE KNOWN SOMETHING...
I'LL MAKE A LITTLE MORE MONEY WORKING FOR GARY...
...AND THEN I'LL GO BACK.
OR MAYBE I'LL TALK TO THE POLICE. I'M SURE THEY'D HELP ME...

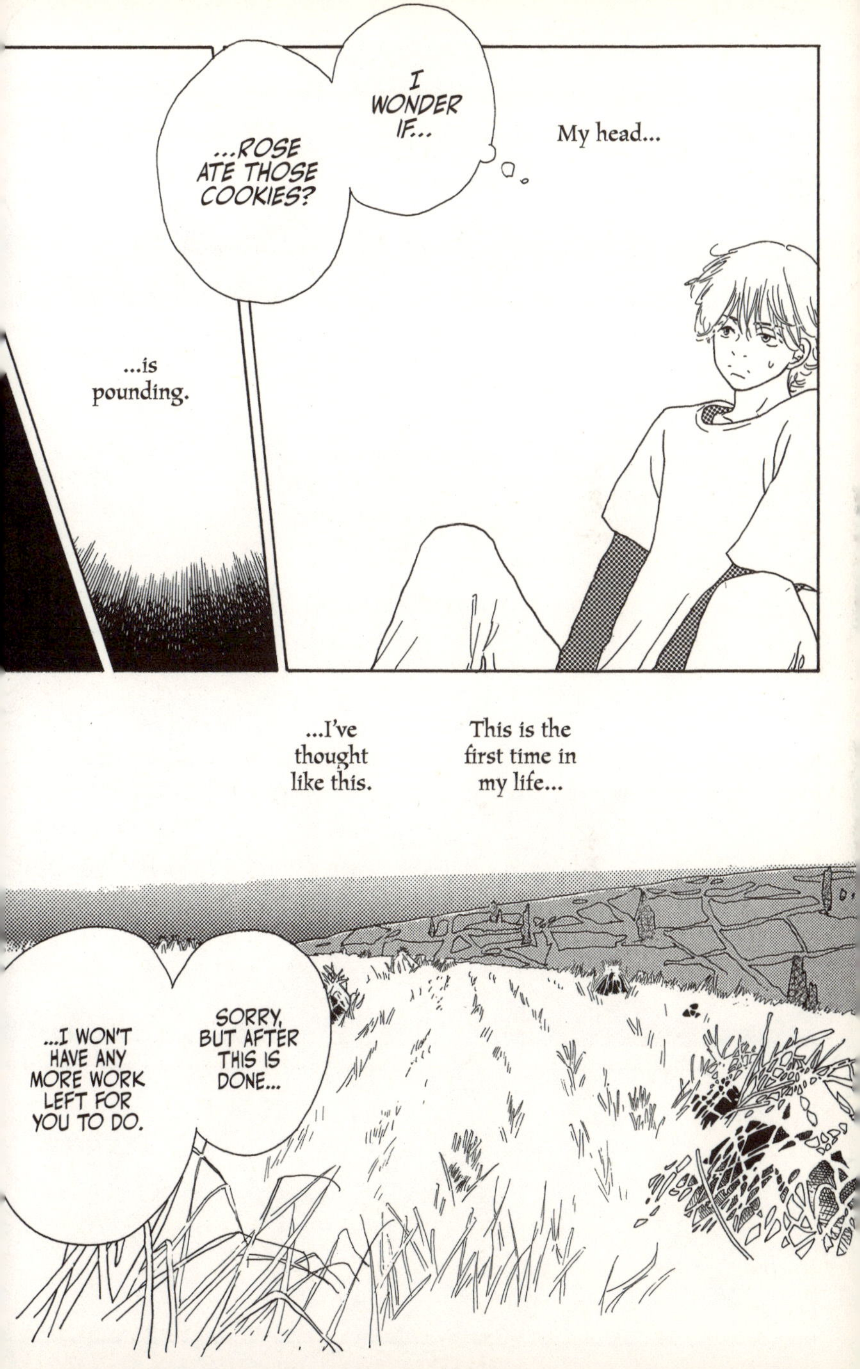
My head...
I WONDER IF...
...ROSE ATE THOSE COOKIES?
...is pounding.
This is the first time in my life...
...I've thought like this.
SORRY, BUT AFTER THIS IS DONE...
...I WON'T HAVE ANY MORE WORK LEFT FOR YOU TO DO.

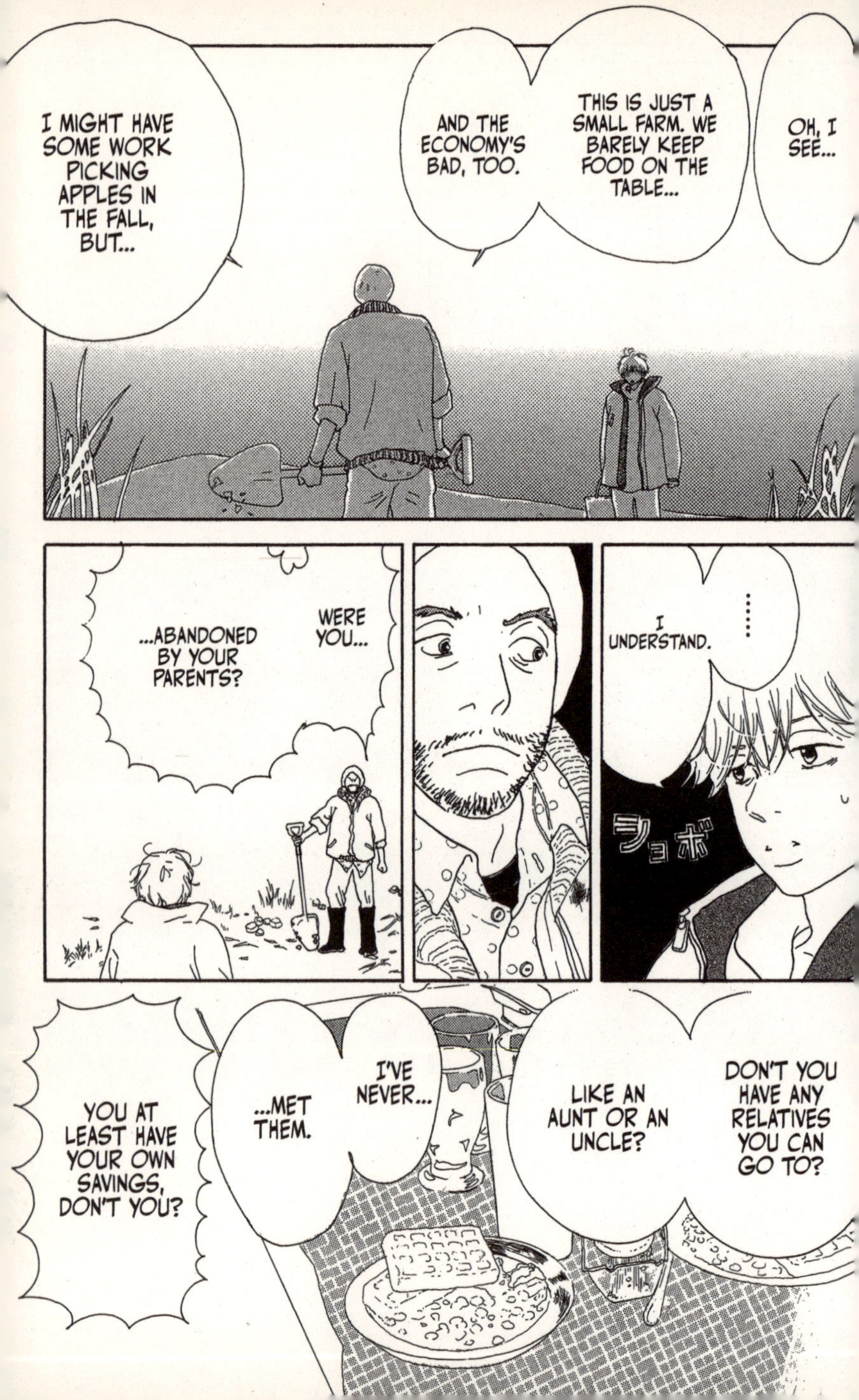
OH, I SEE...
THIS IS JUST A SMALL FARM. WE BARELY KEEP FOOD ON THE TABLE...
AND THE ECONOMY'S BAD, TOO.
I MIGHT HAVE SOME WORK PICKING APPLES IN THE FALL, BUT...
......
I UNDERSTAND.
ジョボ
WERE YOU...
...ABANDONED BY YOUR PARENTS?
DON'T YOU HAVE ANY RELATIVES YOU CAN GO TO?
LIKE AN AUNT OR AN UNCLE?
I'VE NEVER...
...MET THEM.
YOU AT LEAST HAVE YOUR OWN SAVINGS, DON'T YOU?

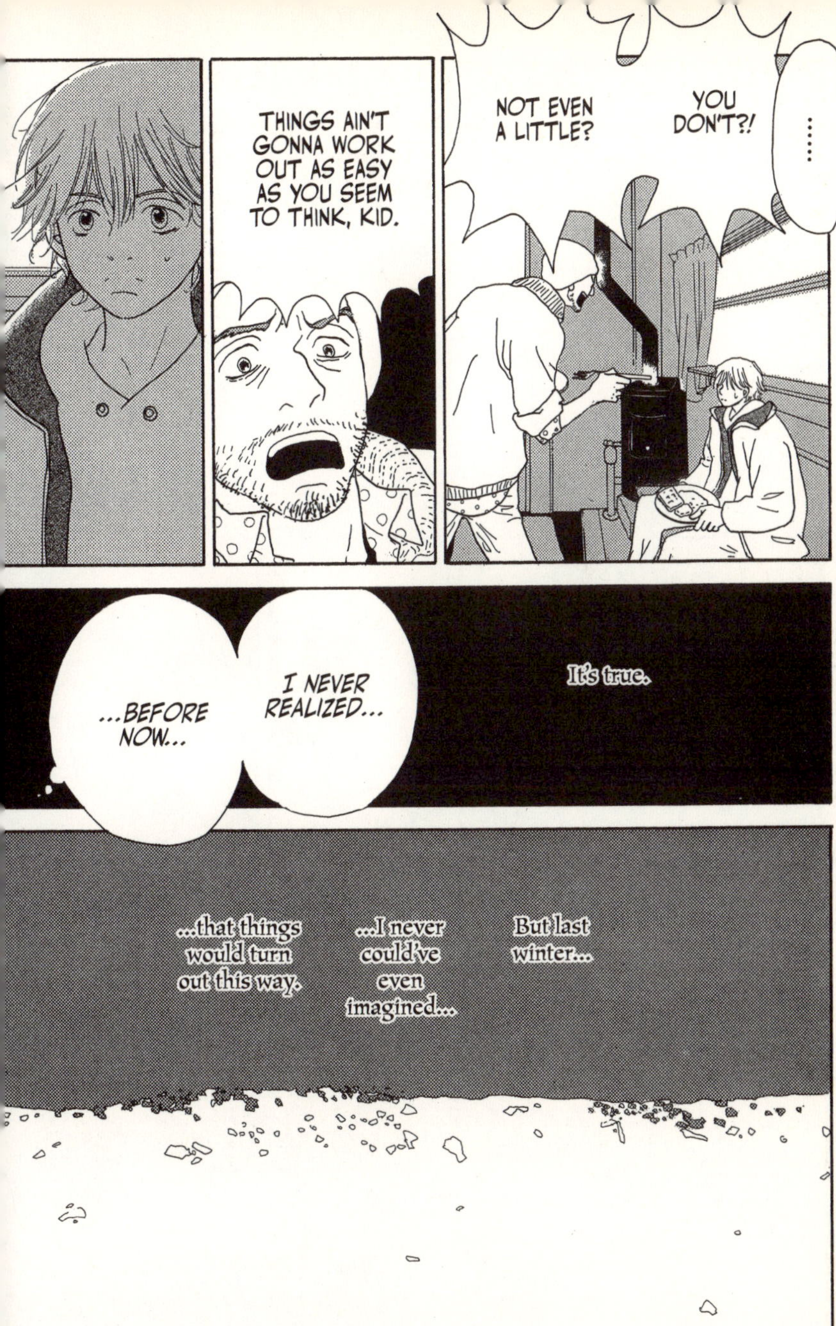
......
YOU DON'T?!
NOT EVEN A LITTLE?
THINGS AIN'T GONNA WORK OUT AS EASY AS YOU SEEM TO THINK, KID.
It's true.
I NEVER REALIZED...
...BEFORE NOW...
But last winter...
...I never could've even imagined...
...that things would turn out this way.

...Rose?

What about you...

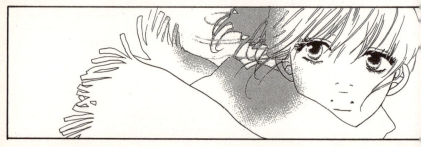

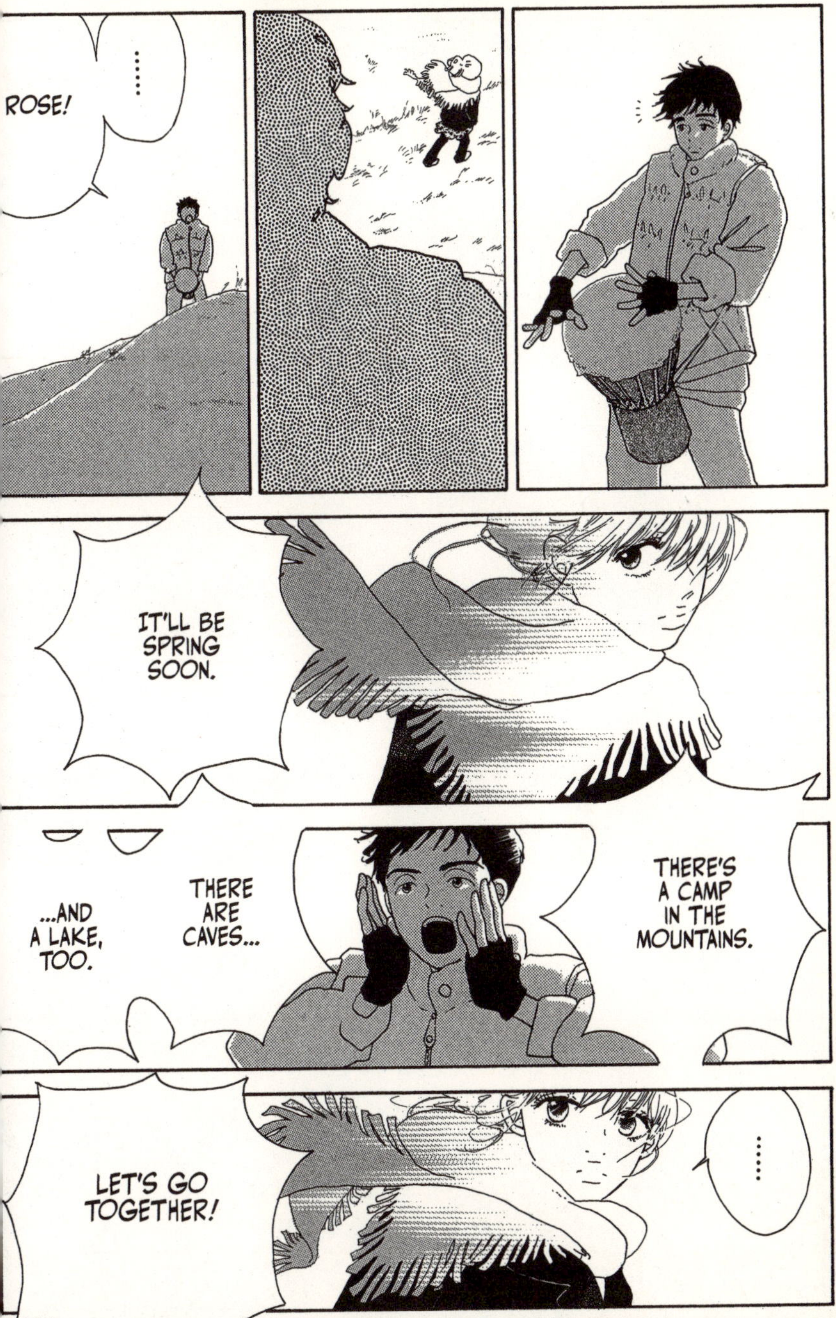
......
ROSE!
IT'LL BE SPRING SOON.
THERE'S A CAMP IN THE MOUNTAINS.
THERE ARE CAVES...
...AND A LAKE, TOO.
......
LET'S GO TOGETHER!

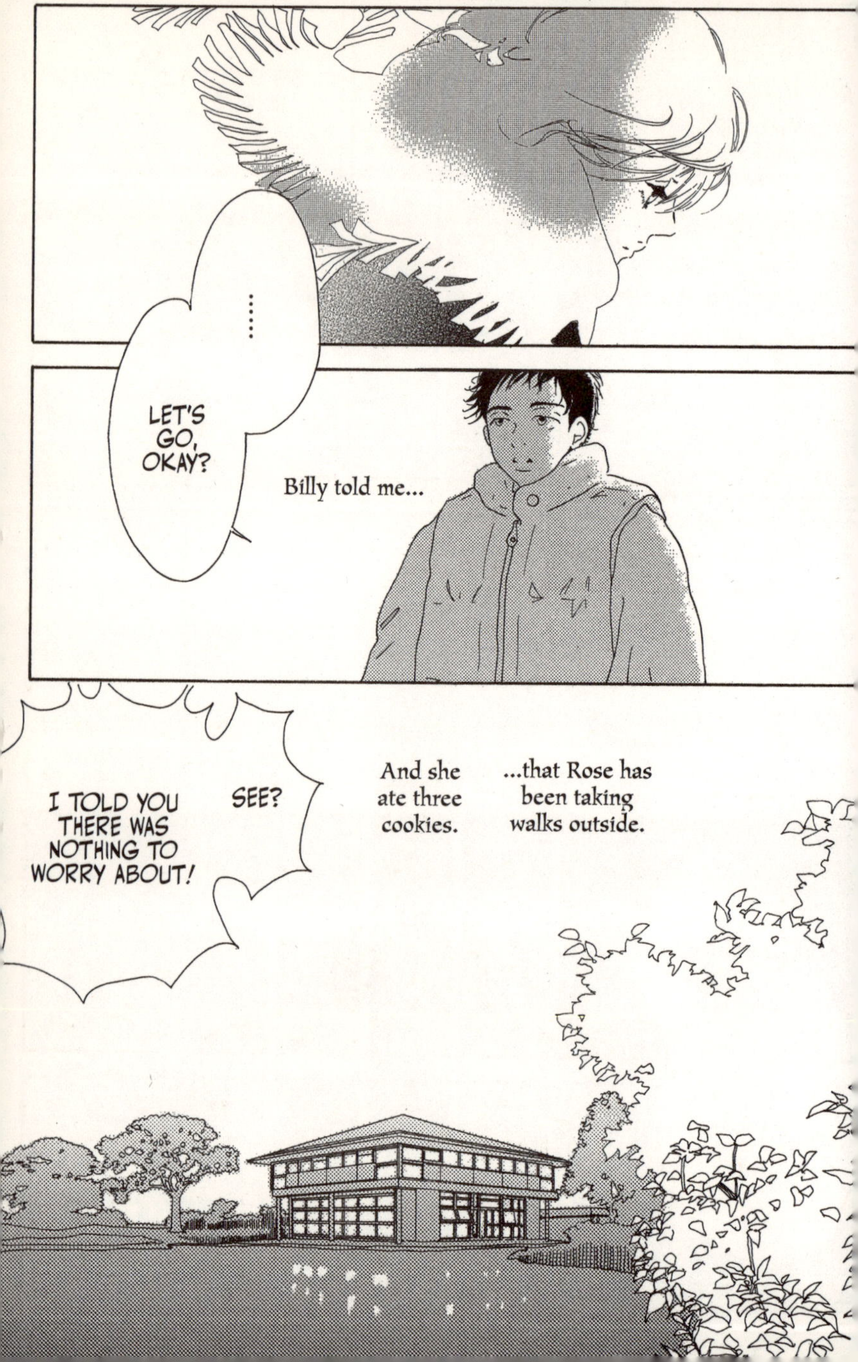
......
LET'S GO, OKAY?
Billy told me...
...that Rose has been taking walks outside.
And she ate three cookies.
SEE?
I TOLD YOU THERE WAS NOTHING TO WORRY ABOUT!

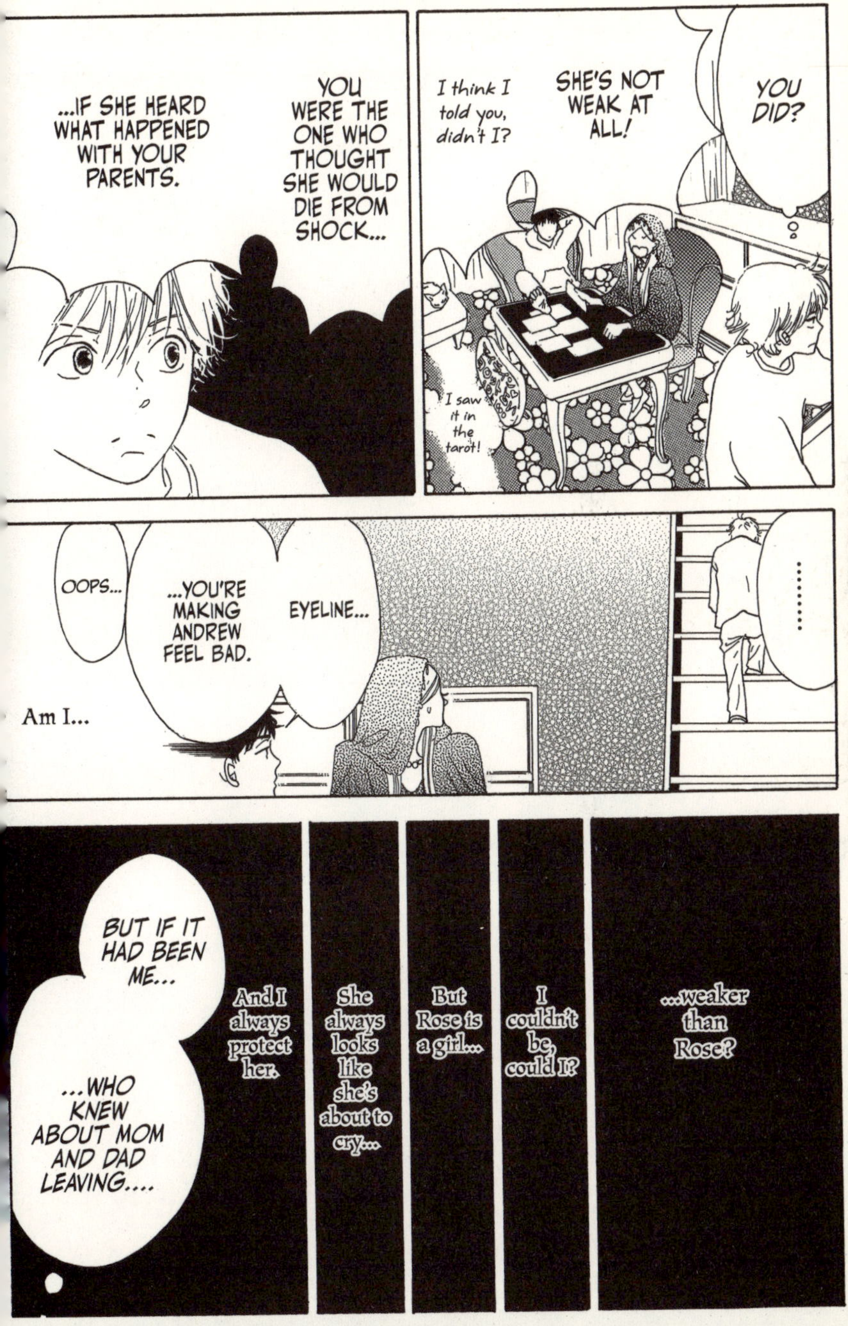
YOU DID?
SHE'S NOT WEAK AT ALL!
I think I told you, didn't I?
I saw it in the tarot!
YOU WERE THE ONE WHO THOUGHT SHE WOULD DIE FROM SHOCK...
...IF SHE HEARD WHAT HAPPENED WITH YOUR PARENTS.
....
EYELINE...
...YOU'RE MAKING ANDREW FEEL BAD.
OOPS...
Am I...
...weaker than Rose?
I couldn't be, could I?
But Rose is a girl...
She always looks like she's about to cry...
And I always protect her.
BUT IF IT HAD BEEN ME...
...WHO KNEW ABOUT MOM AND DAD LEAVING....

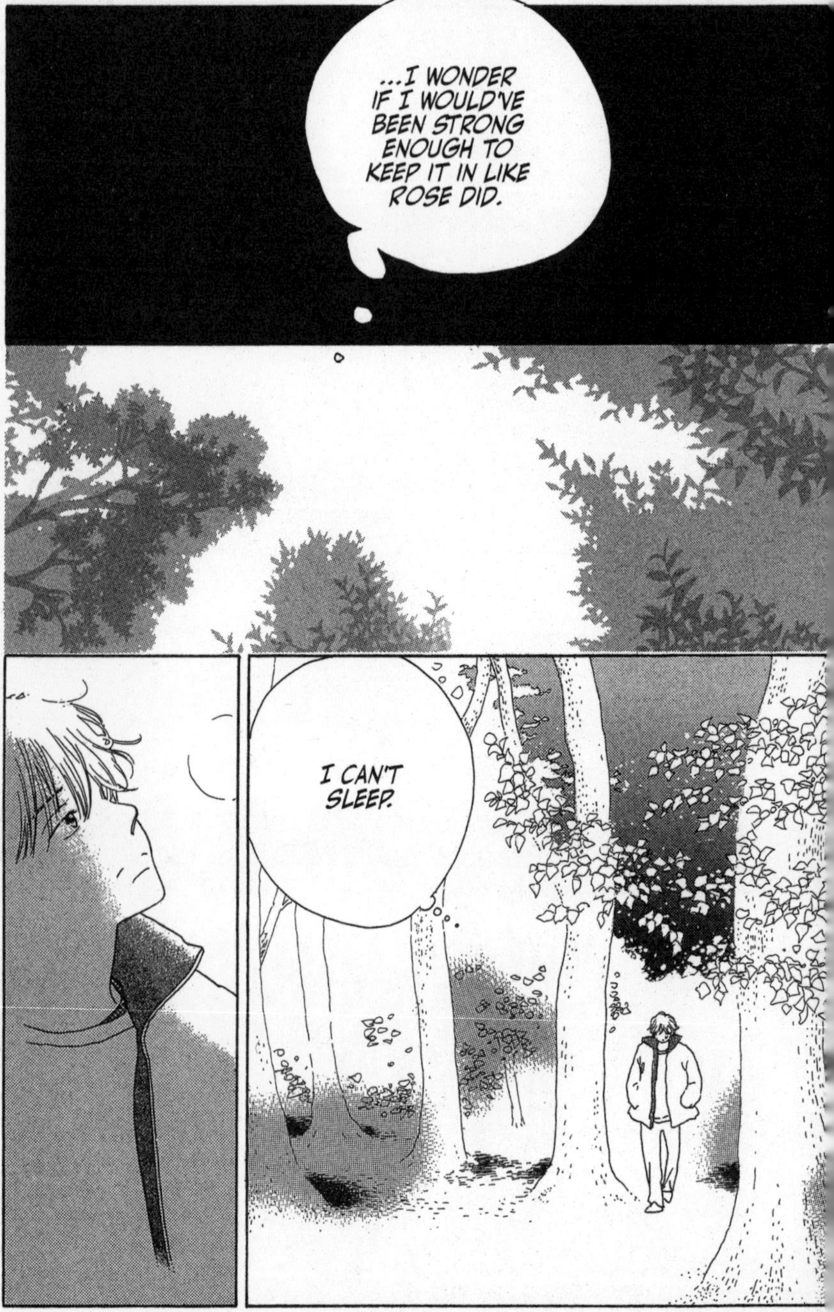
...I WONDER IF I WOULD'VE BEEN STRONG ENOUGH TO KEEP IT IN LIKE ROSE DID.
I CAN'T SLEEP.

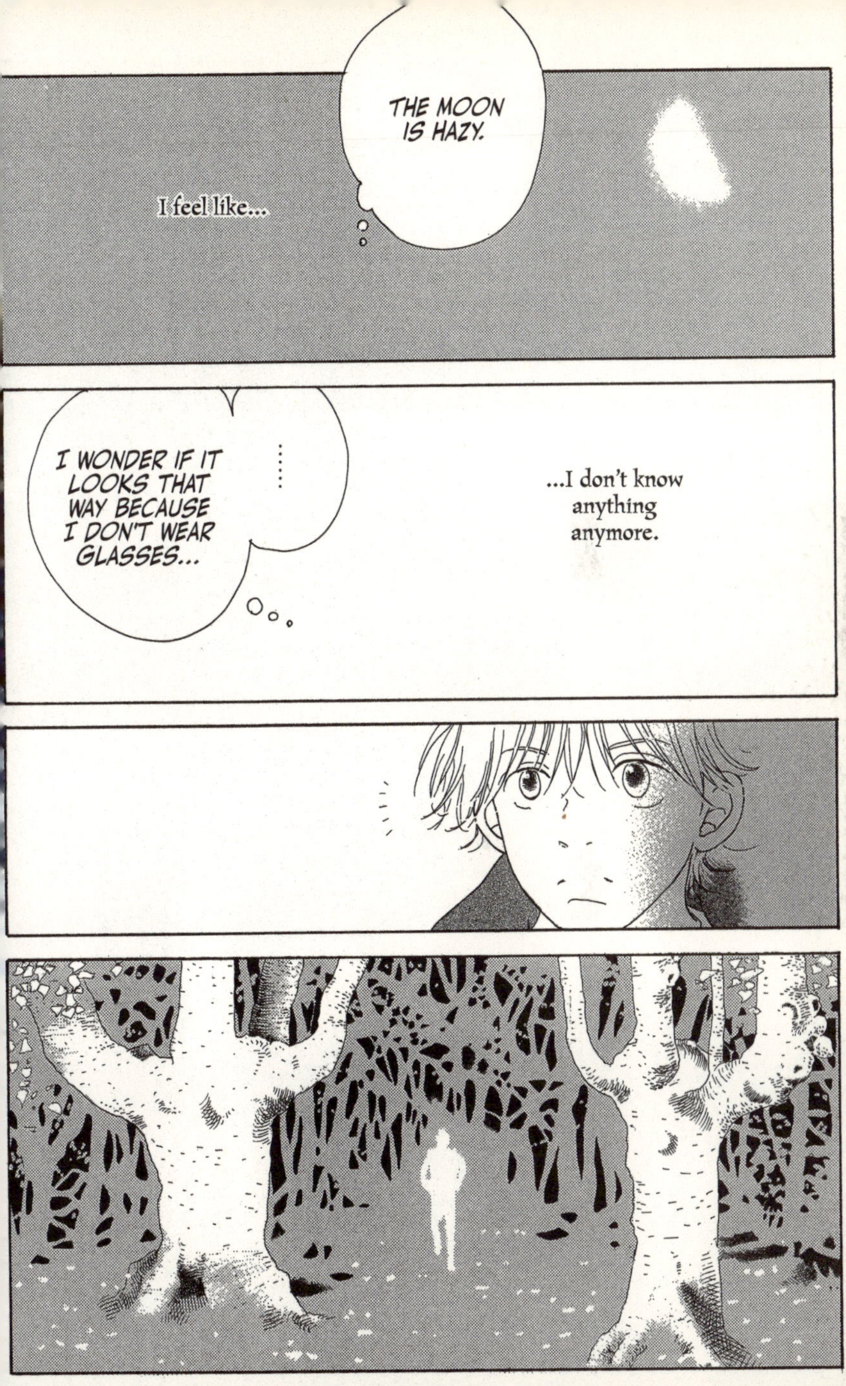
THE MOON IS HAZY.
I feel like...
...I don't know anything anymore.
......
I WONDER IF IT LOOKS THAT WAY BECAUSE I DON'T WEAR GLASSES...

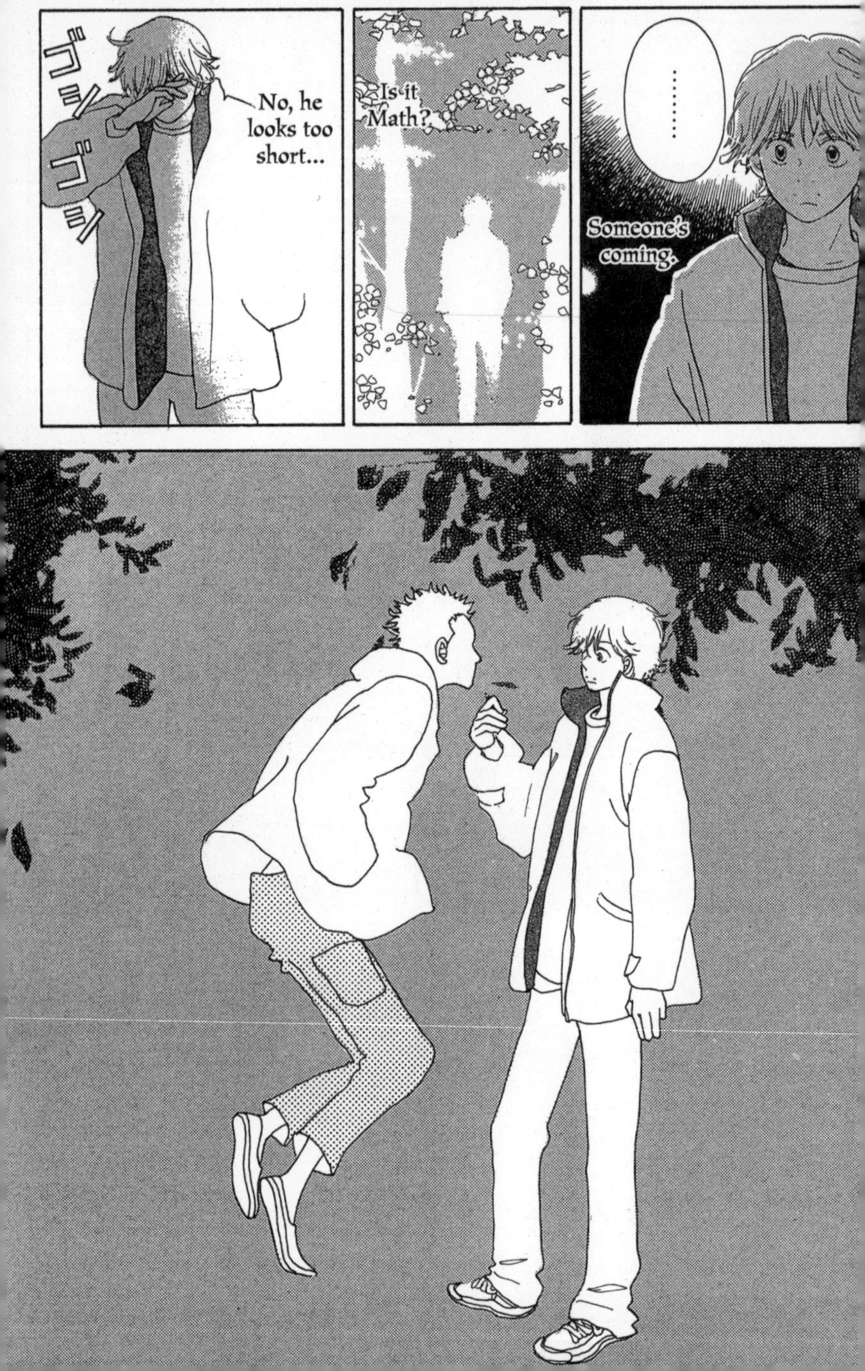
……
Someone's coming.
Is it Math?
No, he looks too short...
ゴシゴシ

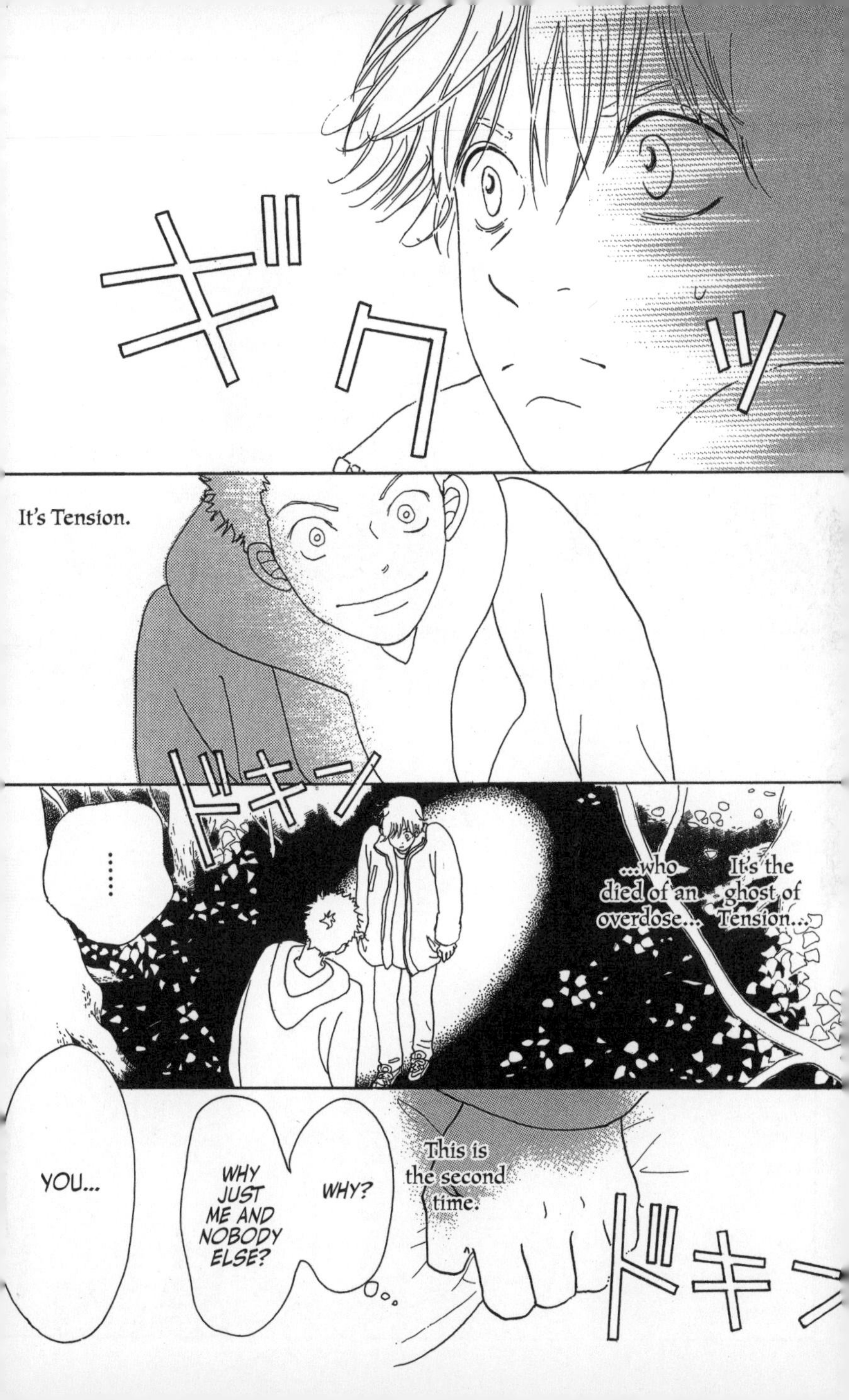
ギクッ
It's Tension.
ドキーン
It's the ghost of Tension...
...who died of an overdose...
......
This is the second time.
ドキン
WHY?
WHY JUST ME AND NOBODY ELSE?
YOU...

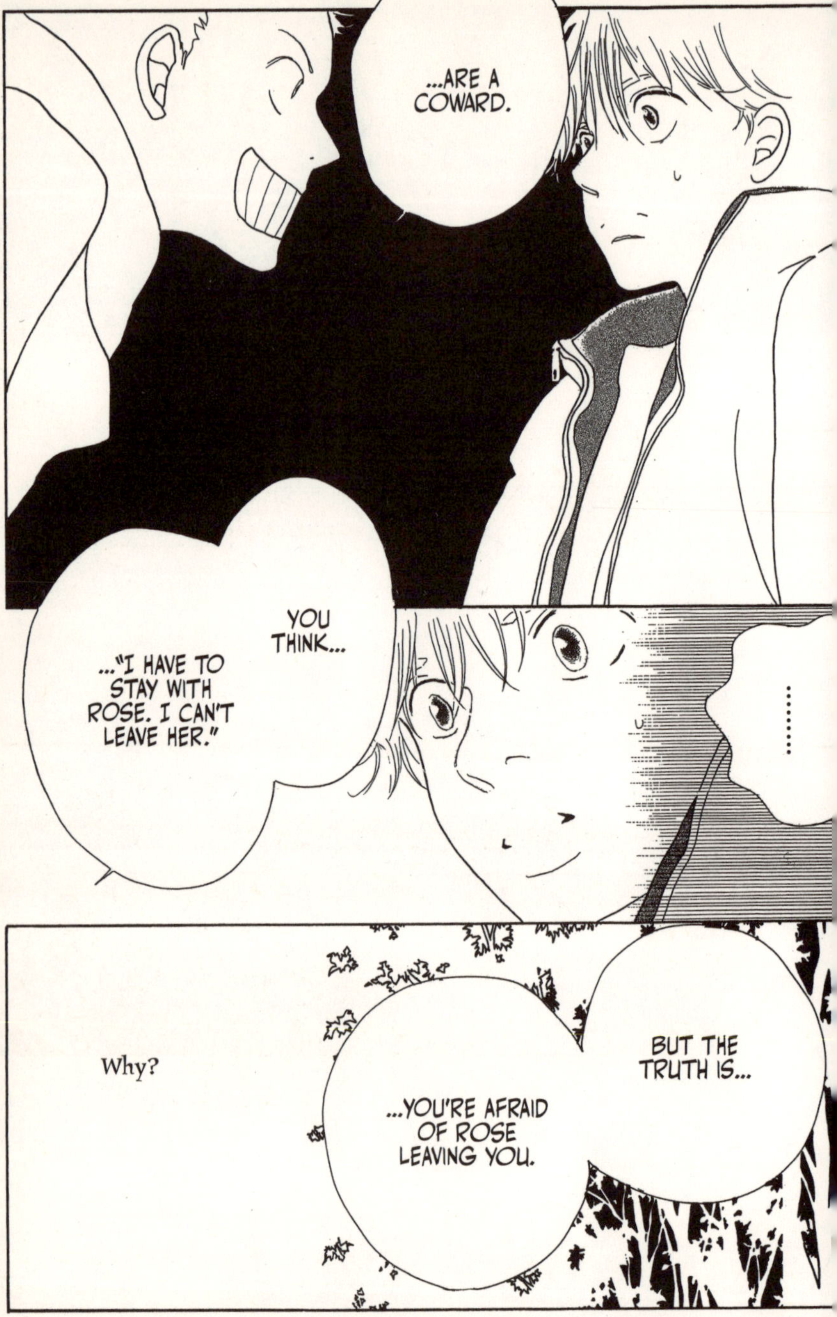
...ARE A COWARD.
YOU THINK...
..."I HAVE TO STAY WITH ROSE. I CAN'T LEAVE HER."
Why?
BUT THE TRUTH IS...
...YOU'RE AFRAID OF ROSE LEAVING YOU.

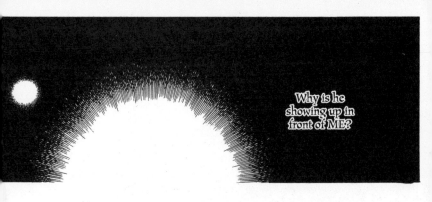

Why is he showing up in front of ME?

ANDREW.

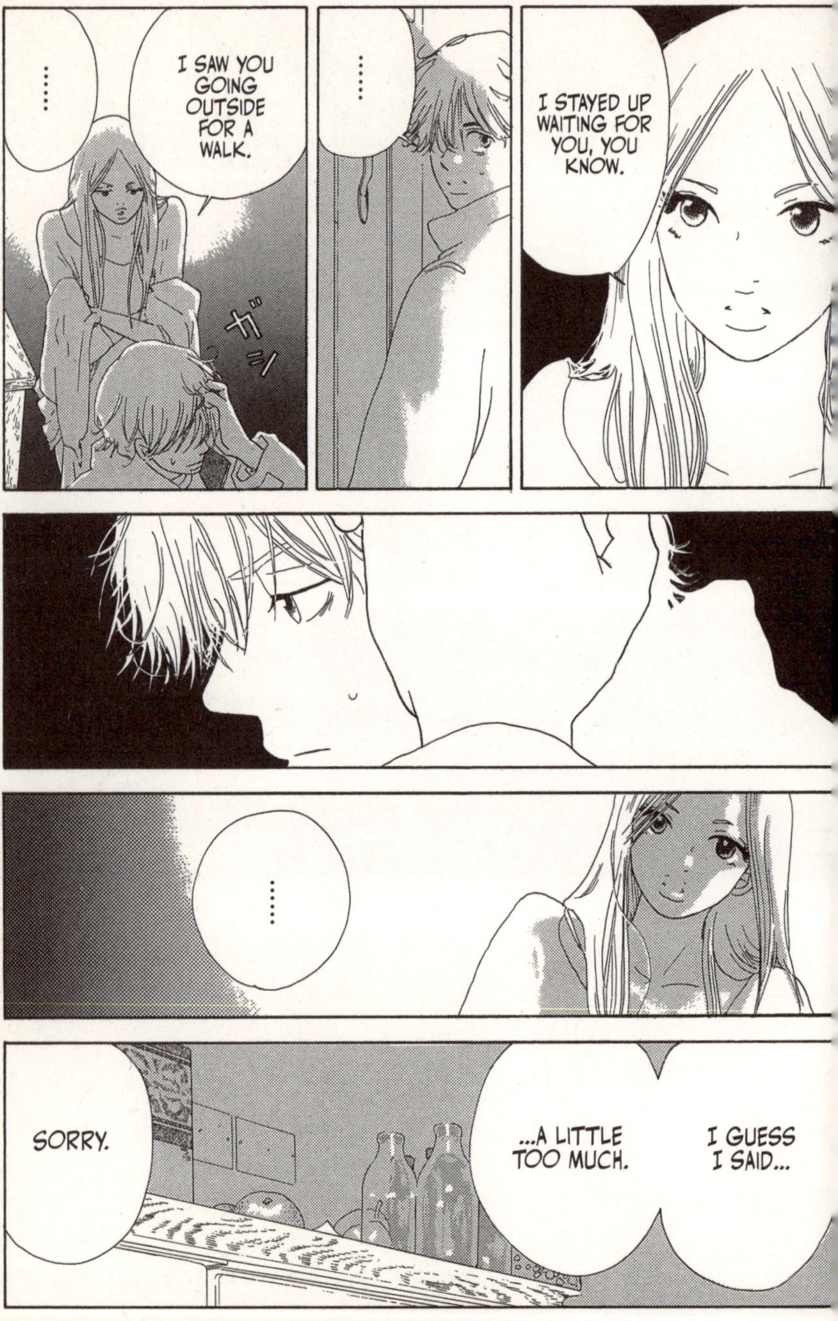
I STAYED UP WAITING FOR YOU, YOU KNOW.
......
I SAW YOU GOING OUTSIDE FOR A WALK.
......
......
I GUESS I SAID...
...A LITTLE TOO MUCH.
SORRY.

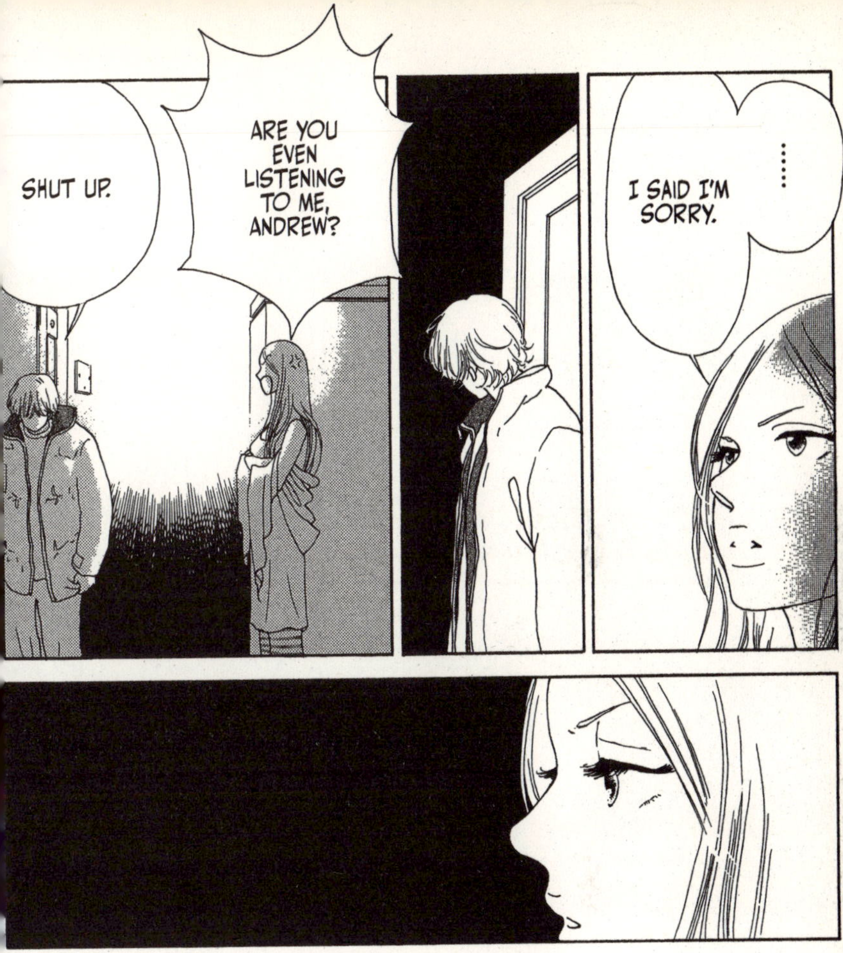
......
I SAID I'M SORRY.
ARE YOU EVEN LISTENING TO ME, ANDREW?
SHUT UP.

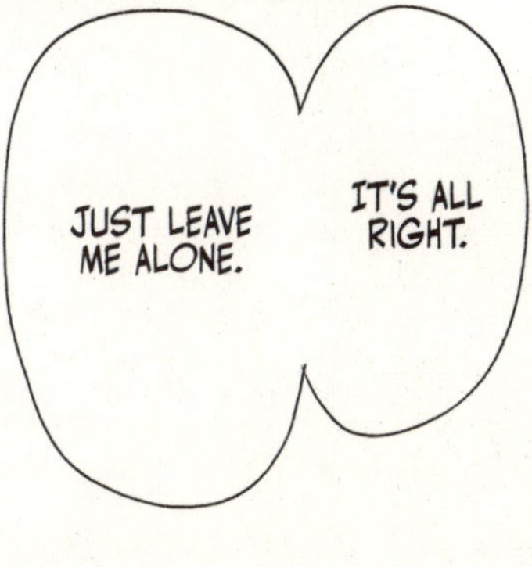
IT'S ALL RIGHT.
JUST LEAVE ME ALONE.

Right then...

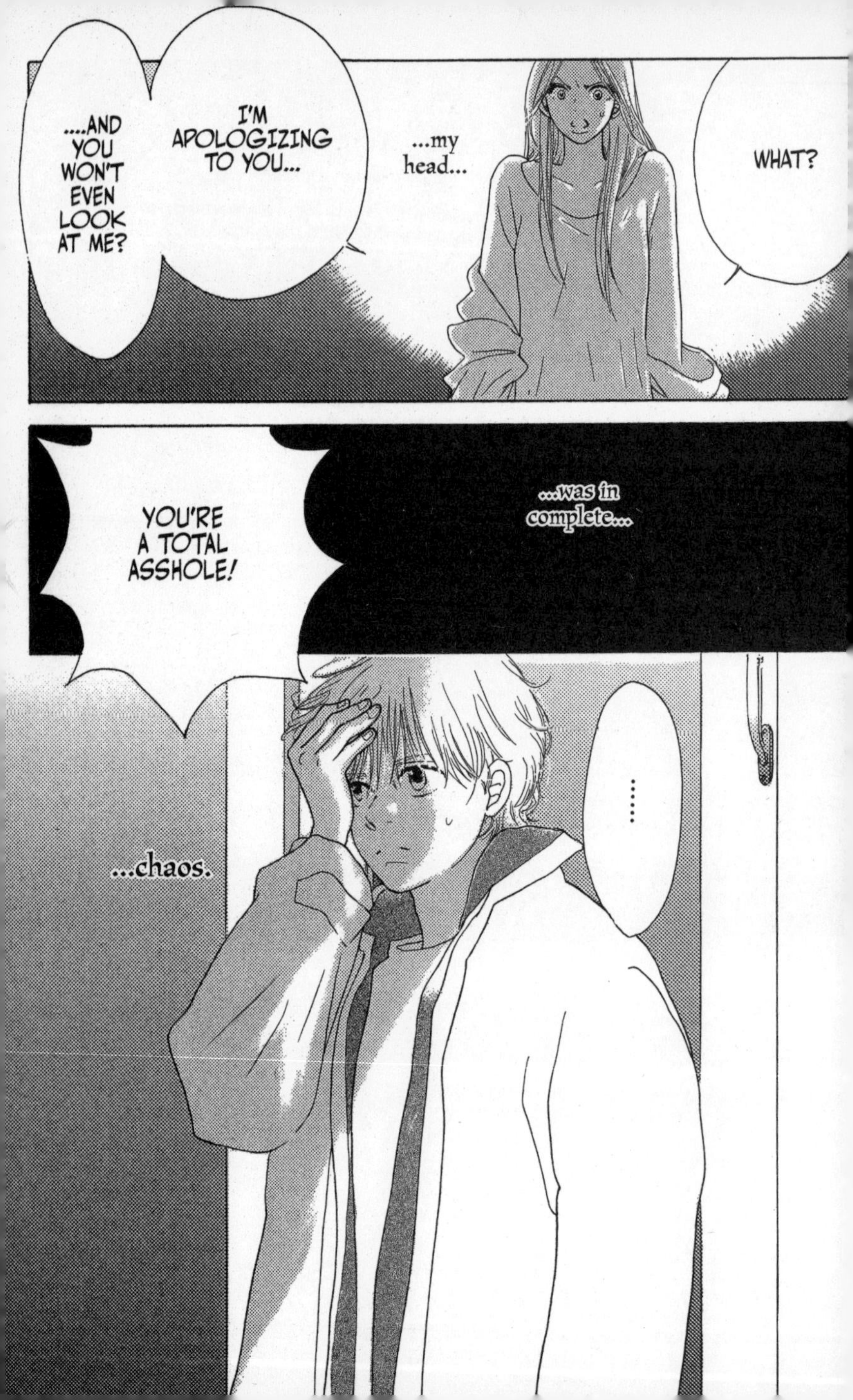
WHAT?
...my head...
I'M APOLOGIZING TO YOU...
....AND YOU WON'T EVEN LOOK AT ME?
...was in complete...
YOU'RE A TOTAL ASSHOLE!
......
...chaos.

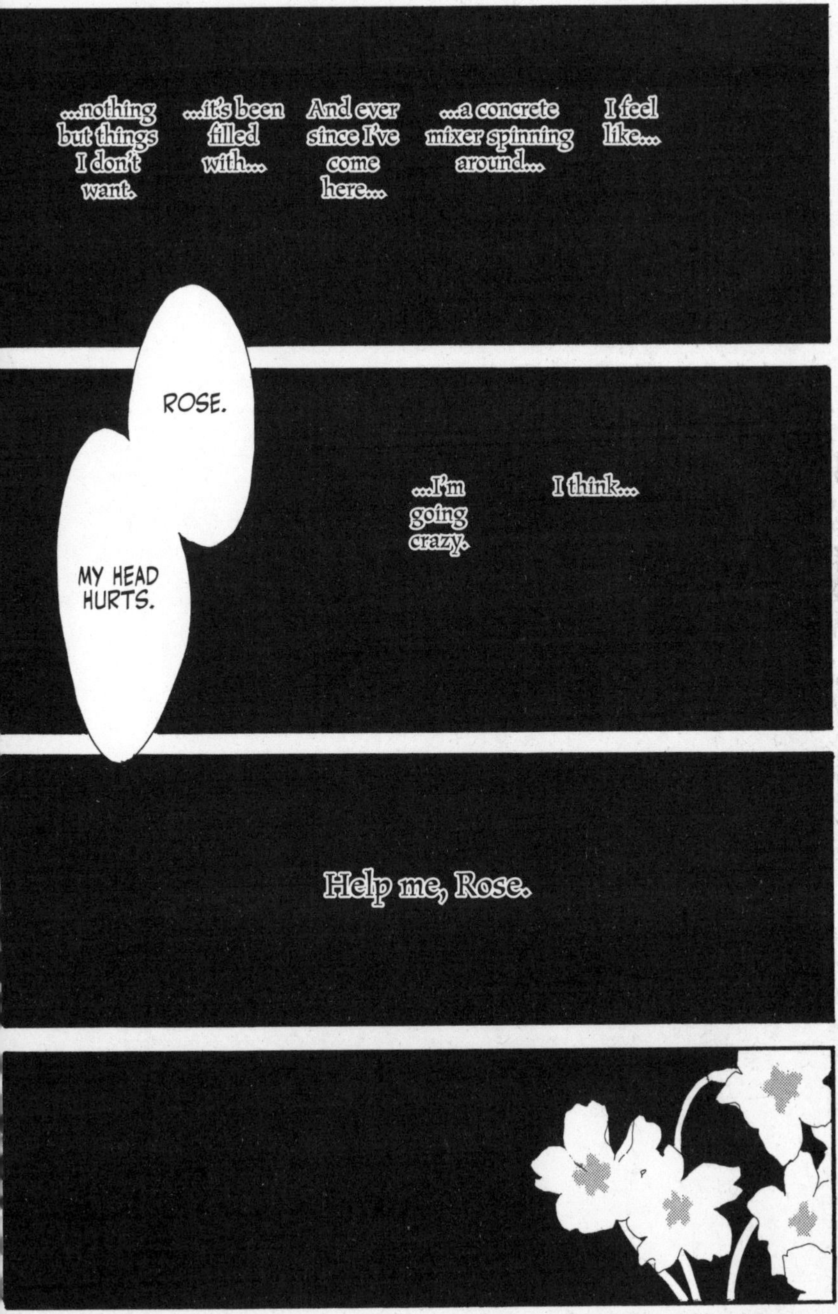
I feel like...
...a concrete mixer spinning around...
And ever since I've come here...
...it's been filled with...
...nothing but things I don't want.
I think...
...I'm going crazy.
ROSE.
MY HEAD HURTS.
Help me, Rose.

Club Hurricane Final Adventure

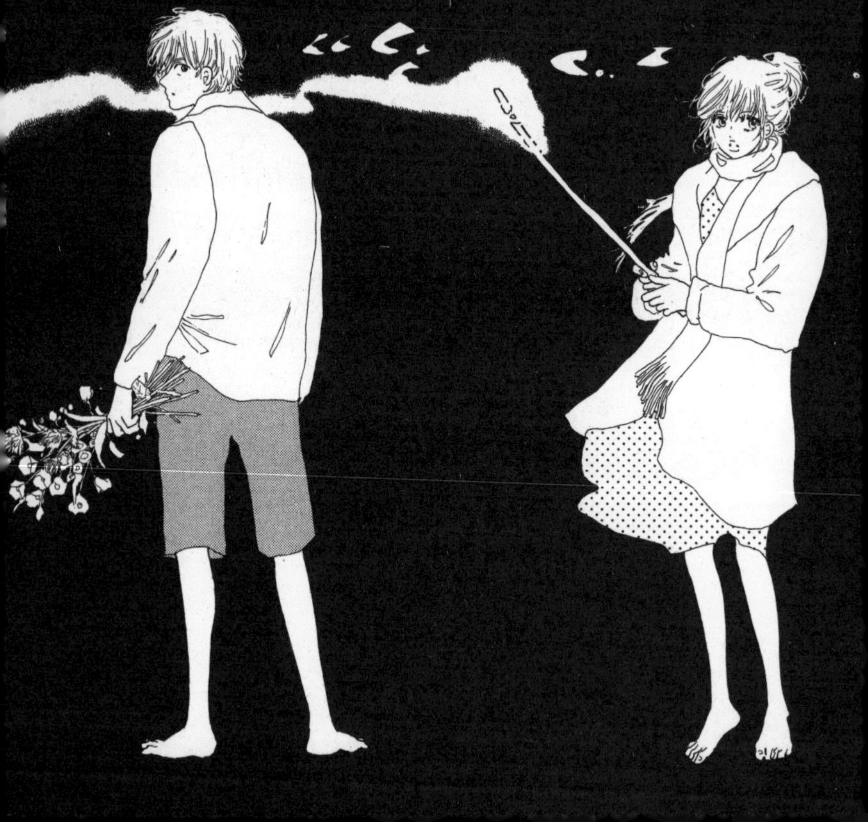

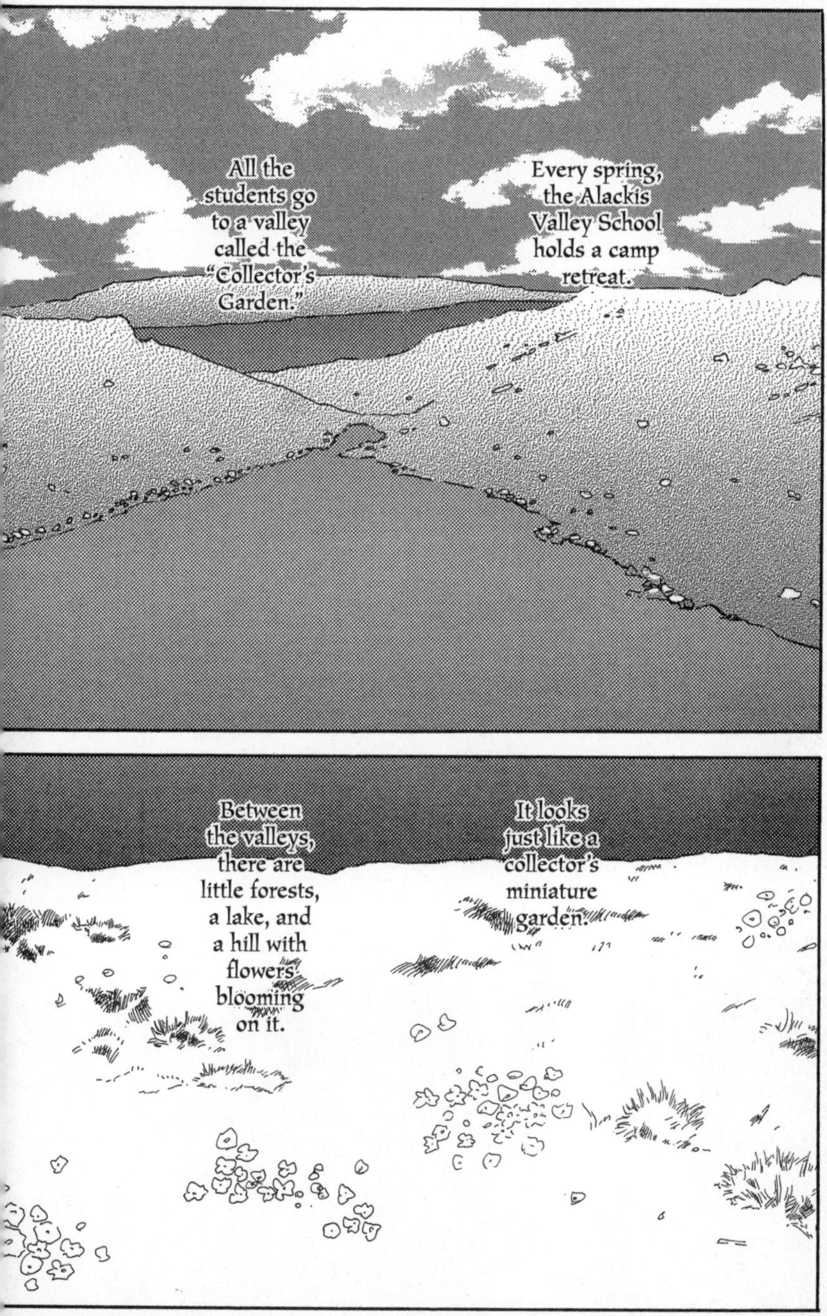
Every spring, the Alackis Valley School holds a camp retreat.
All the students go to a valley called the "Collector's Garden."
It looks just like a collector's miniature garden.
Between the valleys, there are little forests, a lake, and a hill with flowers blooming on it.

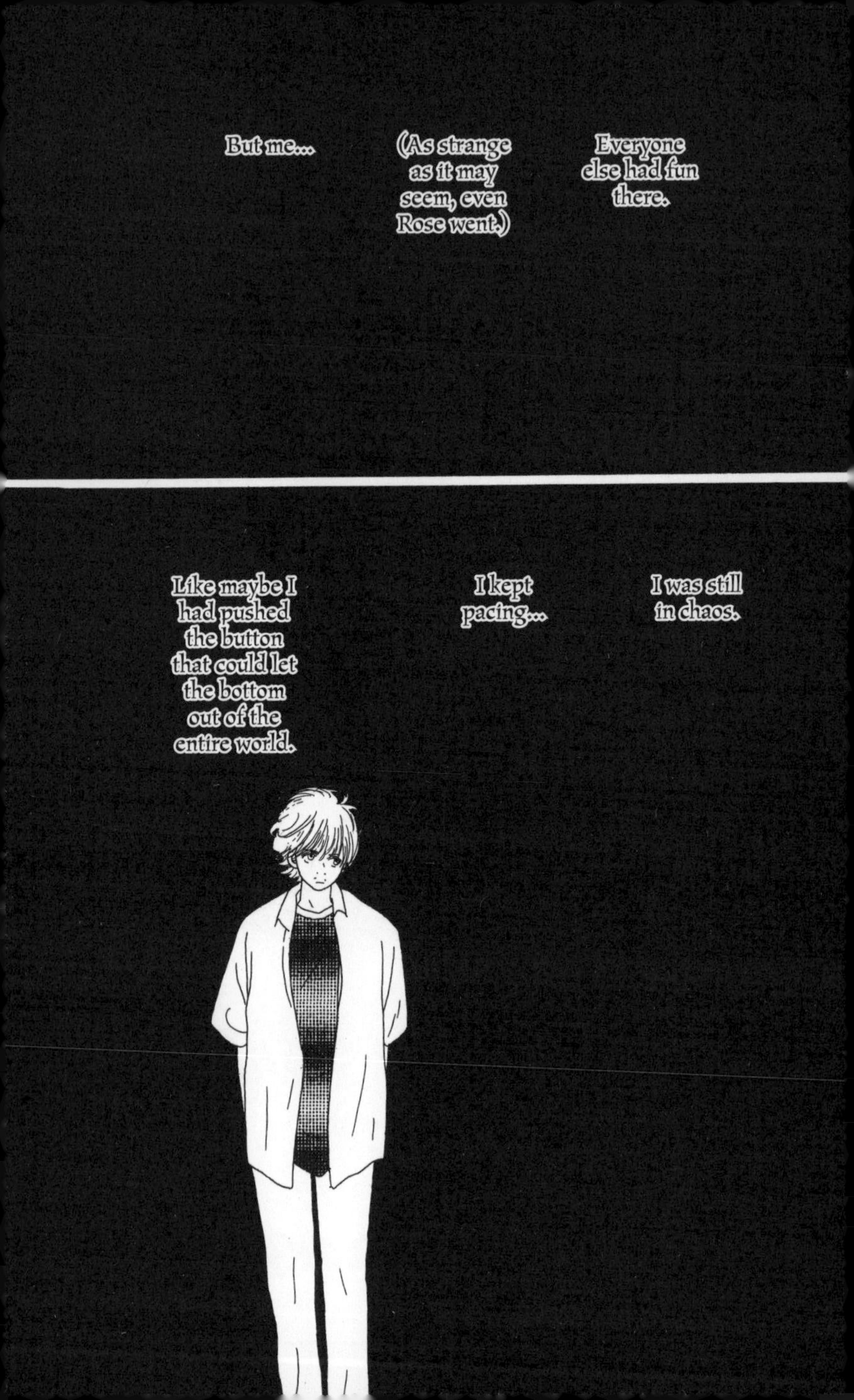
Everyone else had fun there.
(As strange as it may seem, even Rose went.)
But me...
I was still in chaos.
I kept pacing...
Like maybe I had pushed the button that could let the bottom out of the entire world.

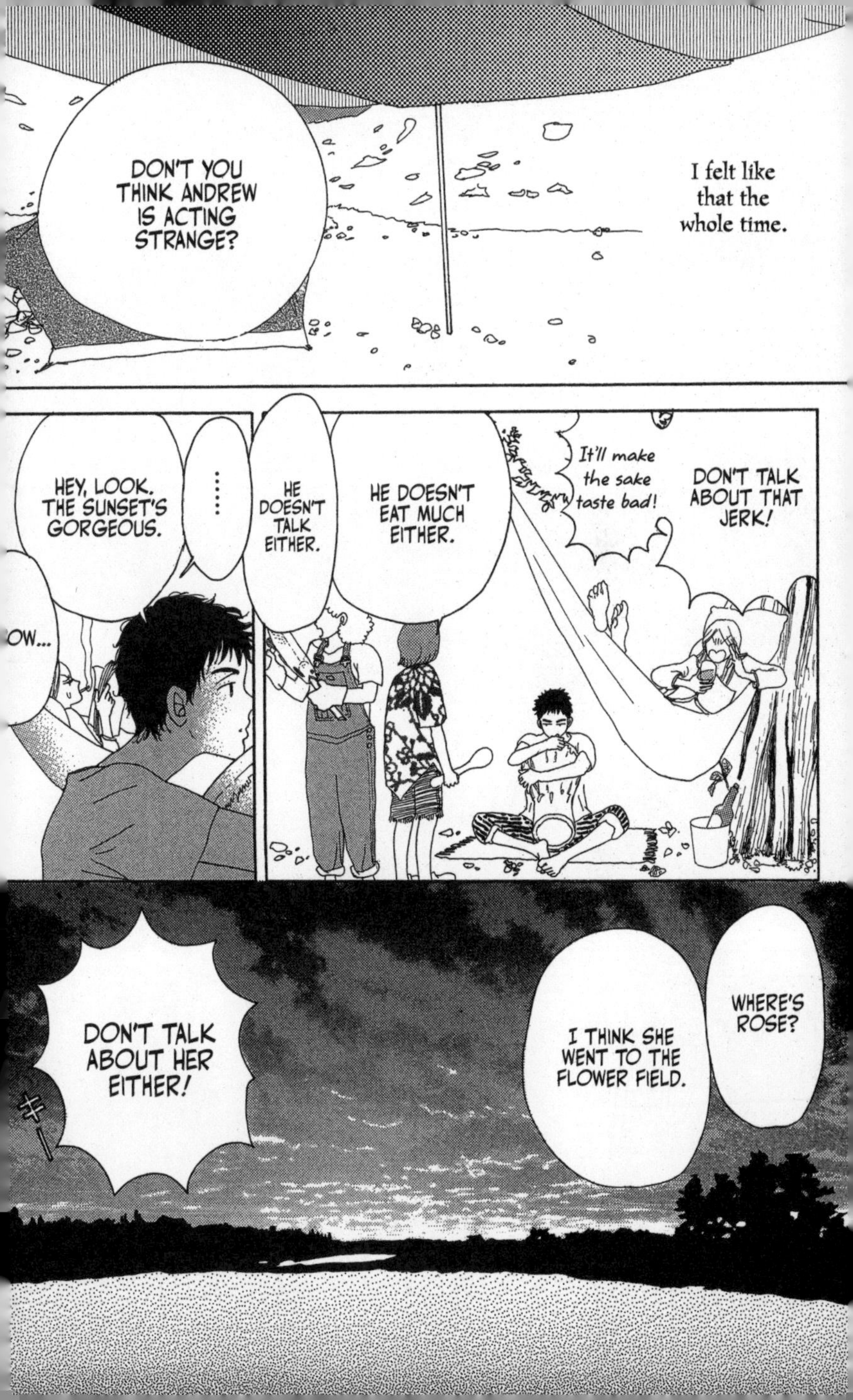
I felt like that the whole time.
DON'T YOU THINK ANDREW IS ACTING STRANGE?
DON'T TALK ABOUT THAT JERK!
It'll make the sake taste bad!
HE DOESN'T EAT MUCH EITHER.
HE DOESN'T TALK EITHER.
......
HEY, LOOK. THE SUNSET'S GORGEOUS.
OW...
WHERE'S ROSE?
I THINK SHE WENT TO THE FLOWER FIELD.
DON'T TALK ABOUT HER EITHER!
キー

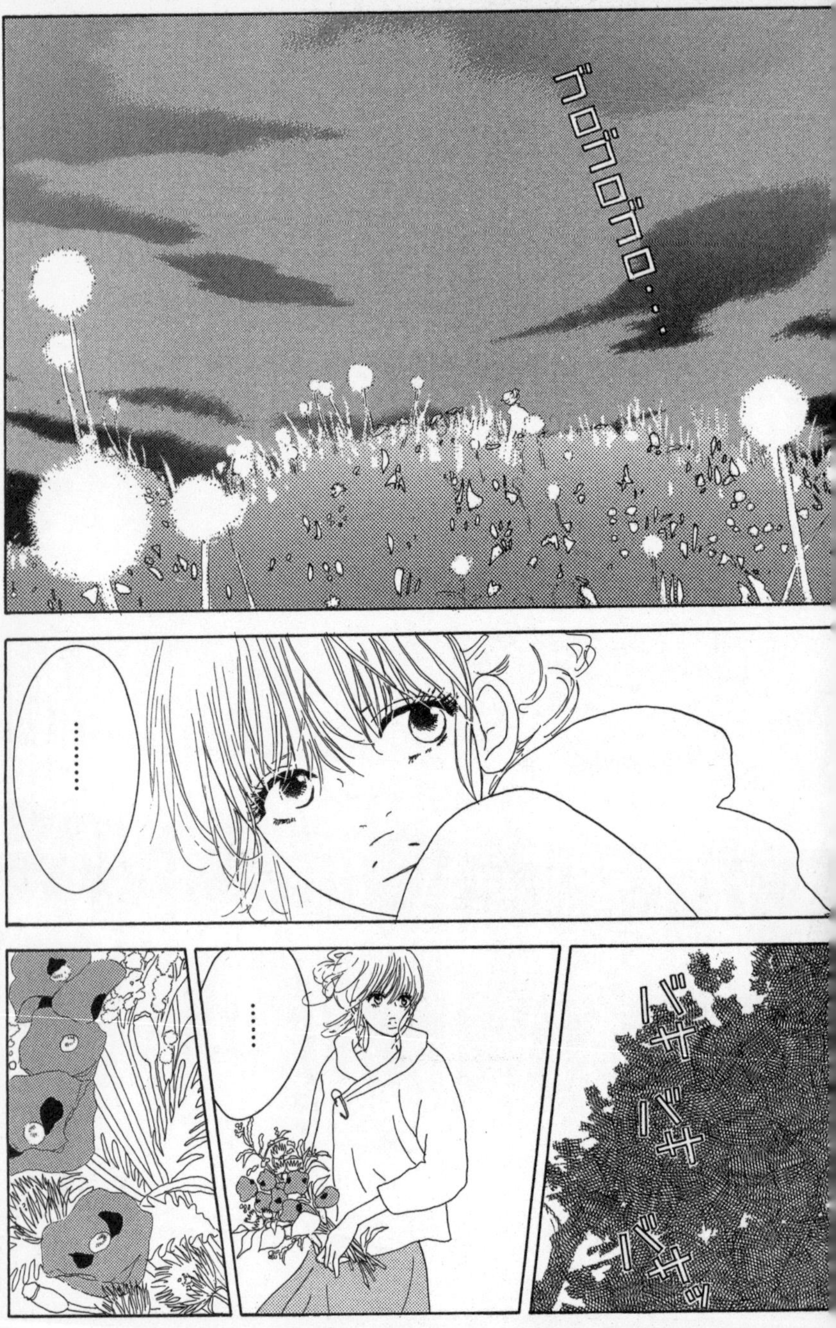
ゴロゴロゴロ・・・
……
バサーバサーバサッ
……

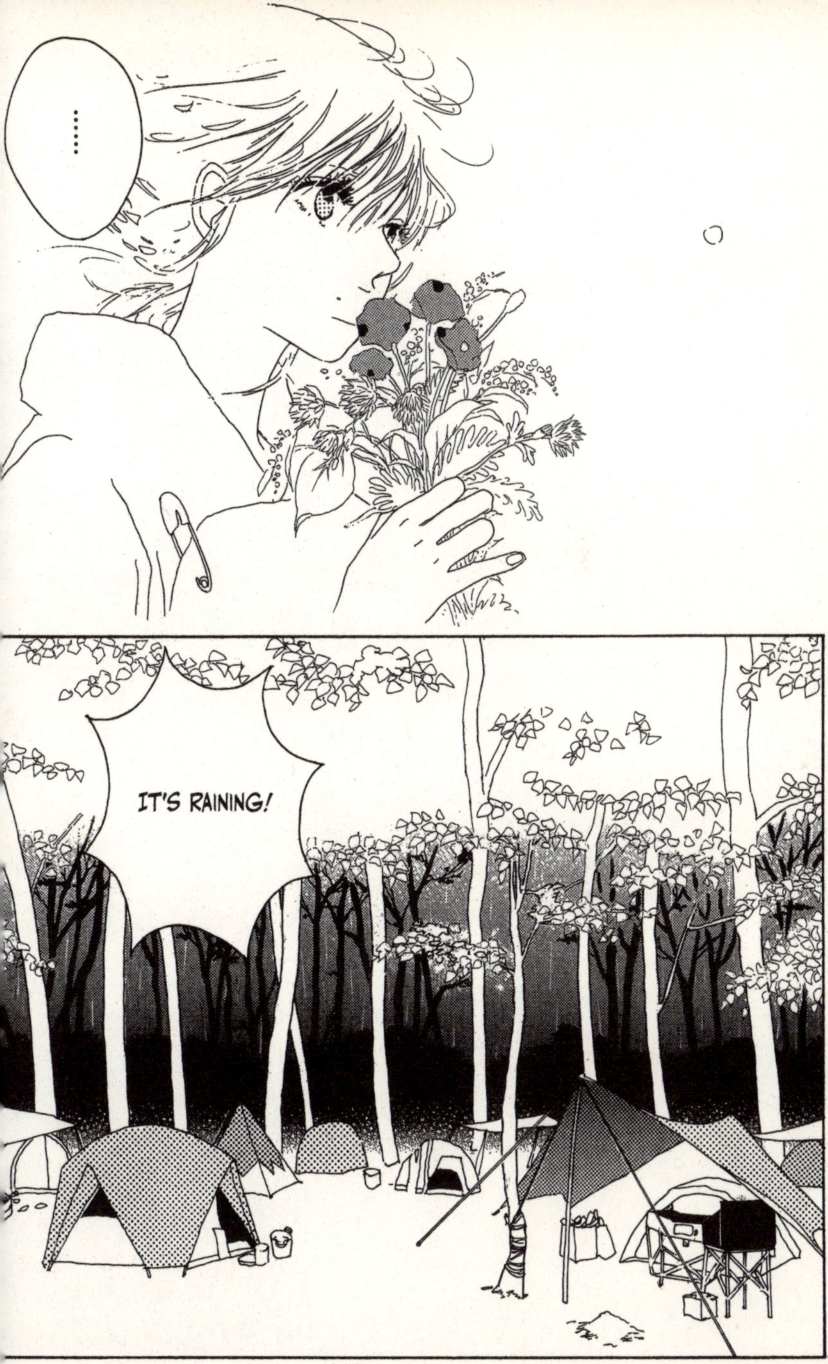
......
IT'S RAINING!

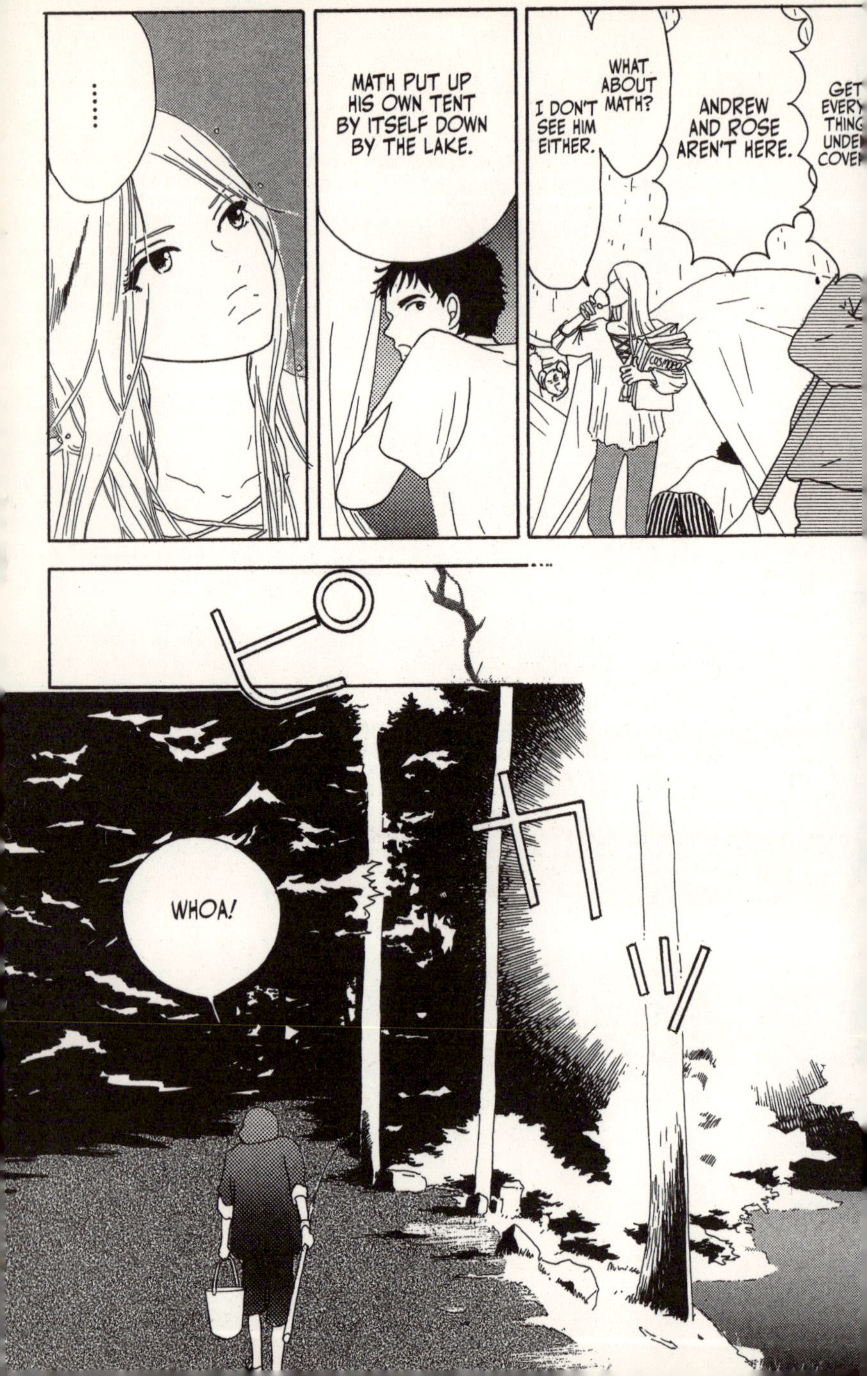
GET EVERY THING UNDE COVE
ANDREW AND ROSE AREN'T HERE.
WHAT ABOUT MATH?
I DON'T SEE HIM EITHER.
MATH PUT UP HIS OWN TENT BY ITSELF DOWN BY THE LAKE.
……
WHOA!

IT'S AMAZING...

BUT...

SCARY.

‥

GOLGODA HILL...

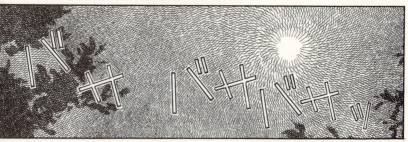

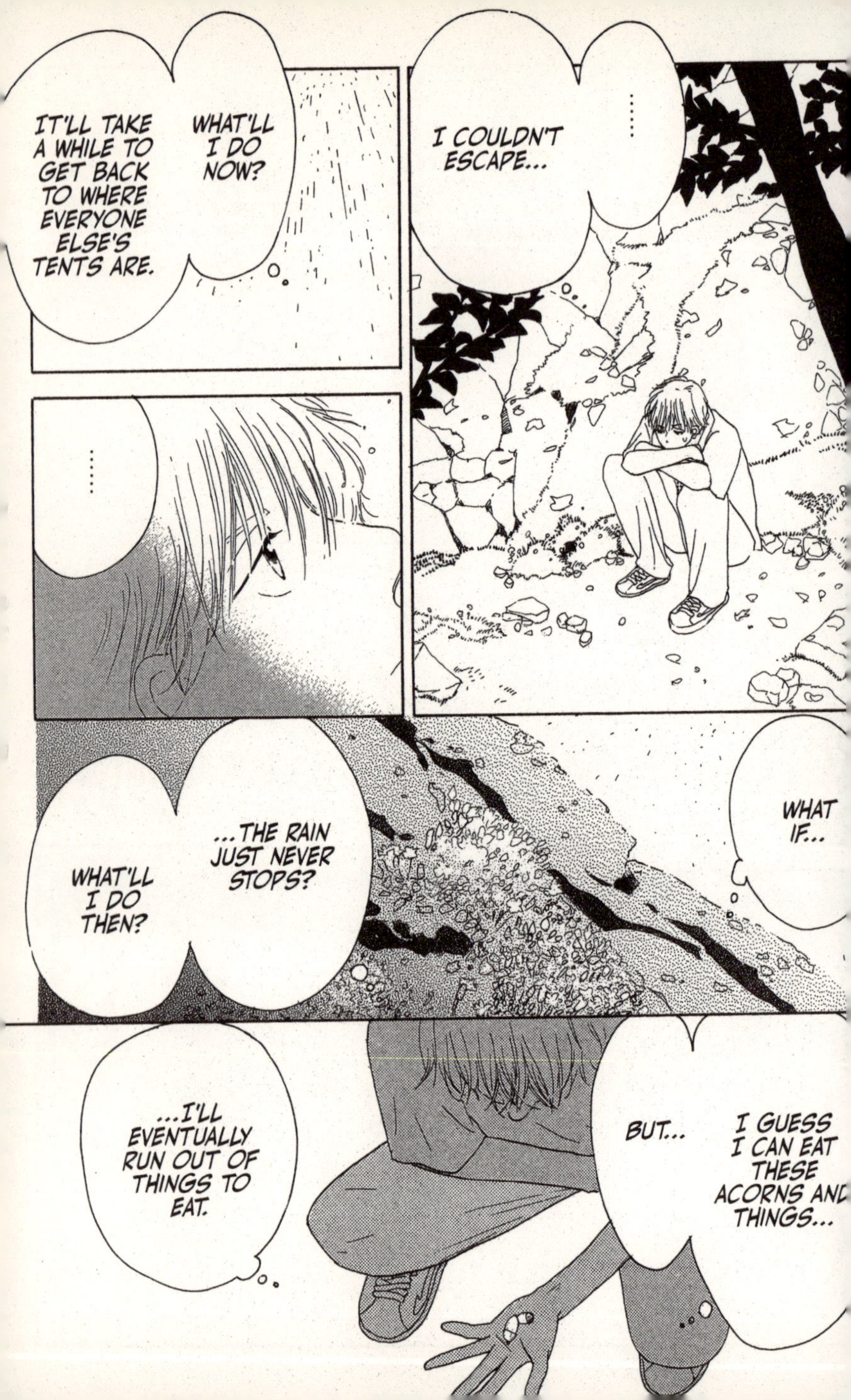

......
I COULDN'T ESCAPE...
WHAT'LL I DO NOW?
IT'LL TAKE A WHILE TO GET BACK TO WHERE EVERYONE ELSE'S TENTS ARE.
......
WHAT IF...
...THE RAIN JUST NEVER STOPS?
WHAT'LL I DO THEN?
I GUESS I CAN EAT THESE ACORNS AND THINGS...
BUT...
...I'LL EVENTUALLY RUN OUT OF THINGS TO EAT.

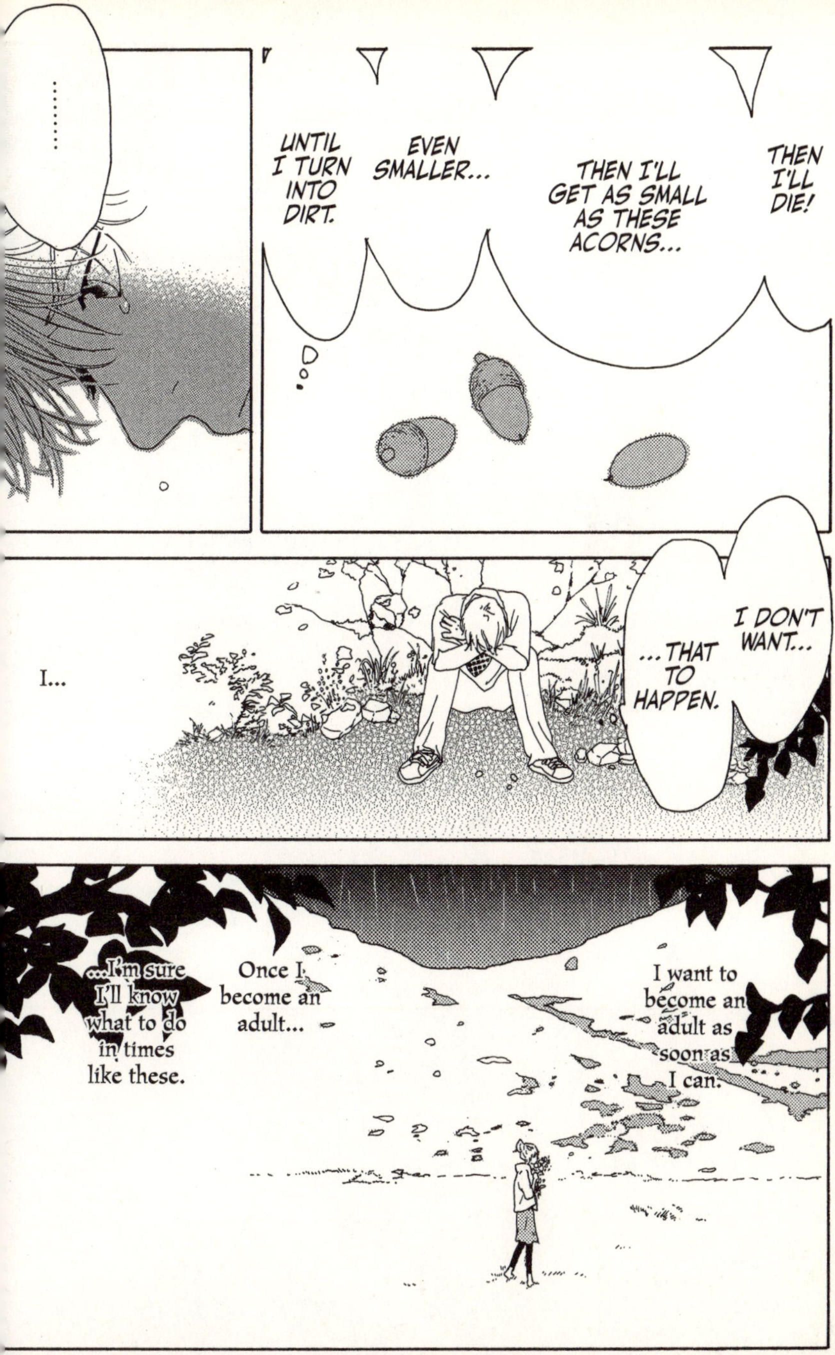
THEN I'LL DIE!
THEN I'LL GET AS SMALL AS THESE ACORNS...
EVEN SMALLER...
UNTIL I TURN INTO DIRT.
......
I DON'T WANT...
...THAT TO HAPPEN.
I...
I want to become an adult as soon as I can.
Once I become an adult...
...I'm sure I'll know what to do in times like these.

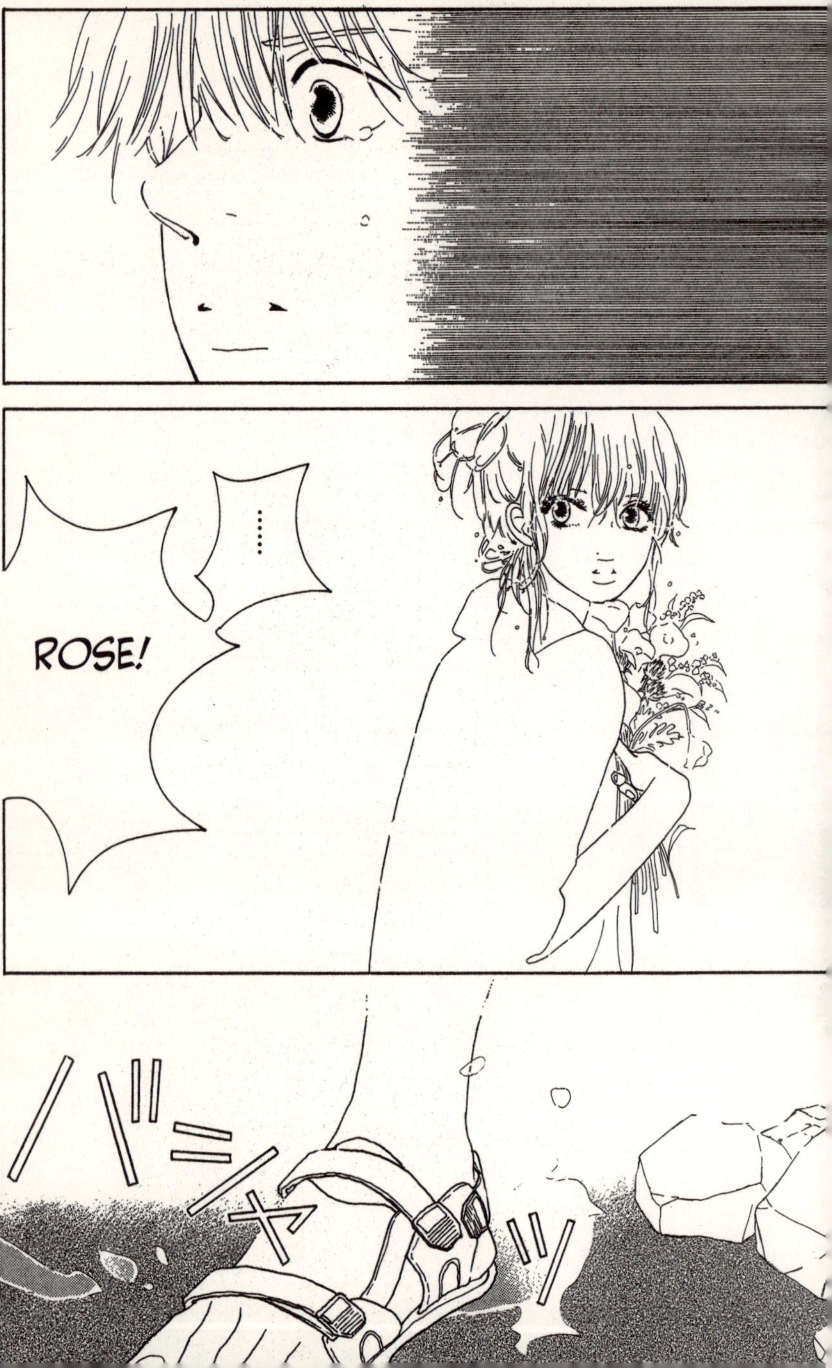
......
ROSE!
バニャッ

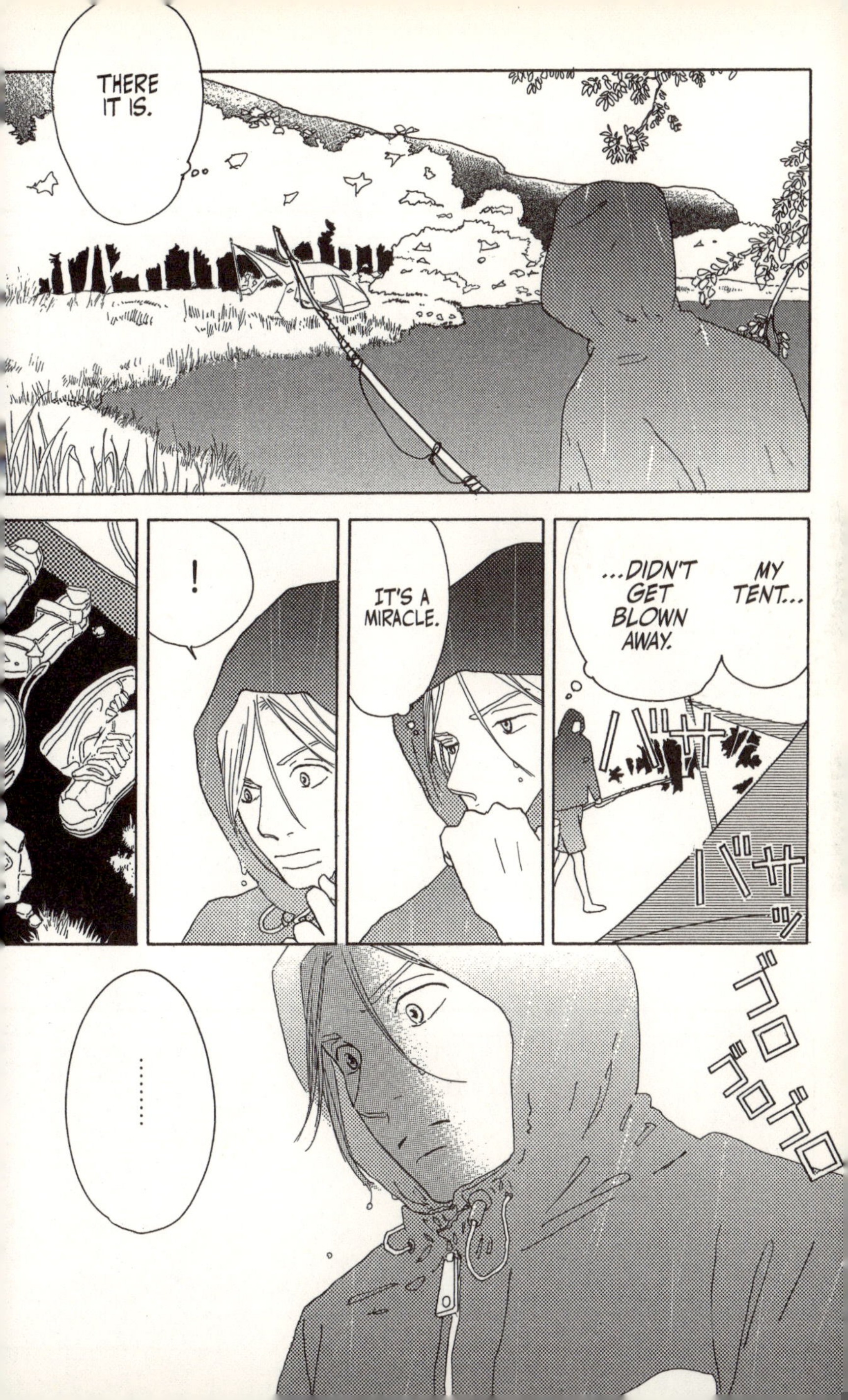
THERE IT IS.
MY TENT...
...DIDN'T GET BLOWN AWAY.
バサ
バサッ
IT'S A MIRACLE.
!
ゴロゴロゴロゴロ
......

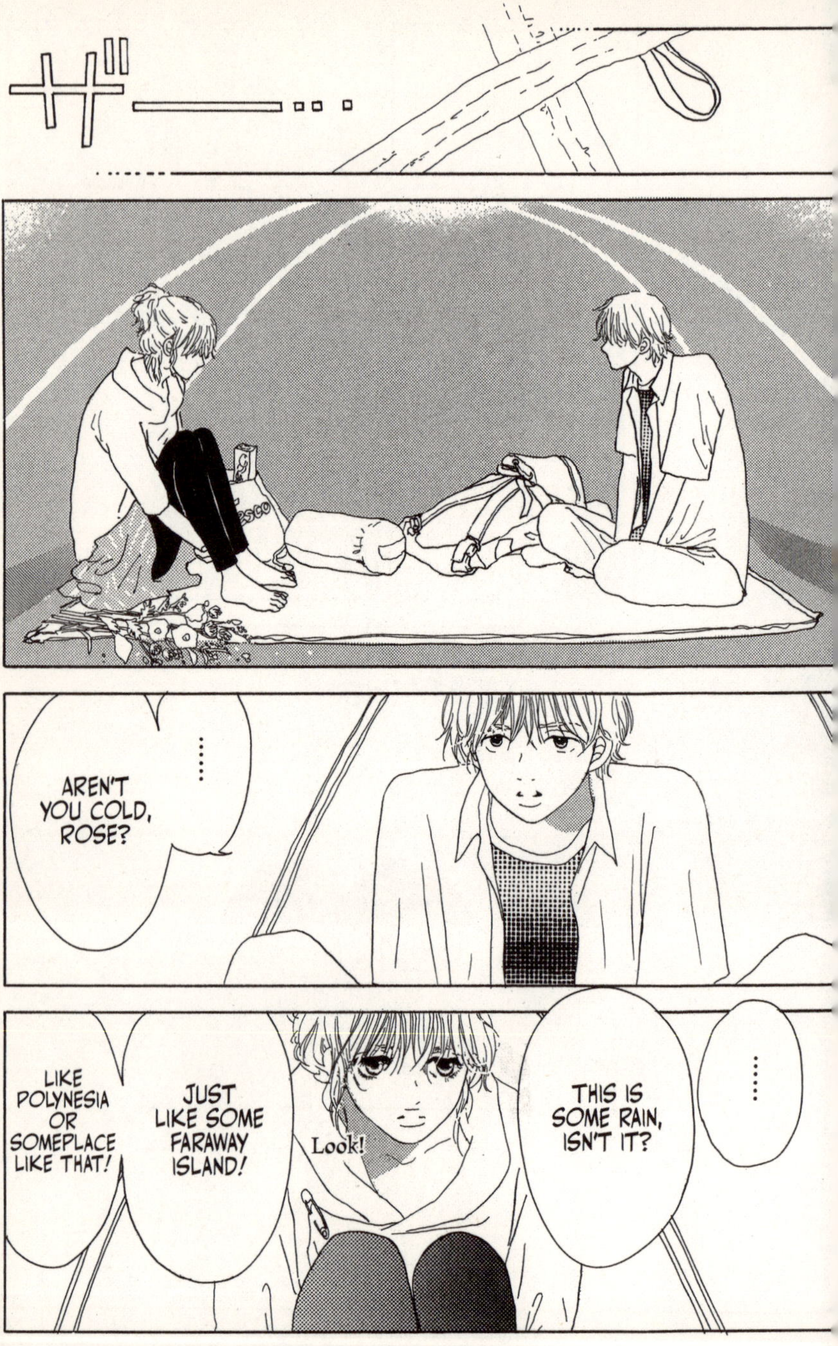
ザー…
……
AREN'T YOU COLD, ROSE?
……
THIS IS SOME RAIN, ISN'T IT?
Look!
JUST LIKE SOME FARAWAY ISLAND!
LIKE POLYNESIA OR SOMEPLACE LIKE THAT!

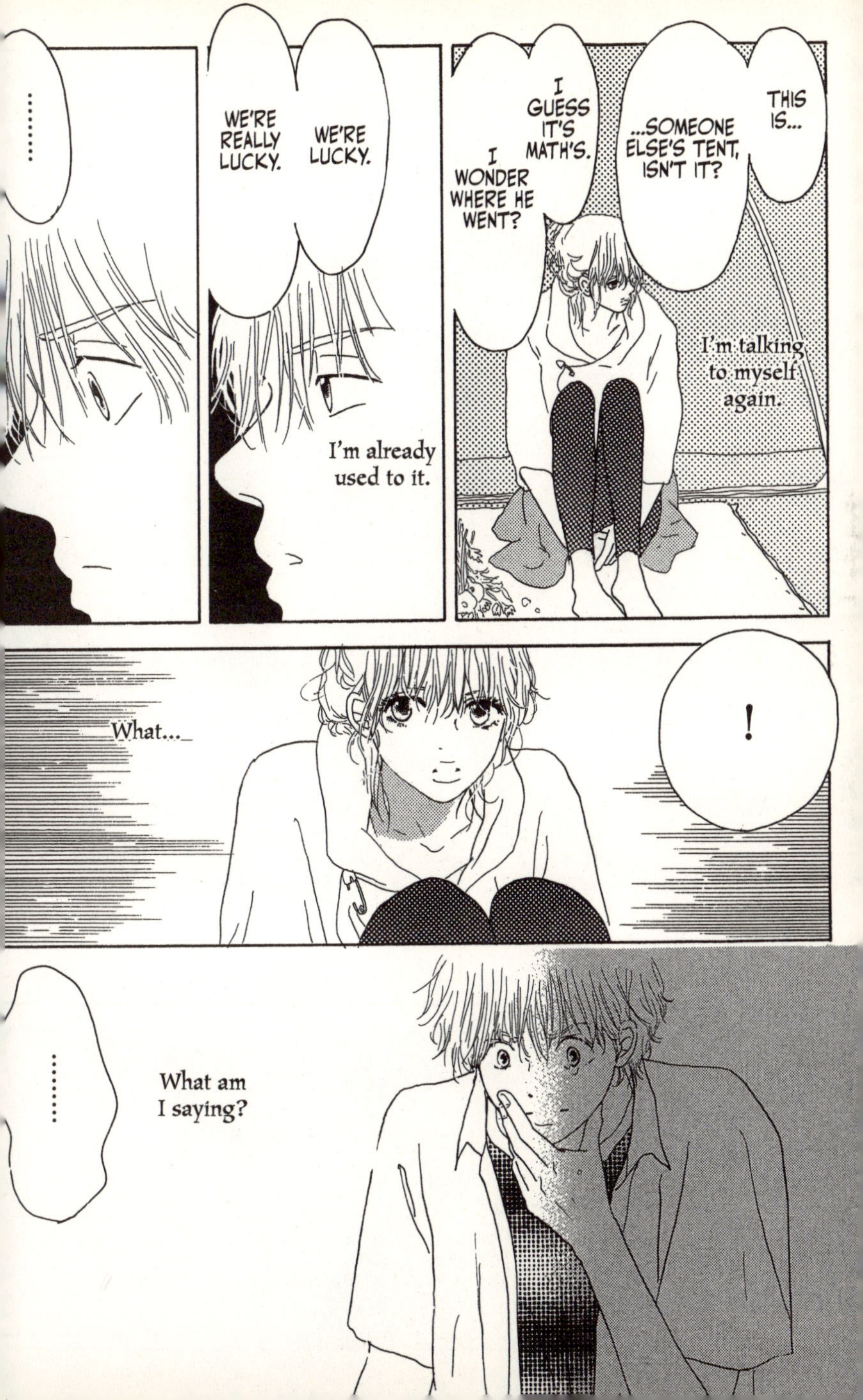
THIS IS...
...SOMEONE ELSE'S TENT, ISN'T IT?
I GUESS IT'S MATH'S.
I WONDER WHERE HE WENT?
I'm talking to myself again.
WE'RE LUCKY.
WE'RE REALLY LUCKY.
I'm already used to it.
....
!
What...
What am I saying?
....

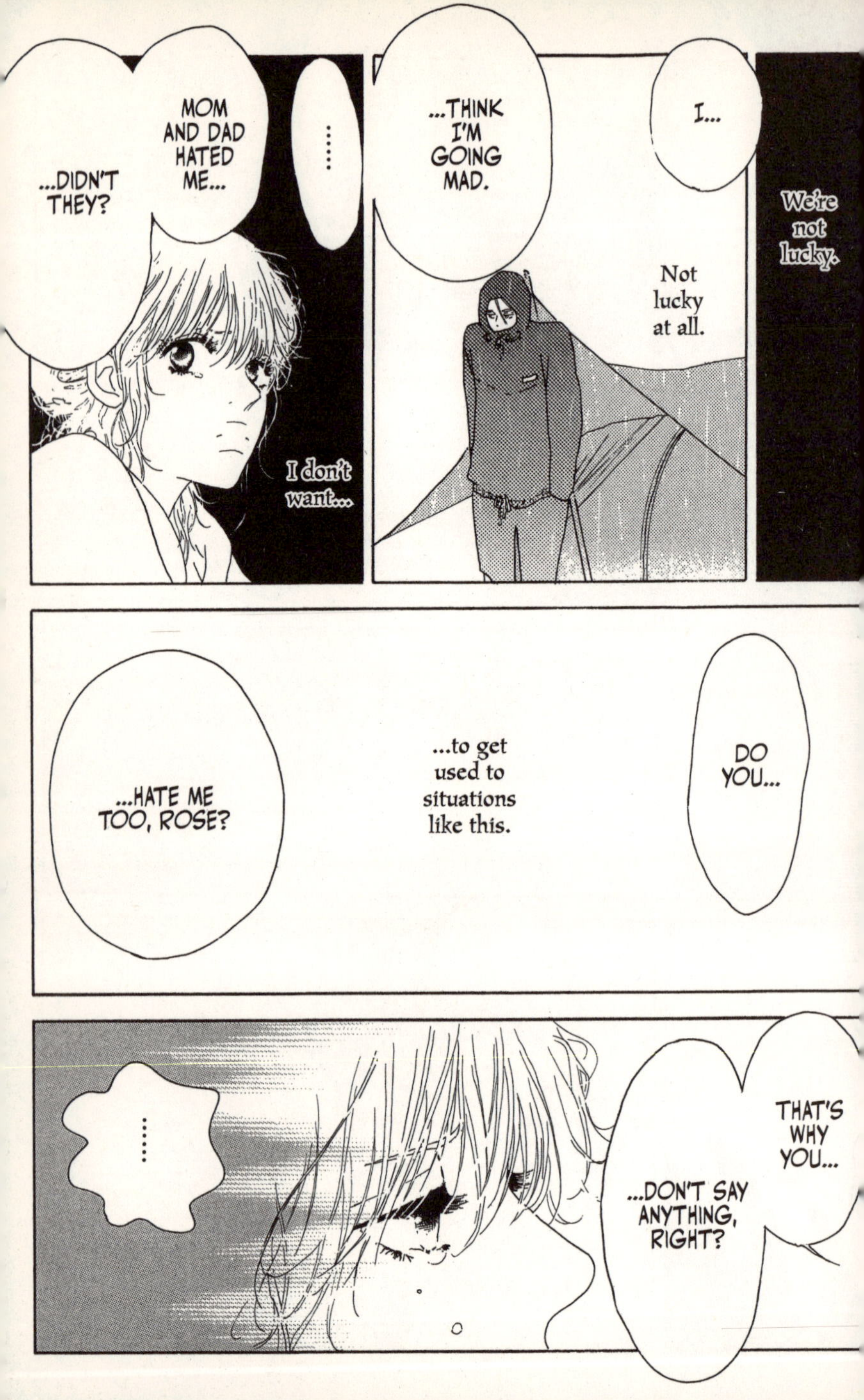
We're not lucky.
I...
...THINK I'M GOING MAD.
Not lucky at all.
......
MOM AND DAD HATED ME...
...DIDN'T THEY?
I don't want...
DO YOU...
...to get used to situations like this.
...HATE ME TOO, ROSE?
THAT'S WHY YOU...
...DON'T SAY ANYTHING, RIGHT?
......

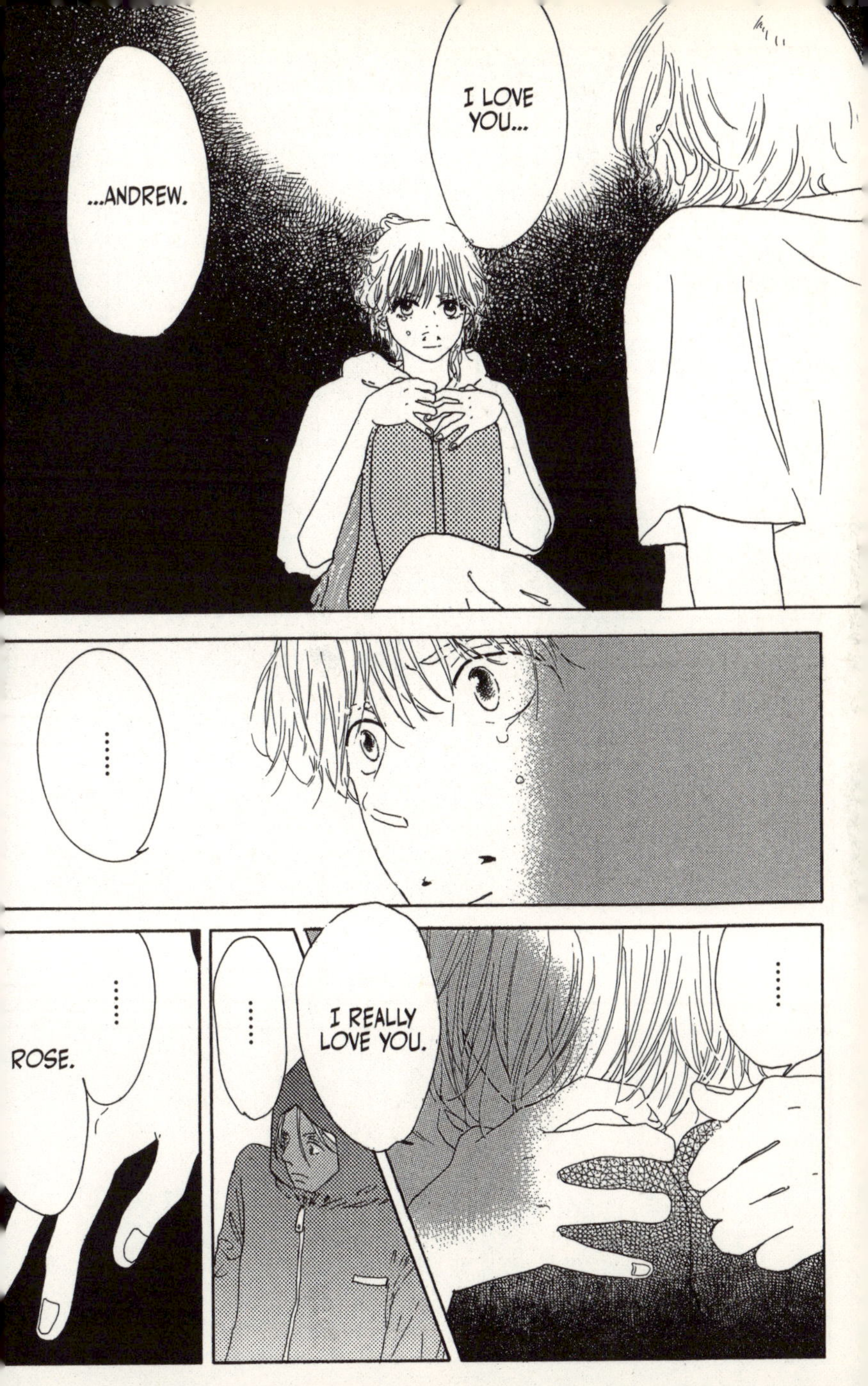
I LOVE YOU...
...ANDREW.
......
......
I REALLY LOVE YOU.
......
......
ROSE.

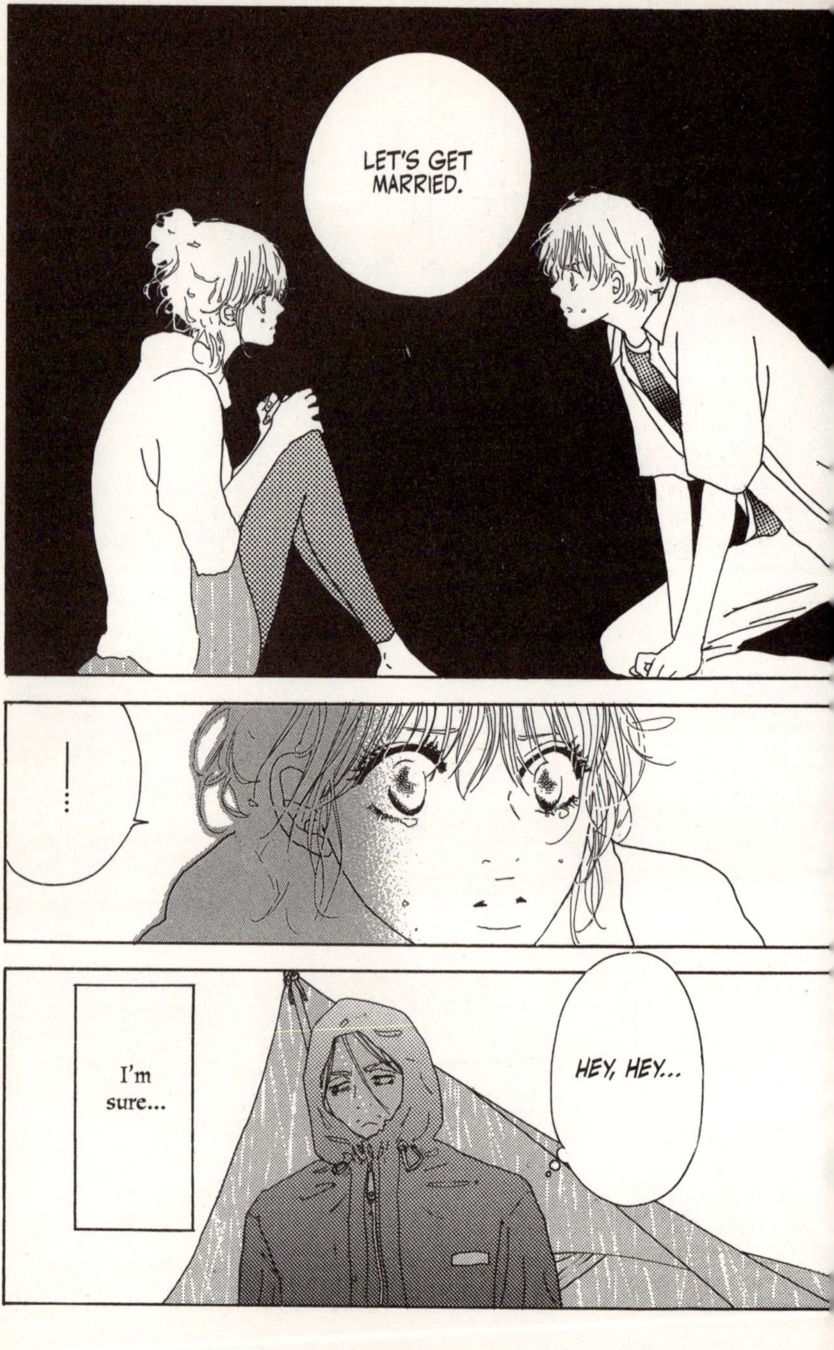
LET'S GET MARRIED.
...!
HEY, HEY...
I'm sure...

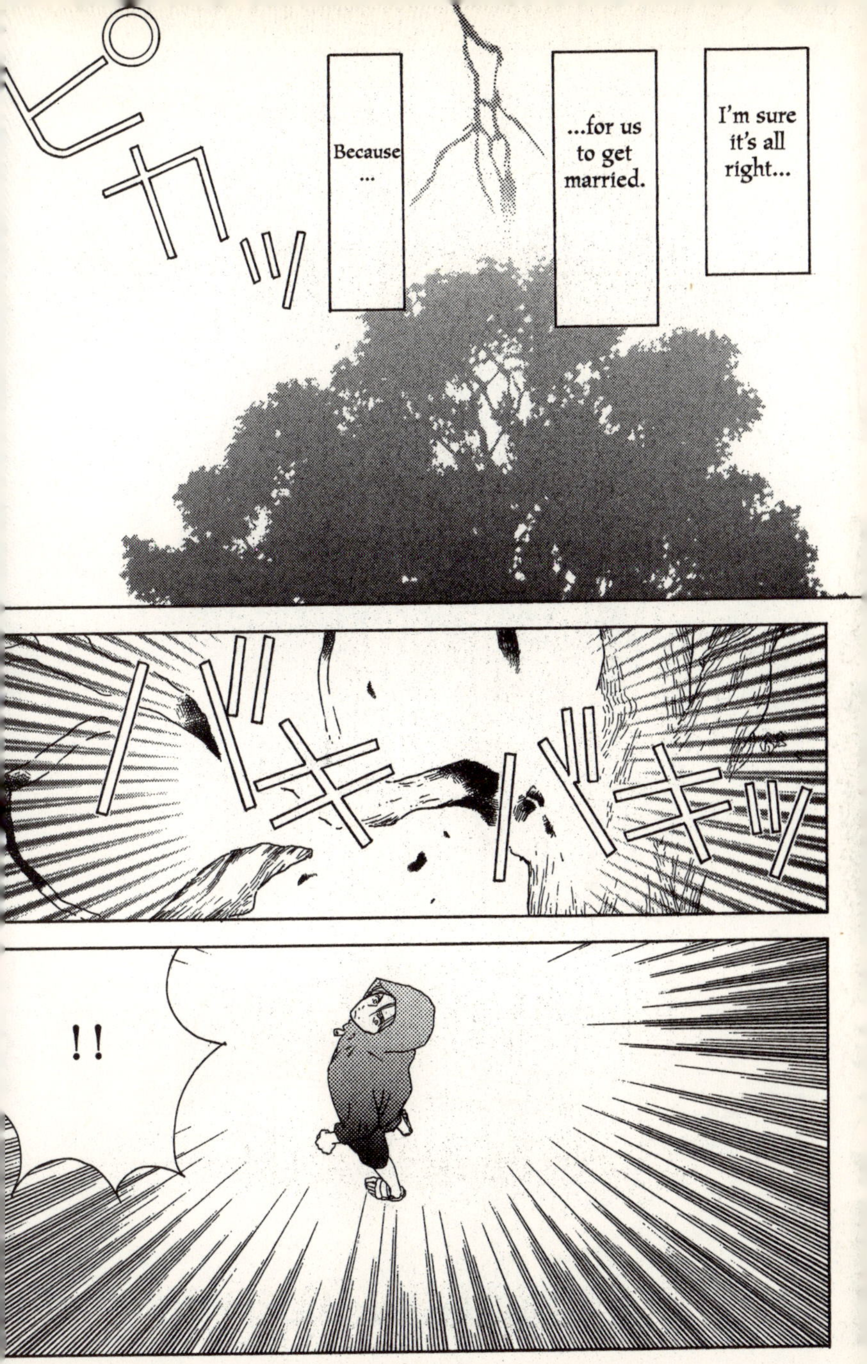
I'm sure it's all right...
...for us to get married.
Because ...
ピカッ
バキバキッ
!!

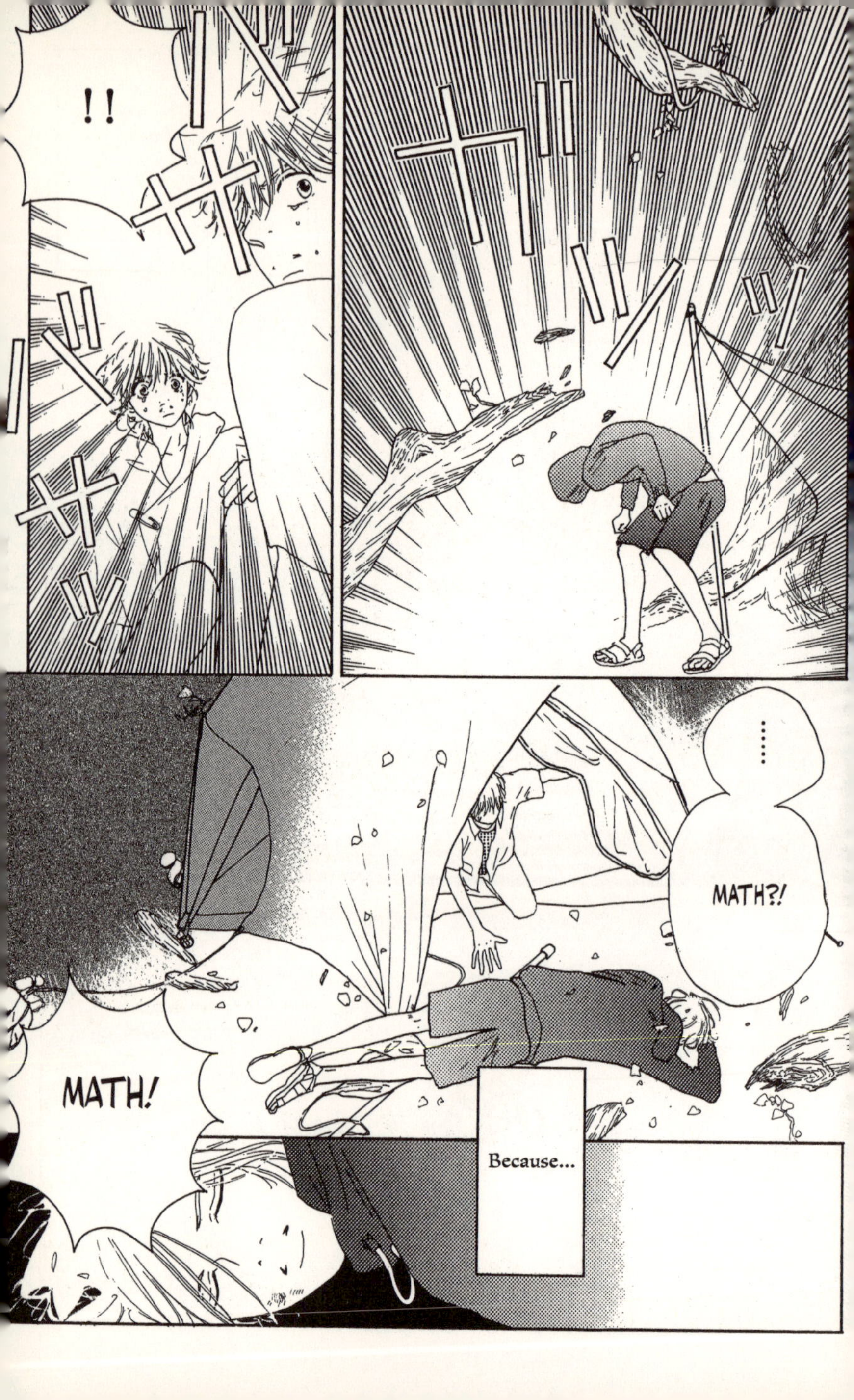
!!
……
MATH?!
MATH!
Because...

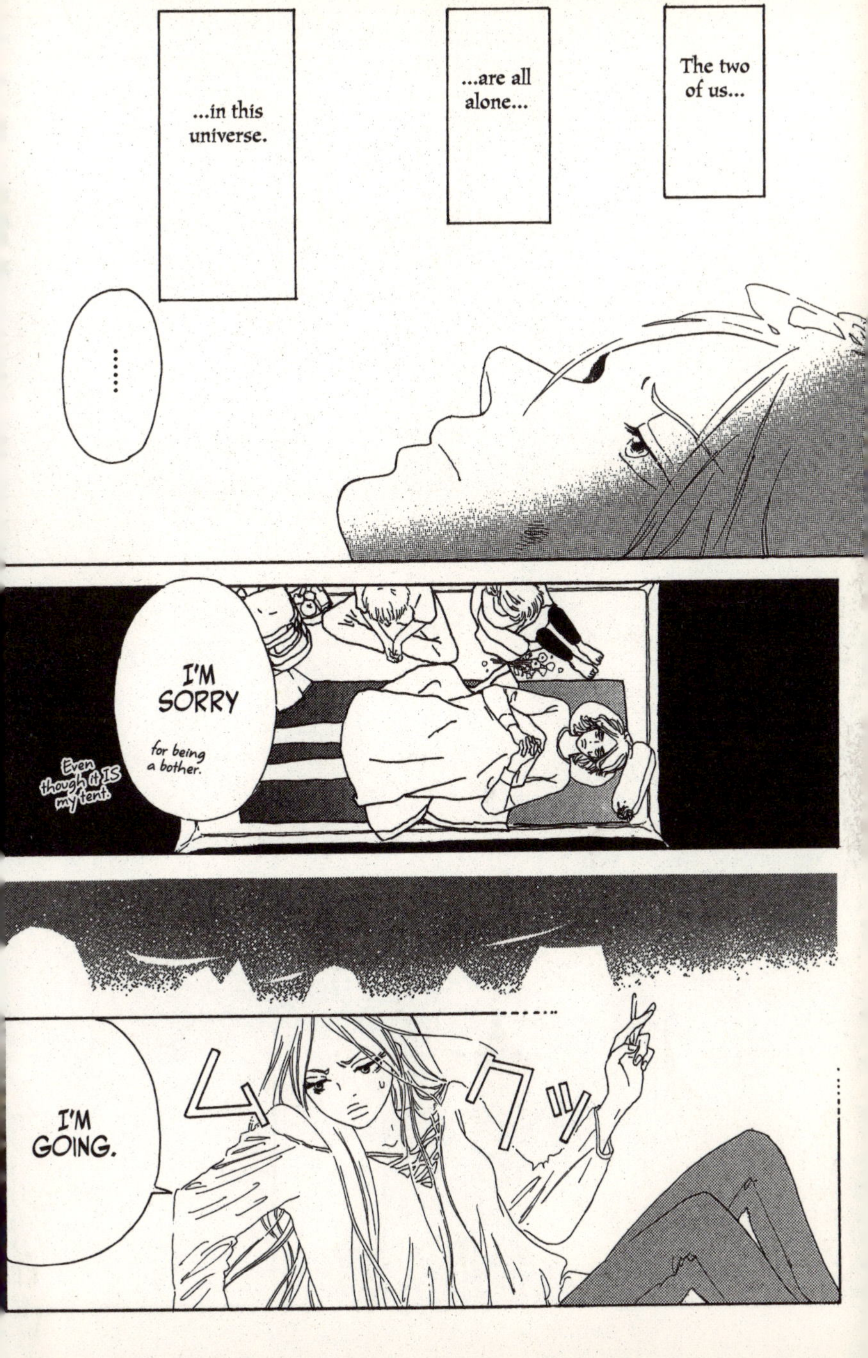
The two of us...
...are all alone...
...in this universe.
......
I'M SORRY for being a bother.
Even though it IS my tent.
ムクッ
I'M GOING.

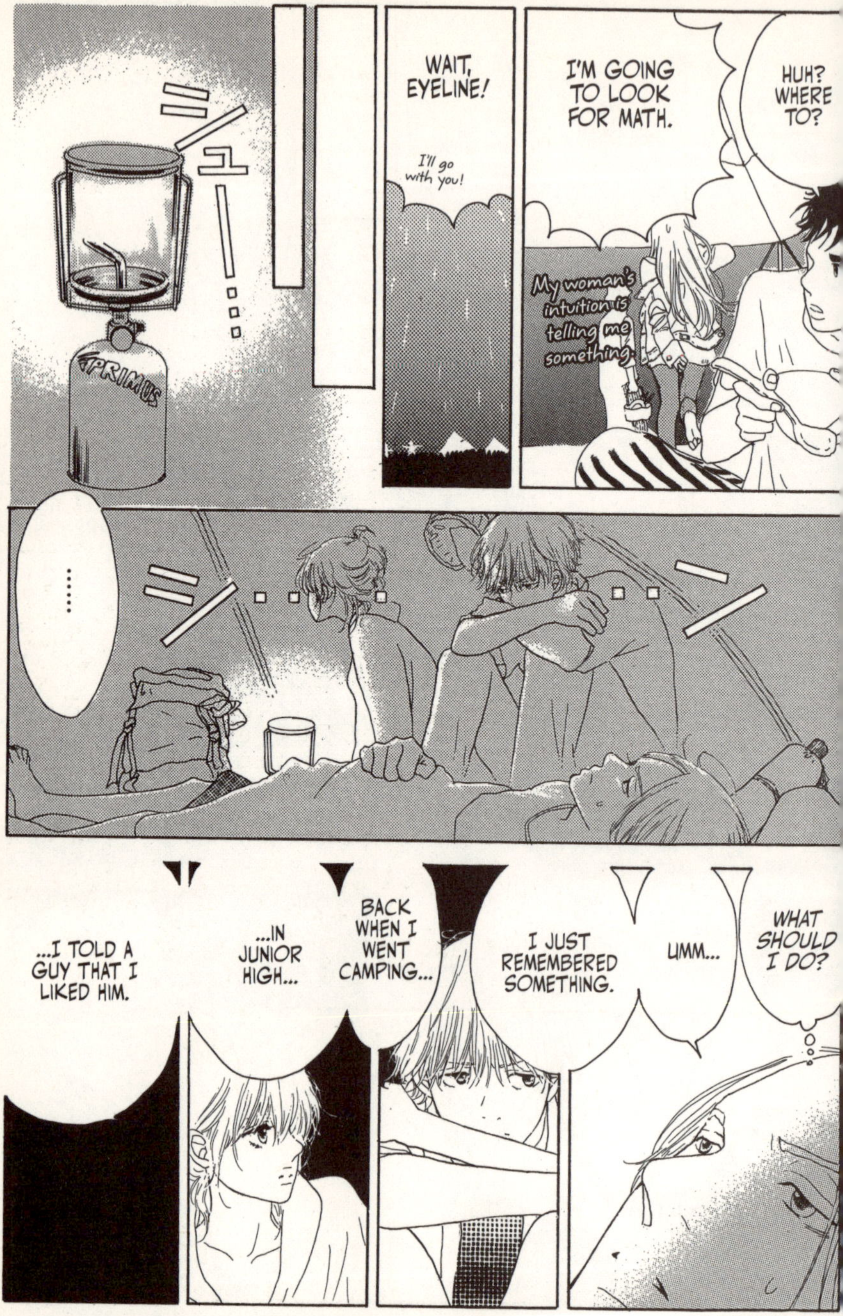
HUH? WHERE TO?
I'M GOING TO LOOK FOR MATH.
My woman's intuition is telling me something.
WAIT, EYELINE!
I'll go with you!
ジュー・・・
PRIMUS
......
シ・・・ン
WHAT SHOULD I DO?
UMM...
I JUST REMEMBERED SOMETHING.
BACK WHEN I WENT CAMPING...
...IN JUNIOR HIGH...
...I TOLD A GUY THAT I LIKED HIM.

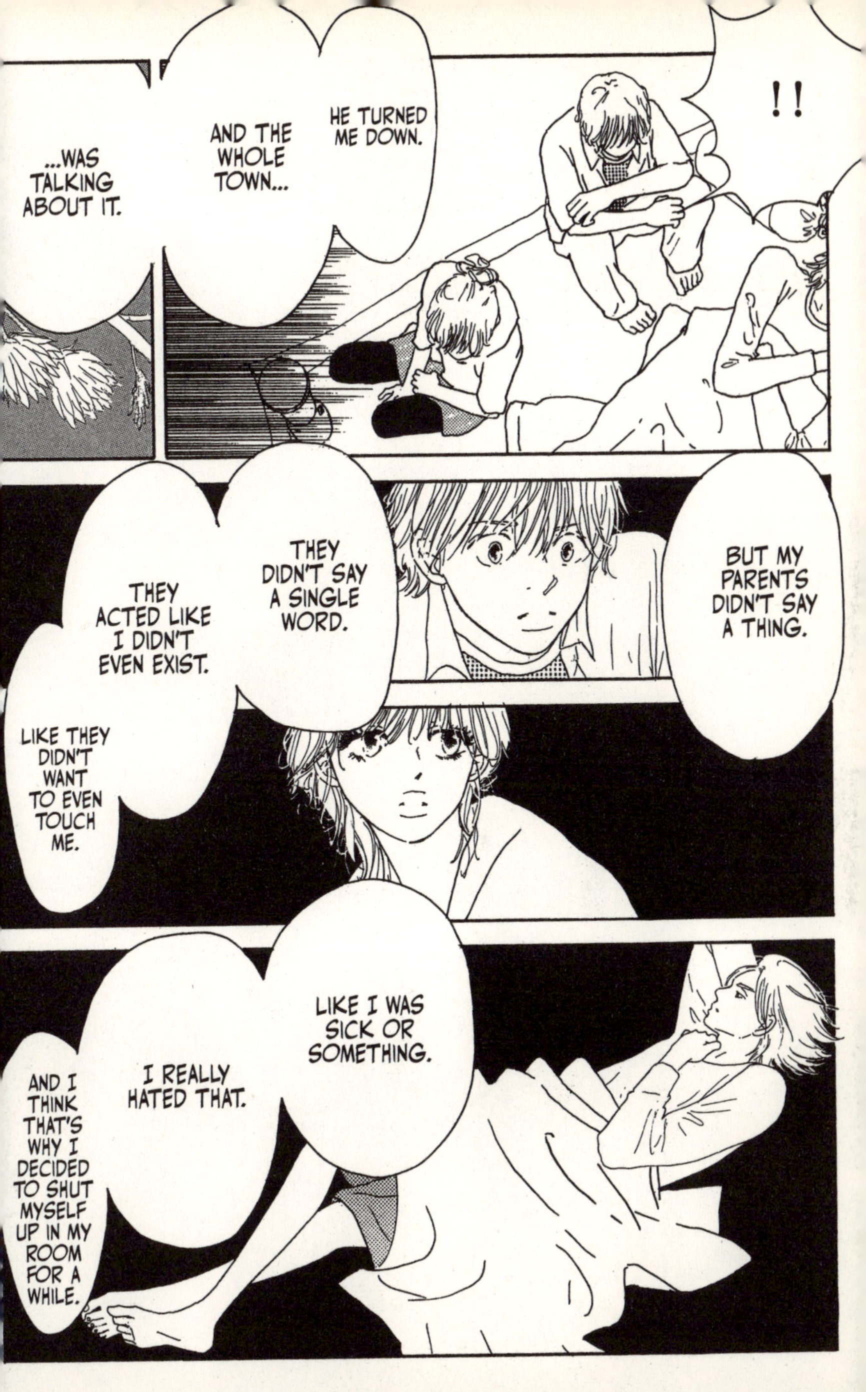
!!
HE TURNED ME DOWN.
AND THE WHOLE TOWN...
...WAS TALKING ABOUT IT.
BUT MY PARENTS DIDN'T SAY A THING.
THEY DIDN'T SAY A SINGLE WORD.
THEY ACTED LIKE I DIDN'T EVEN EXIST.
LIKE THEY DIDN'T WANT TO EVEN TOUCH ME.
LIKE I WAS SICK OR SOMETHING.
I REALLY HATED THAT.
AND I THINK THAT'S WHY I DECIDED TO SHUT MYSELF UP IN MY ROOM FOR A WHILE.

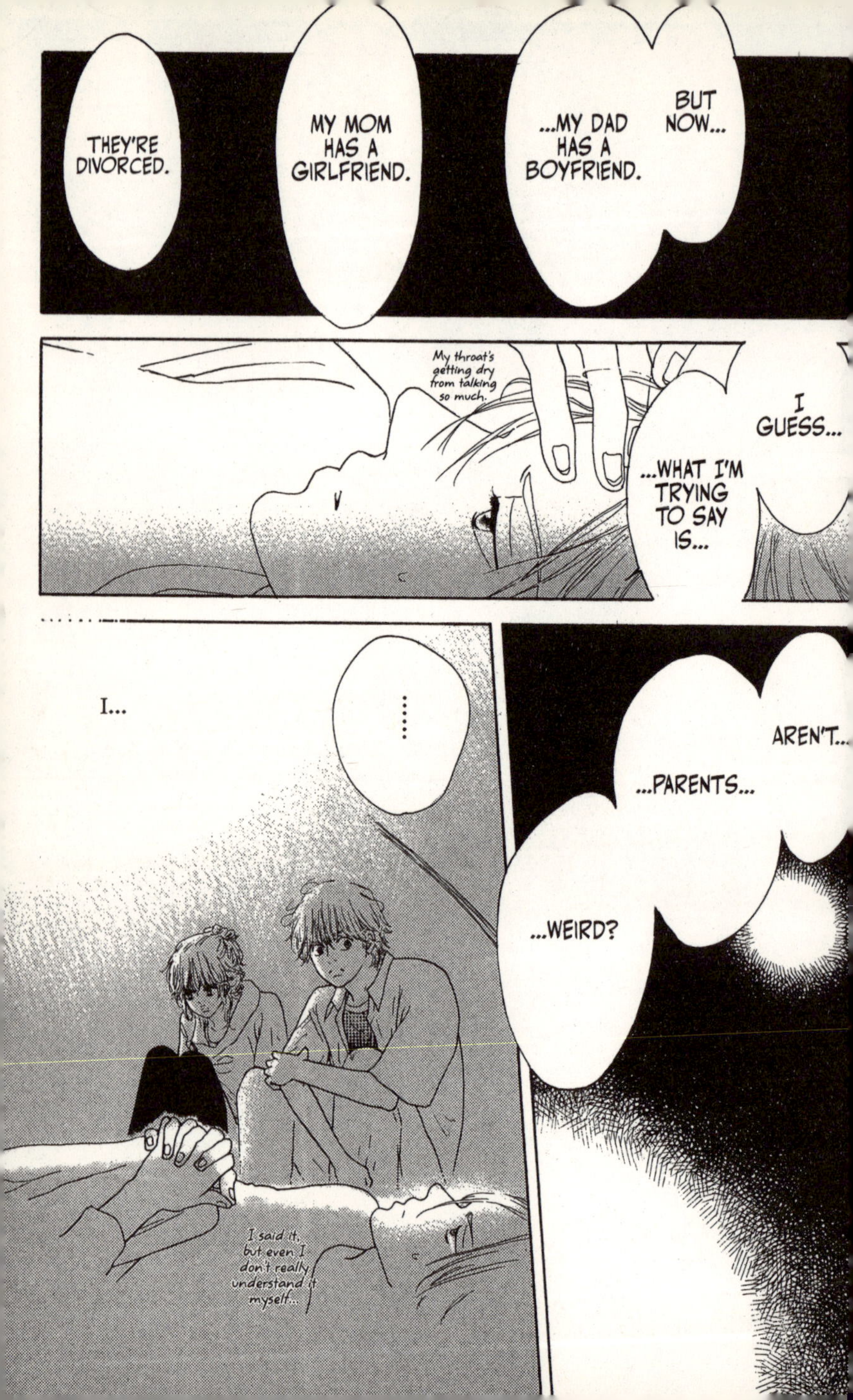
BUT NOW... ...MY DAD HAS A BOYFRIEND.
MY MOM HAS A GIRLFRIEND.
THEY'RE DIVORCED.
I GUESS...
...WHAT I'M TRYING TO SAY IS...
My throat's getting dry from talking so much.
AREN'T... ...PARENTS... ...WEIRD?
......
I...
I said it, but even I don't really understand it myself...

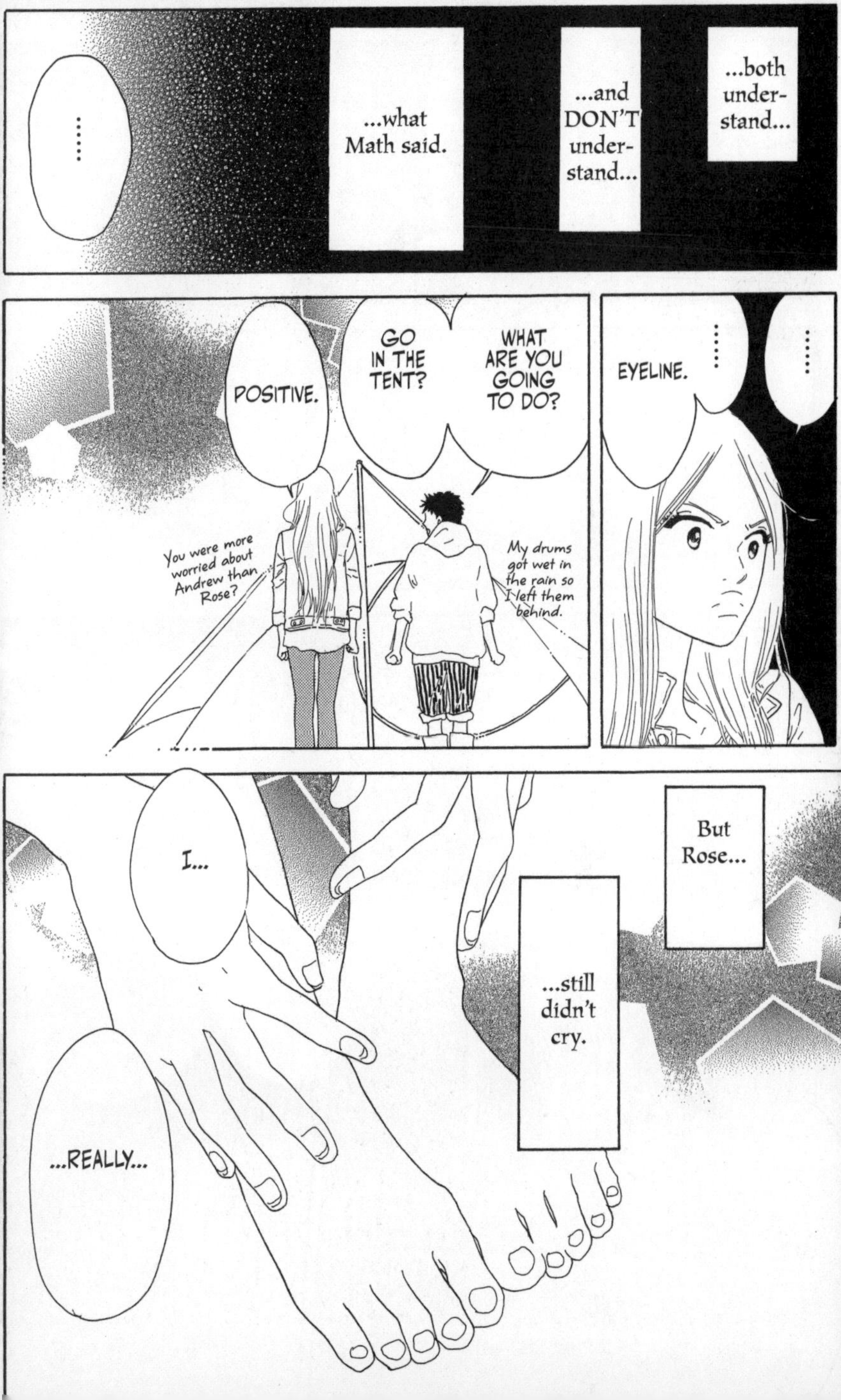
...both understand...
...and DON'T understand...
...what Math said.
......
......
......
EYELINE.
WHAT ARE YOU GOING TO DO?
GO IN THE TENT?
POSITIVE.
My drums got wet in the rain so I left them behind.
You were more worried about Andrew than Rose?
But Rose...
...still didn't cry.
I...
...REALLY...

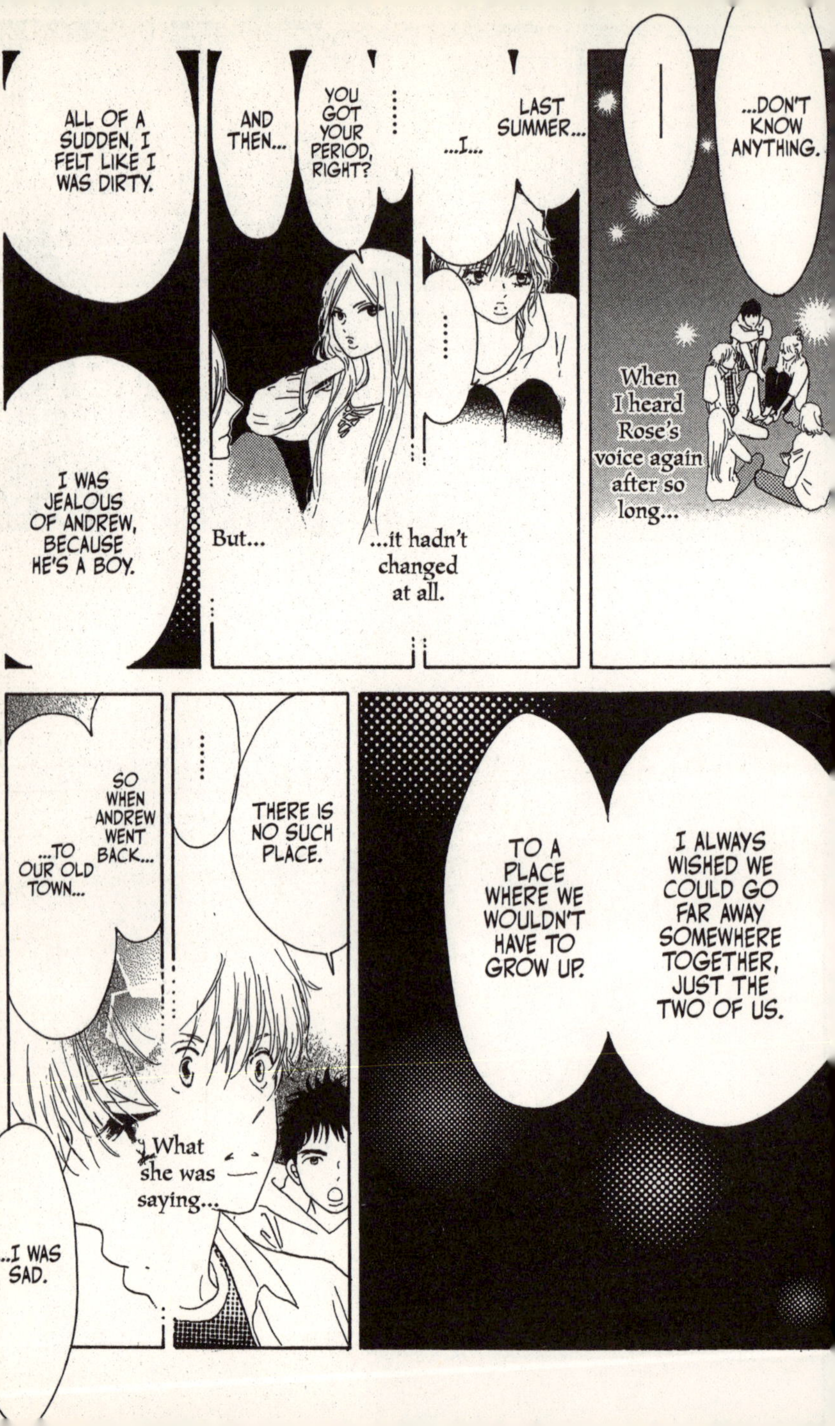
...DON'T KNOW ANYTHING.
When I heard Rose's voice again after so long...
LAST SUMMER...
...I...
......
YOU GOT YOUR PERIOD, RIGHT?
AND THEN...
......
But...
...it hadn't changed at all.
ALL OF A SUDDEN, I FELT LIKE I WAS DIRTY.
I WAS JEALOUS OF ANDREW, BECAUSE HE'S A BOY.
I ALWAYS WISHED WE COULD GO FAR AWAY SOMEWHERE TOGETHER, JUST THE TWO OF US.
TO A PLACE WHERE WE WOULDN'T HAVE TO GROW UP.
THERE IS NO SUCH PLACE.
......
What she was saying...
SO WHEN ANDREW WENT BACK...
...TO OUR OLD TOWN...
...I WAS SAD.

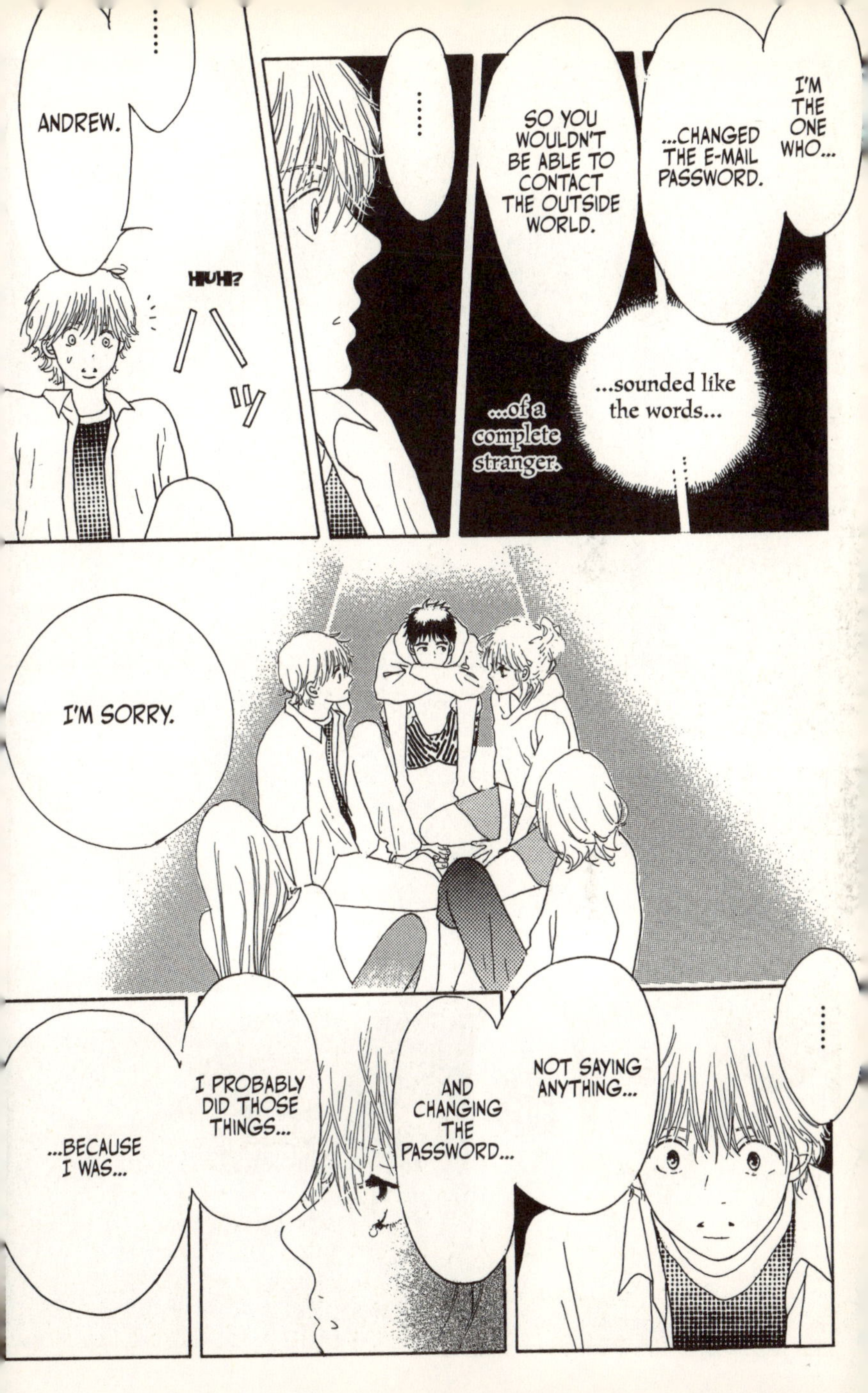
I'M THE ONE WHO...
...CHANGED THE E-MAIL PASSWORD.
SO YOU WOULDN'T BE ABLE TO CONTACT THE OUTSIDE WORLD.
...sounded like the words...
...of a complete stranger.
......
......
ANDREW.
HUH?
I'M SORRY.
......
NOT SAYING ANYTHING...
AND CHANGING THE PASSWORD...
I PROBABLY DID THOSE THINGS...
...BECAUSE I WAS...

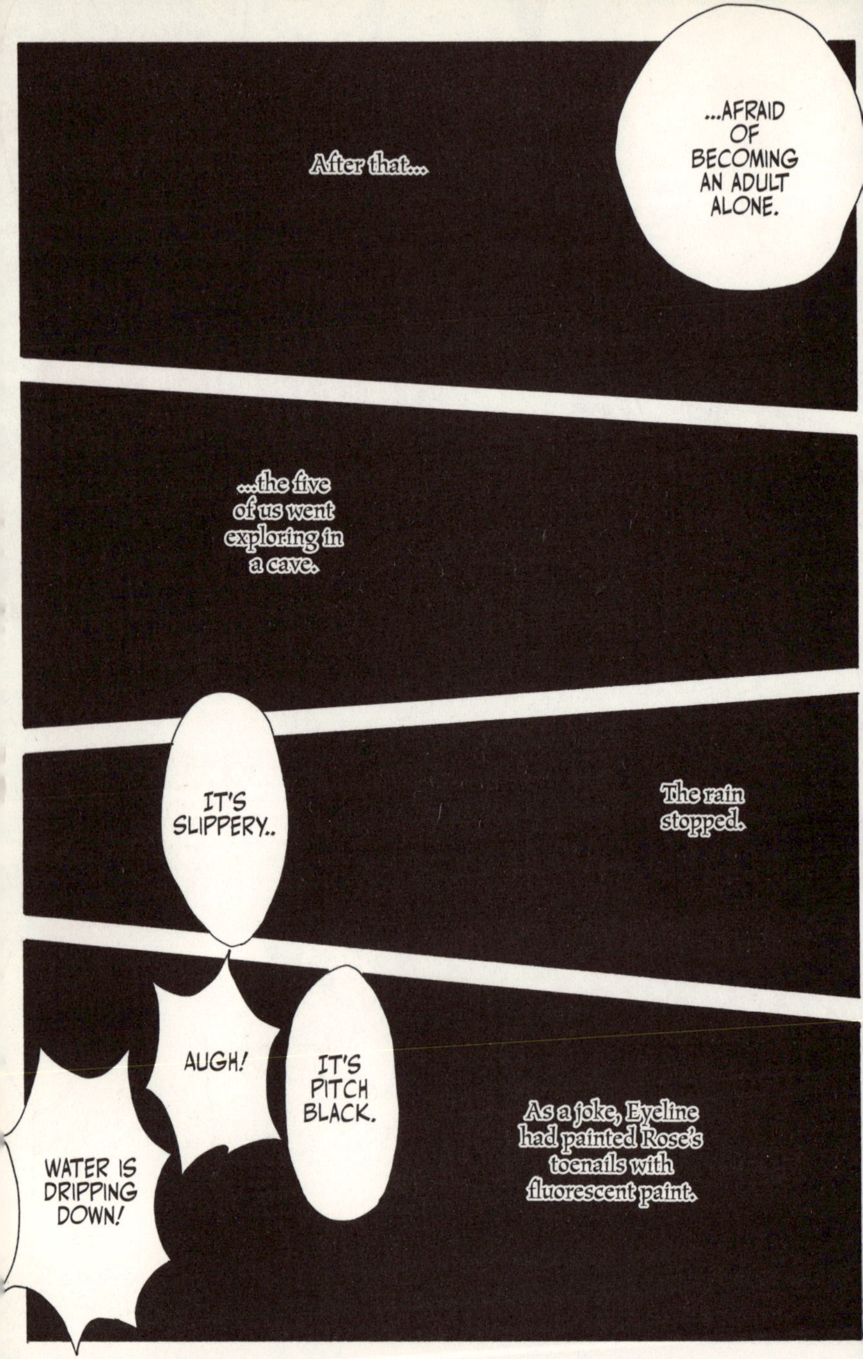
...AFRAID OF BECOMING AN ADULT ALONE.
After that...
...the five of us went exploring in a cave.
The rain stopped.
IT'S SLIPPERY..
As a joke, Eyeline had painted Rose's toenails with fluorescent paint.
IT'S PITCH BLACK.
AUGH!
WATER IS DRIPPING DOWN!

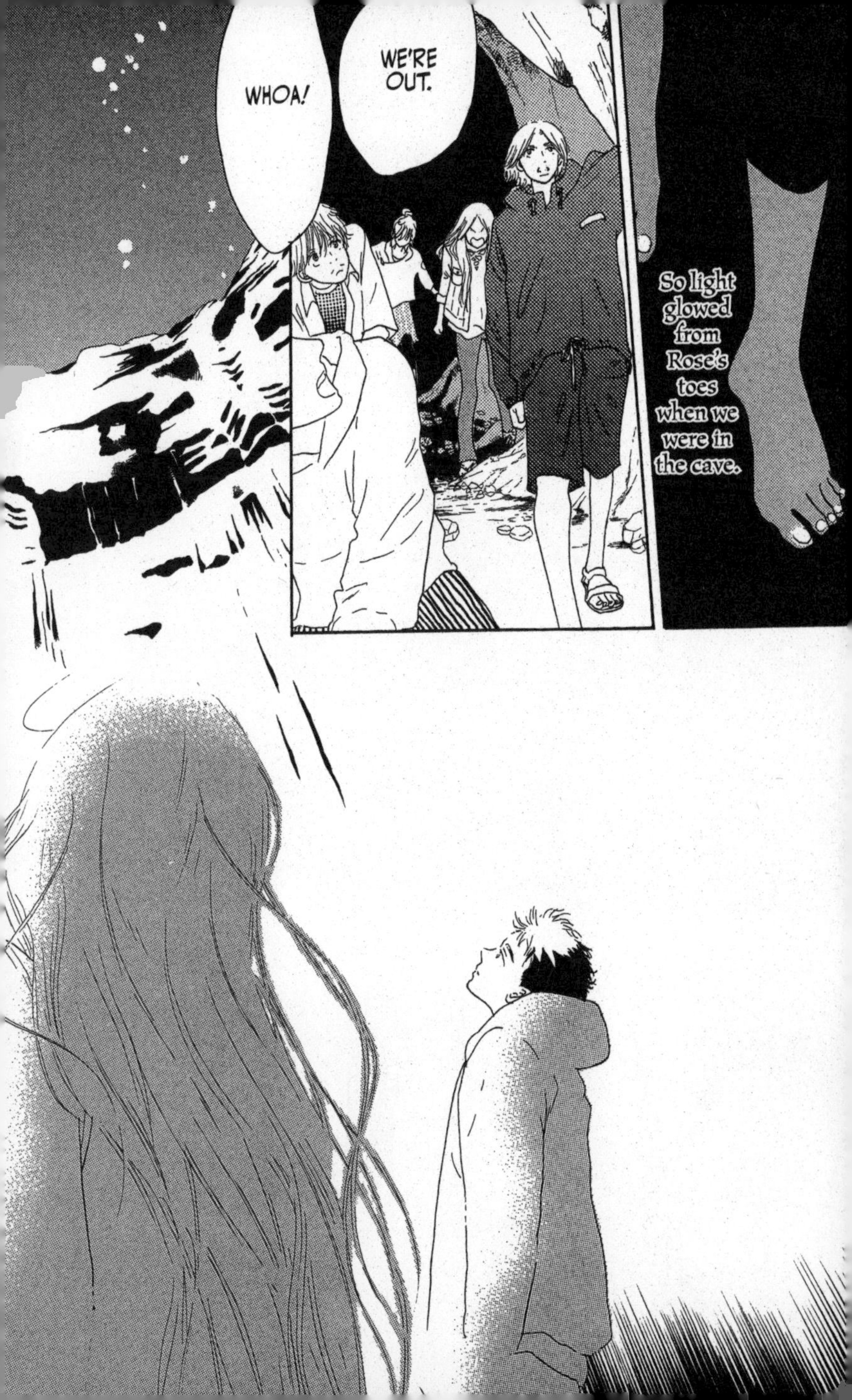
So light glowed from Rose's toes when we were in the cave.
WE'RE OUT.
WHOA!

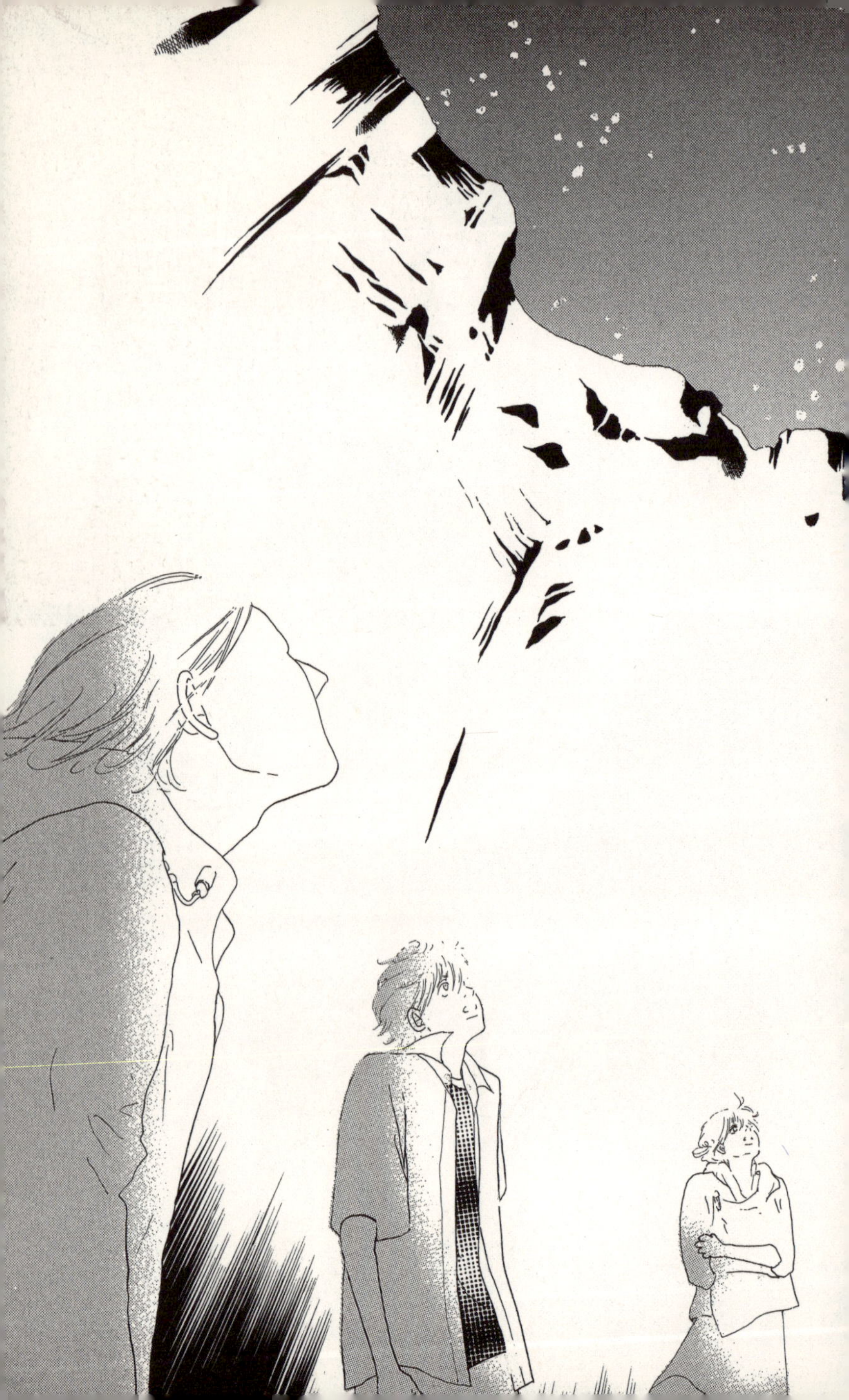

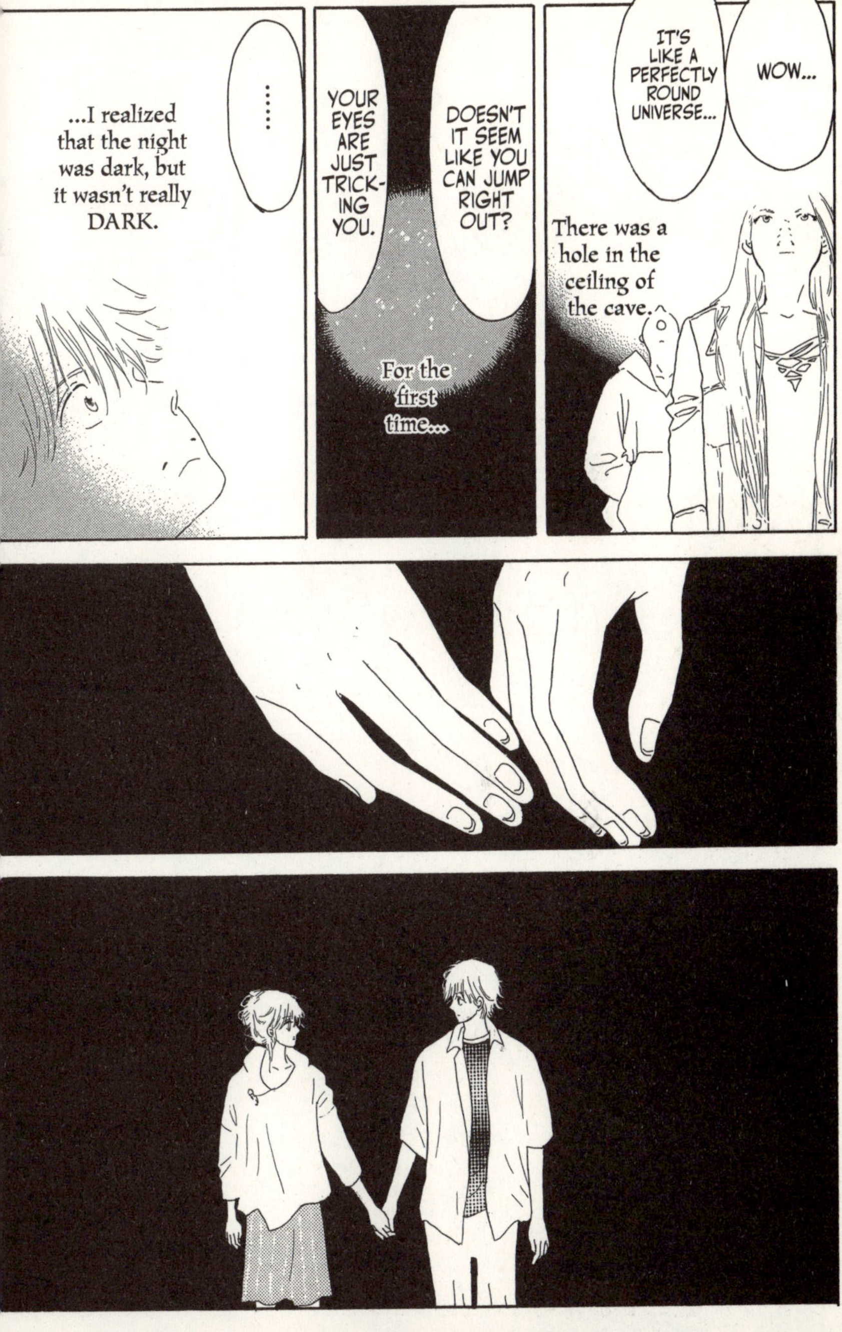
WOW...
IT'S LIKE A PERFECTLY ROUND UNIVERSE...
There was a hole in the ceiling of the cave.
DOESN'T IT SEEM LIKE YOU CAN JUMP RIGHT OUT?
YOUR EYES ARE JUST TRICK-ING YOU.
For the first time...
......
...I realized that the night was dark, but it wasn't really DARK.

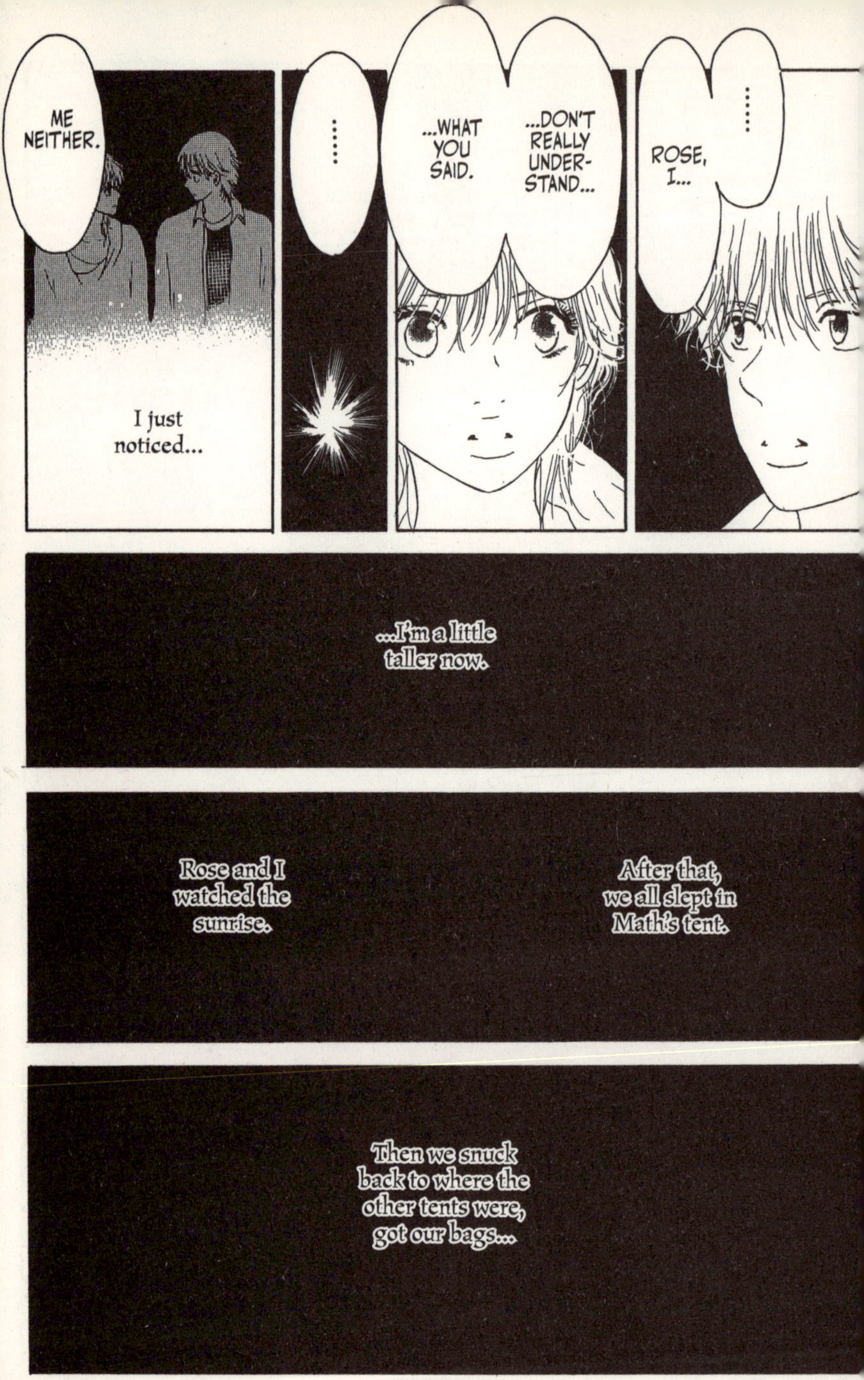
......
ROSE, I...
...DON'T REALLY UNDERSTAND...
...WHAT YOU SAID.
......
ME NEITHER.
I just noticed...
...I'm a little taller now.
After that, we all slept in Math's tent.
Rose and I watched the sunrise.
Then we snuck back to where the other tents were, got our bags...

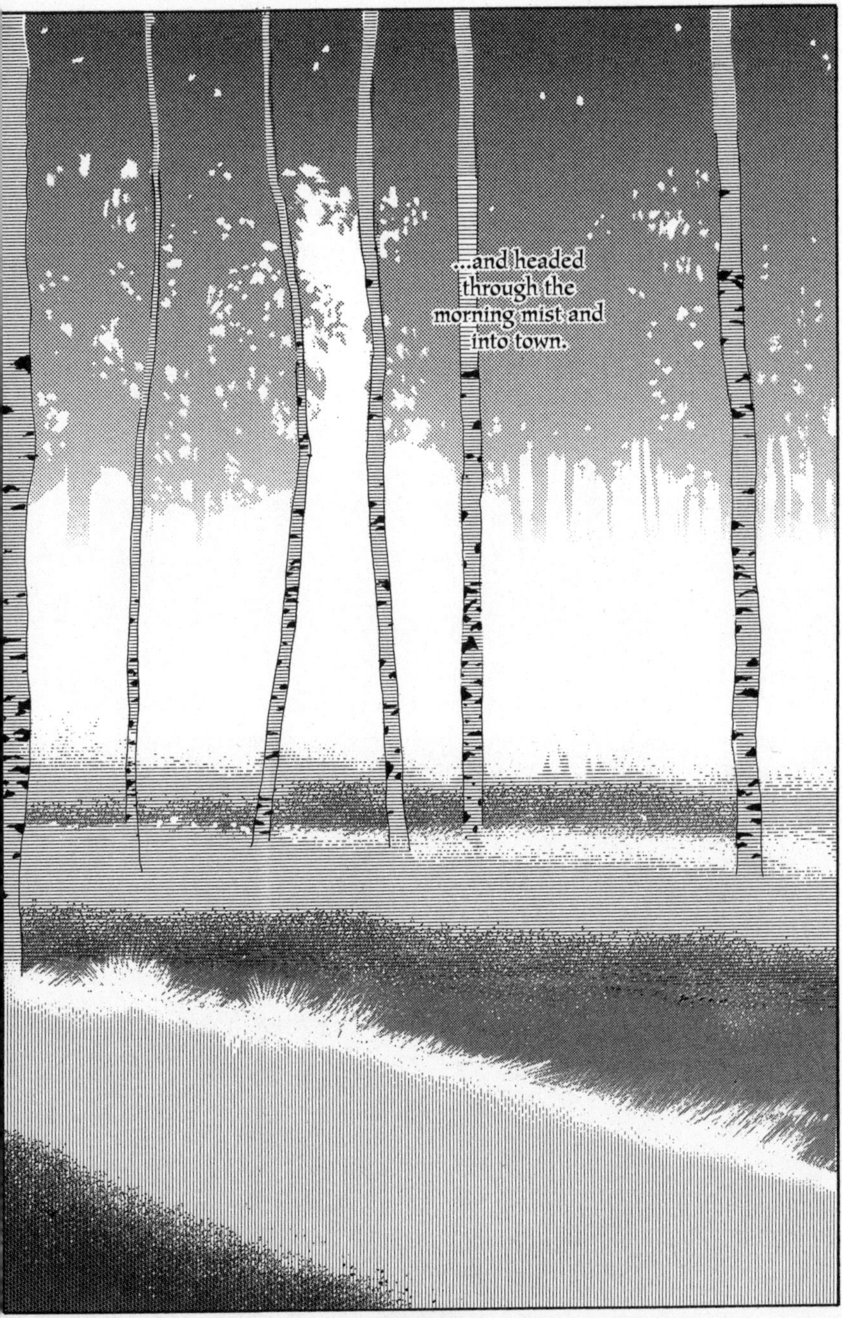
...and headed through the morning mist and into town.

THE END

A★f★t★e★r★w★o★r★d

This is my fifth graphic novel, and it turned out to be like a fairy tale (which I think is a good thing). I had intended "Club Hurricane" to be only three installments, but I felt maybe that wasn't enough. And when I asked about doing a fourth installment, I was told, "The Zipper Comics deal is done now, but please finish the story." I included everything I wanted to, but I wish I could've gone into more detail. (But then again, maybe I'd never finish...) I enjoyed it.

And sometimes I start without really thinking things through first.

"The Laidback Person I Will Never Forget" is something I somehow managed to finish writing, even though I kept telling myself "No! This is wrong!" Even my editor told me, "I was wondering how it was going to turn out..." Sorry!

"Galaxy Girl, Panda Boy."
My friend rode a Fiat Panda, and I got a picture. The story for this one goes this way and that, too. Speaking of which, it seems writing about puberty is my calling. Cars are nice, aren't they...?

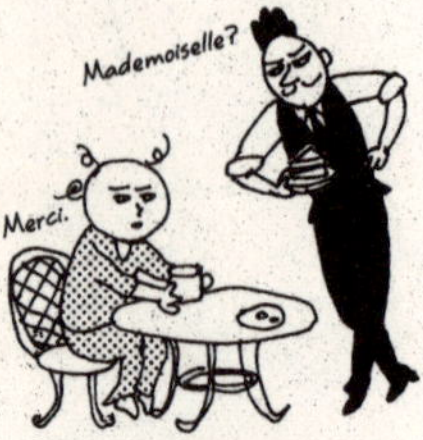

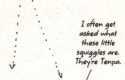

Mademoiselle?
Merci.
A V-neck so low it makes me a magnet for lewd comments.

(So) (by) (the) (way)

I went to Europe again! This summer!
It was the best!

And my "mission" for the trip this time was:
I got stood up by my friend. "Being stood up in Paris" for two days.

My favorite line in this book is
"This is just a small farm.
We barely keep food on the table."
So nobody's listening...

I often get asked what these little squiggles are. They're Tenpa.

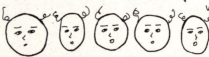

All the Cream Puffs, Joichi Suzuki who did the book design for me, everyone at the office and all my readers... Thank you very much!

Junko Kawakami

TOKYOPOP SHOP

WWW.TOKYOPOP.COM/SHOP

HOT NEWS!
Check out the TOKYOPOP SHOP! The world's best collection of manga in English is now available online in one place!

SAIYUKI RELOAD

.HACK NOVEL

WWW.TOKYOPOP.COM/SHOP

BIZENGHAST

Bizenghast and other hot titles are available at the store that never closes!

- **LOOK FOR SPECIAL OFFERS**
- **PRE-ORDER UPCOMING RELEASES**
- **COMPLETE YOUR COLLECTIONS**

OT
OLDER TEEN
AGE 16+

In the deep South, an ancient voodoo curse unleashes the War on Flesh—a hellish plague of voracious Ew Chott hornets that raises an army of the walking dead. This undead army spreads the plague by ripping the hearts out of living creatures to make room for a Black Heart hive, all in preparation for the most awesome incarnation of evil ever imagined… An unlikely group of five mismatched individuals have to put their differences aside to try to destroy the onslaught of evil before it's too late.

VOODOO MAKES A MAN NASTY!

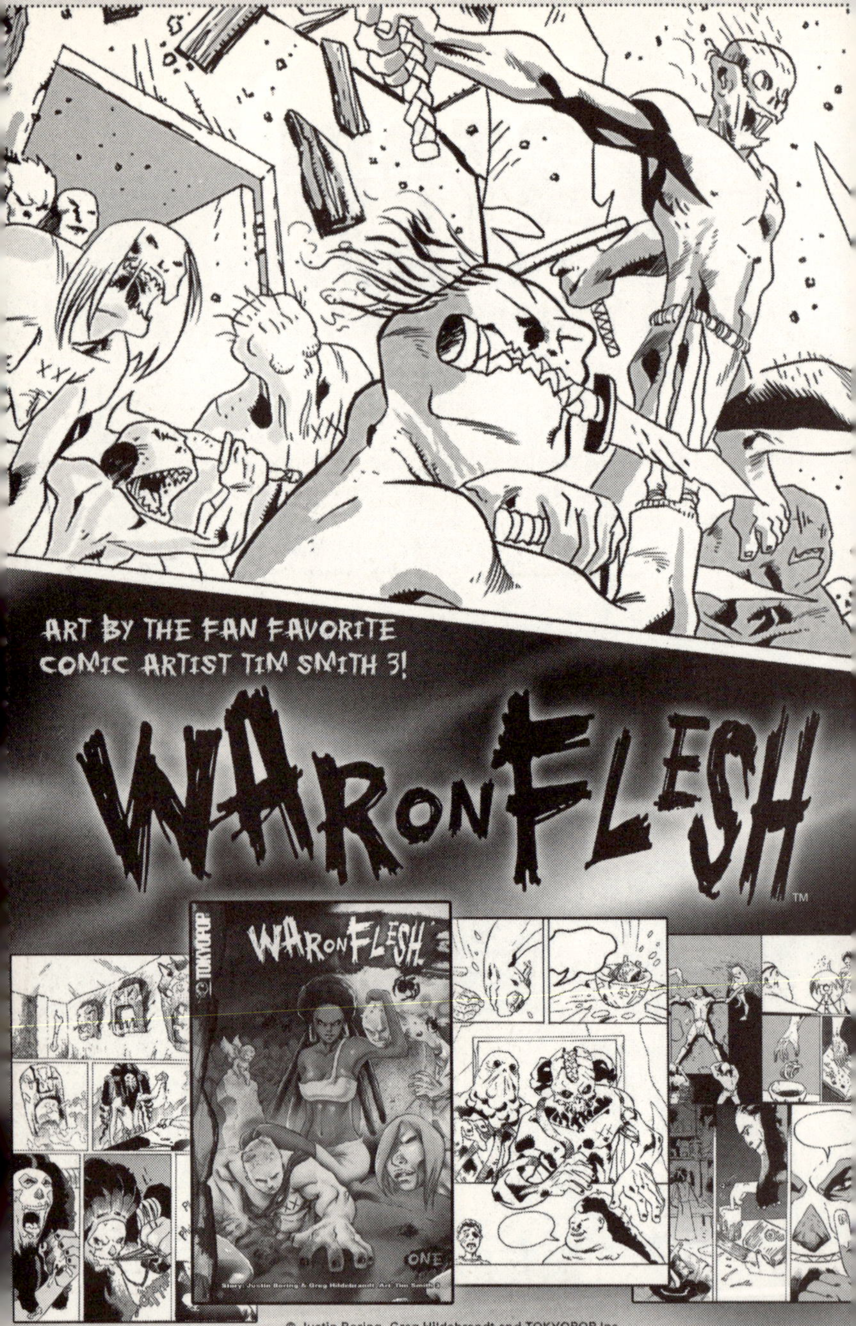
ART BY THE FAN FAVORITE
COMIC ARTIST TIM SMITH 3!
WAR ON FLESH
TM
WAR ON FLESH
TOKYOPOP
ONE

STOP!

This is the back of the book.
You wouldn't want to spoil a great ending!

This book is printed "manga-style," in the authentic Japanese right-to-left format. Since none of the artwork has been flipped or altered, readers get to experience the story just as the creator intended. You've been asking for it, so TOKYOPOP® delivered: authentic, hot-off-the-press, and far more fun!

DIRECTIONS

If this is your first time reading manga-style, here's a quick guide to help you understand how it works.

It's easy... just start in the top right panel and follow the numbers. Have fun, and look for more 100% authentic manga from TOKYOPOP®!